Copyright © 2021 by Steppen Sawicki

All rights reserved. No part of this book may be reproduced in any manner whatsoever without written permission except in the case of brief quotations embodied in critical articles and reviews.

Cover art by Fay Lane

ISBN: 978-1-953997-01-2

First Printing, 2021

BLACK HEART

Steppen Sawicki

Chapter One

Bryan showed his ID at the barricade. The policeman there ushered him in with a frantic wave of a hand and asked something he couldn't hear through the honking of the redirected traffic, the chatter of the crowd he was leaving behind at the caution tape, and his own battered eardrums.

Again he wondered why there were always crowds. Was everyone suicidal? Didn't they know these things often went wrong?

The cop said something else and Bryan nodded to try to get rid of him. Cops were like gnats once they knew who you were.

The cop clung to him anyway, leading him to Andrade as if he wouldn't know where she would be otherwise. She was there at the front of the commotion, nearest the doors to the hotel, where the cops didn't dare venture. She had her cell to her ear and was nodding at what it was jabbering to her, her brown curls falling down her back as her head tipped up to view the building. She was young – twenty-six, same as Bryan – but, same as Bryan, she knew her stuff. He could rely on her assessment of the situation with no worries.

Mr. Cop pointed to her and then stood near the two of them – though sufficiently away from the hotel – as if awaiting a 'thank you' or instructions. As if the cops could be of use.

"You're up," Andrade said when she saw Bryan. "First one here."

"What?" Bryan shouted.

"I said you're the first one here," she said, louder.

Bryan nodded. "You scope it out?"

"I did. Three of them in there."

"How many?"

"*Three*. What's with you?"

He pointed to an ear. "Was at a club. Loud band. Terrible band."

"This is why I don't go to clubs."

"This girl likes this band. It's probably a good thing I got called in."

Andrade tensed and her brow furrowed. "What girl?"

"What?"

Andrade sighed in exasperation. "Never mind. Just get in there. 44th floor. *THREE* of them." She held up three fingers to emphasize.

Bryan nodded and opened his mouth to respond, but a razor-thin and razor-straight suit of a man stepped out past the line of cops and came up to him.

"Are you the, er..." The suit fidgeted with his hands. "Are you responsible for taking care of these things?"

"That's me," Bryan said.

"Ah, good. I have a request. I'm the manager of this hotel and I would like to ask that you take care of this problem with as little mess as possible."

Bryan wasn't sure he had heard correctly. "Mess?"

"We're a well-respected hotel. We can't have just anybody tearing up the walls and floors." He fluttered a hand in the air to illustrate.

Bryan stared at him for a moment, dumbfounded, and then turned to Andrade. "Andrade, how many presumed dead?"

"Current estimate is thirty. But of course it will be higher once everyone is accounted for."

"Thirty?"

"Thirty."

Bryan looked back to the manager.

They finally believe us, he thought, *and now they want to dictate how we work.*

"Thirty people," he said aloud. "I don't give a rat's ass about your floors and walls."

The manager's eyes went wide, but before he could respond, Bryan had stormed away and through the glass doors of the hotel. The police lights flashed against the walls, red and blue flickering over every surface. But as the door closed, he was finally wrapped in silence and he could hear the ringing in his ears. He could remember the awful band and Lily asking him why he was laughing. Him saying it was because the lyrics were shit, and did she really listen to these guys? And then she'd gotten angry and told him, 'Well, I don't see you playing any instruments.' Yeah, he'd told her, but he still knew what music was.

A fight on a first date. Man, he was *smooth.*

Hussein's voice spoke up in his mind. *Don't let the job take you over.*

Oh shut up, Bryan snapped back at his memory. It wasn't anything to do with the job. It had been a dumb girl and Bryan was a dumb guy and they just hadn't gotten along.

But he had also been a jerk.

He watched the numbers climb to 44 above the elevator doors, each number being illuminated in turn. Reaching into his bag, he closed his fingers over the deck of cards. As he took them out, he felt his muscles stiffen of their own accord – his jaw clenched, his stomach tightened, and his lungs took in a sharp breath. His body knew better than his mind what was coming. His whole body was Pavlov's dog, honed to the appearance of a few playing cards. He opened the package and slid out the top card, and, as he still had a couple more floors to go past, he glanced at it. He frowned when he saw it was a joker. He usually took those out, but this one had slipped past him, and it had been too late by the time he'd had to use the deck last night. He could feel a faint pulse beneath his fingers, running the surface of the card as if blood ran through the ink. He could skip it. Could use a different card.

It didn't matter. Why the superstition anyway? It didn't change anything. A totem was a totem.

The elevator doors slid open as he slipped three more cards – empty cards, ready for capture – from the deck into his hand. His eyes defied his rational mind and snuck a peek at them: hearts, clubs, diamonds. Then he looked up.

Before him were five bodies, thin and desiccated as if they had been lying in a desert sun for days instead of a hotel hallway for an hour. They hadn't even had time to start smelling.

He stepped gingerly over them, making sure not to step on any limbs. The lights in the hall were flickering almost as badly as the police lights outside, but the view was still clear enough – bodies scattered down the corridor, all green and yellow, curled into fetal positions or stretched with flailed arms, all with mouths yawned open. They could have been made of paper.

Time to quit stalling. Preparation should have been done in the elevator.

It was a very common mistake in his profession – to wait.

He took the joker in both hands and tore it in half. The demon inside it leapt to his body.

His heart was set afire. His veins burned with acid. His head split apart. A million needles drove in under his skin. His stomach tried hard to dispel its contents, but he was able to keep it down. Possesseds had to concentrate on that part most of all. He cried out and fell to one knee. And then it entered his mind.

The flickering lights flashed darker. A slick, dim grime settled over everything, both outside and inside his body. It was as if the universe and everything in it, including him, was fetid and rotten and turning a burnt black.

He forced his head up. Dimly, through the grime, he saw that there were two red beings... past the walls, down another corridor or in rooms. He looked up further, to the ceiling. The third one was above him, maybe two floors away. He'd take that one last.

It was a struggle to get to his feet, and a struggle to walk down the hall. The demon was making him feel like a stranger in his own body. Every step was torture, every movement a jolt to his nerves.

But I'm alive, he began his mantra. *But I'm alive.* He took steps between the corpses. Some of the rooms he passed had had their doors blown or ripped off, and in these he could see more desiccated bodies – men, women, a child here and there. He growled low and continued down the hall, spurred on. There was a long tear in the wallpaper on his right, and he grinned a grin that wasn't really his. *There's your walls, Mr. Manager.*

The first demon was in the hall, pulsing red and flowing viscous light, only slightly smaller than a man. It hung amorphous in the air as Bryan advanced on it. They always reminded Bryan of the northern lights, though he didn't like the link that association created in his mind. Northern lights were a beautiful memory he had, but they were now tainted by these things. It wasn't right that they looked so beautiful, for what they were capable of, and what they weren't capable of.

It hadn't noticed him yet; his aeon – his lifeforce as seen by demons – was masked by the other one inside him. He reached out a hand, focusing on the power of the demon inside him and thrusting it outwards. The acid pumped through his veins, burning deeper, but he only gritted his teeth against it. The light faded entirely from the hallway, and there was only the blackness and the northern lights flowing. He envisioned a circle of flames around those lights, and it appeared, thrust into existence, licking at the demon and the walls and ceiling, but scorching nothing. The trapped demon screeched like fingernails on a chalkboard that only the demon in Bryan could hear, its light wavering and dipping, but it couldn't escape the circle.

Bryan held up one of the playing cards, and willed the demon into it. The red light was pulled into the card, screaming all the way until it only pulsed faintly red over the laminated surface. The fire whisked once around the card and Bryan's fingers, searing his skin, and was gone.

One demon down. And here came the second.

It drifted through the walls, attracted by the commotion. Perhaps thinking that the excitement meant food. It saw Bryan as he was putting away the sealed card, and then it charged at him, knowing that he was life and ready to fight the demon already possessing him as if they were lions fighting over a kill. Bryan reached into the demon's bag of tricks again, once again stinging his nerve endings and blackening his vision, and sent up a barrier right in front of him. It was a dim transparent yellow, as if it were colored glass, but it flickered and twisted like smoke at the edges. Still, it was strong, and the approaching demon bounced off it and approached again. It pinged against the barrier like a fly at a window, soft red light going forward and back, forward and back.

Bryan growled at the mindless thing. He etched the circle of fire, brought down the barrier in a puff of what could be mistaken for smoke, and, with a flick of his wrist, reined the demon into another card.

He looked up. The third was still above him; it hadn't yet noticed him or the battle. As he let his grip relax on the power his possessor held, light began to seep back into his surroundings, but slowly. He felt more than saw his way to the stairs at the end of the hallway, tripping once over a corpse. He could have used his demon's powers to map out the hotel in his mind, bodies included, but the human body and mind could only take so much abuse, and though things were pretty routine so far, he had to allot energy and sanity for the unexpected. Not that he expected any unexpectedness, but it had been drilled into him: *Only take what you need.*

He remembered Hussein's words to him, spoken in a tiny office stuffed with boxes, one room in a suite of six. *"You could fly and shoot fireballs from your ass with one of these in you, but the consequences wouldn't be worth it."*

It felt like miles to climb two stories, but he made it, and he could see a little better once he had. Not because his eyes were adjusting to the dark, but because his mind was adjusting to the demon. He had twenty more minutes before he absolutely had to dispel it from his body, if he followed the rules.

But who followed rules?

The third was in a room with no corpses, drifting in a corner as if confused. And it might have been, with no more life around. It noticed Bryan too late, and in a moment, it was sealed in the four of hearts. Bryan took a deep breath as he stuck it into the deck, but it was a hard breath, as if he were pulling the darkness into his lungs with it. He took out one more card, thankful to be getting rid of the thing in him until the next time he invited another in. He turned as he raised the card to his lips.

Something was coming – rushing towards him. He hadn't seen it. He threw up a barrier.

It hit the barrier so hard that Bryan could feel the impact, and he slammed into the wall behind him, head knocking hard against it. He blinked stars from his sight and struggled to his knees, head reeling and his possessor eating away at his consciousness. He couldn't black out. If he blacked out....

The demon seemed to have gathered itself as well. It struck again, but this time it tore through the barrier like it was ripping through a sheet of cloth.

Impossible, Bryan asserted, shaking his head to clear it even as the demon poured like a liquid through the tear. He tried to place the containing flames around it, but it was hard to tell where to place them with the demon being so dim; he saw now how dim it was – a pale rose rather than red. As he willed the flames to pin it, struggling against it as it bucked, he realized that's why he hadn't seen it sooner. He hadn't been able to see it until the possessor had taken him over to a darker degree.

What was this thing?

With a final exertion, it flicked the fire aside and leapt at him. It tried to enter him, and the possessor fought back, scratching at Bryan's insides as the demon outside tried to claw its way in.

Bryan had been possessed by two demons at once before. By three and even four at once. But it had never been like this. This was a war inside him. He felt his insides being mauled, torn in ribbons until he was certain that his muscles must be hanging from his bones. The demons screamed at each other in his head – guttural nonsense, no words, just pure emotion that wasn't entirely hate. The darkness grew in Bryan's vision and mind, until all was black and pain and screaming, and some of the screaming was his.

Somehow, Bryan set the ring of fire around the demon; somehow, he got it into the card that was now crumpled in his hand, though he later wouldn't recall doing it. With a shaking hand, he fumbled one more card out of the deck and raised it to his lips, and then breathed the possessor out and into it. The resulting rush of light burned his eyes, and though he felt a loss of weight and pain, he still crumpled to the floor and threw up.

Andrade was the one to point out that he was bleeding, leading him to an ambulance where the long gash on his left arm could be bandaged. He hadn't noticed the wound. He couldn't quite remember the ride down in the elevator. He felt like he had simply appeared in the hotel's parking lot.

"What the hell happened in there?" she asked, looking over Bryan's bloody arm and bruises in shock.

Bryan glared at her through a swimming haze, as if he were drunk. His head was pounding. "You said there were three," he growled.

"I saw three, and I saw you. Until... I don't know. Are you okay?"

He finally noticed the concern on her face, and his anger faded. It wasn't like she'd put the demons there.

"There was a fourth," he said.

Andrade shook her head in disbelief. "But I saw..."

"I don't think you could have seen it. It was pale, and powerful. It broke through my barriers. Tossed me across the room."

Her face turned white. "Did you catch it?"

"Of course." He tried to give her a cocky grin, but even he could feel it came off as a pained grimace.

"Can I see it?"

He had her hand him his bag, and he took the deck from it. His fingers burned when he touched the wrinkled card, and something struck his mind just for a second. Anger? Joy? It was hard to tell which, and once it was gone, it was hard to tell whether or not it had come from the card. He slid it out of the deck and held it up for her.

She stared at it for so long that he felt he had to say something.

"What is it?" He wasn't sure whether he was asking about the demon, specifically, or the situation in general.

"It looks different. Not pale to me, but different. Like a shadow on a white page. I've never seen anything like it. This is why I didn't note it in the building." She looked past the card to him. "Bryan, this might be a beta."

The possibility had been in his mind all along, but hearing it said aloud, in some way confirming the thought, made his blood run cold. "I thought those were only in Japan and Germany. Not Chicago."

She looked at the card again, her voice far away. "They're supposed to be."

"Are you sure it's a beta?"

"How can I be? I've never seen one. But what else could it be?"

Bryan knew her sight was different from what he saw when possessed. Andrade and her Spotter comrades didn't see the demons as red lights, but as things which were more abstract, almost in a fourth dimension... like a tesseract emitting emotion.

Unexplainable, indescribable. So, any description of a beta from the point of view of a Spotter was pretty useless. It had to be seen by the Spotters themselves.

He studied the card, noting the pulse running over its surface. It was stronger, deeper than the usual demon. He shivered and shoved the thing back in the deck, not wanting it in his hands anymore.

"You need to show this to the office," she added. "And then take the rest of the night off. No more hunting until tomorrow. You look like hell."

"I feel like hell." There had been some physical damage – the cut on his arm, a minor concussion – but the mental damage couldn't be measured by anything in the ambulance. He was utterly exhausted, as if he hadn't slept in days, and his ability to focus was dulled. This wasn't typical; he could feel sick and slimy after a possession but he'd experienced nothing like this in the past. It was the result of the fourth demon trying to fight its way into his body. He couldn't imagine what it would have been like to let it possess him.

"You could have died," Andrade said. "Betas killed four Possesseds in Germany alone, and Japan's worse off even than that."

"Maybe I'm a prodigy." Again, he meant to appear cocky, but only came off tired.

Andrade studied him, making him fidget. He knew what Andrade was looking at, and that she wasn't admiring his face, expression, or even his deep brown eyes or tousled hair. She was looking at his aura, reading it to see how injured he really was. And there was apparently a lot to read.

"Scratch going to the office," she finally said. "Go home and rest. I'll put in a report tonight, and tomorrow you can do the show and tell."

"That's ridiculous." He stood up in protest, but his legs gave away the act and he had to steady himself against the ambulance's doorway.

"Is it, now?" she asked with a raised eyebrow.

"Look, if there's one, there could be more, so I need to bring it in right away."

"Which is why I'm making the report as soon as I leave you. And once they get it, it'll take a day to arrange a meeting of all the Spotters to view the demon. So, it's not even going to be needed until tomorrow night. And how would I look if I sent you to collapse in the office?"

"But Hussein, at least–"

"Will get my report. This is an order. You're going home."

Bryan sighed. It was easy to forget that, in the end, Spotters had authority over the Possesseds' actions. As he had never been hurt so badly, the situation had never come up. But tonight, on his first call of the night – his first possession of the night – he had an order: go home and rest.

Andrade took his sigh as resignation. "Come on, I'll drive you home."

He nearly fell asleep on the ride, and Andrade asked whether he would make it up the stairs okay.

"Yeah," he said. "I'm feeling better. Unless you want to come up."

"For what?" She raised her eyebrows at him. "Coffee?"

He felt his cheeks flush. "No, um... I didn't mean it like that. Forget it."

He might have caught a glimpse of a smile on Andrade's lips as he opened the car door, but he was never sure. He stepped out of the jet black year-old Audi, thinking the same thing he always thought when he stepped into or out of it: ten years ago, their single company car had been a used Dodge van. Now they had a fleet of Audis. He shut the door and poked his head back in through the open window. "Are you sure? I really am feeling better."

Andrade turned deadly serious. "You're really pressing that coffee."

"No! Not..." He ran a hand through his hair. "I mean about me not going to the office tonight."

Andrade flashed a grin. "I know. I'm just messing with you. You're so cute when you're flustered. But you still look like you've been dragged through hell. Go rest."

He nodded, unable to argue, and waved goodbye. He watched the car retreat into the night. His failed date at the club flashed through his mind and he again lamented the fact – as he so often did – that joke as she did, Andrade would never really accept any advances on his part, even if he could stand to make any. No Spotter would take a chance on a Possessed; they knew too much.

The climb up the stairs to his apartment winded him, making him think maybe he wasn't feeling better after all. Despite his previous protests, it would probably take hours for him to recover fully. And this *had* been his night off originally.

Black Heart

Remember when you didn't get nights off? he thought to himself as he unlocked his door. *Maybe that's why you go on dates that you're certain will fail. Because you don't know what to do with yourself on a night off.*

His apartment was deadly quiet. Even the noisy upstairs neighbor was asleep. He went straight to the remote and turned on the TV. He wanted to flop down on the couch right away, but pushed himself to the pantry first to grab a nutrition bar. He had meals ready in the fridge, meals he had to make on days off or right before work because of how drained he always was after working, but he felt the standard Clif bar worked best when he was at his lowest.

Bryan tended to check CNN before heading out in the evening, and it clicked back on whenever he turned the TV on after work. He often regretted it, finding the content infuriating. Today was no different.

A woman was on the TV, gabbing to the camera. "Well, it's not working, is it? There were 75,000 deaths two years ago, and last year, the toll skyrocketed to 126,000. That's more than deaths from firearms. And I'm not talking about India or Brazil or God forbid Somalia; I'm talking about the U.S. So, what are these guys doing? Why are we funding them?"

A man in the panel beside her interrupted. Bryan knew his face well; he was an apologist for their office, always getting yelled at on news shows. "Now, I'm not denying things are getting worse. After all, you'd be hard-pressed to find a denier these days, compared to ten years ago. The proof is all around–"

"Assuming these 'demons' are the supernatural beings your office claims they are and not just a physical phenomenon," cut in the shrill woman.

The moderating newscaster stopped the both of them. "Such arguments about the nature of the problem aside, what is the office doing to fight back?"

"Look," the man said, clearly exasperated to find himself repeating explanations he had spoken a hundred times before. "The picture is bleak, but let's look at countries – like Somalia – who had no infrastructure to battle this. There's widespread death and resulting disease for the remaining population. People can't even enter the area without a very high risk of attack. Now, look at the U.S., at Korea. People are... understandably worried, but they work, they go to the movies, they go shopping."

"Are you suggesting we institute martial law like Korea?" the woman asked.

He held up his hands. "That's not what I said–"

Bryan switched the channel to a stunning knife set on sale for only $49.99. He had heard the arguments almost as much as their media control guy had. He would like to see Ms. Shrill try out for a position as a Possessed to see how real demons were. And if she failed, all the better.

He smiled at the thought before he caught himself. That was the demons speaking. He also didn't like the thoughts the knives were bringing up. He switched the channel again, and again, and again.

◆

His cell rang, waking him. He'd left it in his coat pocket, and he had to stumble over to the chair he'd tossed the coat onto. When he fished the phone out, he answered without looking at who it was.

"'Ello," he murmured.

"Bryan, it's Hussein. Did I wake you?"

Bryan straightened up as if Hussein had walked into the room. "Naw – no, sir."

"Of course, I did. I had to check on you, though. Are you okay?"

"Yes, just a bit murky still. I'll be fine by tomorrow..." Suddenly, he noticed the dim light of morning seeping through the curtains and amended his answer, "tonight. Are you still at work?"

"It couldn't be helped. First Andrade's report and then.... Well, you'll find out tomorrow."

"Do you need me in now?"

"No, I need you to rest." Hussein paused, and when he spoke again, his voice was hushed. "It was very dangerous, what you went through. You didn't sleep with it near you?"

"No, sir." Bryan glanced at his bag, where he had dropped it in the hall just inside his door. As far away as could be.

"Good. If it speaks, don't listen to it."

"So, they *do* speak?"

"Not all of them, but it's been known to happen. Just be careful when you carry it." He paused again, as if in thought. "Tell me what happened."

Bryan told him, only omitting how he had thrown up his guts at the end. It was strange to tell the story, being separated from it now. Clinical.

"You did well," Hussein said when he was done. "You kept your head. Had you panicked, it could have destroyed you."

Bryan knew what he really meant when he said 'destroyed.' Destroyed was just easier to say aloud. But even as he was chilled by the connotation, he was buoyed by the praise. "Well, I didn't know what it was. I thought it was a regular demon, just stronger."

"In a way, that's what they are. But there'll be plenty of time for all that in tonight's meetings. Go back to sleep. We'll want to see you in the office early, before shifts start. 4 pm."

"Yes, sir." He hung up, feeling better after the short conversation. That was probably why Hussein had called – even knowing he would be asleep – to make him feel better. He hoped that wasn't the only reason for the praise.

He wasn't sure he would be able to fall back to sleep, so he sat down in front of the TV again. Next thing he knew, he was waking up. It was 2 pm, so he had some time. He kept the TV channel on sitcoms, not wanting to stress out over the news again, and put together a large breakfast-dinner. Eating it ravenously, he wondered why he hadn't eaten anything after the phone call. Once he was done cleaning up, he assessed himself: his thoughts were clear, lighting wasn't giving him a headache, and his pulse was higher than normal but good enough. He couldn't expect to be a hundred percent so soon, but he was decent. The long day's sleep had helped. He glanced at the bag by the door and gave it the middle finger before taking a shower.

He rode the Elevated to the office, watching out the window as the buildings grew taller and denser. As the ride dragged on, he thought he could feel some imprint of a mind from the bag tucked next to him under his arm.

If it speaks, don't listen to it.

Bryan knew about what had happened to the first agent who had caught a beta. Everyone did. Every agent had followed the story in Germany when a demon started speaking to its captor. It had been exciting – a new development in demon-hunting. The man was encouraged and given questions to ask the thing, though the answers never made much sense. That man was dead now, having set himself on fire with his own matchstick totems. Agents didn't speak to their betas anymore.

But if it could speak, surely it *did* have a mind? More so than the regular demon that just wanted to eat. Or was he only imagining things, looking for something he expected to find? He hadn't touched the card itself since showing it to Andrade. He probably should have; he would soon have to hold it up in front of a room full of people and it might make a fool of him. He should have prepared. Would he have to make a speech?

He got off at Madison/Wabash and walked the three blocks to the unassuming building. "Office of Demonic Defense" was printed in block letters on the glass doors, but other than that, nothing differentiated it from any other building in the area. A decent Indian restaurant sat a few doors down, and some attorneys were stationed above that, with a bank down and across the street. On any given day, people walking the sidewalks were unaware that anything other than a paper-pushing office was behind and above these doors.

Well, that perception wasn't that far off from reality, really.

However, people weren't walking the sidewalks unaware today. Today, reporters approached him as soon as they saw him steering towards the doors. They hounded after him, shouting vague questions about what his thoughts were, but they couldn't follow as he ducked inside. A few people were milling in the lobby, but they were security guards and office workers. Other workers were filing through the door behind Bryan, fighting through the reporters as he had, just trying to go to work.

Clipping his ID to his lapel, Bryan nodded to security as he set his bag on the strip. He felt a moment of anxiety as it slipped through the x-ray, as if it would vanish upon being out of his sight for a moment, and stepped through the metal detector.

"Hi Jones," he said to one of the security guards as he stepped through, even as he kept an eye on the x-ray. "Something going down?"

Jones shook his head. "You're about to find out."

Bryan looked at him. "Cryptic."

"Sorry, man, if I were to tell you the whole deal, I'd hold up the line."

Bryan frowned but nodded, grabbing his bag and ironically feeling more secure for it. Part of the whole deal was probably about him anyway, and Jones just didn't know it yet.

He rode the elevator, pressed in by people getting on and off at every other floor. They kept bumping against his bag, too, even as much as he tried to hold it against himself, and he growled under his breath every time it happened. He got off on the eighteenth floor and almost immediately heard his name shouted.

"Ivers!"

He rolled his eyes as he turned, but was relieved to find it was only Cameron Knowles approaching him from down the hall. There was no mistaking the short flat-top haircut, that ridiculous multicolored neon jacket, and the pair of massive headphones wrapped around the man's neck. As always, Cam looked like he had just stepped out of the 80s. Which was ridiculous, because Cam hadn't even been alive in the 80s.

"Business casual, I see," Bryan commented as he grasped Cam's hand and gave him a slap on the back, and Cam drew him in for a bear hug as if they hadn't seen each other for months.

"We can't all wear those sloppy ties all the time," Cam said, pointing to Bryan's loosely knotted tie. "How are you?"

"So, you know?" Bryan smiled thinly, sliding his keycard and opening the door to the section of offices where evening briefings tended to be held.

"Man, *everyone* knows. Have you heard about—"

"*Ivers!*" This was practically screamed from a group of women – Jen, Jill, Jess, and Missy – standing outside their cubicles, who all turned their attention on him. Jess ran up to him ahead of the others, her brown hair falling loose from her usually immaculate ponytail.

"Are you okay?" she asked him as if she had just witnessed him getting hit by a truck.

"I'm fine," he said, his smile fading as he noticed that Jen and Missy were both crying. He had seen Missy cry before, at news of deaths or agents being overtaken, but Jen was typically stoic. This commotion wasn't just about him. "What's going on?"

"Rogge's dead," Missy burst out, which sent fresh tears down Jen's cheeks.

"What?"

Jess took him aside, down the hallway between the cubicles and away from the other three, and Cam followed. "Late last night," she explained. "The police had to take her down."

Bryan stared at her in shock. "But I didn't hear she was having trouble working or anything."

"It was something else," Cam said, suddenly serious. "I mean, something worse, like what you caught."

"But," Jess broke in, "much worse."

"Worse than a beta?" Bryan asked, shifting from shock to anger at all this news. "They must be exaggerating. Most people haven't even seen a beta."

"No, I talked to Rubina. She was the Spotter, and she's half-mad over what she saw."

"He said, she said," Bryan spat. His head was throbbing, the beginning of a headache, but he didn't recognize the warning sign that his temper was already out of hand before his work shift had even begun.

"Maybe. Maybe not. And Gennick...." Her eyes widened as she remembered something. "Have you spoken to Hussein yet?"

"I was on my way there."

"He's not in his office. He's in a meeting, room A-4. I'm sure he'll want to see you there."

"How would you know?"

"Chill, man," Cam spoke up.

But Jess only put a hand on Bryan's shoulder. She was used to snippy, short-tempered Possessed agents. She was a liaison for communication between the office suits and the Spotters and Possesseds. She saw a lot of Possesseds go through her office.

"Take it easy," she said. "We're all reacting differently."

Bryan took a deep breath and nodded, unable to look her in the eye. Then he turned to head back to the elevators. Cam followed him.

"They could have called me in," Bryan growled to him, giving voice to what was really bothering him. "I wasn't infirm."

"You couldn't have done anything. You're assuming you would have gotten there in time. And what if you had gone and gotten possessed by the thing that drove Rogge over the edge and gotten her shot? It could have overtaken you easily considering your state."

"Well, we'll never know, will we?"

"*I* know. I was there."

Bryan stared at him. "You didn't say you were—"

"I didn't want to announce it. I don't want to talk about it. But Rogge wasn't the only one to die or get messed up. You would have been mincemeat."

"Is Andrade's report on my condition that bad?" He tried a broken smile.

Cam's brows were knit as he seemed to study Bryan. "Did it almost get you?"

There was silence as Bryan wondered how to respond, and with how much information. The elevator dinged as he stalled, and the doors popped open to reveal a crowd. Three people got off and Bryan got on, grateful to leave Cam behind with the question unanswered. Even if he did get a few stares from the group in the elevator. Celebrity of the night. His achievement felt like nothing now, Hussein's praise from earlier suddenly being forgotten.

The conference room Hussein was in was packed. As he came in, everyone looked up and the guy standing beside the projection of a map of Chicago stopped talking. They probably would have stared silently for some time, except that Hussein stood and waved him over. He even had the man next to him stand so that Bryan could sit. He then waved for the speaker to continue, and Bryan had to listen to an in-depth plan of how many Spotters would be at which blocks on the map, according to which packs of demons had cropped up where. It was deathly boring, but he tried his best to listen, thinking Hussein may have wanted him there to hear it. Then a woman discussed numbers of demons in D.C., New York, San Francisco, Toronto, and so on and so on. Despite all the sleep he had gotten, Bryan had to suppress yawn after yawn. After what felt like hours but was probably only thirty minutes, Head Coordinator Dover spoke a few parting words and thanked them all.

Hussein and Bryan escaped into the hall before anyone could stop either of them.

"It's good to see you." Hussein clapped a hand on Bryan's shoulder as they walked. "We need to get with Andrade and go over what exactly happened, and then we'll have some more meetings."

Bryan took a good look at him. Hussein was pale, and dark shadows ringed his eyes. "Did you get any sleep today?"

"I think I dozed off for five minutes in a teleconference with D.C." He gave Bryan a smile, but it was thin and exhausted.

"Well, now I feel bad for almost falling asleep during that meeting just now." As soon as the words were out, he regretted them. He was probably supposed to have been paying attention to the meeting. Surely, Hussein had.

Hussein sighed as if disappointed. "You always were impatient."

"I mean, I was listening..." The defense sounded hollow even to him.

"Oh? How many demons this week in Atlanta?"

"Um..."

"I'm kidding." Hussein smiled again, easier this time. "I don't remember, either."

They walked a few steps more before Bryan asked, "Sir, how many died last night?"

Hussein didn't answer right away, as if he didn't want to answer. "Not counting civilians? Three Spotters and four Possesseds."

Bryan's feet stopped, unable to walk further. Hussein stopped and turned to him. A clerk with an armful of files strolled past. "How many civilians?" Bryan asked.

"Current count is at 160."

"A hundred and sixty?" Bryan's voice was barely above a whisper.

"Many of the casualties were police officers responding to the scene."

"Then the Possesseds and Spotters?"

"A Possessed went in and, though they survived, they failed the capture, so three more were sent in at one time. Those three were killed. The fourth was hit later on along with the Spotters."

"Then who caught it?"

Hussein's face had been blank up to now, a mask. But now it fell, and he turned away to hide it and started walking down the hall again. "No one. It's still out there."

Bryan didn't move. He only stared at the geometric pattern on the carpet, his mind full of could-have-beens. He could have been there. If he hadn't gotten injured. If he hadn't gone to the hotel. If his date hadn't been a disaster and he hadn't decided to respond to the general call.

"You did your part last night," Hussein said.

Bryan looked up with a start. Hussein had walked back to him. A pair of people from the meeting passed by, and Bryan caught a snippet of their conversation: the compiling of pie charts and statistics.

"How many more would have died last night, had you not caught the one you did?" Hussein continued. "And you would have died, too, had I let them include you on the call for back-up."

Bryan's face betrayed his thoughts.

"Yes," Hussein said, the creases around his eyes deepening as his voice remained level. "That was my decision. Hate me for it if you want, but I would make it again. I wasn't willing to lose you last night."

"Why? Because then you wouldn't get to parade me around as the guy who caught..." He trailed off and averted his eyes from Hussein's own. He hated all these things he was saying today. It wasn't him.

Was it?

Hussein studied him silently.

"I didn't mean," Bryan began, and then stopped. "I know you..."

"Is it affecting you too much?" Hussein asked. "We can lock it up if the benefits don't outweigh the risks."

Hussein's meaning was clear even if the true question remained unspoken: Is the beta driving you insane? Are you at risk of reaching the same end as the first man to ever catch a beta? Bryan had seen it happen to others time and again, and not even with a beta, but rather with regular commonplace demons – the dissociation, the loss of self, the madness. He knew it well. But could he recognize it in himself?

He briefly looked inside himself. He hadn't felt any imprint of the beta's... mind? But it was certainly affecting him. Was it any worse than the usual, though? Maybe this was all just the usual. And what if Bryan didn't keep the card on him? Without his latent energy exerting power over the demon trapped in the card, it could break out. Ten days was the given minimum that a Possessor watch over the demon in its totem, after which it was fully attached and could be stored in the basements of the office.

If it broke out, and killed more, how could Bryan live with the fact that he had traded it in for a bit of comfort?

There was no comfort in his job. He was used to this. Others had kept and contained their betas just fine before him and his.

"I'm just always this ornery," he said aloud, smiling thinly. "And anyway, there's too much risk in storing it tonight. It's not like I'm the first to catch one of these. I can take it."

Hussein nodded. "All right. But I want you to be honest with yourself, and with me. If you feel yourself slipping, we'll figure something out."

Bryan nodded back. He searched again in his head to see if something else was there, focusing on the bag at his hip. Nothing... just him.

Two hours before sunset, all 47 Spotters and 29 Possesseds – what remained of their office after last night – were crowded in classroom 1, which was a room typically used for training and seminars. The tiny, uncomfortable seats with those little desktops that rotate into place were all filled, and some people had notepads or laptops out, expecting crucial information they shouldn't forget. Cam waved to Bryan from the standing room at the back as he passed by, and as he waved back, Bryan made his way to his saved seat at the front by the podium. The position promised that he would be called up before the group.

Hussein was seated behind the front desk along with a couple of other higher-ups. The room hushed expectantly when he stood, as if everyone held their breath at once.

"First order of business," he said, "is the beta that was caught last night." He recounted the events from what Bryan and Andrade had told him. Thankfully, he left out details of the beating Bryan had taken, only saying that the demon was very dangerous, and had broken through a barrier and attacked. Then he called Bryan up front.

As he stood, Bryan felt like a student called up for doing something wrong. Hussein had told him to show everyone the demon before anything else, since they might not listen to his words for expectation. He almost dropped the pack of cards, his palms were so sweaty, and he found himself looking to Hussein for some sort of encouragement. Hussein did give him a smile and a nod, but that only made him feel silly for looking at him at all. People in the audience chattered in low voices, and he had to wonder if some of it was about him. He didn't look up at them.

Instead, he focused and reached into the deck, and as his fingers touched the card he was looking for, he gasped and pulled away from it. The thing inside had snarled at him; it had thrown hate and loathing at him. It had been like touching a rabid dog and discovering the mistake only too late. But what shocked him most of all was the curiosity and... something like admiration in how it had looked at him, *seen* him. Not at all like a rabid dog.

The deck fell to the carpeted floor, cards scattering. The sound of it startled Bryan back to reality and he looked up at the crowd. A couple of the Possesseds chuckled, but mostly there was silence. Everyone was staring at him. He felt his face grow red-hot as he bent and started to pick up the cards. The beta's card lay among the others, crumpled but otherwise looking the same as all the others. But Bryan knew better.

"I would help if I could," one of the Spotters said to him from the front row.

"I know," Bryan said. "Thanks anyway." No one but him could touch the cards. He had to pick them all up himself, and it felt like he picked them up for an hour as everyone watched him silently. He left the worst for last, but was prepared this time when he touched the crumpled three of clubs. It watched him and spread hate through him, hot in his hand and in his head, but Bryan swallowed it all and held up the card.

Every seat in the room creaked as every body leaned forward to study it. Even the Possesseds, though they couldn't see anything but the three of clubs in their normal, unpossessed states. But the Spotters could see it, and they began chattering excitedly to each other about what they were seeing, their conversation full of metaphors and symbology and words like 'dimension' and 'aura.' As it had earlier, Bryan's head began to pound. The phantom eyes of the beta were trained on him like every pair of eyes in the room was trained on the card, but Bryan felt like everyone was watching him. He was aware he was sweating, and wondered if anyone was noticing. He wasn't sure which was worse – the demon investigating him, or everyone else staring in his direction.

After a full minute of this, Hussein held up a hand to silence the room, and the conversation died down with reluctance.

"That was for the Spotters," he said. "Now, the Possesseds will need to listen. Bryan's going to tell you what it's like."

And here was this speech Bryan was dreading. For a moment, he wished he had just stayed in that horrible night club with the horrible band instead of running off to a hotel full of demons. Then, he set that aside and talked, haltingly, about how the demon had been too pale to be seen until it was on him, about its strength, and about how it had tried to enter him and nearly succeeded. How much power he had had to sap from the demon in him to capture it, and how it almost hadn't been enough. In the end, he was certain he hadn't gotten any of it put into adequate words – and how could he have? – but when he finished, no one spoke and many of the listeners had a stunned look to them.

"Thank you, Ivers," Hussein said, his voice like a thunderclap in the silence. Bryan nodded and gratefully went back to his seat. Hussein needlessly added a few words about how everyone should be careful, that one demon signaled more, and so on. Then Ruggeri took her turn.

Ruggeri was the no-nonsense Lead Spotter. Much like a librarian or boot camp instructor, she was never seen without her hair in a tight bun. She stood stiffly and spoke in a clipped tone. "Ivers was able to capture this demon. Our other team last night was not so lucky."

Bryan gritted his teeth against that phrasing, but he couldn't expect Ruggeri to part with praise easily.

"Most of you," she continued, "if not all, have already heard some part of what happened. We're here to set the facts straight.

"At 4:15 early this morning, a Spotter and Possessed responded to a call at the Caltrop Apartments on Westwood. Note that this is three miles from where Ivers captured his beta. The Spotter was unable to view any demon, but noted several deaths in the vicinity. The Possessed entered the complex with caution. Nine minutes later, the Spotter lost sight of and communication with the Possessed. This Possessed is currently alive in the hospital."

Bryan's heart skipped a beat. Everyone in the room knew what 'in the hospital' meant. That Possessed wasn't in the hospital for physical ailments.

"A second Possessed," Ruggeri went on, "was on hand at this time, and two more were called in along with additional Spotters. Three Possesseds entered the complex at 5:05 AM. Three minutes later, two of them were dead. The third exited the building under influence, and attacked our agents and the police force stationed outside, killing an additional Possessed, three Spotters, and numerous police and civilians. The police were forced to open fire and eliminate this Possessed, after which the demon was free to roam again. Further efforts to contain the demon by additional Possesseds failed, and the demon retreated.

"We believe it traveled east, but we are uncertain since our Spotters were unable to view it. Possesseds described it as little more than a filter, *very* dim. Current death count is at 170, 32 of those being police or SWAT, with four Possesseds and three Spotters. Information is still coming in."

She paused, and the silence was deafening. She had rattled it all off with such a cold and calculating tone, like a newscaster with no relation to the situation.

"This demon," she went on, "is unlike anything seen before. It carries little to no aura. Its psychic attacks are powerful and widespread. Similar to the attacks you're all used to, simply stronger. Along with the deaths, a large number of police cars were compacted. Many of the policemen were killed not by the demon inhabiting and devouring them, but by its psychic blast. The people it did enter were devoured at an incredible rate.

"We have termed this demon a gamma."

The silence in the audience collapsed as everyone began speaking at once. A gamma – there was no such thing they'd ever heard of. Even Hussein had trouble bringing calm back to the room. But all Ruggeri had to add to her remarks was a command for everyone to be careful, and if there was a call but no apparent demon, they should be vigilant, etc. Nothing any of them needed to be told.

First a beta, and then something completely new and more destructive. You didn't have to be a Spotter to read the atmosphere in the room.

Everyone was terrified.

Bryan jumped up as soon as the meeting was over. No one else was really moving around; they mostly just stood and murmured to each other, still in shock. He shoved his way through them and found Cam in the back, and grabbed his arm to pull him out of the room.

"I'm sorry," he told him. "I know you said you don't want to talk about it..."

"But you have to know what I saw," Cam groaned. "Are you ever gonna owe me."

"Well, we knew we had a man down."

They were seated on a bench in the courtyard, coffees in hand. The last light of day was swiftly fading, and the wind sweeping through was chill but not yet wintry.

"We didn't know yet that it was Gennick in that building, but everyone had been called. I got there just as they were deciding which three would go in. I guess there were six of us there at that point. Rogge and Schoettmer and Mokri were the ones to go in. The rest of us didn't think we would even be needed. Three Possesseds are more than enough to take down a beta if they have notice, and we didn't even know if that's what it was. It could have been an alpha and Gennick had just been taken by surprise. We were just security.

"Until the Spotters said that everyone inside was dropping. Rogge killed Schoettmer and Mokri. That's not official, but we know that's what happened. It got her, and just stabbed or crushed or whatever... the two of them. The Spotters saw it happening – well, saw the auras vanishing, and I suppose that's just as bad. And we all started talking about what to do, and we didn't know the answer. We could go in, the lot of us, but we might just get cut down like the others. And Rogge is – was – prime talent, and look what happened to her. We were fucked if we went in. So, we started thinking containment, to get more people there. Everyone and their mother was still on their way.

"We didn't have to make a decision. She came out. I hear it collapsed the floors and just dropped down to the lobby. The Spotters called our attention to it; said she was coming down fast. Then she came through the doors, smashing the glass, and she just stood there looking around, and we didn't need the Spotters to tell us she was under the influence. Her eyes were burning fierce. But it seemed confused, like it hadn't expected half of Chicago's finest to be out there even though fifty red and blue lights were flashing. Me and the other Possesseds ringed it and put up containment fire, but the fires just sputtered and faded out like smoke. Like when we were still training and couldn't figure out how to make it stick."

Bryan barely remembered his own training, but he had watched plenty of other recruits train. He had, while possessed, seen many attempted captures in controlled environments fail, watched the containing flames of supernatural power – the power of the demons – whipping around a target, tightening briefly, then falling away, fading and wafting off as if on a breeze. And he had failed a containment himself just last night, with the beta. He remembered the demon waving the flames aside as if they were a nuisance, and how they had vanished like they were nothing. How weak he had felt. How had Cam felt, confronted with something even stronger?

"Maybe it's my fault," Cam went on. "Maybe I should have tried again. I don't know. But I saw its anger on Rogge's face and I could swear I saw fear there, too. I put up as large a barrier as I could, and so did Gennisson. That's the only reason we're still here."

He suddenly looked at Bryan. "Shit, I didn't mean to mention him. Don't go to him and start demanding his side of things."

Bryan shook his head. Even if he did, Gennisson would probably tell him to go fuck himself.

"Anyway, it sent out a psychic pulse, but it was so *powerful*. Just raw and unfettered. And the weird thing is the demon inside me was disgusted at the display of it. Like it was inappropriate. Like this was some fancy dinner party and someone had eaten the salad with the dessert fork. But the pulse went out and just flattened everything. Crushed cop cars like tin cans. Shattered every light in the area. And the people... there's nothing left of the bodies. Gennisson was blown five hundred feet. He's still in the hospital, broken in a dozen places. Physically, thank God, not mentally. But I got the lesser of the blast. I wound up slammed against a crowd of cops.

"I didn't have time to try anything else. Everyone still alive opened fire. I saw Rogge ripped to pieces by the rounds, and it tried to take a few steps before her legs were shot out. It threw out another pulse, and there was another deafening sound of metal crumpling and people being crushed to pulp or screaming – and then she was down and it was free again.

"I thought it was gonna come for me. I was certain. And my demon just kept tut-tutting all this behavior. But it didn't come for me. It fed."

He stopped. Their coffee had been forgotten in their hands; Bryan's cup no longer seared his fingers. Cam was staring at the cobbles in the walkway. Bryan thought he might be done, and was about to speak when Cam continued.

"I didn't do anything."

He'd said it so quietly, the wind almost took it away, and Bryan thought he might have misheard. "What?" he asked.

"I didn't do anything," Cam repeated. "I sat there on the street and watched people drop like flies until it escaped. Me and everyone around me. We just huddled there like children. But I could have done something."

"You could have died. And taken more with you." Bryan wanted to say more – Cam had thought fast in putting up a barrier, saving lives. But the words didn't come. It was like all words had been taken from him, leaving him hollow.

"Maybe," Cam said. "Maybe." He stood and walked back to the office, leaving Bryan on the bench.

Bryan's phone chirped, and he pulled up the message. Orders for the night. "Partner with Andrade." Another message popped up, this one from Andrade: "I'll be in the lobby." He typed back an okay and leaned back to peer at the sky, which was swiftly turning dark.

Possesseds and Spotters almost never worked together two nights in a row. The Spotters would have had no problem with such an arrangement, but Possesseds built up an animosity for anyone they spent time with. That was why no Possessed in the office could handle a steady relationship, let alone marriage. It was literally dangerous for anyone to hang around a Possessed for too long.

So, it was no coincidence that they'd put him with Andrade again tonight, but it was silly. Did they expect him to have a heart-to-heart with her? Talk things out? Have a psychological moment? Or did they think she would be the only one able to handle him tonight? He supposed he should just be happy they were letting him work. As if that was a reward.

"No time to waste," she said as he joined her by the shrubs in the lobby. "Late start, and we're way over on the west side."

"West?" he nearly shouted in response.

"Yes, west." She glanced back over her shoulder as he caught up. "Oh, you want to go east. After the new one."

"They're keeping me away from it," he protested.

"Of course, they are. You were under terrible strain last night. They're giving you a break. Take it."

He growled, but had no response. She was right, of course. But he didn't have to like it.

The first call came as soon as they hit Garfield Park. Several demons in a commercial area in Oak Park. Andrade pulled up alongside the police block and they got out. The two cops there gave their badges looks of immense relief.

"They've been drifting from shop to shop," one of them explained. "We think they're in the Jewel now."

Andrade looked down the road towards the grocery store. "I think you're right." She turned to Bryan and added, "But get ready in case they come out. Most everyone in there is dead."

"Most?" Bryan prodded as he reached into his bag and took out a deck.

"It's hard to tell from this distance, but there may be human auras. Two inside the Jewel, two further down the street."

Bullshit. People were still alive in there. Andrade just didn't want him to rush in, like she thought he was some kind of idiot. Fucking Spotter psych shit. Fucking bitch.

He looked down, and might have screamed had his throat not closed up on him. Instead, he let out a croak and dropped the card he'd held in his hand and been about to tear.

The three of clubs. The beta.

Andrade stopped and looked back at him. "What?" She looked down at the card on the concrete and back to him, reading his aura. "What happened?"

Sweat stood out on his forehead. "I was about to tear it. I don't remember taking it out."

"Ivers..."

He looked up and saw the Jewel beyond her, just a couple silent shops and a parking lot away. He shook his head and snatched up the card, shoving it back into his bag. "We don't have time for this." He strode past her, making sure to pull a regular demon from the pack.

"Ivers!" Andrade called.

He looked back. She had stopped ten steps back, judging her distance from the danger. He was on his own now.

"Be careful," she said.

He felt a twinge of irritation that she had stopped him just to say that, but he only nodded and turned back to the store, tearing the card he held. The incredible pain of blunt aches and sharp needles and strained muscles flooded him and darkened his mind and vision, and he nearly toppled over, but he managed to only waver drunkenly before continuing down the sidewalk.

He entered the store from the front doors, like he was just strolling on in to pick up some frozen pizza. The demons were among the aisles. He could see their drifting red waves, belying their hunger and ferocity. It was like they were shopping, too, browsing cans and boxes. The store's speakers were still belting out "I've Got My Mind Set on You," but other than that, everything was silence.

In the produce, fruits and vegetables had withered and shriveled here and there, picked at by the demons and judged not quite as tasty as humans. Bryan could see the faint green glow of the plants' aeons — a shadow of what animals held. And then he nearly tripped over the first dead body, taut and gray and sprawled out beside a display of cakes and scones.

Around the corner, in the breads, was one of them. He had it encircled and captured before it even saw him, and he felt both confusion and amusement coming from it as he put it away into the deck. He smiled along with it, though later he wouldn't know why. It was one of those demon things that only made sense while you were possessed. There were more bodies around now, sucked dry and uninteresting to him. There was nothing left there for the demon in him to find appetizing.

Another demon was wandering towards the other end of the store. Bryan passed more aisles as he approached it, and was almost to it when he heard a clatter from the pharmacy, punctuated by a strangled cry. He went to the counter and peered over it at the little bottles that sat on the shelves or had been spilled onto the ground. He couldn't see human aeons through solid objects like he could see the demons, or like a Spotter could with auras, but he knew he had heard somebody.

"Someone there?" Bryan called low. "I'm from the O.D.D."

No one replied. He glanced back at the demon, but it hadn't moved far. Probably sleepy from its meal, lazily sniffing around for dessert. It wasn't causing any current problem, so he clutched his bag close so it wouldn't make noise as he hopped over the pharmacy's counter.

"I'm coming to you," he quietly reassured any possible person. "Don't panic, you're safe where you are."

He rounded a shelf and there she was, huddled in the back corner, under a table. She was maybe all of fifteen, and her dark eyes were wide and frightened. They locked onto him.

"Are you alright?" he asked, hungrily noting her intense aeon glowing bright in the dim grime of his vision.

She was frozen. He repeated the question, and after a moment, she shook her head no sharply.

He glanced around. The demon in the aisles was still browsing. He saw another demon drifting somewhere in the back of the store, but it was far away. The rest that Andrade had pointed out were far off, past even the back rooms, possibly outside or next door.

He held out a hand to the girl. "Hang on to me. I'll show you outside. We have people out there."

She shook her head again, even more forcibly.

Did he have time for this? His head was pounding. He could be done with the demons and then deal with her.

"Okay." He knelt down and looked into her eyes, hoping she was listening. "But stay here and..."

She saw something in his eyes. Her own widened even more than he would have thought they could and, almost in slow motion, her mouth opened and she screamed.

He cursed and stood as he turned, and saw the demon rushing at them through the shelves and aisles and into the pharmacy, drawn by the noise. He encircled it, but it took concentration to slow its advance and hold it. It bucked like a bronco to try and break free, and he pulled hard from the demon in him in order to gain the power needed to settle it. It wasn't so much a battle with the demon that possessed him, but a battle to use its powers without falling into the darkness and the hunger – a balancing act done under the intense pressure of the demon attacking him from outside. The thick grime settled over everything in Bryan's vision as he tried to center the containment fire, and a thought that occasionally crossed his mind at these times crossed it again: it would be easier to give in.

The girl screamed again, but it wasn't a scream of terror this time; it was a scream of pain. Bryan risked a glance over his shoulder.

The other demon from the back had come after all, and it had her. Its red glow pulsed over and around and inside her as she contorted on the floor.

He cursed again, louder and stronger, and turned back to his task. She was good as dead now. He used his anger to quell the contained demon and sealed it in a row of diamonds. Then he turned to the girl.

She was still screaming and writhing on the floor. The demon was now fully inside her, and Bryan realized with a start that it was trapped.

He cursed a third time, and fell to his knees beside her, fishing an empty card from his deck.

"Girl, hold this." He wrapped her hands around the card and held them there. "You have to listen to me."

She moaned and cried, but stopped screaming at least. Still, she didn't look at him. He held her hands with one of his, noting how tiny her own were, and used his other hand to turn her face to his.

"Listen," he said, "you can push that thing out of you, into this card in your hands. Drive it out."

She whimpered and shook and tried to turn away. He gripped her chin. Her eyes were no longer wide. Her entire expression was twisted in agony, tears smearing her cheeks.

"You can do it. Just think about the card and push it out into it."

She closed her eyes tightly, apparently concentrating and trying. But she moaned and rolled her head. Bryan could see the demon still in her, red under her green aeon, roiling and swirling as if in a pool.

"Again. Concentrate on the card. Imagine the demon flowing out of you and into the card."

He looked to the back rooms again. Where the other demons roamed, still far away. They hadn't advanced in his direction. That was all well and good, but he still had a demon in himself. He couldn't tutor this girl indefinitely.

The girl sobbed. Bryan gripped the back of her head, driving her face into the card. "Do it," he snarled. "Drive it out. I know you can, so do it."

She whined, snot falling from her nose onto the card. But this time, Bryan watched the demon move from her insides to the card. Emptied of demon, the girl began convulsing and coughing. Bryan set her down on her side. He flicked on his radio.

"Andrade," he said into it, "I've got one of us in here."

The gamma didn't strike that night, and the rest of Bryan's work was uneventful, if 'uneventful' could include two more possessions and twenty-one deaths. He told Andrade the details of finding the girl – the new possible Possessed – and, after the last call of the night, she went back to the office to file yet another report. The girl herself had been whisked away in an ambulance, only just starting to come to her senses. Four other civilians had been found in the back rooms of the Jewel, having managed to hide from the demons... their lives changed forever, but alive.

As Bryan entered his apartment and flung his bag down beside the door, he thought again of the beta inside it. It hadn't bothered him again that night, settled in the bottom of the bag, but it had been watching him. He had felt it, noticing its attention in quiet moments, and had felt it slink back. Nine more nights until he could relocate it to the office as a fully bound capture. If the office didn't demand he keep it on himself longer to make doubly sure it wouldn't escape the card. Though Hussein was unlikely to let that happen, judging from how apprehensive he had been about Bryan keeping it for the normal amount of time.

He turned on the TV, and sure enough, the attack from last night was everywhere on every morning news program. As he ate his dinner-slash-breakfast he listened to the anchors prattle on about how the office had dropped the ball on this one. They were crowding outside the office, hounding anyone who looked like they might enter the building. Bryan wondered how Andrade had fared, getting back in there.

The police force's news conferences contained a lot of 'We-don't-have-all-the-information-yets,' and even Bryan wasn't sure how much the office's police liaisons were letting on to the cops. Probably, a battle was raging there. Chief Marchette wouldn't appreciate thirty-two dead cops and SWAT with no explanation.

But nothing about tonight. The gamma seemed to have gone into hiding. Scared? Or just full from last night's feast?

He switched the channel to Nickelodeon and fell asleep on the couch to the sound of SpongeBob. But he was plagued by nightmares of his sister, and of a cabin with a demon somewhere inside of it. He could sense it, but couldn't tell where it was, and so he went running from room to room – too many rooms – trying to find his sister. But all he found before waking in a cold sweat was a girl with dark eyes who convulsed on a bedroom floor and screamed when she saw him.

◆

"Another night spent together. They're trying to tell us something."

Bryan grumbled in response to Andrade's quip as he got into the passenger seat. She could most likely tell he was irritated, and was trying to lighten the mood. But his mood wouldn't be lightened enough for him to even get embarrassed at her tease. He didn't like this idea of the office having Andrade babysit him for the third night in a row.

She didn't say anything more as she started the car, but she did look a little too long at the shadows under his eyes, and likely at his aura, as well.

It wasn't just the partnership that annoyed Bryan; they were also assigned to the west side again, in what felt like a futile attempt to keep him out of harm's way. With the night past having offered no sign of the gamma, it was anyone's guess where it could be now. Hell, it could be in the Jewel that Bryan had been in last night for all anyone knew.

And Bryan knew why he was here in Andrade's car for the third night in a row, too, though it was something practically unheard of among Possessed and Spotters. Only part of Andrade's report on last night would have been about the girl in the Jewel. The other part of it would have been about a short moment in time where Bryan had very nearly allowed a beta to possess him without his knowledge, about him gasping and dropping a card before shrinking back from it in terror of what could have been.

He couldn't blame Andrade for reporting it, but he could be angry, and he was.

"So, how's that girl from last night?" he asked, trying to be civil, but not entirely happy with the topic of conversation he'd come up with.

Andrade looked at him in surprise. "They didn't tell you?"

Panic gripped him. "They told me I was partnering with you tonight. That's all." He braced himself for bad news: she'd died after all, gone crazy, killed herself....

"She wants to talk to you," Andrade said. "That's why we're on the west side again."

"To me?" Surprised but relieved, he relaxed in his seat. "Why?"

She shrugged. "The office psychologists went to see her in the hospital – she *is* doing alright – and she said she wanted to talk to you. Before committing to anything, I guess."

"Then why isn't Hussein going? He usually deals with anybody on the fence."

"He's kinda busy." She gave him a sideways *Duh* look.

"Oh. Yeah." He looked out the window at the passing apartment buildings, offices, and shops, and his mind automatically jumped to how to defend them – where he would enter, the path of hallways and stairs he would take, and where the demons might be. He had to intentionally shut off the thoughts and think instead of the girl. *The girl* – he didn't even know her name and she wanted to talk to him about hunting demons. The girl who had looked at his eyes and screamed at what she saw. What would he tell her? He wasn't Hussein; this wasn't his job.

He took a deep breath. *Don't get angry over this, too*, he told himself, though he wasn't sure if he was angry or just nervous.

Andrade drove them to the far west end of Garfield Park, deep into a network of broken houses, their siding crumbling and roofs in shambles, with bars on windows and debris on lawns and cars ready to fall to pieces. She stopped in front of one such house. They climbed the disintegrating steps to a front door whose screen was torn in two places, and knocked. An elderly woman answered, her gray hair tied back under a kerchief. She looked at them with some apprehension... because she knew who they were, Bryan guessed. But she only said, "Yes?"

"Hello." Andrade held up her badge. "I'm Aries Andrade and this is Bryan Ivers with O.D.D. We're here to speak with Ms. Sonia Reeves."

"My granddaughter, yes." Her face didn't change, but she moved aside. "Please come in."

They entered an immaculate room decorated with furniture that had seen better days but was polished to a shine. The old woman went to a chipped but sparkling set of stairs and called up them, "Sonia! They're here!", and then directed them to a worn sofa that had an elaborate quilt folded over its back.

"She's been waiting for you," she said. "Have a seat."

"Thank you," Andrade said.

"Thanks," Bryan managed, wondering if Sonia might trip and fall on her way down the stairs, so he wouldn't have to do this.

But she came down just fine, and he looked at her only momentarily before casting his eyes down.

She looked entirely different from the terrified girl he'd met in the pharmacy. This Sonia was still a teenager, but carried herself like a young woman, a smile on her lips if not in her eyes. Wary but confident. Already dealing with what she had gone through. He and Andrade stood to shake her hand and introduce themselves, and he felt the girl's eyes on him, studying him as if she was looking for something in particular, but he wouldn't meet her gaze.

"Thank you for meeting with us so soon," Andrade said as she sat back down. "We know things are difficult for you right now, and if there's any part of it you'd rather not talk about..."

"It's okay," Sonia said, her voice not entirely steady. "Your psych guys already brought up everything."

"I'm afraid that's a necessity these days. But we're glad you're considering the position."

"To be Possessed?"

"Yes, you show an inclination to tolerating demonic possession. It's quite rare, and we need all the help we can get."

"I'll bet. It's not like it's fun." She gave an awkward smile that Bryan caught out of the corner of his eye.

The grandmother entered with a tray of iced tea and cakes. Bryan snatched up a plate of cake and shoved a forkful in his mouth as if it would prevent him from having to speak. He barely noticed that it was delicious.

"Can I ask why you're considering it?" Andrade went on.

That awkward smile came back. "Well, it pays good, right? I mean, I'm sure you guys don't live in Garfield Park."

It was Andrade's turn to avert her eyes. "Yes, but there's a lot that comes with the pay. You've already experienced a part of it. You'd get used to it, and you'd be trained to handle it, but you'd still be going through a measure of physical pain and mental disturbance every work night."

Sonia shifted in her seat, as if remembering the pain from the night before. Sure, she had won the lottery, with the promise of a high-paying job, all training expenses covered. She just had to step into it. But what was the price?

Still, she looked directly at them as she responded. "A person can get used to a lot of pain, ya know?"

Andrade watched her for a moment, then looked at Bryan, who was still shoveling cake in his mouth. "I know I'm not the one you wanted to talk to. So, I'll let you two talk alone, okay?"

Bryan glared at her, but she stood and went to the kitchen, where the grandmother was clanging dishes together as if to drown out the conversation in the next room. Bryan didn't look up from his plate.

"Good cake," he said to fill the silence.

"Nana made it," Sonia replied.

The silence stretched out to seconds.

"Aren't you," said Sonia, "supposed to convince me to work for you?"

"Not my job," he mumbled.

"You just... catch demons."

"Yeah."

"Why do you do it?"

He munched on a bite of cake. "Pays good."

"I'm serious."

"Weren't you serious when you answered money?"

"I don't know. I don't even know if I'll do it, never mind why."

He finally looked at her. She was so small, maybe all of 5'3. She sat with both feet planted on the ground, as if ready to jump up at any moment. She had a little snub nose and short hair that rose in a halo of curls around her head. Her gaze was unsteady, caged and haunted.

"A demon took my family," he said. "All of them in one moment. Possesseds didn't even get a steady paycheck back then. But I joined because of that."

She thought about that. When she spoke again, her voice was low and quiet. "My best friend was in Jewel with me. I lost track of her when it happened, when we heard screams from the front of the store and everyone started running. I only found out afterward that she's dead. I probably heard her screaming and didn't know it was her."

She took a gulp of the iced tea as if it were whiskey. Bryan's cake sat on the arm of the sofa, forgotten.

"How do you do it?" she asked. "When there's so much death and screaming?"

"If I didn't do it, how much more death would there be?"

"That's a lot of responsibility."

"I suppose so, but..." He moved across the couch, closer to her. "Look, sometimes you fuck up, sometimes a demon gets away, and sometimes people die because you did something wrong. But you're trying, and that's all anyone can do at any job."

She took another pull of the iced tea, swallowed, and asked, "Does it always hurt like that?"

He had expected this question. "Yes, but you learn to control it, to deal with it. If you have a good reason to do it, the pain is nothing. The problem is the mental toll."

"Mental?"

"There are no physical scars when a Possessed invites a demon in. But even after it's gone, some of it remains in your mind. A shadow. A remnant. It becomes a part of you. One possession, two, you'd get away with remaining a normal human being. But night after night of possessions, it builds. It warps you. No Possessed is the same as before they took their job. You'll find yourself thinking thoughts you never would have imagined a year ago, feeling emotions at times when you never would have before. Its influence stays with you and it changes you."

His eyes held her own, hers wide and uncomprehending. He was scaring her, and he thought that was just fine.

"So, you'd better have a damned good reason to invite them in."

Chapter Two

"You scared her," Andrade accused on the way to the car.

Bryan stuck his hands in his pockets petulantly. "Letting a Possessed talk about possession. What did you expect to happen?"

"I'm sure that's not how Hussein would have handled it."

"Well, I'm not Hussein!" he snapped.

But she didn't notice. She stopped walking and put a hand to the mic in her ear.

"What?" he asked, too sharply.

"They're calling everyone. North side. Must be the gamma."

She didn't have to say anything else. They leapt into the car and were on their way. Bryan turned on the car's radio to hear the developments. A demon – the radio didn't use the term 'gamma', but that was obviously what they were dealing with – had taken over a Possessed and was hiding out in a college as if everyone outside would just forget about it and head home. Absolutely everyone was to come to the spot and do a gathered containment. It was unprecedented, but clearly they wanted to make sure a repeat of the other night didn't happen. The demon needed to be caught tonight.

Fucking PR, Bryan thought. *That's why they want it caught. Can't risk the funding getting cut.* He shook his head to clear the thought.

Well, it pays good, right?

Was he angry at the girl? Was that it? What did it matter to him if she joined for the money, anyway? Why was he being so high and mighty about it?

Easy, you don't want her to join. You saw her scream and writhe when it went at her, and you don't want her to go through that again. She's too young.

You were younger.

He focused on the lights of the houses passing by as the radio talked and the GPS quipped directions. Turn left, turn right, continue on, continue on....

The place was a circus: squad cars, SWAT vans, reporters, and the daring and curious – and stupid – students. All were swarming the parking lots and the lawns and the garden beds that were turning brown from the fall chill. Red and blue lights flashed against the walls of the buildings, alerting the demon that everyone in the world was just outside.

"It's still in there?" Bryan thought aloud.

"Can't be," Andrade said, as if he had asked her. "It would have moved on by now."

Bryan watched out the window as Andrade flashed her badge and their car was were waved through the roadblock. No panic, no dead bodies. The ambulances were idling, the paramedics smoking cigarettes. It was still holed up in there. What demon just sits in a corner with such a feast right outside the door?

They were snatched up by Connors as soon as they opened the car doors. He had his usual air of barely controlled panic under a veneer of calm, the sweat already standing out on his forehead despite the weather. It had been his default state of being for as long as Bryan had known him. Certainly, a heart attack was in the near future for him. The cop lights reflected red and blue off of his bald head.

"Andrade, you're to the left. Keep back with the other Spotters. You guys won't be able to do anything anyway – you're blind here. Ivers, I really didn't want to use you, but we need everyone here."

"Thanks for the vote of confidence," Bryan deadpanned.

"Shut up. We think it got Keeler, so keep your eyes peeled in there for her. You're around in the back parking lot with Caplin and Brogan. You're senior there. Attack starts in twenty minutes. On my signal, we're going to contain this whole building, and then restrict the circle in tune with everyone else until we can pinpoint the demon. Keep your radio on."

Bryan grumbled under his breath, but didn't lash out. Connors was a good guy underneath all the gruff, and they were all already on edge. This wasn't the time for one of the department's well-known Possessed-on-Possessed fights.

Connors knew what he was thinking, though, because he shouted after him, "Thanks, Ivers!"

Bryan waved in response, but didn't look back. He was studying the building as if he could see inside it. Six stories, as wide as tall. Science building. Classrooms and labs and professors' offices. Which would the demon be in?

He took a wide curve around the building to reach the other side, passing a couple of other groups of Possesseds awaiting the signal. But when he saw the shadows of Caplin and Brogan, he remembered that he would be in charge of the two of them and his heart skipped a beat. In charge? What experience did he have being in charge? The only time group containment was done was for training purposes, and this was no training exercise. And he'd never trained anyone. He'd certainly never led a charge. He had gone in and captured while other Possesseds waited outside, but that wasn't this, either.

Calm down. All you have to do is keep the radio on. Connors is the one leading.

"So, what are we doing?" Brogan asked him, his dark eyes expectant.

"We're, um, waiting on the signal," Bryan said. "Connors said twenty minutes. Waiting on as many Possesseds as we can get into place, I think."

"I think we've got enough already," Caplin argued. He had blond hair that he kept slicked back. It always made him look even younger than he already was. "How many people does it take to catch one demon?"

"And what happened before, shithead?" Brogan shot back. "We've already got the cops breathing down our damn necks."

"Fuck off, Brogan."

"Hold it, hold it." Bryan stepped in between them and waved them a couple of paces away from each other. They stomped away as Bryan peered up at the building across the parking lot and lawn. Spotlights were running over it, but they weren't illuminating anything but empty windows. He heard Caplin spit into the grass.

This was what being in charge meant, Bryan told himself. Keeping the kids from throwing punches at each other. He was a babysitter. He looked at the other groups in the distance. Each of them had their own babysitter. The real danger here was all the Possesseds having to work together, every one of them on edge and every one of them knowing they were staring madness in the eye.

Bryan made sure Caplin and Brogan said no more as they listened to the radio, which first squawked that everyone should come to the college, then cut that instruction off to announce that they had as many people as they were willing to wait for and everyone should get ready. Then Connors laid out the plan for everyone, finishing by stating that he himself would capture the thing.

Bryan cursed under his breath. He didn't envy Connors that task. With it adequately contained – and by so many people – the capture shouldn't be a problem, but even if Connors didn't go mad initially, having the responsibility of it in the days to come....

Connors told them to take their demons. Cards ripped, pages were torn, and plastic was cracked. Bryan heard glass shattering over to his left – Stenger breaking one of her glass marbles. People cried out. Caplin fell to the ground and leapt back up as if no one would notice. Bryan managed to keep down a shout by biting his lip, though he did draw blood. Then it was silent again, save for Connors's voice on the radio – rougher and strained now – repeating the instructions once again, laying them out like directions for building an Ikea bookcase.

"You'll have to work together to contain the entire building," he added. "Don't compete. Don't fight for sections. Don't get cocky and try to contain more than you're able. We're all screwed if too many of us mess up their part.

"Contain the building now."

Fires sprang up. Edging around the building, swirling into being around corners of the roof, down in the grass at its foundation, settling into windows. An ethereal conflagration any regular bystander wouldn't see or feel. But Bryan could see it licking at the bricks and glass as if the structure really might burn and crumble. Bryan added his fire, pulling from the demon inside him, and the well of power seemed so shallow as his fire raced across the sky to the building. It was nothing after experiencing a beta wrestling inside him. He thought again of the card hidden in the bottom of his bag, shoved under his wallet and keys and two packs of other, lesser cards.

There was a pause while they all waited for something to happen, for the demon to leap out a window or cause an explosion to try to escape the containment, but no sound or movement came from inside.

"Are we sure it's in there?" Brogan scoffed.

"Shut up and concentrate," Bryan spat at him.

"Leaders, move in," said the radio. "Everyone else, tune in. Wait for notice of where it's found."

Bryan went to the entrance before him, which was one of four entrances to the building. Two other Possesseds joined him there and they entered and spread out to search, separately but haphazardly. They weren't trained to search; they typically had Spotters to tell them where the threat was while they had their own demons to pinpoint danger. Here, neither worked, because this thing they were looking for was invisible to all of them. It was like they were all

groping around in the dark. But they could see the desiccated bodies crumpled at the bottoms of the stairs and gathered in the corners of classrooms. A professor's office revealed a teacher slumped over his keyboard as if asleep. But the halls kept the most corpses, everyone having run from the classrooms and labs and offices in the panic, some halls so full that the agents had to tiptoe around the bodies. The only sound was the crackle of the radio as people announced 'first floor south clear', 'second floor east clear', etc. Their voices shook from the exertion of carrying their demons.
Or from fear. This is suicide.
Bryan wiped the sweat from his face. The containment fires followed him up another floor, the agents outside closing their containment around the floors everyone had left to check, closing around where the demon would be hiding. How many more floors? Two? He suddenly wasn't sure, his thoughts muddled. He had to strain to remember the building held six floors.
Where would it hide?
Top floor. In the lab.
He stopped. He had suddenly been so certain. His gaze fell on his bag again.
If it speaks, don't listen to it.
Had it been a supposition from his own mind, or...
I should go look. I can handle it. It would kill Connors. I just need to use...
He glanced up the stairwell, up to the topmost floor. He couldn't go. Not yet, not on a hunch. He looked back to the level of the current floor and saw red shapes moving behind the doors and walls —

demons inhabiting the agents as they searched. If he climbed the stairs, everyone would see and demand to know what the hell he was doing going ahead.

But if he was a demon, wouldn't he hide on the top floor?

But if he was a demon, why would he hide? He'd be more likely to roam the halls wherever he found himself, searching for food. Was this one really hiding? Hiding was a human concept, not a demon one. Demons didn't consider danger, threat, or the possibility of capture.

But it's on the top floor, in the lab.

He entered the doors marked with a 4, trying to ignore the idea, but it nagged at him. He went through the rooms of the fourth floor and then the fifth floor, automatically, his mind elsewhere. If the demon had been on either of those floors, he would have been screwed from being so distracted. But both floors were cleared and they all continued on to the top floor.

They could all feel the energy of the containment fires now, having abandoned the lower floors and focused on a smaller area, one floor. It made the demons in them restless and itchy, and made them want to get the hell out of there on some instinctual level, while also being comforted by the energy. Another one of those things that only made sense when a demon was inside you.

The lab.

Bryan made a beeline for the lab, knowing it was in the center and to the right, to the east. He thought briefly that he should tell the others that that's where it was, but then considered the fact that he might be wrong after all, along with what he was going on (what *was* he going on?) and the other rooms needing to be checked, as well.

He entered the lab, the door swinging shut behind him with a click. There was destruction here – tables and stools flipped over and shoved against walls, water spraying from torn basins and pooled on the floor, glass cases shattered. And blood, from bodies torn and ripped to pieces.

He reached for his radio, and held it to his lips.

They'll die, too.

He heard a clatter from the far side of the room, and though the space between him and that wall was perhaps forty feet, it felt like miles.

They'll die and you'll have called them here.

He took a step forward, and then another step.

You can take it. You just need to–
If it speaks...

An animalistic growl sounded from behind a row of cases partially filled with microscopes, the majority of them already lying broken on the floor.

His radio slipped from his hand and thumped to the floor as he reached into his bag.

You just need to use...

It slumped from around the corner, shuffling and dragging its legs, its clothes torn and tattered, its hair hanging over its face. It had no color, either demon or human, but its eyes burned.

...just need to use...
...don't listen...

Bryan looked down, realizing too late what he was doing, and it was too late to tell his hands to stop because they were already tearing the card.

The beta leapt into him and immediately started a war with the other demon that was already housed there. He screamed and fell to the ground, his mind shredding away in ribbons, his veins bursting, and his heart thundering in his ears. He forgot the gamma. He had to do something with what was in him or he would be lost.

There was a deck lying on the floor, in the middle of a scattering of things that had spilled from his bag at some point. He reached out for it as if grasping for a rope to pull himself out of darkness, but it sat just out of reach. It was too far away. It was miles away, states away, countries away. Then it was in his hand. He'd find out later that the rest of the Possesseds were called there by his scream, and that someone had handed the deck to him. He shook the cards out of it and grasped one, crumpling it, and the lesser demon was practically thrown into it by the beta.

He grabbed more cards – a handful – but the beta would have none of it. It tore into his brain like a rat tunneling through meat, and he screamed again, had never stopped screaming, but he could hear something else over his own screams and the sick sliminess of the demon rooting in his head.

They were fighting *it*.

He willed himself to stop screaming, to look up. The fire was around the gamma – around Keeler, he could see now that it was Keeler – but the demon was pushing back against it and refusing to be captured. Connors was shouting at it, his book held up like a Bible in front of a poltergeist, trying to will it into a page. But the fire was dissipating and people

Black Heart

were taking steps back. It was winning. Soon, the place would be drenched in blood.

He could end it.

Bryan embraced the demon in him, and he felt part of himself slip away. He wasn't sure what it was or whether he would ever get it back, but that didn't matter. He stood, his legs like unruly stilts and his hands still clutching playing cards, and he looked at Keeler, at the gamma in her. It was writhing as much as Keeler was writhing, pale rose pink under pale sickly green, but Keeler stood, ready to lunge forward at her attackers. Just waiting for an opening.

He threw fire around it, the demon he was pulling it from protesting and ripping at him again, but he felt that ripping only from a long ways away, like sound through cotton.

He pulled it out of Keeler, and it came kicking and screaming and refused the card, entering Bryan instead.

Detached, beaten, Bryan saw the two fighting. Before his eyes and behind his eyes, red and pink, blood and rose, whirled colors wrapping around each other and around him. But though he felt them in every heartbeat and in every vein, it was like they were fighting inside of someone else, he only a spectator. They clawed and bit at each other as he looked on with a trace of sadness and defeat.

He had one last ounce of strength... the strength of a child sufficient to topple building blocks. Still, he used it, and pushed at them. He put to his lips two playing cards, and when that didn't work, he bit them hard enough to leave indentations in the corners, in the 6 and K, a spade and a heart. Then, he passed out.

◆

He was thirteen again, and his parents and sister lay green and shrunken on the floor of the cabin they had rented. He lay curled up in a fetal position, sobbing and screaming at the thing inside him.

He was thirteen again, and he couldn't cry anymore, couldn't fight anymore. But he had separated it from him; he could ooze the thing out of him and into the straps binding his wrists.

He was thirteen again, and he sat in a courtroom with the lawyers making speeches, but he wasn't listening – was lost in his head, empty and alone.

He was thirteen again, and Hussein had found him.

He woke blinking at the bright sunshine that spilled in through the blinds in the windows. Everything was white. It didn't make sense, all this white. He turned his head and saw the colors of a sea of flowers and balloons. Flowers on a table. A white table. He was in a hospital room.

He turned his head to the other side and saw Hussein, head resting on an arm, using the bed as a pillow. He was asleep.

Bryan tried to think, but his mind was numb and his thoughts cloudy. He had gone into the science building with the others. And then...

He looked to his bedside table, but it only held a lamp and a glass of water. Where were his cards? What had happened to him? Had Connors caught it? He remembered the beta getting hold of him, and then pain.

He looked down at Hussein, sleeping peacefully by his left arm. Surely, Hussein had better things to do than sit here with him.

He wanted to get up, but he felt numb, exhausted and unstable, like a stranger in his own body. It wasn't a common descriptor for normal people, but among Possessed it was well-known. It happened a lot when they first started training... when they first allowed demons in.

The door from the hallway opened and Andrade walked in. Her eyes widened on seeing him looking at her, and he held a finger to his lips to hush her before pointing to Hussein. She covered her mouth with her hands and literally bounced over to him like he was a puppy left to her as a birthday present.

"You're looking so good!" she whispered. He knew what she meant – his aura. "You were touch and go for a bit there. You got very pale."

"What? From the beta?"

She peered at him quizzically. "Do you not remember?"

"I remember I let the beta take me, and then..."

And then...

He remembered. He shot upright, gasping for breath as if drowning. It woke Hussein.

"Bryan!" he mumbled hoarsely, half-asleep and confused. "Bryan, what..."

"It's okay." Andrade put her hands on Bryan's shoulders and eased him back down onto the bed.

"But it... it..." he argued, not sure what he was trying to say.

"It's caught. You captured it."

He stared at her, stunned into silence.

Hussein rubbed at his face. "Did he just wake up?"

"Before you," she said.

He grinned sheepishly. "Sorry, Bryan. I'm not a very good bedside guard."

"I can't believe I was here when you woke up," Andrade said. "Us Spotters have been switching out to keep an eye on you, but Hussein's been here 24/7."

"For how long?" Bryan asked.

The grin fell from Hussein's lips. "Five days. Two of them stable. The Spotters said your aura was nearly depleted."

Bryan looked down at his hands as if he could see the aura there. "But I caught it."

They both nodded, Hussein gravely and Andrade energetically. Bryan looked to the flowers and balloons. There was an enormous pile of them, the arrangements spilling over onto the floor. It was a strange sight. Before today, he would never have imagined getting anything more than a card signed by the office, should he have ended up in the hospital. "Was anyone hurt? Other than the civilians who died before we moved in?"

"There was an energy wave sent out from you," Hussein said. "But it caused little more than bumps and bruises. Except for Andrew..." Hussein looked to the window as he mentioned Keeler.

"Andrew got the worst of it, and he's in the hospital. He's alive, but gone."

Bryan took a sharp intake of breath. He looked down at the white sheets that covered him, and bunched the fabric in his fists. "I only caught it because I let the beta take me over. I didn't even realize it was happening. It was like I was hypnotized."

Hussein took his hand. "It doesn't matter. All that matters is you got it and you're safe. After the loss of Andrew, we weren't sure if you would make it through."

Bryan felt his cheeks grow red at the caring words. "Where is it now?"

"In quarantine at the office."

Bryan shot up again, though with less energy. "But that's... what if it got loose? In the office?"

"It would have destroyed you, had we kept it near you. It very nearly did already. It's a risk we had to take." Hussein leaned back in his chair, looking to be easing a crick out of his back. "We have several people keeping containment on it."

"They won't be able to do a thing if it manages to break out," Bryan argued. "It needs to be with me. And the beta... the beta, too? Both in quarantine? This is—"

He had thrown the sheets back, swinging his legs over the edge of the bed – meaning to stand and somehow dress and march out of the hospital and on to the office. But the movement and anger made his head spin, and he would have fallen to the floor if Hussein and Andrade hadn't caught him and laid him back down.

"You're barely yourself," Hussein said, one hand on Bryan's chest as if to hold him there on the bed. "You haven't had the latent energy to keep them contained on your own, not without them overtaking you."

"Bullshit," Bryan mumbled, staring at the ceiling. "I could do it."

"That's your position talking. I want you to close your eyes and breathe."

Bryan scoffed, but did as Hussein said. He closed his eyes and took deep breaths, and focused on the place where he could always find himself. He was on the lakeshore, waves rippling in the sunlight and lapping at the graveled sand. The tiny bits of pebble biting into his feet.

He covered his eyes with an arm, feeling tears welling up in them and not wanting Andrade to see them. "I didn't mean to capture it. It was a mistake. It was only because of that beta. Because I couldn't control it. How can I control this thing if I couldn't control a beta?"

"Andrade," Hussein said quietly. "Can you...?"

"Oh," she spouted. "Yes."

Bryan heard her heels tap away and the door open and close, and he felt Hussein's hand on his arm. He lowered it. The tears hadn't fallen. Instead, he blinked them away fiercely.

"You've learned," Hussein said, his eyes boring into Bryan's, "an alpha can stick with you, but a beta can overtake you. But now you know. You can see the signs of it trying to overtake you."

"But what does a gamma do?"

Hussein leaned back and crossed his arms. "We don't know yet. This is new territory for everyone. We considered putting you in quarantine along with it."

"Oh, come on."

"I know. No one would have liked it. And I think isolation would only have a negative impact on you. It went poorly when they tried it in Germany. The demons just talk to you all the more in isolation." He sighed. "But I think it's not necessary anyway. I think you can handle this. You need to know you can handle this."

They were dancing around stating it directly, but Bryan knew what 'this' was that Hussein thought he could handle. They couldn't keep the gamma at the office. They didn't know how easily it might break out of the card it had been captured in. Like any other demon, it might be more containable in the hands of its agent, Bryan's energy and will still working on it without him knowing or trying anything. Latent energy. Another thing they didn't fully understand. And they didn't understand a gamma either.

It wasn't like any other demon.

But they'd have to treat it like one in the absence of any other information.

Bryan turned his head on the pillow, looking to the window. The sunlight hurt his eyes, but he held them open. "Can I?"

"Bryan." Hussein's voice was sharp, authoritative.

Bryan looked at him with some surprise.

"Do you remember what I told you when you first started?"

"Yeah. 'Don't piss off anyone.'"

A corner of Hussein's mouth twitched up, but the rest of him remained serious. "Before that."

"That I can do this." Of course, he remembered. "That if I ever think I can't, I'm wrong. I can do it. Because..."

"Because?"

"Because I'm alive. As long as I'm alive, I can act. And because... well, you said I would have to find the second reason for myself."

Hussein nodded. "And you did."

"Yeah. But..." Bryan swallowed the lump in his throat. "But Gennick thought he could, too. So did Rogge, and Keeler."

Hussein didn't answer right away. But he looked deep into Bryan's eyes as he thought. Then he said, "I know. But they did all they could. That's all we can do. That's all any of us can do. You can be scared. But you have to be strong. You walk through fire every day without flinching. You just have to walk a little further now. Just remember why."

Bryan nodded. He was very tired. The conversation had taken all of his energy.

"I know this has been lonely work," Hussein added. "And you might need help on this one. Don't think you can't ask for it."

Bryan frowned as he shut his eyes. What a strange thing to say. How would he even ask for help, or receive it? These were his demons now.

They threw him a party on his return to work two days later, as he was mortified to discover. It was bad enough going to work and expecting to be the center of attention, but he had expected to deal with one person at a time, not all of them at once with a cake and a sign proclaiming 'Welcome Back, Ivers!'. He got pats on the back from the men and hugs from the women and 'Good jobs' and 'How are you feelings', and the whole time, he wanted to just crawl out of the room and into a hole. As it was, he tried to shrink into himself, hunching his shoulders and hanging his head to appear smaller in a sea of Possesseds in jeans and t-shirts, Spotters in business causal, and office workers in suits and ties.

"Sorry, man," Cam told him when he was finally able to pull him away from the others. "I wanted to tell them you'd hate it, but they were so excited about planning it."

"Office parties should be banned," Bryan said. He held an untouched piece of cake on a bright red plastic plate. He had dropped the fork somewhere, but he didn't care. He wouldn't have tasted it anyway.

"I hate to say this right after you've left a hospital," Cam said, "but you look awful. Even if you are at a party for you."

Bryan looked at the crowd before him, making sure not to make eye contact with anyone. "I'm going to be seeing that demon I captured right after this. Actually, I was ready and steeled for it, but this has thrown me off."

"They meant well." Cam scratched his nose. "You can't blame us for being grateful."

"I didn't even mean to catch the thing." Bryan sighed. "Look, it's a long story."

"I don't doubt it. But we're Possessed. We're tough guys. You can take it."

"I can't even take a welcome back party."

"This? This is your real enemy. But demons? You beat them up for a living. They're nothing."

Bryan couldn't help but smile. "You're always right."

"Ivers?" It was Andrade, appearing from the chattering party-goers. "I hate to pull you away from the party, but Hussein thinks we'd better not wait."

"*Please* pull me away from the party," Bryan said, leading her out of the room.

"You look better," she said in the elevator.

"Is that why Hussein sent you?" he asked without malice, only curious. "To check me out beforehand?"

She shrugged, and with her hands behind her back, she looked adorable doing it. "Possibly. He always has reasons for doing what he does. All I know is that he told me to go get you."

"Meaning he knew about the party," Bryan mumbled.

"What?"

"Nothing."

Quarantine was a sterile white block of the building. It always seemed to Bryan like people there should be walking around in hazmat suits studying petri dishes, but they were just dressed in regular office attire. There was added security – they all had to sign in at the small desk with the bored-looking deskwoman, who looked less bored at the sight of Bryan. She looked at him for a moment before asking Hussein, "Should I expect anything, sir?"

Bryan thought of the party downstairs. One last blowout before Ivers fucks everything up and a demon tears through the place?

But Hussein smiled. "I assure you everyone involved is fully prepared. No worries."

Oh God, why does he have to lie like that? Bryan thought feverishly. *I'm not prepared. He hasn't prepared me. I haven't prepared myself.*

A hand landed on his shoulder and he jumped, but it was only Andrade, who of course could tell he was nervous. She smiled at him, trying to be reassuring, but he was only embarrassed that the nervousness he felt was showing.

Hussein led them down the hall, indoor windows to either side displaying the scenes inside the little rooms. Two or three people gathered around a table holding anywhere from one to one hundred little totems. This was where fresh demons were stored when a Possessed had a breakdown and went into therapy, unable to handle their newest demons. Or when a Possessed died. Bryan saw Gennick's candles and Keeler's notebook on one table, an agent staring at the collection, watching until the day the demons were set into the things.

It was boring work – Bryan had done his share of it – but it was necessary. If a demon got loose while their owner was already half-crazed, it could take them over. And if a demon got loose while their owner was dead or emptied of mind? Well, then you had a loose demon who was a little smarter when it came to how capturing worked.

They came to two rooms across from each other, one housing two people and the other five. Bryan knew which one held the gamma. Hussein opened the door to that room.

The five looked up, and Hussein greeted them and started explaining that they were to stay alert, etc.,

etc. Bryan wasn't listening. He had stopped in the doorway, his eyes locked on the card on the table, sitting there with five people staring at it like a holy relic. He had felt something from it on entering the room, or... no, he had felt it all along, from the moment he had entered the building. He just hadn't noticed it. A barely controlled rage and fear – a numbing fear. A mind, contemplating each of them as if searching for an opening. For an escape.

"Bryan."

His eyes snapped to Hussein. Had Hussein said something to him?

"What?" he asked, his voice sounding small and tinny to him.

Hussein motioned to the table. "Go ahead. Pick it up," he said, as if offering some party favor instead of a crazed demon that could rip his mind to shreds.

Bryan swallowed hard and stepped forward. He felt all eyes on him but, looking up, he saw that most of the people in the room were watching the card. He glanced back at Andrade in the doorway. She *was* watching him, waiting to see what color his aura became when he picked up the card. She nodded at him, and for a moment, he hated her. He swung back around.

I don't need your reassurance, his mind snarled. *I don't need your permission.*

Eyes on the card. Reach out and pick it up. But, oh God, what if I fuck it up?

He watched his hand reach out as if it didn't belong to him. As if someone else was going to pick up the card and deal with the demon, and that would have been just fine with him except that it wasn't. It was him, and everyone – including Hussein – was watching to make sure he didn't fuck it up.

His fingers brushed the glossy surface of the card, and something in it jumped and retreated like a dog huddling into the shadows of its kennel. And Bryan could feel its eyes on him, but that was all. And that was enough, because it really *saw* him.

He picked it up in his hand and looked at it. It looked back, from the depths. But he had it.

Everyone in the room breathed again.

He looked to Hussein, who looked to Andrade, who gave a thumbs-up. Bryan wondered whether she would really be able to tell anything about what was happening with this demon. Gammas were – no, *the* gamma was – still invisible to Spotters. Would she be able to detect any change in him if it came from the demon?

Still, Hussein clapped him on the back and dismissed the five Possesseds, all of whom told him 'Good job' or 'Way to go.' He put a plaster smile on his face and hoped it looked convincing enough.

Hussein ushered them all out, including Andrade, and then unexpectedly closed the door. He looked out the window, across the hall to the room with the other card, two Possesseds around it.

"Are you okay?" Hussein asked, still not looking at Bryan.

Bryan momentarily considered the question, which had been asked of him several times already that day, but those other times didn't matter. Hussein wasn't being sympathetic or initiating conversation. This was business. This was *work*, he reminded himself.

"I think so. It's—"

"Don't tell me what you think. Tell me what you know."

Anger flashed through him at the interruption, but it was a quick burn and then it was gone. This was work.

"It's watching me," he said. "There's an intelligence behind it that's unlike the other demons. It's like it's trying to hide from me while also watching me."

"Like a predator?"

"Yes and no. It seems curious."

"Seems?"

"It *is* curious."

"Hm." Hussein still watched the two Possesseds across the hall as if they were doing something interesting, something other than watching a prone playing card.

"I think we should keep the beta here," he said.

"No!" Bryan nearly shouted. "I can deal with it."

"I'm still not sure how you managed when it took you over before."

"It didn't take me over!" he did shout.

Hussein finally looked at him. "It did, though. Otherwise, we wouldn't be here." He'd growled the words, his voice low like the snarl of a wolf.

"Otherwise, I wouldn't have saved everyone's asses!" Bryan crossed the room to stand eye to eye with Hussein, towering over him by half a foot.

"So, I should allow you to put everyone's lives in jeopardy?" Hussein spat. "To keep your image?"

"I don't want my image!" Bryan spun away from him and circled the room, stomping out each step. Like a toddler having a temper tantrum. "I don't want other people having to clean up after me. Having to watch my garbage. It's bad enough I was in the hospital for days." He stopped, clenching and unclenching his fists. "I need to do right this time."

He breathed. In and out, in and out. When Hussein didn't speak, he looked up.

Hussein let out a breath and hung his head. "I wish you had punched me so I could refuse."

Bryan reeled. "You... were testing me?"

"Partially. What did you get from the demon?"

"Not very much. There's anger there, but it's only watched me. Felt me."

"I don't like this, Bryan."

Bryan looked across the hallway, to the other card, but he concentrated on the gamma. It slunk back into its hole, as if it had been spotted approaching him. "You think I do? But that demon is mine, too. And I know its tricks now."

Hussein didn't respond. He watched Bryan, chin in one hand, thinking.

Bryan smiled at him, a little bit sheepishly. "Well, after all, I didn't punch you."

Hussein watched him a moment longer, until Bryan was very uncomfortable. Then he turned and opened the door as if the conversation hadn't happened. "Let's go pick up the beta," he said.

They did, and it felt like nothing compared to picking up the gamma. It didn't even snarl this time. Cowed, perhaps. Bryan barely felt it at all.

◆

"Time to get to work," Bryan told Hussein as they signed out the two cards and the rest of Bryan's deck. "Let me guess – Andrade is my Spotter again tonight?"

Hussein gave him an unreadable look out of the corner of his eye. "Walk with me, Bryan," he said.

Bryan did, a bit confused.

"But no," Hussein said on the way. "You're not paired with Andrade tonight. I know you've had enough of her for now."

"Obvious, huh?" He slumped against the wall of the elevator. "I don't mean to be angry at her."

"It's the demons. At least you haven't tried to choke her, like... well, you remember."

"Gavin and Brobst? They both should have known better than to date."

"They should have, but we can't really forbid it. Anyway, I'm trying to say you're doing well."

"It's hard to tell," Bryan said, though he really wanted to thank the man for saying so. Still, he felt he didn't deserve what Hussein had just said. He felt sick with hate, hate at Andrade just for being around and being able to see what she naturally saw, with his hate for her growing as much as his camaraderie with her. His strengths and weaknesses, flowing around him in a rainbow of colors. It wasn't her fault. Was it his fault he had this turmoil of emotion? Or was it the fault of the demons? Was he himself or just an amalgamation of other beings?

He didn't say any of this. Hussein already knew it all. The discussions had been had, through the late-night arguments over cheap beer when that had been all any of them could afford, until they'd

had commiserations over cheap beer because that was what they'd grown used to.
Who am I?
You are Possessed.
Hussein led him to his office, and the sight of the woman sitting beside the door shocked him out of his thoughts. She was stunning. She stood and bowed when she saw them.
Hussein held up a hand, smiling awkwardly. "That's not necessary."
The woman's face turned red behind her glasses. "I apologize, sir. It becomes automatic."
"No worries. Bryan, this is Kiyoko Harper. She's an outstanding agent from Tokyo. Possessed, Spotter, and keeper of a beta. Kiyoko, this is Bryan Ivers – whom you're familiar with, I'm sure."
Bryan's mind reeled. "Wait, did you say...?"
"All three, yes."
Bryan knew full well of Possessed Spotters, but a beta keeper on top of that was unheard of. He hadn't known such a combination existed in one person. He looked her over incredulously. Dark hair in a pixie cut, tall, and attractive as hell. The blush had passed, and looking now at Bryan, she wore a stern expression as if she were already rejecting him with no words spoken.
"I suppose you won't mind," he said, holding out his hand, "if we would just shake hands."
She gave him a look that could freeze fire, but shook his hand, gripping it so hard that he had to cover his grimace with a smile, which only deepened her angry look.
"Let's go in," Hussein motioned and escorted them in to his office. He closed the door behind

them, and Bryan was starting to wonder what this was all about when he sat behind his desk and announced, "You two are going to be partners for a time."

"*What?*" Bryan exclaimed.

Harper said nothing; in fact, she gave no reaction at all, save for generally appearing to lament the situation, and so Bryan inferred this was no surprise for her.

"For how long?" Bryan continued.

"For as long as needs be," Hussein said.

Bryan gaped at him.

Hussein spread his hands open. "Well, out with it. We're here to hear your protests so that they can be out of the way."

"What can I say? It's ridiculous."

"It's necessary. I want eyes on you, and who better than a Spotter?"

"We'll kill each other!"

"That's why she's also Possessed."

"Great, we'll level the city when we kill each other."

Hussein stood and walked around his desk. "You're both professionals. You both know your limits. It will be a trial, but no more so than anything else you've done. Especially after capturing a new species of demon."

"If that's true then I don't need a babysitter. 'Cause that's what this is." Bryan suddenly remembered Hussein's words from earlier – the ones he had found odd, but thought little of: *You might need help on this one.* Hussein had already thought of giving him a partner when he'd been lying half-dead in a hospital room. Had probably already been reviewing candidates. His hands closed into fists as he imagined throttling Hussein. Hussein had planned it all along, all the while keeping that 'I'm your friend' face on.

"This is how I kept you out of quarantine," Hussein explained, dead calm before Bryan's rage. "Not to say I don't like the idea. I do want eyes on you. Experienced and capable eyes."

"You'd rather I set down all my cards in quarantine and let other people watch them while I do nothing!"

"Don't be unreasonable."

"Don't be... so fucking... calm!"

Hussein's voice lowered, pure steel. "Am I? Then, what are you?"

Bryan sputtered, turned, stormed in a circle, and fell into a chair. He was angry, of course. Angry and unreasonable, hurt and... throwing a tantrum.

He looked up from the floor and saw the two of them, Hussein leaning back against the desk, Harper with her hands politely clasped in front of her and her face blank.

"Is it so terrible to have a partner?" Hussein asked him.

"Well, it's... it's not..." *Not done.* He saw Harper again, and he realized that all along she had been regarding his moods coolly. "I guess not. I just..." he murmured, not really feeling the words, but ashamed at how he had just acted. He passed a hand over his mouth and looked directly at Hussein. "Do you think I can't do this?"

Hussein looked down at the floor. "No one knows if you can do this. Because no one's done it before. That's why we're giving you help." He looked up and into Bryan's eyes before adding, "I know you're capable, and don't think I don't know how you feel about having a partner, but this is the solution to a difficult problem."

Bryan looked again to Harper, but couldn't hold her gaze. Had he acted like a child? Would he act like a child again? Probably. Had it been the gamma? He searched it out in his deck. It was merely watching him – a frightened feral cat in a corner.

"You're not hunting tonight," Hussein broke into his thoughts.

Bryan leaned back in the chair and shook his head. "You're killing me."

"Don't pretend you're not relieved. You're going to Caltrop Apartments. Investigative work. Betas have been known to transfer vague memories to their hosts. Take this gamma and see if it recognizes anything at the apartment building. This may be our chance to find out where all these things we chase are coming from."

"Better detectives than me have tried. Or is Harper a star detective along with everything else?"

"Funny. Now, I want you to get a feel for this gamma, but under no circumstances are you to let it out of that card. You got me?"

"Yeah." In other words: Don't screw up like you did with the beta. "Hell, it'd be easier to just hunt."

"An assignment here and there won't kill you, and neither will having a partner. Now that you've screamed and cried and gotten it out of your system, deal with it." He waved them out, and Bryan went grudgingly with Harper following behind.

Bryan signed for a company car and the two of them piled in it without so much as a word. Bryan's anger was barely controlled in tapping the steering wheel and repeatedly wiping his mouth with his hands. All the while, Harper sat in the passenger seat like a stone, hands folded neatly in her lap. It only made him more furious.

"Look," he finally said while stopped at a red light, "I'll tell you now. This will be a disaster. We tried partners, back in the beginning. It didn't work. I mean, how long have you been doing this?"

"I'm well aware of the problems Possesseds have working in pairs and groups," she said, avoiding the question. "Japan tried it, as well, and they tried harder to make it work."

"If it doesn't work, try and try again, eh?"

"There had to be a death before they caved."

"Yeah." He glanced over at her out of the corner of his eye. She was looking out the window, something almost sad about her. "Promise not to kill me, 'kay?"

She looked at him, but he didn't look back. "I'm not psychic," she said flatly.

The light switched to green. His fingers tap-danced over the steering wheel. "What are you getting out of this anyway? Why come all the way over here for this, to be stuck with a partner?"

She turned her head to look out the window again. "I have my reasons," she said softly.

He sighed and turned his attention back to the road, gray beneath the streetlights. So, she wasn't interested in giving away information about herself. Meanwhile, she had probably learned everything about him. She had probably been given an entire file on him, everything from "no remaining family" down to "loves chocolate chip cookies." He felt like a bacteria in a petri dish, being studied and tested.

Neither of them spoke again until they stood in front of the apartments.

"Are you getting anything?" Harper asked.

"Of course not." Bryan peered up at the building. Middle class set-up. Concrete and glass, nothing special. Not even any patios. The place was ringed with yellow caution tape and traffic cones and smashed cars. Condemned signs were stuck to the first-story windows. The front doors were gone, as Cam had said, and the jagged hole where they'd used to be had been covered over with boards. As the two of them walked closer, they passed glass and bits of concrete littering the ground over splashes of blood. Crime scene. Don't clean anything.

He studied the blood as best he could in the darkness. Did he feel something? Some hungry, ravenous memory almost there and then gone, like a dream that slips away the more it's searched for? He looked down at a long splash of blood as he walked. How had that one died? Throat ripped out? Stomach? Had it started with the legs?

He stopped, jerking with the motion. One of them was watching him, its attention like a prickling at his skin – the back of his neck and down his spine. Hard to tell which one, as it shrank back as soon as he noticed. But it had been watching, looking around with... what? Interest? Amusement? Indifference? It slipped away from him again.

"What?" Harper asked.

"Nothing," he said. "Nothing of interest."

A flashlight shined in his eyes, startling all memory he'd almost had away.

"Get out of here. This is a crime scene," came a voice from behind the light, short and gruff, as if it had already said these words five times that night.

"Office of Demonic Defense," Bryan said, flipping out his badge. "We're investigating the area."

"Oh, sorry about that." The voice lowered the light out of their faces, and Bryan could see that there were two officers – the gruff one who'd been speaking and another who lingered behind and was younger. The latter was wide-eyed at their badges. A rookie. "We get a lot of rubberneckers at these scenes. Amateur demonhunters and kids on dares and such."

"I'm sure you do," Bryan said. "Were you two here on the night of the incident?"

"No, but... we all heard about it. We all know the officers who were here and didn't make it out."

Bryan nodded, but he was thinking of the memorial service for the office's agents that he hadn't attended because he'd been unconscious. Instead, for him it had been replaced with a welcome back party. It made the event that had happened here distant, removed. It also made him certain that he wouldn't recognize anything here, demon or no demon.

"Is it true it was caught?" the rookie asked, voice eager.

"Yes," Bryan answered, the word sticking in his throat.

The rookie breathed a sigh of relief. The other said, "And I hope you lock the damned thing away."

Bryan held back a laugh, struck by the absurdity of the conversation, of him being here with these affected men who had given silent prayer in memorials while he'd slept. Him here with the culprit demon. "Can we go inside?" he asked.

"Well, it's dangerous." Gruff cop waved at the place. "The structure's punched clear through on several floors. Stability's compromised."

"We'll be careful."

"Yeah, you guys are known for being careful. There's a gap in the boards in the front door space. But seriously – I know it won't stop you, but I would recommend staying out of the place."

"Thanks for the concern."

"Besides, something falls and crushes you, it'll be on our heads."

"I'll keep an eye on him," Harper said, starting for the building.

The cop huffed and held up his hands in surrender, and Bryan followed after Harper.

Broken glass crunched under their feet as they made their way to the door. They ignored the *Condemned: No Trespassing* signs and squeezed through the gap in the boards, Bryan turning on his flashlight to scan the inside. It was pure rubble; nothing resembling a lobby remained. Everywhere was plaster, glass, dust, and twisted metal. Splinters lay against the crumbling remains of a wall. And ahead, through what had once been walls or an elevator – it was hard to tell – was a hole in the ceiling. Bryan walked to it, trying not to trip or lose his balance on the debris and failing a couple of times. He looked up into the jagged darkness above and tried to imagine blowing such a hole open.

"Anything?" Harper asked.

"No," he said shortly, annoyed at her pestering.

"Then don't stand there waiting for something to fall on you."

He glared at her, but it was too dark to show and she wasn't looking at him anyway.

"Let's go up," she said. "It started on the seventh floor."

The stairs were at the sides of the building and unaffected. On the seventh floor, exiting the stairwell, Bryan could see the cavernous hole ahead, down the hall. He started for it, but Harper brought him up short.

"Here," she said. "Room 720. This is where it switched hosts."

"That's Gennick and Rogge you're talking about," Bryan growled at her.

She shrugged and went through the doorway, the door of which was lying in splinters on the other side of the hall. "Whoever. I didn't know them. I just read the report."

"I'll bet the same report names me as a 'host', too."

"Perhaps." She turned to face him. "Have you never considered that the Office of Demonic Defense considers its agents to be items?"

"Then you know nothing about the office," he spat. "Maybe that's how Japan operates, but not us."

She turned away and shone her light into the dark apartment. "Or maybe you don't want to admit that you're expendable?"

He wanted to spin her around and pin her against the wall, to shout in her face that just because she thought *she* was worthless... but he just shook his head and mumbled under his breath, "You're not worth it."

She either didn't hear him or didn't care to respond.

He swept his light over the apartment. Everything was in shambles – tables overturned, pictures fallen off the walls and smashed, window broken, curtains torn. He wondered if Gennick had done it, or Rogge, or some combination of both. But one or both of them had done it when taken over by the gamma, the demon tossing their bodies around in pain and madness.

Bryan swallowed hard. Gennick was still in that madness if not the pain, locked away in a padded room to gibber and scream. It could have been him, if he hadn't used the beta. Gennick had been there, under the window, with the soft nighttime glow of the city seeping in like a shroud over the contents of the living room, over the tossed coffee table and the pile of magazines that had been thrown from it.

Bryan started. The image had been so clear, as if he had been looking out of Rogge's eyes, looking at Gennick. He went to the window and turned around to face the room. There was the table, legs sticking up in the air, the magazines, and a broken figurine of the Virgin Mary in the corner, with a breeze ruffling his hair from the smashed window. He knelt. Definitely, Gennick had huddled here. And Rogge had come in. And Gennick... he had been so far gone that the gamma had been able to leave him and go for Rogge, the demon only seeing her aeon's lifeforce and not realizing that she was another Possessed, another prison.

But that wasn't what Bryan was looking for. He didn't want to go forward, towards Rogge and the massacre outside. He already knew what had happened there. He stood and faced the window, trying to imagine how it would have gone for Gennick, step by step. Under the window – he would have crawled there. Where had Gennick been possessed? He couldn't find the exact place. He kept coming back to the scene viewed from beneath the window – the scene through Gennick's eyes, but no more. And each time, he felt more and more of Gennick slipping away, his torture, the clawing at his brain, tearing it to shreds. The demon overcoming his mind and dissolving it... dissolving him.

Bryan tottered and tried to grab at the table legs, but they went with him. Harper leapt over nimbly and caught him before he could go down.

"I'm fine," he said, not feeling the words. "I just need some air."

He pushed Harper away and went to the window to breathe in a few lung-fulls of city air – crisp night wind tinged with smog. The torn curtains twisted and whipped beside him like snakes trapped in the jaws of a mongoose. City lights blinked in the night. Apartment lamps blinking off for bedtime, and head and brake lights speeding below. Normal people coming home from work or going out for a night on the town. What must that be like?

Don't start. You chose this.
You were thirteen.

He shook his head and took another deep lungful of sooty air. *Don't start doubting. It won't make things easier.*

Yet, if he had never found these particular demons, the beta and the gamma, he wouldn't have been doubting the work at all. He had been just fine catching little alphas every night. Had been used to it.

It was simple. It was practically on par with a filing job, if filing involved walking through corpses. He hadn't been happy, but he had been okay.

But now... now those things in his bag were watching his every move. Possibly his every thought, with the presence of mind to ruminate over the observations. Or so he suspected. It certainly felt that way to him. It felt that way right now.

A car below beeped its horn, and he looked down at it as it swerved around another car that had stopped in the middle of the road.

And a memory hit him with the force of a truck. A memory of diving around cars, not understanding this insanely fast source of light and noise, falling through one and getting a blast of even greater noise and a rush of air and an energy source inside it but knowing the thing itself had no life energy. Machinery both terrifying and monstrous.

He leapt away from the window and darted from the room, nearly tumbling over the little Mary figurine.

"What?" Harper called after him as she followed.

"The road. I was down there." He took the steps in the stairwell two at a time and tried to run through the lobby, but he tripped on debris and went sprawling on his hands and knees, cutting his hand, and mild as the pain was, it seemed to hush the memory of the cars and the road. Cursing, he pushed himself up and through the door.

Circling the building, they dashed past the night watchmen, and the gruff one waved and asked how things had gone. Bryan didn't answer, trying instead to dredge the memory back up, and Harper didn't seem to know what to say in answer, so they both rushed on without responding.

Bryan broke upon the road so fast that he stepped off into it before he could stop. But no car was going by, and he stood off to the side of a lane wracking his mind.

Lights.

Horns.

Confusion.

It was all gone.

Harper watched him silently, as if knowing he needed to think. He turned in the street and looked about him, but only saw a car turn the corner and come his way. He stepped out of the road as if the action admitted defeat.

"Are you sure it was this road?" Harper asked.

"Of course, I'm sure," he said. The car zipped past them.

"Then why not cross it?" she asked.

He peered across the road at the other side.

Why did the Possessed cross the road?

"Okay," he said, and stepped back into the lane. Harper followed.

On the other side, he didn't stop, but kept his inertia moving forward. There were houses here, and he was able to walk between them, the grass rustling at his shoes. He hadn't been here on this path; maybe the demon hadn't crossed the road at all, but the sound of the grass touched something in him. He seemed to see something ahead that didn't make sense, too. A place with no grass at all, an empty desert with empty sand and empty dirt. He rushed forward, breaking into a run. He knew it was somehow directly ahead – a dead place among the city, a place opposite to this place. He *felt* it, though he didn't know where he was going. He didn't let himself think about it. He kept his mind blank, as if meditating. It was difficult; he had never been one for meditation, much as the office touted its benefits.

The darkness helped. He didn't have the chance to inspect his surroundings, save for the little bit illuminated by streetlamps and porchlights. The sound of crickets and the grass amplified the dichotomy up ahead, convincing him that this was all new, and that he had been astounded by all this, had fed upon little blades of grass and ants as if they were a feast. And they had been, compared to what he'd been used to, where he had been blasted from... that beginning somewhere up ahead.

He crossed one more street and came to a stop in front of a building, and he thought it was a church until he saw the two Stars of David engraved above the windows. Again, he stood in the street and stared at it, somewhat in awe.

Something had happened here. Both of the demons practically confirmed it as they looked upon it.

"Harper," he said quietly, as if not wanting to wake something. "Can you see anything?"

She didn't respond right away, as if searching. "Just an old synagogue."

He wasn't sure what he had expected from her. He hadn't expected there to be demons here, after all. But it did seem like there should be demons here.

Why did he think that?

He was getting a headache.

There was a fence around the building, the type with the horizontal bar up towards the top, and Harper had to help him over and vice versa. Bryan tried the doors, but of course they were locked. They circled the building, moving quietly, again as if a monster slept inside. Several of the windows were broken.

"It's abandoned," Harper whispered.

"Yeah," Bryan said. "But why?"

"Shifting neighborhoods. Economy."

"No. Something happened here." He took off his jacket and wrapped it around him arm so that he could clear a windowpane of glass.

"What are you doing?" Harper was incredulous. It was the first emotion he had heard from her.

"Breaking and entering." Bryan hoisted himself through the window. The glass pieces cracked underneath his boots as he landed. It was dark outside; it was pitch in here. He took out his flashlight again and shone it back and forth. Pews, a platform, balconies. Nothing out of place. No dead bodies. No commotion.

Harper was climbing in after him. "We could just come back with the keys," she said. "We could look up records, find out what happened."

"And if something happens tonight? We need to check it out now."

"But what would happen?"

"I don't know!" he shouted, dropping the whisper.

"Well, tell me what you *do* know." Harper didn't shout, but her voice was tight and constrained. "Was the gamma here? What was it doing here?"

"Yes, it was here!" He stormed out into the aisle between the pews, looking up at the empty wall at the head of the space, where tablets might have hung once. "But it wasn't here."

"That doesn't help," Harper said, her voice even again.

The words he was speaking didn't make sense to him, either. He didn't know what he was trying to say. He breathed in deep, and something in the air seemed to enter and lodge in his lungs, and the desert flashed in his mind again. "It was here, but then it wasn't. It was in the road and it was confused. This wasn't the right place; it wasn't supposed to be here. This place had energy everywhere and the cars came... and I crawled into the grass. Eating." His voice had dropped. He didn't quite believe what he was saying. What place would have been the *right* place?

The place it had come from. The dead place.

But that wasn't possible. What place was like that? A desert? Even a desert had sand lice and lizards. Even the sand had nutrients. The place he envisioned was entirely devoid of life energy.

But that was crazy.

"Ivers, are you talking about... where it came from?"

He looked back at her. He couldn't tell if it was the poor lighting or not, but she looked deathly pale. He felt pale, too. The source of the demons had always been a mystery. What he had just babbled was crazy talk. But he knew it was right. He knew there was a dark, dead place. He knew he had been there, hungry... *starving*.

Not he. The demons. The gamma and the beta. He had to stop inserting himself in their thoughts.

But surely these were his thoughts?

His head was hammering now.

He tried to empty his mind again, but it was racing with thoughts of countless sources of energy, of gobbling a trail through the grass to the apartments, eating for the first time in... how long?

Harper had accepted his silence at her question and walked to the platform – the bimah, where a rabbi would read from during services – where a lectern and a couple of scattered chairs rested. She didn't use her own flashlight. She seemed to be looking for something, and using the dark to her advantage. Bryan followed her, switching off his light so as not to interfere.

"What about you?" he asked her. "See anything?"

"No," she said in the gloom. "But I can only see what's present at a given moment, not history."

"Right." He was disappointed. He wanted someone else to back him up. He felt like the office was going to stick him in the loony bin. Like Gennick. He winced at the thought of his colleague.

"But we'll need to report this. Maybe have the place watched. Maybe it could happen again."

"You mean another gamma?" He gaped in her general direction. He wasn't sure why he should be so shocked. The idea had always been there in his head; he just hadn't given voice to it until now. But hearing it said aloud seemed like the equivalent of making it happen.

"Let's get out of here," Harper said. "Place gives me the creeps."

Back in the car, his brain was finally able to settle down a bit, though it was still pounding away. He didn't want to think any more about the synagogue and the dead place, though he knew he probably should. But he could handle only so much at one time.

He glanced at Harper. She was watching the buildings go by out the window, hands folded neatly in her lap. So proper.

"So, tell me something," he said. "Anything. Just get my mind off of this gamma for a couple of minutes."

"Like what?" Her voice was even, devoid of emotion. Like a robot.

"Like... anything. Okay, where are you really from? You don't have an accent, and your last name isn't Japanese."

"My father was American," she said, but offered no further information.

"Oh." He tapped at the steering wheel like he had earlier. "You grow up here?"

"I moved back and forth. But mostly I schooled here."

"Mm." He didn't know what else to say. He was veering dangerously close to family history territory. He certainly didn't want to bring that topic up. "So..."

"Stop! Stop the car!"

Bryan slammed on the brakes, the inertia throwing him against the seatbelt. The car behind them blared a long and angry honk. "Harper, what the hell?"

She was already jumping out of the car and running back the way they had come. He jumped out after her and danced back and forth a bit, trying to figure out whether to follow or park the car. He decided to follow, leaving the car stopped in traffic and the other drivers shouting at him as he passed.

He spied Harper ducking into a door, and he tried to go in, too, but was held back by a flood of people who were running outward and screaming bloody murder. He was nearly knocked to the concrete, but flattened himself against the window. A part of his brain registered the sign on the window – a Thai restaurant – and then he saw Harper inside, waving her arms about in the midst of prone bodies. Capturing.

He already had a deck out, and he had a moment to think that Hussein had told him no hunting tonight. Then a woman on the sidewalk screamed – not in fear, but in pain. He turned to see her fall to the ground and whither, growing pale yellow and green and dry.

He tore a card. The effect of being Possessed after a dry spell of a week was debilitating and strangely intoxicating, like getting drunk after swearing off alcohol. The thing in him saw the gamma and beta watching from their cards – their eyes on him so much clearer in this state – and was defensive of its host and yet invited them closer.

He came to his senses lying on the ground, terrified of how the beta and gamma would respond to the invitation. Bryan had no time to think about it. He captured the demon sucking the woman dry as words filled his head.

There are more.

You need me.

Harper burst out onto the sidewalk, looking around. "You got it?" she asked Bryan.

"Yeah." He took stock. The gamma hadn't responded to the demon in him. It had merely watched. The beta was still whispering sweet nothings, thinking his conscious mind wouldn't notice the intrusion. But he had noticed. And judging from it still being in the card, it couldn't do anything without his assistance.

"Fuck off," he told it, and threw the demon in him into another card.

He turned to see Harper's eyes narrow behind her glasses.

"Not you," he told her.

A wailing suddenly came from the dead woman. Bryan spun around, but saw that the sound came not from the corpse, but from a small girl who knelt next to it, shaking and sobbing. It was just them and the girl and the dead now.

Harper had pooled her own demon back into a totem – what looked to Bryan like some sort of little nut. She looked at the child as if not comprehending her. "It got away from me," she said, and it sounded like she was defending herself to the girl. "There were six of them and it–"

Harper's voice broke off and she turned away, covering her mouth with a hand. She seemed about to sob, but instead she screamed and threw her fist at the restaurant's window. Its glass shattered and cascaded to the sidewalk, and the girl looked up at the two of them, wide-eyed and afraid.

But it didn't surprise Bryan. He knew the outburst hadn't come out of nowhere. He had practically expected it.

Steppen Sawicki

Chapter Three

Hussein scratched at his beard as Bryan finished his briefing on the synagogue. He was silent for a moment, as if expecting Bryan to keep talking. Under the scrutiny, Bryan fidgeted and coughed, then opened his mouth to keep talking even though he wasn't sure what to add.

But Hussein held up a hand to stop him. "You say it wasn't supposed to be there."

"I think so. I mean, yes."

"Then where was it supposed to be?"

Bryan wasn't sure how to answer, but he suspected it was a rhetorical question anyway.

Hussein swiveled his chair to the window, though the blinds were closed against the night. Not that they had ever been opened. "I'm going to see what I can do about getting eyes on that place. Kiyoko's right. It could happen again."

"I'll want to check in there tomorrow night," Bryan said. "To see if I can pick up anything else with my mind clearer."

Hussein swiveled back to look at him. "Why was your mind not clear enough tonight?"

Bryan flushed. "I... um, got a headache."

Hussein raised his eyebrows, but didn't remark. "Alright. Anything else to report?"

"Yes, sir," Harper broke in. "We encountered several demons in a restaurant on the ride back. Ivers had to capture one."

Bryan scowled at Harper.

Fucking tattletale.

Hussein threw his hands in the air in exasperation. "*One* night, Bryan."

"I had to," Bryan argued. "It was—"

"It was my fault," Harper said. "I was unable to contain them all myself. One escaped me and exited into the street. Ivers was forced to capture it to prevent further casualties."

Hussein looked from one of them to the other and gave a prolonged sigh. "Then you're a fucking hero, Bryan. Fantastic. Anything else?"

"No, sir," Harper and Bryan said in unison.

"Then, Kiyoko, you're dismissed."

Harper gave a nod and stood. Bryan didn't look at her, still angry at her for mentioning the restaurant, even if in the back of his mind he knew that Hussein would have gotten a report on it from clean-up anyway. And she *had* claimed responsibility.

Hussein watched him as the door clicked shut, than kept watching him.

Bryan uncrossed his legs and then crossed them again. "Um, sir?"

"What did the gamma do when you took in a demon?"

He shook his head. "Nothing. Just…"

"Watched."

"Yeah."

"That's all?" His eyes bore into Bryan's, watching him like the gamma watched him.

Black Heart

"Look, the demon in me even invited it in for shits and giggles, and the gamma did nothing. The beta did more than the gamma did, so..." His voice trailed off as he saw Hussein's expression, and he knew he shouldn't have said anything about it.

How does he do that? How does he get this information out of me, every time?

"Bryan, how am I supposed to supervise you if you don't tell me you have demons inviting other demons into yourself?"

"Is that what this is? Supervision? Is this kindergarten?"

"This is a *job*."

"This is a mother *dead* on the sidewalk, and twenty others alive because I *did my job*."

"I'm not saying you did the wrong thing."

"Then what are you saying?" Bryan crossed his arms, petulant.

Hussein spread his hands. "Can I be worried about you, Bryan? Please? Can I? You want to be the tough guy, fine. But you still have to report. If this thing gets control of you, how many dead will that be?"

Bryan looked away, and he swallowed hard. "The beta tried to convince me to let it out, but I recognized it. Its voice did nothing to me. And the gamma didn't accept."

"Why not?"

It was defensive, too.

Bryan shook his head. "I couldn't tell."

After a pause, Hussein spoke again. "You watch it like it watches you. Got it?"

Bryan looked at him again. "Yeah."

Hussein looked him over for another minute, and this time Bryan held his gaze. "Are you okay to go home today? We can put them in quarantine while you rest."

Bryan looked at the closed blinds again. It was concern in Hussein's voice, and Bryan knew it. This was a job. It was supervision. Maybe he could leave just one
the beta
in quarantine.

Why the beta?
It's the one that talks to you. You don't need it.
Well, of course, he didn't *need* it. He wasn't sure why that had crossed his mind.
Don't listen if it speaks.
"I'm fine," he said aloud. "I'm watching them."

He let his bag fall to the carpet beside the door and, as if escaping it, crossed the room quickly. He collapsed onto the couch, half-expecting to fall asleep right then and there, but he was too hungry. He had barely eaten a lunch. Still, he lay there for a few minutes, relishing being able to stretch out and bend his mind away from the gamma.

Except that it was still observing him, from across the room.

He turned on the TV, barely looking at what had come on – *The Golden Girls*, of course, because it was 4 AM. He went to the kitchen and, tired as he was, cooked chicken cacciatore from scratch to keep his mind busy. The chopping and frying and portioning (he always measured exactly – that was part of what helped keep his mind focused) and the sounds of Betty White and Beatrice Arthur calmed him, reminding him of who he was underneath the demons. Almost convinced him that he *could* have a decent conversation that didn't result in him or the other person getting pissed off. Because that's what normal people did. They talked and laughed non-sarcastically and had lives and families that they'd eat with.

He ate with the TV.

He slept and dreamed of the cabin, but there were too many rooms. A maze of rooms. He was lost and there were demons around every corner and he had nothing to capture them in and he could only run from room to room. At one point, he thought he found his sister, but it turned out to only be Harper, and he was angry with her for being there doing nothing – just kneeling on the floor with her hands tucked together on her lap. But he wasn't doing anything, either, only rushing from room to empty room. He yelled at Harper anyway.

She looked up at him, her eyes dark behind her glasses.

"She's behind you," she said.

He woke with a start on the couch, bathed in sweat. He pulled himself up to look at the bag by the door. He wasn't sure what he was expecting, but it just sat there, unmoved and unopened.

Harper was already there when he got to the synagogue, alongside Skinner and Phan, the day-watch team. The latter two were seated in a car across the street like they were working a stake-out, Harper talking to them through a window.

Phan – the Spotter – lit up when he saw Bryan. "Ivers, man of the hour. How ya doin'?"

"Leave him alone, Phan," Skinner said. She stifled a yawn as Bryan reached the car and peered through the window opposite Harper. "I've had to deal with this all day. Why are Spotters always so damned cheerful?"

"They aren't," Bryan said. "It's just comparison."

"That right, Phan?" Skinner asked her car-mate.

"Hey, it's hard work propping up you guys' attitudes," Phan replied, peering at Skinner over his sunglasses. They were all wearing sunglasses, despite the sun having already dipped behind the buildings around them. Still, the fading daylight seemed too bright.

"But hey, Ivers." Skinner turned back to Bryan. "You okay?"

Bryan tried not to huff at the question. "Fine," he growled.

"Well, that's good," Skinner said. "Me, I haven't been awake in daylight for this long in years. It's horrible."

"That's just the demons talking," Bryan said.

"Whoever's talking, it's horrible."

"I like it," Phan said. "I miss working in daylight."

Skinner rolled her eyes and looked up at Bryan as if for commiseration. "I've gotten this all night. I mean day. What are we even looking for here?"

"Our orders were basically 'Don't blink and be careful,'" Phan said. Bryan noticed he hadn't really looked away from the synagogue except to greet him and respond to Skinner.

Bryan shifted on his feet. "It's the first memory I can get from the... thing. It was here. And before that, it was somewhere else."

Skinner was still peering up at him. "Thanks, man. That makes total sense and explains everything."

"Look, I don't know, either. It's a demon. You get easy answers from yours?"

"Alphas don't give answers, remember?" Skinner looked back across the street. The sun was below the horizon now, the pinks and baby blues fading from the sky to give way to blacks and grays.

Harper said nothing, as if she wasn't required to converse now that Bryan was present. Like Bryan wanted to converse. But at least Skinner had left the topic alone rather than pressing him. Because that was the sum of his knowledge; nothing else from the gamma had cropped up in his mind, and he still didn't know where or what that dead, empty place had been.

A car pulled up behind them, an Audi. Company car. Skinner checked them out in the rearview. "Hallelujah. Our relief is here."

And that's when it happened. Bryan felt it only as a silent explosion, as if a bomb had gone off across the street – it was that sort of power. Then it was gone, and the synagogue still stood as if to defy the incident. Bryan blinked at it to make sure the building really was still there and not an exploded pile of rubble. But it was there.

"What the hell was that?" Skinner asked.

"Did you guys see that?" Andrade shouted as she burst from the car that had just arrived.

"Yeah." Phan exited his car, too. "But..."

"What?" Skinner demanded. "What was it?"

Finally, Harper spoke. "There was a sudden appearance of many demons in that one space. And then they were gone."

"No," Andrade said. "Not gone. They..."

"Exploded out," Bryan finished.

"Like they rushed out from here." Phan spun around, searching about him as if he could spot the demons. "Like they were pushed out."

"It was like there was a wind as they went past," Harper said quietly. "But there wasn't."

Everyone was out of the cars now, with all sunglasses off. Skinner slapped her hands on the roof of her own car. "None of you make any sense!" she shouted.

"Everyone," Bryan said, "stay here." He started across the street. Harper followed him, and he turned around to tell her to stay before realizing she was *supposed* to follow him. That was her job. But Andrade was following them, too. He pointed at her and to the cars, but she shook her head.

"No, I'm going," she said.

"We have a Spotter already," he replied.

"You have two Possesseds, as well." When he squinted at that, she added, "And you might need an extra pair of eyes."

Whatever. There was no time to argue.

Skinner and Phan had been there earlier to see the gate and doors unlocked, so all Bryan had to do now was walk in. As he approached, a dog barked in the distance and a car drove by in the street, offering reminders that he was still in the regular world, where life went on as usual.

He stopped at the door. "Anything in there?" he asked Harper and Andrade.

"Not that I can see," Andrade answered. "But that doesn't mean as much these days."

He looked at the door, thinking. Then he took out his deck from his bag.

"That's not necessary," Harper said. "I can possess."

"You can see already," Bryan said. "I'm useless here unless I possess."

"But none of us can see a gamma," Andrade said.

He had taken out the wrong pack. Opening it and looking in, he saw only two cards lying in it, tooth indentations marking the corners. "Damn it," he said, stuffing it back into his bag and fishing out the other pack full of recently-caught alphas and empty cards.

"We're wasting time," Harper said, suddenly and with venom, and opened the door. She marched through it as Bryan and Andrade shouted and hurried after her.

"What the hell are you doing?" Bryan exclaimed as she stopped between the pews.

She turned around and held out her arms. "You can either waffle on outside about whether or not there's a gamma inside, or you can just go in and find out. And wouldn't you know it, nothing's here."

"And if there had been?" He looked around at the pews and up at the bimah platform. Nothing had changed since last night.

"If there had been, I'm as Possessed as you are." She turned in a circle, taking in everything just as he was.

"You think I—"

He was cut off by Andrade touching his arm, which made him jerk. "No power plays, guys," she said. "Is anything different from yesterday?"

"Nothing!" Bryan shouted at her. "It's just as much a wreck as it was before!" He crossed his arms and stalked up the aisle.

Harper was to the side of the platform, inspecting it. "It happened around here, towards the back."

Bryan stomped onto the stage and looked around yet again. What was he even looking for? The demons were gone, so what was his purpose here now? What had he wanted to be here for this evening? Had he thought he was going to solve 'The Mystery of the Synagogue' by staring at it once night fell? He looked down at the floor and kicked at the dust that blanketed it. It was a lot of dust, and it went up in a fog and drifted lazily down in Harper's direction. She looked up at Bryan in irritation.

"Ivers," she started, and coughed and turned away down the aisle as some of the dust entered her mouth.

Bryan smiled – a slow grin that grew to feel slimy on his face. He forced it away. "I really didn't mean to kick it at you," he told Harper as if apologizing for the grin.

She was still coughing, retching even. She spat twice and pawed at her face.

"It wasn't *that* much," Bryan complained.

"No, but..." Harper spat again. "It tastes dead."

Dead.

He saw it again, just for a moment. The dead place. Then it was gone.

He got out the right deck this time, and took a card from it. Harper barely got out a protest before he tore it.

It hurt more than it should have. He shrieked and fell to the floor, and dust churned up around him as he flopped into it. It entered his mouth and eyes, and he was repulsed by the stuff, by its absolute absence of life, even as he was struck by the strongest recognition. He knew this death... had been immersed in it for hundreds or thousands of years, had drifted among it hungry and cold, starving and freezing. He saw the landscape again and it was so, so dead, all metal and dust.

"Ivers!" he heard from a million miles away, and again, "Ivers!" right above him.

He realized he was screaming, and made himself stop. His eyes were full of dust, and it hurt to open them.

"My eyes," he said, and coughed. He could still taste it.

"Hold still," he heard Harper say, and then she was pouring water into his eyes, holding them open. "That was a stupid thing to do."

"We thought that was the gamma you let in," came Skinner's voice.

"Scared us near to death," Phan said.

"It was the dust," Bryan said, as if making a weak excuse.

"Yeah," Harper said. "The dust made you freak the fuck out."

He sat up, wiping his eyes. They still stung, and he blinked rapidly to try to dispel the remaining dust. But the taste in his mouth was worse. He saw everyone standing around him. Phan and Andrade were wide-eyed. Skinner looked annoyed. Harper was holding a water bottle, and he snatched it from her and alternately drank and spat.

"It did," he admitted. "I remembered that place again. We've been there. For millennia."

There was still dust floating around, getting in his eyes and mouth and nose. He stood and made his way down the aisle to the other end of the room.

"So, it *is* where they come from," Harper said, following him. She and Skinner had their hands over their mouths, though Andrade and Phan seemed unfazed by the dust. Bryan could see all of their aeons, a soft pulsing green.

"What does the dust have to do with it?" Andrade asked.

Bryan downed the remainder of the water and looked up at the bimah, and then he did what he had intended to do. He focused on the energy of everything around him, saw the faint glows in and around everything, and let the place light up like Christmas. The glow was always there for a demon, but you could ignore the weaker parts, unfocus from them just like most things in your vision unfocus and fade and don't wind up in your memory. But he focused on all of it now – the life source that made the demon in him drool. Metaphorically.

"Does an ant have an aura?" he asked.

"What?" Andrade squeaked. "Um, if you're asking me..."

"I am."

"Well, yes. But only if I really look for it, or watch it in my peripheral vision."

"How about a dust mite?"

"No, they're too small. But demons can see their energy. Is that what you're getting at?"

He grumbled under his breath. That *had* been was he was getting at. "Yes," he said louder. "Even mites and microbes, bacteria, individual cells have energy, if you look for it. If you watch from your peripheral vision."

"Then this dust..." Harper suggested.

"Is completely devoid of life. It emits no sign of aeon. Only spare bacteria, and I assure you it only has those from lying in this location."

"This location?" Skinner echoed. "What location would it have come from?"

"The dead place," Bryan breathed out, and shoved the demon into a card. The aeon around him fell away as if collapsing into itself, and all that remained was a ruined synagogue with rotting wood and broken glass and peeling paint and dust in the air.

Outside, across the street, a gray-haired woman was walking past their cars achingly slowly, as if she really wasn't up for the walk she was taking. She saw them come out of the synagogue and stopped.

"Oh, did something finally happen in there?" she asked as they reached the cars.

"Do you live in the area?" Andrade asked.

"Yes, right there." She pointed to a house almost directly across from the synagogue, neat and trim with a little garden in front. "I don't like being at home at night. So I go for a walk every evening until it passes."

"Until what passes?" Bryan asked.

"Well, it's hard to say. It's just a feeling. Something happens in there at night." A look of comprehension snapped onto her face. "You're with the office, aren't you?"

"We are," Bryan affirmed. "Would you say this something happens every night around this time?"

"Certainly every night. But the time varies. Sometimes at sunset, sometimes a little bit later on. Unless the weather's awful or I'm sick, I walk around the block to sit in the park down the way where it doesn't hit as hard."

"What is it you feel?"

"Well, it's... like a hurricane kicks up, but there's no wind. But dreadful. Dark. Oppressive." She shook her head. "I don't even like to talk about it. It must be something awful if you're looking into it."

"I wouldn't worry about it, ma'am," Andrade said.

"Really? But it has gotten worse. It used to be I could barely feel it on the other block, but now I do. Very much so. I would walk further, but my knees aren't up to it."

"I'm sure it's nothing," Andrade said. Bryan left her to crowd-control the one old lady and got into a car, Harper following.

"Still think it's abandoned due to the economy?" he asked her.

◆

They knocked twice before the door was answered by a slight man who seemed to be in his 30s despite sporting a head of gray hair.

"Rabbi Daniels?" Harper asked.

"Daniels, sure," he said in a baritone. "The jury's still out on the rabbi part."

"Ah, well, I'm Agent Harper and this is Agent Ivers with—"

"The office. Yes. I already unlocked the doors for you all earlier today. Come in."

He moved aside and waved them in. Bryan's first impression was that the man was in the middle of packing. There was sparse furniture, showing only the bare essentials – couch, chairs, dining and side tables. And nothing on the tables, nothing on the walls. Then he realized there were no boxes. Everything was eerily and spotlessly clean, too. He felt he was dirtying up the place just by standing there.

"We wanted to ask you about the synagogue," Harper said.

"You want to know what went wrong," Daniels said, falling into an armchair.

"Well, yes." She and Bryan sat on the couch, both of them doing so gingerly, as if worried about breaking it.

"Where do I start?" He suddenly threw his hands in the air. "Where are my manners? You want some coffee?"

The taste of the dust still lingered on Bryan's tongue. "Yes, please," he said eagerly.

"Milk and sugar?" Daniels asked as he pulled himself out of the chair.

"No, thank you," Bryan and Harper said in unison.

He went into the kitchen. Bryan leaned over to Harper and said, "Doesn't seem like a rabbi."

"She raised an eyebrow at him. "You know many rabbis?"

"Um. No." He felt his cheeks flush, and turned away to find something to study, but only saw the empty dining table. He didn't say anything else until Daniels came back with two mugs of coffee and a glass of iced amber liquid.

"I hope you don't mind," he said. "I need something a little stronger if we're going to talk about this."

"It's your house," Bryan said, taking a swig of the coffee. He wouldn't have minded some whiskey himself. He was grateful Harper was there to ask the questions.

Harper placed her mug on the table without drinking from it. "So, you knew something was happening at the synagogue?"

"Something, sure," Daniels said. "But damned if I know what."

"When did it start?"

"That's just it. It didn't *start*. There wasn't a defining moment. It just grew without our noticing." He gulped from his glass. Bryan was struck by how old he seemed in his mannerisms, even though he couldn't be over 35 judging by his face. But what had happened in the past seemed to have worn him down.

"But surely it was noticed eventually," Harper pressed.

"Oh, yes, it was noticed. Well, no, not even noticed." He sighed. "Look, when I joined Agudas Achim, I was mostly interning with Rabbi Sobol. He was old and not in the best of health. He was on his way out, but he still had a good year left in him. I was fresh out of school and excited. I had a shul in the heart of a major city. Everything going for me, you know, and everything going for our synagogue. So what if there was a chill in the air in the evening? So what if there were unexplained sounds or smells or... *feelings?* We had a good congregation, and they really appreciated what I was doing – made me think I was doing right by them. Things were fine."

He gulped at the glass again, and then wiped his lips. "Then people quit coming to night Shabbat. Plenty were still coming in the next morning, just not as many to the sunset service. And I would ask people why the sunset service was thinning out, and they would always have some excuse – the kids were sick, the car broke down, so on and so on. But I knew the real reason, and I felt bad for even pointing out their absence, because I felt it every Friday night when I stood at the bimah. Felt it even in the office if I was around late enough. A stifling feeling of total oppressiveness, forming there and then blown out over the city.

"Now, keep in mind this was before the office, before anyone knew much or thought anything of demons as we know them now."

Bryan was skeptical of that. The office in Chicago had been around before regular people had become familiar with it. But he couldn't fault someone like Daniels for not knowing that, and he didn't say anything.

"Back then," Daniels went on, "the demons that were mysteriously killing people were the mythical religious demons, evil spirits working against Hashem. My thoughts at the time... Well, it might be silly. Might be vanity to think my own synagogue might carry such a weight. But, I had thoughts that this immense power must be the Almighty. This was a synagogue, after all. What else would visit such a force on us?

"But if it was the Almighty, why were people refusing to show on Friday nights? Why did the same people stop coming to Saturday Shabbat, as well? Why did the shul dwindle away more and more? Why did the rabbi himself decide to retire earlier than expected, leaving the place to me? And why did I not want it? Was this the power of the Almighty? The hand and beneficence of the Almighty?"

He downed the rest of his drink and gazed at the spotless carpet. "Fuck. You didn't come to hear that."

"But you know now," Bryan said, "that it had nothing to do with God. It certainly has to do with demons. A great number of them. We saw it tonight."

Daniels grinned wryly. "Damage already done, I'm afraid. What god would... hmm. Never mind. You didn't come here to debate either, I think."

"No," Harper said. "We'd like a time frame, though. Were there any problems before you started interning at Agudas Achim?"

He shook his head. "No. Well... I don't think so. At least, I don't like to think so."

Harper huffed. She was clearly losing patience with his unsurety. "So, when did it start?"

"It didn't start," Bryan said. "He already said that. But it was happening before people generally knew demons were around."

"But..." Daniels didn't lift his eyes from the carpet as he spoke. "But it seemed to begin when I started my interning. I don't like to admit it, and maybe I just didn't want to think it had anything to do with me starting there, and maybe it was going on before then and only started to get noticeable when I arrived..."

"All right," Harper said. "Then when did you join the synagogue?"

"Thirteen years ago," Daniels answered.

Bryan gave a start. Harper looked at him questioningly, but he only stood and gulped down the rest of the coffee in his mug.

"Thanks for your time, Mr. Daniels," he said.

"Thank you," Daniels said.

Bryan blinked at him. "What for?"

"For not calling me rabbi."

Cold rain was beginning to patter the ground as they stepped outside. Harper studied Bryan as they walked to the car.

"What's with you?" she asked.

He opened the car door and looked at the impeccable house, paint and plants and fence all in order. "Thirteen years ago is when I joined the office."

"That's thin correlation," Hussein said, leaning back and twirling a pen. "I was in this business five years before you joined, and reports of death by demons can be identified up to twenty-five years ago."

"I'm not saying," Bryan said, "that it started when Daniels joined the synagogue. That's only when it became noticeable. Or started to become noticeable."

"Then quit flopping your words around and say what you're saying."

Bryan took a deep breath and tried to compose himself and all of his thoughts. The appearance of the demons in the synagogue, their immediate dissipation. The dust. The dead place. "I just think... that we're on to something here. And it very well could be a source or origin point for all that's been happening."

"An origin point, right here in Chicago?" Hussein looked at him skeptically.

"Well, maybe... maybe it's not the only one."

Hussein sighed and set his twirling pen down. He was clearly on edge, irritable. And Bryan assumed it was because of this crazy theory of his. True, he didn't have any proof beyond his own intuition, but wasn't that what Hussein had wanted him to be listening to?

"What do you think?" Hussein asked Harper. "I haven't heard a peep from you."

Her eyes flicked to Bryan, then back to Hussein. "I only know what I saw, which was many demons appearing in the building and being pushed outwards. It could be due to the place being a point of origin. They do have to come from somewhere, after all."

"But?" Hussein prompted her.

"But... this 'dead place' they would have come from is suspect. I mean, it sounds like another planet."

"Is that so crazy?" Bryan shouted. "Look at what we do every day!"

"Bryan," Hussein said, "we need to know where this place is."

"I don't know!" He jumped out of his chair. "I don't know where it is! You think that isn't driving me nuts? And why does it matter anyway? You don't even believe me!"

Hussein slammed a palm down on his desk, and both Bryan and Harper jumped and shut their mouths. Hussein's hand became a fist which he set against his forehead.

"Harper," he said through gritted teeth. "Out."

She got up, stealing one more glance at Bryan, and then left.

What did I say? Bryan wondered with a certain amount of panic.

Hussein didn't look at him, and didn't speak for nearly a minute. He chewed at a nail on the hand that had slammed the desk. Then he said, "Sit down," in a tersely controlled voice.

Bryan sat, his heart pounding.

"They won't give us time," Hussein said, staring at the wall.

"Sir?"

Hussein looked at him, and his eyes changed. They became haggard, almost sad. "The council wants to interrogate you under possession of the gamma."

Bryan's breath stopped. "But... what if I can't handle it? What if someone gets killed? What if *everyone* gets killed?"

"They seem to think you can handle it."

"Why? Because I handled it so well before? Because Gennick and Keeler handled it so well?"

"They tell me betas are well tolerated the second time around."

"This isn't a beta!" He was shouting again.

"I know that," Hussein said, his voice level and cold. He was clearly controlling himself.

"Then why... why would they risk this?" Bryan gripped the armrests of his chair. His palms were sweaty. He couldn't even remember being possessed by it the first time around. He had no idea what he could expect. How could he be expected to keep his head?

Hussein clasped his hands together on the desktop. "You're seeing things that just aren't seen by other Possesseds. Alphas don't keep memories like this. Betas give vague impressions and speak, but they certainly don't *transmit* memories to their holders. I had to tell them you found this synagogue and everyone knows what happened there tonight. I told them...." He spread out his palms on the desk. "I told them that, given time, we could extract more. But they don't want to give us time. The media is going crazy; the government is breathing down our necks. The demons are proliferating faster than we can catch them. We're losing the war, no matter how many hundreds of battles we win a night. And now I'm supposed to go to them and tell them you saw some 'dead place' that could be another planet, for all we know and you don't know anything about it but that demons are rushing here from it...." He looked down and took a breath.

"But they couldn't *make* me do it," Bryan said. "Could they?"

Hussein stared at the desktop.

Harper's words came unbidden to Bryan's mind: *Have you never considered that the Office of Demonic Defense considers its agents to be items?*

"Hussein?" he prodded.

"They're considering it a matter of national security. I'm not even supposed to be telling you about it."

Bryan felt light-headed. Forcing him to do this was akin to torture, with the possibility of death for all involved in the interrogation. Were they really that desperate? Were things really that bad? Somalia and Nigeria were terrible, and China was having a bad run, but the U.S. couldn't reach that level, could it? But then, five years ago, he wouldn't have expected China to be falling behind.

"Bryan."

He looked up. Hussein was finally looking at him again, and his eyes weren't as defeated as Bryan had expected them to be. "Bryan, if you decide not to do it, I will fight tooth and nail for you."

He was in a daze as he walked the halls, so he didn't notice a girl with a halo of dark curls dart out a doorway until she had run into him.

"Omph, I'm sorry!" she cried, looking up at him. Then she exclaimed, "Bryan!"

He was so out of it, it took him a moment to realize it was Sonia, the Possessed he had discovered.

"Or, I guess I should call you Agent Ivers," she said.

"So you accepted," he sighed.

"Yeah. I mean, yes. Though it's just been lectures and meditation so far. So much meditation. Do you really still meditate that much?"

"Not much time for it, no."

She looked hideously innocent hugging her notebooks to her chest, a thick binder sitting on top of them. Bryan knew what was in there: demon theory, meditative theory, the processes your body undergoes under possession.... He had been one of the test subjects for the last. Seemed things were coming back around full circle.

"I don't think I actually ever thanked you," she said, tucking a curl behind her ear, "for helping me back in the Jewel. They said some Possesseds have to wait for hours or even days before their first demon is extracted."

Bryan felt his face tick, and hoped Sonia hadn't noticed. "That's far less common these days. The office is known well enough."

"Still, thank you." She peered up at him with sudden concern. "Are you alright? They say you had to catch some new kind of demon."

"Fine," he grumbled. He scratched at the back of his head, thinking of a topic change. "So, I guess you found a better reason than money, huh?"

"Oh, the money's still up there on the list of reasons." She grinned up at him, her brown eyes dazzling.

He glared down at her. "Have you already forgotten what I told you?"

The smile left her face and she took a step back from him. She shook her head. "It is a *list* of reasons."

He tried to stop glaring as best he could. He hadn't meant to scare her, had he? "I guess you can have more than one."

A more cautious smile crept onto her face. "Anyway, I should get going. Long ride home, and I'm not used to staying up all night."

"It grows on you," he said, and then waved as she backed off with her own wave goodbye. When she turned away, his hand fell slowly to his side.

He realized then just how badly he hadn't wanted her to join.

He didn't know why he did it, but upon leaving he rode the Elevated for a few stops and walked into Stoddard Mental Hospital. It wasn't his first visit there; it didn't take a beta or gamma to empty a Possessed. But he was there tonight to see Gennick.

It was well outside visiting hours, he was told, but he spoke with his badge and was shown to a gray room that was empty of all but bed, table, chair, and man.

Gennick lay on the bed with his eyes open despite the time, staring at the ceiling. Bryan set his bag on the floor and set the chair beside the prone man and sat – his eyes never leaving Gennick's, willing them to move. But they only blinked occasionally.

"Hey, Gennick," he said. "Hope they're treating you well. Especially since I might end up here myself eventually."

He hadn't known Gennick particularly well. Theirs had only been a working relationship, and Possesseds didn't really work together. Still, he had wanted to see Gennick, to see this first person who had tangled with a gamma and come out scathed. As if to say to himself, *See, this is how bad things* could *be.*

It wasn't his first time seeing it, and wasn't his first time in this hospital. There was practically a whole wing dedicated to comatose, ruined Possesseds, ones who'd either been struck down in the line of work or had never survived their first possession intact. But Gennick had fallen to a gamma' he'd experienced what Bryan could barely remember, what his mind had locked away to protect him.

"What is it like, Gennick?" he whispered, because the little room was so silent, so dark, so gray and lifeless... like Gennick. "What's it like when it eats away at you?"

Gennick didn't respond.

Bryan sighed and lowered his head. "I don't know what to do, Gennick. They want me to put that thing back in my body. And I don't know if I can handle it. *You* couldn't handle it, and you were always capable enough. Now look at you."

Gennick stared at the ceiling, but blinked once as if to say, *Yes, look at me now.*

"I guess I just had to talk to somebody about it. Even if they're just a body. I can't just turn my back on the office. They need me, and they need this thing I have, but I'm scared. I'm a fucking coward. After everything that's happened, I'm still a frightened child."

Full circle. He leaned back and looked at the empty gray wall. Why *wasn't* he in here? What made him so damned resilient? Why hadn't those three days at age thirteen destroyed him?

He stretched his mind out to the gamma across the room in his bag. It was watching, regarding the scene with two of its holders here. Just for a moment, his vision doubled as if he were sitting where he was but also sitting across the room, looking at himself.

He blinked and it was just his eyes he was looking through. He turned back to Gennick lying in his bed. He wasn't going to find any answers here.

"Thanks for listening," he said, and reached out to pat Gennick's hand. "Sorry to interrupt your slee—"

Gennick's hand jerked away.

Bryan had been half turned away to leave. He looked back to see Gennick looking directly at him, his eyes wide and cognizant.

His mouth opened.

And he screamed.

Bryan was on the Elevated before he felt his breathing and heart rate return to normal. He put his head in his hands and sucked in deep breaths. Meditative breaths. But his head was reeling and he couldn't get to where he needed to be, to the lakeshore with the waves and the sun. He wanted to get drunk and pass out, to pretend none of these problems would be with him when he woke the next night with a hangover.

Gennick's moment had passed. Bryan had heard the screams die away from his place in the hall, and the nurses had told him Gennick had returned to his usual state, and asked what Bryan had done.

Nothing, Bryan had said.

He had done nothing.

He had just been there.

He rubbed at his face and peered through his fingers at the windows of the train. Everything outside was a shade of blue – morning twilight. Soon, the sun would rise. It was usually his favorite time of the day – or night – but right now, it looked sickly to him, uncanny. Like a drowned corpse. Like someone whose face he knew, but that hid a stranger's soul behind it.

He had done nothing.

He woke hours before sunset, tense and drenched in sweat, but he couldn't remember what he had been dreaming. His thoughts immediately turned to the events of the previous night, and he threw Howlin' Wolf on the record player to distract himself. He cooked Eggs Benedict and pancakes and grilled cherry tomatoes and ate a third of it all. He didn't want to head out early to the synagogue, but he found he couldn't avoid it. He also didn't want to be alone.

The place was swarming with agents. Skinner and Phan were there again, but so were several other Spotters and Possesseds. And Cam was there, his jacket standing out in the crowd.

"How you holding up?" he asked Bryan.

"I'm walking and talking," Bryan responded, thinking again of Gennick. "What's with the circus?"

"We were just about to head in. We're all here to observe the inside. We hear some demons just popped up and vanished last night."

"Something like that."

"You found it, didn't you? They didn't say so, but we all kind of figured."

"Yeah." Bryan spoke quietly. He didn't want everyone there to hear about it. "I can catch its memories sometimes. Hussein sent me to the apartment it wrecked, but I don't think he expected me to really catch quite so much. It's like it has a mind and I'm reading it."

Cam was staring at him, a little disbelieving and a little fearful. "Fuck, man."

"Yeah, fuck."

"Just remember it goes both ways."

"What?"

Cam looked to the synagogue. The last of the sunshine lit up its stained windows. "It'll be looking at your mind, too."

Harper was approaching them, so Bryan didn't respond. She stopped before them and spoke without offering a greeting.

"We're all heading inside now."

The inside had been transformed. Office agents milled about, checking on cameras and sound recorders and thermal imaging and Geiger counters and all the other old ghost-hunting equipment that must have been pulled from storage and dusted off. There were people taking samples of the dust from the podium and people inspecting the pews and windows as if they likewise held some mystery.

And everybody looked at Bryan as he entered.

Bryan Fucking Ivers. Man of the Moment.

If only the floor could open up and swallow him.

"What exactly has everyone been told?" he asked Cam.

"Pretty much what I told you. A 'disturbance regarding demons.' But everyone knows you found it. We're all to possess and watch the show."

"It's not a show," Harper said from behind them.

Cam indicated the cameras and agents and stereos with his hands. "*This* isn't a show?"

"Ain't no fuckin' show," came a voice from their left. They looked over to see Skinner regarding them coldly, brows knit. "I was here. I felt it. Felt like every damned demon in the city rushed out and should have knocked over the building. I don't see why we aren't setting up a group capture."

"Maybe," Harper snapped, "because we aren't prepared to capture every damned demon in the city." Her tone on those last words was mocking, clearly forgetting that Skinner had been on her side of the argument. Her voice was a sheen over rage in a way that Bryan hadn't heard before.

"Hey," Skinner snapped back, "maybe you're too chickenshit to capture some demons, but–"

"Shut your mouth!" Bryan shouted. "You're just talking about yourself."

"You couldn't handle shit," Harper put in, though it wasn't clear who she was talking to.

"Possesseds, separate!" came an order from a Spotter situated by a camera. "You haven't even been together in here for five minutes!"

They all cursed, and Skinner spat, but they walked away from each other. Bryan silently raged that Cam had kept his own mouth shut as if he were better than the rest of them, and couldn't or wouldn't sling mud like the rest of them. Him and Harper both, they acted so high and mighty and–

Something was watching him. Something was whispering these words in his ears.

He spun around, hitting his hand on a pew hard enough to send sparks of pain shooting up his arm, but he barely noticed. He had felt eyes burning into the back of his neck, and had heard a voice like hard iron blowing cold into his ears. But no one was behind him, and the only people gazing at him were the ones who'd looked when he had spun around like his ass was on fire.

He lowered his head sheepishly, but reached out to the beta. *I know that was you*, he told it.

It didn't say anything. It was like it was pretending nothing had happened.

So, he thought about what Skinner had said. If they *could* throw up a net right here for when all the demons appeared, wouldn't that save a lot of trouble? Assuming that demons really did "appear" here. 'Point of origin,' Harper had called it. But if they threw up a net, could they keep hold of it? Or would the demons just tumble out into the synagogue, their push outwards halted by the Possesseds themselves? A city's worth of demons jammed into a single building. With a sizable chuck of Spotters and other agents to snack on.

No, they would have to study it out first – size it up. It was necessary, if damned inefficient. Meanwhile, people would die. Tonight, in apartments and houses and shops and offices, people would die.

Bryan's hand throbbed where he had struck it. He concentrated on the pain, needing it, though it was nothing compared to the pain of possession.

Connors was picking his way from person to person, checking on everyone, rubbing his arms with his palms as if he were cold, scratching at the back of his bald head. Never still. If Bryan hadn't known him better, he'd have thought the man was either going to fly into a rage or start blubbering.

"Ivers, you okay?" he asked, as if Bryan had bullet holes in him.

"Fine," Bryan answered.

"Good. Good. You're not possessing here. Ah." He held up a hand to shut Bryan up. "There's a reason. We want to see if you can catch anything from the gamma. If you were possessed, that demon would interfere with what you could gather. Understood?"

"Yeah," Bryan agreed sullenly. But what Connors said made sense. "Though, I didn't gather anything last night."

"You did, once you were inside. This dust. You're right; it reeks of death. You'll find something else tonight, too, I bet."

Bryan frowned at him. "I'm not sure I like you being so positive."

Connors sniffed and scratched at his cheek. "I don't want to treat you different, Ivers, but I have to. You've got certain things to do here."

Before Bryan could respond, Connors clapped him on the back and stalked off to a Spotter who was next in his line of sight.

Different. That's what he was now. Different.

"You okay, man?" Cam asked, suddenly beside him.

Did *everyone* have to ask him that?

"Christ," Bryan barked, "leave me alone! Nothing's wrong with me."

"I was just asking," Cam said, his face souring.

"Well, don't."

"Fine! Maybe there *is* something wrong with you!" Cam stalked off fuming. He bumped into another Possessed on the way and the two had to be separated by Connors.

Great fucking idea, Bryan thought. Let's put half the Possesseds in Chicago in a single room. He noticed Harper and Andrade both checking him out and wanted to scream. Everyone was watching him. Everyone was studying him. He was like some little experiment, no longer a person. The Possessed with a gamma.

"Okay, everyone settle." Connors jumped up onto the platform and caught everyone's attention. The chatter and tantrums died away. "Sun's about to go down. We're going to take turns possessing in teams of three until we see something. Whether you're currently possessed or not, watch and concentrate. I want silence."

He jumped back down quickly and began assembling teams, as if he hadn't liked being up there. Bryan realized people *had* been avoiding that area, whether it was due to the dust or something else.

Cries of pain sounded as the first Possessed group set up, breaking and tearing totems. Bryan huffed out a sharp breath. Not him. He didn't get to possess. The Spotters cast curious glances at him, noticing he wasn't possessing or standing in any team. He was separate. He wasn't a part of any team.

Then they were all watching the front of the synagogue, silent and waiting. Bryan and the others from last night were in the middle of the space, close enough to get a good view but far enough away to indicate that they knew what was going down. Except for Phan, who was all the way in the back at the building's entrance, as if to say he wanted nothing to do with any of this. Bryan realized the guy had been suspiciously taciturn, as he normally would have been bouncing off the walls in greeting everyone.

The light through the colored windows dimmed, going baby to ocean blue, pink to crimson, orange to ochre. Agents stared, readied cameras, and held their breath.

After thirty minutes, the teams switched off, the second team possessing and the first taking a break. After another thirty minutes, the third team took over. Then the first again.

The sun set. The sky blackened. Spotters and other agents started chatting quietly to pass the time, but any Possessed who spoke was silenced by Connors.

At 10:30, people started grumbling in disappointment. They had been expecting a near-sunset occurrence like what had been reported last night, and instead they were standing around for hours. The eyes of the teams not currently possessed started wandering, and at one point Cam found Bryan's eyes and they shrugged at each other, their spat already forgotten.

At 11:20, it happened.

Bryan saw nothing, but he felt a wave of chilled air, stale and empty so that he had the sensation of suffocating within it. And with it came the scent of death. Not the smell of rot, but of absolute death – the absence of life, life long gone eras ago. He had the powerful feeling that he knew these sensations, and had drifted among them. He had been there, in...

He grasped at it, but it fell away from him like a dream. Like a nightmare. One he *needed* to remember, even if he didn't want to.

He stretched his mind out to whoever might be listening. *Where is that?*

There was no answer. He shouldn't have expected one.

"Ivers."

Harper was there, looking at him with genuine concern, her brows knitted behind her glasses. She didn't ask him if he was okay, but it was in her expression.

He wiped at his face and his hands came away wet. He had been crying.

"Sorry," he said, not sure what he was apologizing for but needing to say something.

Everyone around them was chattering excitedly, asking each other what they'd seen, checking equipment, getting into little fights.

"Did you see anything?" he asked Harper. "Were you possessing?"

"I was, but it's hard to say." She looked back up at the platform. "There was a sliver, some sort of rift of nothing, of no aura or aeon. I'd swear the demons were thrust out of it, but it happened so fast, and then they were pushed out around us."

Bryan hadn't even noticed the explosive force of the demons being pushed into the city. He had been so focused on that land. But he had gotten nothing for it.

"We don't get to hunt tonight, do we?" he asked Harper.

She looked at him quizzically, but only said, "No. We have to write reports on what we saw here. But other than that, the two of us aren't doing much."

He nodded. "Want to go get a drink?"

She frowned, conflicted. But after studying him a moment longer, she said, "Okay."

"This is weird," Harper said. She had an open Miller in her hands, but she hadn't taken a sip yet.

They were out on Dusable Harbor, feet hanging over the water, listening to the waves lap the piers. Watching the lights of the shore to their right, the lights of the boats drifting in front of them, and the absolute darkness beyond that.

"What is?" Bryan asked.

"I just... thought you meant you wanted to go to a bar."

"Oh." Bryan couldn't remember the last time he had been in a bar, save for a month ago when he had captured some demons in one. The location wouldn't have occurred to him. "Naw, isn't this better than a bar?"

She seemed to think about it, then answered, "Yeah." She finally took a sip of her beer.

He took a gulp of his own. The breeze picked up and ruffled at his hair, blowing cold. For an instant, he thought again of the cold dead wind that had brushed past him in the synagogue – the same wind that blew through the dead place.

"I wanted to thank you," he said, "for not asking me if I'm okay. Whether you realized it or not."

"I noticed your reaction when others asked it."

He gave a short laugh. "My aura."

"Yes."

"Everyone's been asking me if I'm okay. It might not bother me so much if I had an answer."

"You seem distressed a lot, even for a Possessed."

He flinched. "Do you have to be so damned blunt?"

"Sorry."

The beer was cold in his hands. He shifted it and turned it, fiddling. "Were you possessed by your beta?"

It was her turn to flinch. "I was careless. Caught off-guard. So, yes, it possessed me."

"What was it like?"

She turned her head to look at him. "You've been possessed by one, too."

"Yes, but I want to hear from you."

She was silent for so long that Bryan thought she was refusing to answer. Then she reached behind her into her bag and brought out a walnut shell. She held it up before her.

Bryan gaped. He knew she had caught it long enough ago that it should be in the office storage in Tokyo; Hussein had told him so. "They made you bring it with you?"

"In case you go out of control with your gamma. The idea is that I could do something other than jack-shit." She turned it in her fingers, holding it perilous over the water. "It is so tempting to think I could just throw it into the lake."

"It talks to you, doesn't it?"

She nodded. "It's realized that my father's voice gets the best reaction out of me."

"Fuck." He looked away from her, from the shell. "I'm sorry. It's because of me you have to–"

"I agreed to this assignment." Her voice was still level. It had been matter-of-fact all along. "It took something when it possessed me. Some part of me that... I don't know what it was, but I miss it regardless. People call me a cold bitch. Maybe that's why. But who knows?"

"That's how it was for me, too. I mean, without the 'cold bitch' part. But everything's just been... wrong ever since. Harder. Nothing makes sense anymore."

"But you have the gamma, as well."

"Yeah, and it doesn't really talk. If it does, it tries to go through my thoughts. But mostly it just *watches* me. Like it's trying to learn *Bryan*."

"It can't do anything. It's in that card."

He sucked in breath sharply, so that she looked at him. He wrestled inwardly for a moment.

"Harper, can I trust you? Like, you're not going to secretly report what I say back to Japan? Or even to the office here?"

She studied him, then sighed and looked out at the water. "I'm not some secret agent if that's what you're asking. My job is to support you and make sure you don't go crazy."

"I'm saying..." he said too loudly, close to shouting, angry, "I can't just figure this shit out on my own! They put me in a glass case and then they..." He stood and threw his can of beer out into the water. Still half-full, but he didn't care. He'd thrown it so hard that he nearly fell in the water himself, and

Harper rose in case she had to pull him back. But he righted himself and stood there breathing hard.

"I'm your partner," Harper said.

He looked at her, expecting her face to spell out concern or – worse – pity. But she only regarded him with cold discerning eyes, as if to say it was up to him whether he talked or not. It was what he needed.

"They want me to possess with the gamma so they can question me – it. They haven't given me a choice, really, but Hussein said he would fight them if I wanted to refuse."

Her mouth dropped open. She turned away from him, and then back again. "*Kuso!* That's insane! It could take you. People could die. *Agents* could die. And then where would we be if another gamma...." She stopped, and drew in a breath and let it out slowly. "I'm sorry. I'm thinking too far ahead again."

"No, you're right. What if another gamma appeared? What if I could give proper information on it? Or that rift in the synagogue – what if I could tell where that was going to? That *place*. It's in my head, driving me crazy. I need to know where it is."

"Who cares where it is? There's nothing there!"

"*I* was there. I need to–"

"You weren't there!" she shouted over him. "You were never there. That demon was!"

"Maybe it's the same thing."

"No, it's not. You'd be risking your sanity and the lives of who knows how many people just to find out where some place full of dust is."

"But the demons are coming from there. More and more of them. You must know – we ignore it the best we can and soldier on, but we're gonna be overrun before this is over, the way things are going."

"And you're going to solve all the problems? You're going to possess and find out how to stop the demons showing up?"

"I don't know! It's all I can do!"

"Listen to you – you've made up your mind to do it already!"

"Maybe I have. So what?"

She grabbed the collar of his shirt and swung him to the edge of the pier as if she would toss him into the lake, and he caught hold of her hands and fought her to the edge, as well. She was smaller than him, but he had been caught off-guard and was unsteady, so they were in even danger of falling over as they pushed and pulled at each other before they both fell on their asses on the boards. They sat there then, breath puffing into the cold air.

"I haven't made up my mind," he gasped. "I can't. I'm fucking terrified!"

The water lapped at the pier, pointing out the silence. Harper grabbed her beer and downed the remainder in one go.

"We do ignore it," she said when done. "We just keep going out every night and capture until dawn, but we know we don't get them all anymore. They carry over into the next night. But we just go out the next night and do the same thing."

"We need to know what that thing is in the synagogue," Bryan said. "I thought if I was there tonight, I would remember something. Find out something. But I only thought of that place."

"What if you possess and it tells you nothing? What will it get from you?"

Black Heart

He wished he hadn't thrown his own beer into the lake. He could get up and get another from just a few steps away, but the act of standing seemed impossible.

"When I was thirteen," he said, "demons killed my family. My parents and my sister. And one possessed me. It was in me for three days before I found a way to push it out and into the cuffs on the bed I had been strapped to. I was strapped to that demon in that cuff for three more days before I could pretend to be sane enough to be unstrapped. Ever since that happened, I've said no more dead parents and no more dead siblings and no more Possesseds tied to demons. And I do the best I can, but people still die and we still recruit. And if I can do something different and help in a different way, then...."

Harper's voice was quiet, and wavered the slightest bit when she replied. "You're Possessed. We can shout and scream all night, but you'll make your own decision."

The night wind blew through the space between them, cold, like the wind through the dead place.

Steppen Sawicki

Chapter Four

He slammed the door shut behind him. He let his bag fall to the floor, making a soft *whump*. And then there was silence in the apartment. He didn't turn the lights on. Only stood in the entryway in the dark and the silence.

The fight with Harper had been bad enough. The fight with Hussein not long after had been worse. Hussein hadn't taken Bryan's decision well. They had both of them tossed aside profession and shouted a barrage of curses at each other. Then they had momentarily thrown a barrage of punches at each other. Bryan might have clipped Hussein's jaw. Hussein had definitely cuffed Bryan's ear and struck his left arm straight-on before throwing him out of the room. Bryan couldn't remember much of what either of them had said, but none of it had been productive. Only on the train ride home had he realized he'd wanted to talk with Hussein. He had wanted a real discussion about his decision – and it was *his* decision, regardless of what Hussein wanted. But Hussein had objected flatly and Bryan had gotten defensive... and it had all gotten out of hand.

He passed his hand over his face and walked further into the dark apartment, to find the curtains and pull them open. It was still dark out, but the city lights gave the room a dim glow. He looked at the gray, washed-out city sky and considered calling Cam, but he knew he would still be working, busy like a Possessed should be. Not moaning about in his apartment in the dark. Bryan knew he should eat, too, but he had lost all appetite. And besides that, he was tired. Deathly tired, but only in his body. His mind was still a mess, thoughts and regrets and dim memories swirling around in it.

He went into the bedroom, realizing that he hadn't actually slept in his bed for days, even now thinking that he could just lay on the couch staring at the TV again until he fell asleep. But he shoved that thought aside and crawled onto the bed, sitting cross-legged in the center of it.

He hadn't meditated in months.

The idea was to empty out and quiet your mind enough to look inside and pick out what wasn't you – what was lurking inside your mind that might be a remnant of some demon, or some demon trying to set up residence. It wasn't required of most Possesseds, not outside of special circumstances, but it was recommended. This seemed like a special enough circumstance to Bryan. If Hussein hadn't thrown a fit, he would probably have told Bryan to meditate in preparation for the interrogation.

Bryan wondered if Hussein might not tell anyone he had agreed. It occurred to him that he might have to go over Hussein's head to tell them himself. Hussein might want too badly to be some sort of white knight fighting for his subordinates.

Bryan shook his head forcibly. His thoughts were still racing. He took deep breaths, focusing on the silence in the apartment and trying to echo it in

Black Heart

himself. Tried to envision the water washing over the pebbles, the sun on the waves.

His left arm ached. He shouldn't have tried to punch Hussein. Had he thrown a fist first? Or had Hussein? He couldn't remember. But either way, he shouldn't have gotten physical. It wasn't going to affect his career – Possesseds fought all the time and black eyes were a common sight in the halls at the Office. Hell, he had fought Hussein before and gotten his ass handed to him. But this time it had been messy, and neither of them had been in it fully.

He let out a harsh breath. He felt he would never be able to meditate again.

A memory of pale, dead earth illuminated by moonlight flashed through his mind. He seized it, desperate, and threw himself into it. He heard the desert winds blowing, and felt it brush his skin. Dead sand flurried in the air and entered his mouth, and he tasted it and it hurt, but he didn't care. It was a horrible dead landscape where even the moon's skull seemed to stand out, and he hated it and was hungry, but it was home and he was satisfied. He drifted through it, over dirt and sand and gray waters, both repulsed and fulfilled, until he crested the top of a hill overlooking an empty plain. The moonlight spread out thick before him, and in the plain marched a line of hooded figures, and he knew that they were the same as him.

He woke violently hours later, thrashing his arms and searching all around him. There had been someone standing over him, watching him, and he hadn't been able to move or open his eyes to see who it was, or he hadn't wanted to open his eyes to see.

But daylight seeped through even his thick bedroom curtains, and he could see now that no one was there.

Something banged outside the room, in the living room or entryway. Bryan nearly screamed, and then he realized that it was someone banging on his door. That was what had woken him. Had he been screaming in his sleep? It wouldn't be the first time a neighbor had told him to knock it off.

He stumbled to the door, flicking on all lights as he passed even though the living room curtains were still open. He stopped in the hall when he noticed his bag by the door, a wild stray thought passing through his mind: that the demon was knocking on the door.

Then the bang sounded again, and Hussein's voice called, "Bryan, you better be in there!" Bryan could tell it was him even though it didn't really sound like him at all.

And Bryan could see why when he opened the door. Hussein stood there stooped over, disheveled and drunk as hell.

"Bryan, there you are. Here, throw this away." He handed Bryan an empty whiskey bottle. "No littering, you know."

He brushed past Bryan into the apartment and looked around. "You've really made something of this place. It's lovely. This." He pointed to a framed picture on the wall. "Where did you get this?"

"Target," Bryan said. "Hussein, it's the middle of the day. What are you—"

"Oh, crap." He clapped Bryan on the shoulder. "You were asleep."

"That's not the problem. I've never seen you this drunk."

Hussein threw his arms wide. "I've never been this drunk!" he announced.

"Why are you here?"

"Is it in there?" Hussein pointed to the bag by the door. "In your bag? It's all its damned fault."

"Hussein..."

"If we could just set them on fire or shoot them or something, we wouldn't be in this mess. But they just hang around and we can't do anything with them. What are we gonna do when the cards and matches rot and disintegrate? If you had just taken an office job any of the twenty times it was offered to you..."

Bryan watched his boss rave, noting the shadows under his eyes and the lines in his face that hadn't been there years ago, when they had gotten drunk together. But then, Hussein had always politely stopped at tipsy.

"You need to sleep," Bryan said. "You look like you haven't slept in a week."

"Nonsense." He grabbed the whiskey bottle Bryan had set on a table and put it to his lips before realizing it was empty. He put it back down crookedly and it fell to the rug. "I got three hours yesterday."

Bryan put his arm around Hussein's shoulders, noticing for the first time in a long time that he stood half a head above his boss, and led him to the bedroom. He glanced at the clock. It was two in the afternoon. "And you'll get three more today if you're lucky. Though it's not going to help you much."

"This isn't about me. You... I didn't mean to punch you."

"I know. I didn't mean to—"

"But we forget how to talk," Hussein interrupted him. "These damned demons take it all out of us."

"That doesn't mean you had to get drunk." He sat the man on the bed, and he half-rolled over on it before sitting up.

"I used to be a sensible man," he said, pronouncing the words *senslible min*. "I was an architect. I was gonna build my own house."

"Take your shoes off. I'm going to get you a bucket so you don't puke in my bed later."

Hussein grabbed his shirt as he started to walk away. "Bryan. Bryan, I'm not stupid. I know you have to do it. Or that you feel you have to do it. You know how bad things are. But you don't *have* to."

Bryan frowned. This felt like another fight coming. "Hussein, just go to sleep."

"No, listen. It's your choice. I just need to say that I don't want you to do it. You're like my kid. I found you and I pulled you into this business and taught you everything, and if this all goes to hell, it's me that failed you. And I'm worried I've failed you."

Bryan couldn't speak. These weren't sober words. These were truths that only surfaced when you were drunk; words you weren't supposed to say out loud. "I'll..." he said, "I'll be back with that bucket."

Hussein patted his shoulder. "You know what to do," he said.

Bryan wasn't sure whether he was talking about the choice he had made or the bucket.

When he got back, Hussein was passed out on the bed. Bryan had to take his shoes off of his feet.

Bryan fell asleep on the couch as soon as he laid down on it, his mind finally quiet and his fears laid to rest. He woke when the sun was low in the sky, to the sound of Hussein throwing up. Bryan was mixing pancake batter by the time Hussein came out of the bathroom, hand to his head.

"Good morning," Bryan said.

Hussein grumbled under his breath and fumbled his way into a chair at the breakfast bar as Bryan poured him a mug of coffee.

"I'm afraid all I have to mix that with is cheap beer," Bryan told him.

"If I were in anyone else's apartment," Hussein said, "I would be deathly mortified." He took a gulp of the black coffee and winced at how hot it was. "Instead, I'm only hideously embarrassed."

"You act like no one's ever been drunk before."

"I showed up at your place in the middle of the day and woke you up. I acted inappropriately as your supervisor."

"You're not just my supervisor," Bryan said quietly, his back to the bar as he poured batter onto the griddle. "We can talk to each other."

"Fuck, I don't even know what I said." There was a pause, and then he continued, "Fuck, the time. I need to get to work."

Bryan turned just in time to watch Hussein fall while trying to get up, disappearing behind the bar.

"Fuck," he said from the floor.

"You need to eat," Bryan said. "You're still half-drunk."

"I'll throw up if I eat." Hussein pulled himself up, gripping the edge of the bar.

"You might, but you might throw up even if you don't eat. You still not eat bacon?"

"No pig." He sat back down in the chair as if the act of walking away from it was impossible.

"I still think that's silly, with you not being religious."

"I'm not gonna start right now."

"Fair enough." Bryan flipped the pancakes.

"I am so sorry for this, Bryan. You shouldn't have to be cooking me breakfast first thing in the evening."

Bryan shook his head. "It's nothing. I actually kind of needed this. I wasn't sure if I was doing the right thing, but I know now that I am."

Hussein sighed behind him. "Well, at least I was coherent, apparently."

"For just a moment. Then you passed out."

Hussein grumbled and drank his coffee.

Bryan cracked eggs onto the griddle, smiling to himself. Hussein had taught him everything, and Hussein had never failed him. He would be fine.

Bryan entered the room and his breath stopped. The center of the cafeteria had been cleared, all tables and chairs pushed off and stacked against the walls, replaced by a circle of twenty Possesseds. He stopped at the scene, and Hussein clapped him on the shoulder.

"It'll be okay," he told Bryan.

But it wasn't the idea of the possession that made Bryan stop to rethink his decision; it was the fact that he would be doing it in front of a crowd. Still, there was no going back now. The building had been cleared of all office workers, save for the security downstairs. The Possesseds who weren't in this room were gathered in the street and courtyard. Spotters had been told to stay away, along with normal agents and office workers, just in case the whole thing was a disaster. The entire office had been put on hold for Bryan and his demon.

He swallowed hard and stepped forward towards the group. Cam was there, smiling to reassure him, but his expression looked forced. After all, if Bryan screwed up, everyone in this room was already dead. There was Harper, too, who didn't smile, and Connors fidgeting with his book. Along with the Possesseds were three of the four directors – Cantrell, Bey, and Utterklo; they were regular office workers with no skills outside of administrative powers, chosen long ago by Hussein and Ruggeri. They were only here to watch and interrogate, as if to say a round of Possesseds couldn't be trusted.

Bryan knelt in the center of them all, his blood rushing in his ears, trying not to crush the card box in his hands. Everyone around him sat on the floor, as well, except for the directors, who stood upright – or, in Cantrell's case, stooped over – in their suits and studied him. And Hussein watched him, worry set in his face. He had told Bryan, even on the way to the room, that he still had a chance to back out of this, that they couldn't make him do it, not with him there to help. He had still held out hope that Bryan would turn around and refuse to possess.

Connors nervously flicked the pages of his book. "Remember what we discussed," he announced. "All of you stay vigilant. Don't get distracted. It could be looking for just such a moment."

He's right, Bryan thought. The gamma was a damned smart thing. It had kept quiet these past two days, watching silently as if knowing that, if it was a good demon, it would get this possession, and that if it acted up, Bryan could call the whole thing off. Meantime, the beta – he could tell it was the beta, as he had been learning about the two demons as much as they had been learning about him – had been absolutely hounding him. Whispering to him, disturbing his sleep, disturbing his emotions. The past two days had been hell thanks to that thing, and more than once, he had seriously considered taking it back to quarantine.

Bryan looked down at the box, to the gamma hiding inside. What did it really want? What did either of them really want?

"Possess," Connors ordered.

Totems tore, snapped, and cracked. Everyone around Bryan – save for the directors – doubled over, moaned, and cried out. Then they pushed themselves back upright and stared at Bryan, who felt like he was sweating a river.

Black Heart

"Whenever you're ready, Bryan," Hussein said. His brows were furrowed, one hand propping him up. In pain.

Bryan nodded at him, unable to speak. He looked down at the little box, then pried the top flap open. He saw inside the gamma and three blanks, which was two more than he needed, but he wasn't taking any chances. He reached for the gamma's card, remembering standing in front of half the office and spilling a pack of cards around his feet. But he had had to touch this card to move it to this pack, so he was somewhat prepared. As his fingers brushed it, it looked at him, and slinked backward. Hiding something. *No time to worry about that now.*

He slipped it out, noting the crumpled toothmarks at the corner. He held it in both hands, watching it watch him. He looked up at Hussein, and they locked eyes for a moment before Hussein nodded.

He let out a breath.

He tore the card.

The demon blazed through him, burning his veins and the underside of his skin. It crawled into him, burrowing, ripping out a space. He would have screamed, but there was no air in his lungs, so he only croaked and fell to the floor on his side, fetal.

He sucked in air and released it in a laugh. It was shaky and low – almost like a cry, but it was a laugh.

"Bryan, can you hear me?"

He opened his eyes. He hadn't realized they'd been closed. He looked at the people before him, taking in the lifeglow of their aeons.

He was so hungry.

He laughed.

"Bryan?"

He turned his head up slightly, so that he could see the one speaking. *Hussein.* He glowed a deep green.

"Are you alright?" that green glow asked.

Bryan grinned. The action pulled at his skin, stretching the muscles. Contorting them. "Yes," he said in a voice that didn't sound like him. But then, he *wasn't* him. "Perfect."

Hussein looked off over Bryan's body. To Harper. Bryan didn't see her reaction, but Hussein looked back to him. "What can you tell us about this gamma?"

Bryan chuckled. He looked down at the floor under his cheek and saw the aeons of a million little mites, the energy trapped in the linoleum and the steel underneath. He reached out a hand and passed it over the surface. He wanted to lick the floor.

"I can tell you anything," he said.

Hussein threw another glance at Harper. "Why is this demon different from the others?"

"Age," Bryan drew out the word, feeling it on his tongue.

"It's older? That's why it's more powerful?"

"No. Younger."

"Younger? But... then, how do the betas fit in?"

"Oh, they're older, too. But the alphas, they're the oldest."

Hussein's face was scrunched up, trying to work it out. Because he hadn't known who was young and who was old. Bryan saw now that Hussein didn't know anything.

"How old is the gamma?" Hussein asked.

"How could one keep track? Centuries. Many centuries."

Director Utterklo spoke up suddenly, his deep voice jarring. "Then certainly they existed somewhere else, prior to here."

"Where do the demons come from?" Hussein asked.

Memories flitted through Bryan's mind. Memories of death and hunger. All trace of a smile left his lips. "The dead place."

"Yes, but where *is* this dead place?"

Bryan sighed as if this were some longsuffering line of questioning. "Earth."

"What does that mean?"

"Earth means Earth."

"Don't fuck with us," Hussein snarled. "Explain."

Bryan's eyes narrowed at Hussein. He wanted to say '*Or what?*' He almost did say it, but he knew the answer. Those who served no purpose were locked away from human contact. From life contact. That couldn't happen. Not now.

"The Earth next to this Earth," he said. "Next door."

"Another planet," Cantrell said from the group of suits standing outside the circle. He was the oldest of the Chicago directors, with gray hair and a crooked back. He was also the most vocal, usually to unfortunate results.

"No, you fool." Bryan eyed him angrily. "I said Earth. I *meant* Earth."

"Another universe?" asked a voice from behind him. *Harper.*

Bryan searched his own mind and considered. "That's a close approximation."

The room went silent, though Bryan could hear and see them all breathing around him. They exchanged worried looks with each other. This had just gone beyond anything they might have suspected.

"Then, how do the demons travel here?" Hussein asked. "Through gateways, like in the synagogue? Are there more of those?"

"Yes, yes, yes."

"How many?"

"I haven't counted them."

"Many?"

"I just said," Bryan growled. He was sick of looking at Hussein. He rolled over onto his other side clumsily, not quite able to work his body.

"What are these gateways? How are they made?"

"They make them." On his other side, he could see Harper, stonelike and expressionless. He started to grin at her, but his eye caught Cam off to the side. He looked horrified, his body tense. He kept looking from Bryan to Hussein and back to Bryan again, as if something were going wrong here.

Was something going wrong here?

"Who?" Hussein demanded. "The demons?"

Bryan didn't answer. He was looking at Cam, seeing him for him and not for his life. Cam noticed and stared back, shrinking within his frame. He looked as if he might whimper.

"Bryan! Who?"

Bryan put his forehead to the floor in order to stop seeing. He screwed his eyes shut and focused on the cool of the linoleum on his forehead. He didn't feel like laughing anymore. He was starting to realize that he hurt everywhere. "Not the demons. They're Possesseds, like us. But not like us. They're Possesseds all the time. They've been Possesseds since back before eternity."

"What does that mean?" Cantrell asked.

"Shut up!" Hussein spat at him, and then he turned back to Bryan. "How do they make the gateways?"

"Don't know." Bryan was tired, and he ached. He wanted this done with, except that he didn't.

"You do know."

"But I don't!" He wanted to cry. The pain had become unbearable, but a part of him liked it and wanted more. Yet, he wasn't sure what was him anymore. He wasn't sure who was talking. He balled his hands into fists and set them against the floor. "I don't know. But the gates open more every night. They have to work at it."

"We need to stop," Harper announced.

"Not yet," said Cantrell. "We haven't gotten anything."

Bryan opened his eyes and looked to Hussein, who was picking up the card box. He held it out to him before Cantrell grabbed for it.

"We're not stopping," Utterklo said from behind Cantrell.

They were so close. They were bursting with life. And he was so hungry. Had been so hungry for so long. He reached out to them.

Hussein ripped the box from Cantrell's grip and pushed him squarely in the chest, nearly knocking him to the floor. "Always listen to the Spotter," he growled. He opened the box and was about to hold it out when Harper spoke again.

"No! Stay away from him. Slide the card to him."

Hussein glanced up at her briefly before he slid the card across the floor. It stopped inches from Bryan, and he looked at it as if not comprehending. He gazed up at Hussein again and saw that life... how close it was. He could just pull himself a bit further. He reached out a hand and gripped the floor, and pushed with his leg.

Harper stood behind him. "Sir!"

The others in the circle tensed.

Hussein didn't move. He only spoke low, barely above a whisper, as he looked into Bryan's eyes. "You're still alive."

Bryan stopped. His mind separated a fog from itself, then set it aside.

The card was beside him. He touched his palm to it and willed the demon into it. The demon went willingly, almost apologetically easily, even if it didn't want to go.

Bryan didn't want it to go.

The absence of pain rushed over him so that he cried out, and he felt the loss of a part of himself, but this time not literally; this time, the loss was the cutting of a tie.

When he came to, Hussein was bending over him – not an aeon, but skin and hair and eyes. Everyone else still remained in the circle, apparently not wanting to come closer. Bryan felt more alone than ever before in his life.

"You with me?" Hussein asked.

Bryan nodded and pushed himself into a sitting position. He was shivering. The room felt ice cold after the heat of the demon.

"Everyone out," Hussein ordered, "except Harper. Connors, get everyone to work. Someone bring blankets from the lounge."

"I'll do that," Cam said, his voice hollow.

"You shouldn't have stopped," Cantrell said as the others filed out. He and the other directors were clearly planning to stay in the room. "We only got bits and pieces here."

"If you're going to stay here, keep quiet," Hussein told him.

"You may be a Possessed, but that doesn't give you the right to insubordination."

Hussein shot up from the floor and imposed all of his 5'5 frame on Cantrell. "You may be a prick, but that doesn't give you the right to put my men in danger."

Cantrell's face flushed red. Bey laid a hand on his shoulder, as if to tell him not to engage in a fight. She was the only director who ever seemed to know how to deal with Possesseds, and had kept her mouth shut through the whole spectacle.

"Sir," Harper spoke up, "we had to end the session. Ivers's aura was fading. Or changing. But it signified danger."

"Well, since you sound so certain about what you saw," Cantrell said sarcastically, turning away.

Cam arrived with the blankets. He draped them over Bryan, who thanked him weakly. Almost immediately, Hussein was waving him out. Bryan looked over his shoulder at Harper. She actually looked livid, eyeing the suits with contempt.

"We're only thinking of the city," Utterklo said. "This demon is our only lead. This interrogation gave us our only clues. We don't want to have to do this all over again."

"Great," Harper spat. "Next time, I'll let him eat you."

"Enough," Bey broke in. "It's done. Let's move on. Did Ivers catch anything else from the possession?"

Five pairs of eyes turned to Bryan, but he didn't notice. He hadn't been listening to the arguments. He had only clutched the blankets around him, staring at the card on the floor. His mind was fuzzy, half-remembered scenes floating through it.

"Bryan."

"What?" He looked up at Hussein, trying to focus.

"Did you get anything out of this that you didn't say aloud? About the Possesseds on the other Earth or the gateways?"

Bryan shivered. He thought of the hooded figures roaming the dead place in his meditation. "They aren't really Possesseds. Not like us. They've been Possessed for so long that there's no human and no demon. Only one being. Eternally."

"You mean they're immortal?"

Bryan didn't answer. He didn't have the words to explain the horror of those figures in the empty desert, searching for new food for all of eternity, jumping from Earth to Earth to feed. *Only to feed.*

"How do they open these gateways?" Hussein asked.

Bryan shook his head. "I don't know. They use the demons somehow. A great number of them."

"Then how do we stop them?"
Bryan shook his head again.

When he laid down on the couch in Hussein's office, he meant only to rest a few minutes. But when he woke, hours had passed and it was 1 AM. He sat up, rubbing sleep out of his eyes and wondering what to go do now. He desperately wanted some coffee, but it was prime time for people to be milling through the lounge and cafeteria. He didn't want to have to bear the weight of that many eyes. So, he went down the hall to where a new research area had been set up. The space had been a conference room, but was now stuffed with monitors and computers and printers, as well as eight people working hunched over cups of coffee. When Bryan walked in, they all looked up at him and stared.

"Hey, boss," Bandy said. He was a young agent of no talent excepting electronics – part of their glorified I.T. squad. He took off his glasses and rubbed at his screen-dazed eyes. "Good to see you alive."

Bryan mumbled a reply. He was still fuzzy.

"What brings you here?" Bandy continued.

Bryan watched a television monitor showing the synagogue with a crowd of people. "I, uh, was wondering if you found anything new in the data."

"Nothing we haven't shown you guys already. Pressure increases, temperature shoots up, and infrared lights up like a Christmas tree. Typical environmental effects for demons. Just higher than normal because there's so many."

"Can I see the infrared from tonight?"

"Yeah, sure." Bandy put his glasses back on and turned to his computer. He clicked through screens until a video popped up of a blue space with red bodies milling about. "Give it a second," he added.

Bryan watched and waited. Suddenly, there was a flash of red on the platform, which swirled for maybe five seconds and then shot outward.

"That's all she wrote," Bandy said.

"And you still have no evidence for the gate itself?" Bryan asked. "The way they came through?"

"Are we calling it a gate now? No, there's nothing. Just the demons appearing out of nowhere."

Bryan stood up straight and chewed on a fingernail. "But they aren't appearing out of nowhere."

"Conservation of energy says they wouldn't."

"But they have no energy where they're coming from."

Bandy took off his glasses again, glancing up at him. "What's that?"

"Nothing. EVP?"

"Not sure why we even set up the speakers. Demons don't register as voices or noise on them."

A woman Bryan knew only as Caddy peeked at them from around a computer monitor. "Don't knock the EVP. We got something tonight."

"Tonight?" Bryan asked. "Why only tonight?"

"Damn equipment wasn't recording previously," Caddy explained. "No one bothered to check it. Nobody thinks anything of EVP."

"Well, what's on it?" He went around to her computer. After clicking about on it for a moment, she pulled up a sound file. She played it, and the crackle of speaker noise played.

"Wait for it," she said.

After a few seconds of silence, there was an expulsion of sound, deep and rumbly, as of the unintelligible murmuring of hundreds of voices speaking together or of earth moving. It went on for about five seconds, and then there was sudden silence again.

"That from the gate opening?" Bryan asked.

"Yeah. We're not sure if it's the sound of the... gate itself, or something else. Demons don't make sounds, even that many demons. So, I'm at a loss right now on that."

"Hm," Bryan grunted. But he already had an idea what the sound might be from, because it called up a memory of hooded figures gathered and speaking in an unknown tongue.

He left the research room and headed to the classroom where, it seemed like ages ago, he had scattered a deck of cards before showing off a beta to a crowd of Possesseds and Spotters. A ridiculous concept now, to think that betas were the danger. He was nearly to the room when he realized classes might be canceled for the day due to his interrogation, but Ward was lecturing to the new kids – kids in his mind, though at least one of them was over forty years old. Bryan slipped in the door silently and sat in the back row so that no one noticed him.

Ward was prattling on about how to project, how to encircle the other demons with your own demon's power, and how to put up a shield to protect yourself. Everything Bryan had learned from practice, but which these kids were having to learn from

PowerPoint slides. He wondered which way was easier, though in the end, they would have to practice off of paper even if they had been schooled on procedure.

It would have been easier to have died when those demons possessed us.

It wasn't a new thought. Bryan shoved it away as he had before and listened to Ward drone on about the front and back of the mind and how it could manifest outside the body.

"Bryan?"

He snorted awake and looked up to see Sonia. Her unruly hair was pulled back into two puffballs at her shoulders.

"Hey," he croaked, pushing himself up. There was a crick in his neck from slumping in the hard seat.

"What are you doing here?" She smiled, clearly amused that he had been napping in her class. Two other students – a teen boy and girl – stood with her, staring at Bryan in awe. He could practically hear their thoughts. *THE Bryan? Whoa.*

He wanted to slump back down in the chair again.

"I... ah... I'm not sure actually." He realized they were all looking down at him, so he stood up, scratching his head as if confused. "I just needed to go someplace quiet, but not too quiet. You know?"

Her smile turned lopsided. "Not really."

He looked around at the emptying room. A couple of students were gathered around Ward, clarifying some points. Like this was just another college class.

"So, how's training going?" he asked Sonia.

She shrugged. "It's still all lectures. But tomorrow we start practice with the demons we caught." She looked beside her to her silent hangers-on, and then back to Bryan. "Hey, you wanna grab a coffee?"

The cafeteria had been exactly what Bryan was avoiding, but if someone was with him, maybe no one else would bother him. And God, did he ever want that coffee. He nodded, and Sonia told her classmates she'd see them tomorrow.

Seated in the cafeteria, she put a pile of sugar and cream into her coffee as he took grateful sips of his own, black. People were looking at him and whispering. He tried to ignore them.

"What was it like when you did practical training?" Sonia asked, stirring her creation.

"Didn't have any," he said. "There was just a handful of us back then, and even the experienced ones were learning as they went along. We trained in the field."

Her eyes widened as she said, "Oh." She looked down at her coffee. "I guess it's pretty silly for me to be scared, then."

"I'd be more worried if you weren't scared. This isn't a thrill ride. It's not going to be fun."

"You're trying to scare me again."

"Maybe. But anyway, there'll be several Possesseds there to watch you kids in case something goes wrong."

"Yeah, but... will it hurt like that time?"

"Of course, it will. Didn't they talk about that?"

"They did. But I wanted to ask you."

He eyed her over his cup. Her expression changed only slightly, but there was an undercurrent of fear to it. It pressed on him her age – only fifteen – and her innocence. "You'll be prepared for it this time."

"You're not going to be there, are you?"

He blinked at her. "I haven't sat in on training in years. Hell, you see what I'm like."

"Oh," she said, lowering her eyes again.

There was a silence between them, in which Bryan could hear the voices at the tables surrounding them. He imagined they were all talking about him. "Christ, you *want* me to be there? I was starting to think you were stronger than that."

"It's not that." She nearly stood up as she spoke. "I just... wouldn't have to worry if you were there."

"I'm not your dad. There's already gonna be several Possesseds there."

"But you helped me before."

He sighed and rubbed his forehead. "I only told you what to do to capture the demon. To pull it out of you. I *told* you. You did the action yourself. It'll be the same tomorrow, whether I'm there or not."

She seemed to shrink into her chair. "You make it sound so easy. But it wasn't easy."

"But you did it."

She didn't speak right away. She traced her nails along her cup, leaving trails in the Styrofoam. Finally, she spoke quietly, without looking up. "Were you scared today?"

He drew in breath sharply. Then he took a sip of coffee to mask the desire to backhand her and the self-loathing that followed. When he spoke, it was through gritted teeth. "I was fucking terrified. But I did it, because it had to be done."

She still didn't look up, but she nodded.

He looked at her to say more, but saw Hussein stalking towards the table.

"Bryan!" he shouted for the whole room to hear. "Where the hell have you been? I've been looking for you, and your damn phone is off."

"Did something happen?" Bryan asked.

"No." Hussein looked a little defeated by the question as he came to a stop at their table. "No, we still don't have a clue about anything. I just didn't know if you were okay." He looked to Sonia. "I shouldn't have interrupted."

Bryan waved his hand in introductions. "Sonia, this is Hussein Hussein, in charge of Possesseds. Hussein, this is Sonia Reeves. She's in training."

"Training?" Hussein repeated. "I thought they canceled classes today."

"Mr. Ward said they had talked about it," Sonia said, "but we're needed soon as possible. So, we started late tonight instead. Um, sir."

"Oh. Good, good. Well, always exciting to see new faces."

"You don't have to sugarcoat," Bryan said. "I was the one to recruit her."

"Ah, great," Hussein said. "So, you got the 'Welcome to Hell' speech for an introduction."

Sonia grinned in that lopsided way again. "Something like that, sir."

"Well, it is. It's also the most important work anyone can do these days. So, it is good to see you here." He put his hand out and she stood to shake it.

"Thank you, sir." She smiled genuinely at him, and then at Bryan. "Well, I should head home. Thanks, Bryan. I mean, Agent Ivers." She waved at him and slipped away.

Hussein took the chair she had vacated. "Are you okay?"

"Yes, sheesh."

"Well, how am I to know?" he asked, throwing his hands in the air. "They want me to ask you how many parallel universes there are."

"How would knowing that help?"

"Not at all. It's just busy work for me. Have to pretend we're doing something."

Bryan shook his head. "I don't have an answer. Innumerable. They've been going from one to the next, just eating every source of life. The gamma's actually pissed about it, since it's their fault it went hungry for so long."

"But none of these things starve. None of them die."

"I told you, they're not human. Not anymore."

Hussein rested his chin in his hands. He looked past Bryan, eyes unfocused. "And they're coming here."

Bryan looked away from him, to the other tables. The room was thinning out now, everyone going back to their desk to work through the last hours of the night.

"Go home," Hussein said, standing up. "You need the rest."

◆

It wouldn't be dark for long, but it was for now. Lightning was flashing in the distance and rain was starting to fall in a mist that the freezing wind blew around in a frenzy. Bryan ducked his head against it and marched on. The station was just three blocks away. Hussein's words repeated over and over in his head.

Busy work. Busy work.

Is that what they had all been doing all this time? Running around capturing demons that only multiplied more and more every night, proliferating faster than they could be caught. Looking busy. Looking like they were preventing some catastrophe. But the catastrophe was coming regardless.

...they're coming here.

Bryan's brain kept trying to throw up defenses against the inevitable: *We can fight them, we can defeat them.* But he had only to remind himself that countless other Earths had likewise fought and lost. Once the gates were finally open all the way, how many demons and eternally Possesseds would file through? A world-full? How could anyone defend against that?

...been following you.

He stopped on the sidewalk. He hadn't quite heard the voice in his head.

She's behind you.

His breath halted. The voice was so clear now that he was actively listening to it.

He didn't turn around. Instead, he reached into his pack and pulled out a deck.

Yes. Now.

He stopped in the middle of pulling out a card. Was he doing this because the voice was telling him to, or because he chose to? He couldn't tell.

Hurry.

He spun around. The rain was falling in large drops now, spattering on the pavement and in his eyes. But no one was there.

Still, his heart sped and his blood pumped hot.

"There's no one," he said, mostly to himself and partly to the voice.

She's going to kill you!

It had shouted in him with such genuine fear, a fear he felt, that he pulled the card out. He checked it to make sure it wasn't the gamma – of course, it wasn't, because the gamma was alone in its own pack, but still he checked – and after almost dropping it, Bryan tore it. He fell to a knee on the sidewalk and gritted his teeth, and looked up to see something coming his way. Something that was almost a demon, but not quite.

He threw up a protective barrier just in time. A force hit him so hard that, even with the shield there, he was thrown back several feet. The remaining deck flew from his hand and cards scattered down behind him, sticking to the wet pavement. Several landed in the gutter, one directly in the path of a passing car. Bryan felt the tires crossing over it.

Concentrate!

Thrashing, he pushed himself up to standing, reinforcing the barrier. The thing was still there in front of him – a figure that should have been dark in the night rain, but for him glowed a radiant crimson, like nothing he had ever seen before. It was beautiful. But it was stepping towards him, as if stalking him.

He cast a ring of containment around it, and it halted. It held out its arms towards him and, suddenly, there was fire all around him, and he couldn't move or make a sound.

It was doing the same thing back to him. A ring of containment, around him and the demon in him.

But the figure wasn't stopped; it was walking towards him.

It came slowly, in fits and starts, fighting against the containment he had around it, but winning. He strained his own muscles and couldn't move an inch. He didn't even feel that he was standing, but instead that he was pinned in the air, the fire scorching him. He had never been contained this steadily, not outside of training. Possesseds didn't fight each other. Not this way, at least.

Bryan was shocked. He was furious. The demon in him was amused.

And still the thing came towards him. It was covered in a dark hood and a dark robe, like what he had seen in his vision of the desert. But its head was down, concentrating on its steps. It had no weapon out. He wasn't sure what to expect. Then he remembered the cards scattered behind him.

If it got to those cards....

How many demons could he handle inside him?

He focused everything in his mind to a point, looked past the pain of the fire. He thought of the lecture he had fallen sleep to earlier – manifesting the front and back of your mind outside the body. He did it now, throwing all of himself into the fire around the thing. It twitched and was frozen for the slightest moment. Then it continued forward. Slower, jerkier, but forward.

Bryan couldn't move. Every inch of his skin screamed, his flesh searing. People passed by on the other side of the street, oblivious to what was going on.

What do I do?!

Nothing answered him. Maybe there was no answer to give.

It came close enough that he could see its face in the midst of a crimson aura – a woman's face, twisted in a snarl of concentration. It would have been taller than him, but it was slumped over, fighting against his containment. It made to pass him by. It *was* going for the cards.

What was it doing that he wasn't? He couldn't think anymore, couldn't see through the pain of the fire. However ethereal, he imagined he could feel his skin crackling under it. The demon in him felt it, too, and was screaming in his mind. For just a moment, he lost himself, and it seemed the fire overtook him, burning his bones, and then he and the demon thrust it out.

The force of it dented cars and broke windows, and tossed the thing beside him into the nearest building hard enough to crush the bricks. It lay on hands and knees and coughed blood – striking crimson blood. Then the thing was getting up. Its hood had been thrown back, and bright red hair hung down, soaking in the rain.

Bryan was on the ground, nerves singing. He struggled to rise, but his arms and legs were like jelly. He felt for his pocketknife – the one he used to cut open packages and boxes, the little three-inch thing that had never tasted blood. He wanted to gut the thing, and punish it for hurting him. A growl rose in his throat.

It was up, but its limbs sat at odd angles, broken. Its arms dangled and it limped on its crooked legs as it came towards him. That beautifully striking blood flowed from its open mouth, and Bryan reeled at the sight of it. He saw the blood of the thing and salivated.

Again, that fire wound its way around him. But this time he knew what to do with it.

He drew the fire into himself, into his heart and lungs and marrow. Screaming, he launched himself at the thing. He only wanted to destroy it now. Wanted to tear it apart. Wanted that beautiful red blood for himself.

He thrust the knife into it, slicing open a flood of red, and he sank his teeth into the wound... ripping it wide, tearing at the muscle. Blood filled his mouth, drenching his tongue in life that was sweet and bitter and everything at once. The muscle ground between his teeth and the bone cracked, and he was thrilled to the core.

A scream brought him back. A scream and running feet, running away and then gone. And something

...come back...

else stirring in the back of his mind. He slowly came back to himself, coming to a realization of what he had done like he was surfacing through murky water. The copper taste of blood was still in his mouth. The remains of the body lay beneath him, nothing but bloodied meat and empty, open eyes.

He backed to the curb and vomited, spilling blood and raw flesh into the gutter. He stared at it disbelievingly, shaking, his vision wavering and his limbs numbing. About to faint. He stumbled to the cards that were still stuck in puddles, fumbled for an empty one, and threw his demon into it. He hoped he would faint then, in the rush of absence. He wanted to, to just black out and deal with all of this later. But he didn't. He remained on his knees in the rain, copper and bile on his tongue.

When he looked back at the figure, he saw something red moving along the sidewalk, rising from the gutter to crawl towards the body that still sat against the wall. The body whose leg, at that moment, twitched with the snap of a bone fitting into place.

Chapter Five

"Here, drink this."

Hussein handed him a cup of coffee. Bryan grabbed it, his shaking hands spilling half of it onto his fingers and the blanket that lay over him. It burned and he didn't notice. He gulped down the liquid and Hussein had to take it from his lips.

"Careful," he said. "It's hot."

Bryan didn't care. The scalding coffee running down his throat was nothing. He had to wash that taste from his mouth.

Hussein added more whiskey to cool it down and handed the cup back.

Bryan had burst in downstairs drenched in blood, absolutely raving, and though the guards knew him, they hadn't been sure whether or not to let him in. They were half-convinced he was possessed. They'd called Hussein, who'd tried to bring Bryan upstairs, but he'd refused to go.

"She'll kill these guards!" Bryan had shouted. "They can't do anything! She'll kill them. If she comes here, everyone in this lobby is *dead*."

He'd been unwilling to leave the lobby until four Possesseds had been posted at the doors. And even then, Hussein had needed to drag him away.

Now he was back in Hussein's office, back on the couch. The blood was gone from his face and clothes as if it had somehow evaporated. As if what he'd experienced had never happened. As if he were crazy. But he could still taste it on his tongue.

"Okay," Hussein said, sitting on the coffee table. "Now tell me again, and slowly this time."

Bryan told him, in between gulps of whiskeyed coffee. Hussein had to remind him several times to slow down and breathe. When he finished, Hussein put his chin in his hands, deep in thought.

"You're saying this woman regenerates?" he finally asked.

"I'm not crazy. I saw it... I saw pieces of it... the pieces...." Bryan shook his head, and his hands shook so hard that Hussein had to take the cup from him again.

"I didn't call you crazy. I just need your opinion on what you saw. Was she dead?"

"I snapped her fucking neck!" Bryan leapt up from the couch, towering over Hussein. "I ripped her carotid out! You think she might not have been dead?"

A knock sounded at the door, followed by, "It's Harper, sir."

Hussein's eyes didn't leave Bryan. "Come in."

She came in dripping wet and slightly out of breath. She eyed Bryan. She must have heard him shouting. He sat back down, withering under the scrutiny. "We found the scene easily enough," she said. "There's clear evidence of a fight, but no body. No blood, even."

Bryan felt himself pale. He had been right. It was still out there.

Hussein leaned back, hand over his mouth, thinking some more.

"What the fuck do I tell everyone?" he asked.

"What..." Harper stepped forward, then wavered before continuing. "What *did* happen?"

"Bryan happened upon a new sort of Possessed and a fight happened. The Possessed is still at large. Tell everyone to be alert."

Harper's mouth opened and then shut. She didn't leave. Hussein turned to look at her and sighed. "That's my job, isn't it?" he said.

"I wasn't—" she began.

"No, I need to say several things to several people." He stood and put a hand on Bryan's shoulder, though Bryan noticed a nearly imperceptible pause in the motion as he did so. "I think you should sleep."

He went to the door, speaking quietly to Harper so that Bryan couldn't hear, and then left. Bryan imagined it was a warning he'd given her. *Watch your neck.*

She turned around a chair from the desk and sat. She didn't fold her hands primly this time; they gripped the armrests. Her eyes were glued to the wall.

They didn't speak for a full two minutes. When Bryan did speak, his voice seemed to boom in the little space.

"What do I look like?"

Harper seemed to realize the number she was doing on the armrest, and set her hands haphazardly in her lap. She looked at him, studied him, and then said, "Your color is concerning. It's like what I saw earlier today when I stopped the interrogation, but fainter. If it were any darker, I'd swear you were possessed."

"Am I?" he husked.

She started. "You're agitated. That's all."

"Agitated. That's me."

She leaned forward. "They said you were covered in blood from head to toe. But there's nothing on you."

He looked down. She was right. Besides the rainwater and a bit of mud, he was clean. "That 'new kind of Possessed' Hussein mentioned – I think it can pull parts of itself back together. Mend itself. Even from a distance." He looked up at Harper. "Regenerate."

"How did you get drenched in its blood?"

His eyes went wide and he turned away without answering.

"Something happened," she said in that steady voice of hers. "Tell me what."

Again, like he had at the pier, he wondered whether he should trust her. He wasn't certain what Hussein was going to report, but he may very well leave out Bryan's episode. But Harper had to work with him. She deserved to know.

"I possessed to try and fight it off. But that thing got the better of me; tried to contain me. The demon in me took over. Just for a minute. Just long enough for me to rip out that thing's neck with my teeth." He passed a hand over his face as his stomach turned, remembering the blood in his mouth. "I came back to myself and threw it all up in the street. And the things I threw up *crawled* back to the body."

There was silence as Harper processed this. When she spoke, her even tone was gone. Her voice shook. "You came back."

"Yeah." He knew what the next question was, and he didn't want to answer it.

"How?"

"I don't know," he said. As soon as the words were out of his mouth, he remembered that she could clearly see when he was lying.

But she didn't say anything. Instead, she said, "You should sleep."

He gave a short laugh, looking at her. She was unreadable. "I don't want to be alone right now."

"Then I'll stay here. Hussein told me to anyway."

"Is that what he said?"

"Of course."

Liar.

The word seared his mind like a firebrand, so that he jerked.

"What?" Harper asked.

"Nothing," he said.

And again she didn't press.

He laid down, wrapped in the blanket. But he didn't close his eyes. He felt like he could never close them again.

"Harper?"

"Yes?"

"Why did you take this assignment?"

She gave a long sigh and turned her head to the window. It was still dark out, at least another hour until sunrise. Not that anyone could tell with the blinds closed. "It's stupid really."

He lifted his head to look at her. "Tell me anyway. Just to give me something else to think about."

She appeared to think it over, still looking at the blinded window. Then she spoke, her voice as level and even as if she were reading from someone else's story. "I didn't know I was different from other people. I thought everyone saw auras and such like I did. Then I got possessed and joined the Tokyo division, and it became apparent really quickly that I was a Spotter, too. And everyone was so proud to have me on the force, like I was some prodigy. Like I was going to make a difference. And I believed it. But the demons kept coming and I didn't make a dent in them. Then I caught the beta. Well, it attacked me and I happened to capture it. And everyone was so proud again; I had done something really special now. I thought I could use this, that this was just the kick I'd needed. But the demons kept coming more and more, and people kept dying more and more. Then I got news of this guy in the U.S. who'd caught something even crazier than a beta, and heard that they could use me there, so I thought maybe this was our chance. Maybe this was our break. Maybe I could still help. Maybe I could still... be worth something."

    She was still facing the window. Bryan laid his head back down on the couch.

    "I told you it was stupid."

    "It's not," he told her.

    "You don't have to say that."

    "It's not. It's why we're all doing this. Fighting on in a hopeless fight, waiting or looking for a break."

    She turned her face to him, and it was level, serene. Unreadable. "Go to sleep," she said.

He woke with a start, from a dream of torn skin in his mouth. The room was bright with sunlight. Harper slouched in the chair, asleep. She'd stirred

Black Heart

when he'd woken up thrashing, but hadn't awakened. Hussein was at his desk, head in his arms. He hadn't stirred at all.

Bryan tiptoed out the door and to the bathroom, where he pissed a river. He didn't meet anyone on the way there and back. The building was like a tomb in the day. There were daytime workers – analysts and payroll employees and damage control personnel – but they hardly equaled the buzz of nighttime and they worked on the lower floors.

The two were still asleep when he got back. He closed the door silently, without even a click of the latch, and looked them over. Harper's hair was in her face, swaying gently with each breath. He could hear her snoring if he listened hard enough. Hussein was hunched over his desk, arms for a pillow, back rising and falling. Bryan felt bad for him; he had taken his couch.

His eyes roamed to the other side of the room, to the bookcases. And his bag. His bag filled with waterlogged cards he had scooped up in the midst of his gibbering horror, filled only with self-preservation, as if the cards were pieces of his body which he'd had to gather together before running away from the thing that was gathering its own body.

And the gamma. The gamma was in there, too.

He went to the bag and took it out, finding the box immediately, as if he were a metal filing drawn to a magnet. He sat down on the couch and drew it, expecting to feel something when he touched the card, but he felt nothing, as if it were asleep, as well.

He turned it over and over in his hands. Seven of spades.

I know you're there, he thought at it.

It didn't respond. There was only an energy under his fingertips, like with any other demon.

I know you can hear me.

Nothing.

Come on, you cowardly fuck.

Nothing.

He took a shaky breath. Was it trying to make him angry?

What was that thing that attacked me?

He felt something. Its eyes on him perhaps, but that was all.

You helped me. If you want to help me, you'll tell me what that thing was.

It peered out at him. The card was warm in his hand. It was studying him, thinking. Somehow he knew this, and he waited, until its voice rose in his mind, coming up from some depths he hadn't known were there.

You know what she is.

He flinched at the voice. It was toneless, sexless. Like a stray thought in his head come forward.

He licked his lips, which were dry and cracked. *Possessed eternally.*

It didn't answer, but he was right.

How did it get here?

It didn't answer.

Through a gate?

Nothing.

His fingertips pressed indents into the card. Why was he even bothering with it? He was answering his own questions. *I thought only demons came through the gates.*

It's difficult for them, the voice told him. *This early, it is a risk few take, and fewer than that reach the other side.*

He blinked at the sudden information. *Then why do they try?*

Because they are hungry.

He thought of the dead plains and the dead wind that blew through them. Of dwelling there for centuries. *How do I kill it?*

You don't. She is Eternal.

Bull. I can burn her, at least.

The demon tied to her will reconstruct her.

Then I'll drown her in lava or a vat of acid or something.

Even at a molecular or atomic level, she will be brought together.

Sweat stood out on Bryan's forehead. *How is that possible?*

Her demon knows every part of her. That is why she is Eternal.

His whole mouth was dry now. Nothing he or anyone else could do. How was that possible? All these years of fighting demons, just to run into something like this? To end like this?

And there were others.

Why was she after me?

She was after me.

Why?

Younger demons are powerful. Our power wanes as time passes and we feed.

So, she would use you? How? For what?

This is a war, after all.

He was getting a headache. Harper stirred in her sleep and gave a sound that was nearly a whimper.

All this was hard to process when he had to struggle to get answers. But it made sense that the Eternal had been after the gamma – perhaps that was why it had been frightened. But then again, what did it have to be afraid of?

It didn't matter.

Right?

Bryan shook his head to focus. What would a group of eternally possessed people want to be doing, if this was a war?

They're strengthening the gate, Bryan guessed. *So they can come through safely.*

It didn't answer. So he was correct.

When will that happen? When can they come through?

They have 2,000 years to prepare. Then they have their chance.

Bryan licked his lips again. *When?*

Soon.

God, his head was pounding. His fingertips were burning where they touched the card. *When?*

It didn't answer, and he knew it didn't know. He knew because it was in his pounding head, looking out of his eyes, flipping through his thoughts.

He threw the card away in horror, and it felt like he'd used all his strength to toss that card away from his body, like he'd been throwing a fifty pound weight, like the air resistance against it had been a hurricane. But, being a card, it didn't fly, but swayed drunkenly in the air, threatening a couple of times to drift back to him before landing on the corner of the coffee table. It wavered there for a moment and then fell over the edge to the carpet. He had cringed away from it and was breathing heavily.

Stupid, he thought at himself. *Stupid. You didn't even learn anything.*

But he had. He had learned that these Eternals wouldn't die. And that there were more of them.

And more coming.

Soon.

"Are you certain you were overtaken?"

All four directors stared at Bryan. They might as well have shone a spotlight in his eyes. Hussein wasn't watching Bryan, though. He was studying the directors, his eyes moving from one to another.

"Yes," he said. "Due to the... violence I used against the Eternal." The 'violence', so far as the directors knew, was that he'd used his knife to attack. He had been willing to give the whole truth, but Hussein had refused to allow it. Keeping that part quiet would keep him out of quarantine – maybe – but doubt gnawed at him.

Still, this wasn't the time for quarantines. The suits just wouldn't understand that.

Wallmann looked down at his notes; he was always taking notes. "Then how did you come back to your senses?"

Bryan swallowed hard. "I don't know."

"Surely, you have some idea."

"I... heard people screaming. I think that did it."

Another lie. It had been the gamma, speaking to him. But he couldn't tell them the gamma had first called out to him when the Eternal had approached, and second, brought him back when he'd been overtaken. What would they gather from that?

What *was* there to gather from that?

"People screaming," Cantrell said. "That can't be all. People are always screaming when Possesseds are overtaken."

Bryan flinched, but none of them seemed to notice. They were chatting among each other.

"If we only knew what the catalyst was, this would be huge," Wallmann said.

"Well, it's not something we can test in the lab," Cantrell responded.

"Are we certain he was overtaken?" Utterklo repeated.

"We're getting off track," Bey spoke up. She was perhaps the only one in the room who didn't look frazzled, her eyes regarding Bryan coolly and her back straight in her chair, her hands folded perfectly on the table. Though the rest of the suits had already heard Bryan's story hours ago, Bey had only heard it for the first time just now, and her face had been a mask the whole way through, even as Bryan had added in that there was no physical way to kill the Eternal – which he claimed the gamma had told him *during* the fight. Another lie to add to the list. "We're here to discuss the Eternal. Since that's what we're calling it."

"Was there even an Eternal?" Cantrell asked. "It just sounds outrageous."

Hussein stiffened. "Are you saying Ivers pounded those cars and that wall on his own and then lied about it?"

"Well, this whole gamma business is unstable," Cantrell replied.

Bryan gritted his teeth to keep silent. They were saying *he* was unstable.

"I saw the blood on him!" Hussein shouted. "A lobby-full of guards and agents saw the blood on him!"

"I'm saying, let's not ignore all possibilities."

The other directors looked at each other uneasily, as if they wanted to tell Cantrell to shut up. Because they knew what was coming next.

Hussein leapt to his feet and slammed his palms on the table. "We're all insane, all of us that saw it? Is that it? Mass psychosis?"

Bey calmly held up a hand as if to call for silence. "Clearly, *something* attacked Ivers and bled all over him. And I think it's in everyone's best interests to accept that along with the information Ivers gathered at the time from the gamma."

"Right, we need to inform the other Possesseds," Utterklo said.

"Of what?" Wallmann spoke up. "That something may attack them and there's nothing they can do about it?"

The room fell silent. One of them had finally spoken the issue they had been dancing around. What they had been avoiding with accusations and insinuations.

Hussein slowly sat back down. "They deserve to know. They know something happened to Ivers and that it could happen again. Let's not create panic with silence."

Oh, you're one to talk, Bryan thought. *Let's talk about all the stuff you've made me keep silent.* But that was unfair. Hussein was just looking out for him.

But what about everyone else?

"Ivers?"

He jerked his head up. They were all looking at him. They had asked him a question, and he hadn't heard it. His face flushed. "What?"

"I said," Bey repeated, "is there any advice you could give the others on how to handle an attack from this Eternal?"

He looked back down at the table, away from their eyes, to think. "She tried to contain me. I think how I got her back was I accepted the containment. I took it into myself... absorbed it into my body and mind. When I did that, I was able to throw her own energy back at her." He looked up. "But it was terrible to do that. It fed the demon possessing me. Helped it overtake me. Swallowed my own mind. I... don't think it's practical."

They stared at him.

"Noted," Cantrell said.

Harper was waiting for him in the hall, half-asleep. She hadn't slept well in that chair – had probably only gathered about three hours of sleep from it. But she hadn't left him.

"Well, that was pointless," he told her as she stood.

She didn't respond as they walked, but she stole glances at him out of the corner of her eye.

"Stop fucking staring at me," he finally said.

"Did you tell them you spoke to it?"

He stopped to face her, huffing. "I shouldn't have even told you."

"Ivers, what were we told when we caught our betas? That they can speak, that they'll say anything, that they'll lie. That they'll try to gain control."

"Right. Don't listen."

"Right. And here you are *chatting* with the thing."

"It's not a beta."

"It's worse than a beta."

"It's the only avenue we have to gain information."

Her eyes actually turned sad, but maybe they were just tired. "Is that really why you talked to it?"

"Yes! Why else would I? You think I *want* to talk to it?"

"I don't know."

"Look, I don't need this psych bullshit." He turned and started walking again. "They know what I found out. That's what matters. This gamma isn't what I'm worried about right now."

They had reached the elevator, where a couple of agents were waiting for a lift. Because of them, Harper changed the topic. "Are we still containing the synagogue tonight?"

"Yeah. Those plans haven't changed. The neighborhood's already evacuated." In fact, he had completely forgotten about that plan until it had cropped up at the end of the meeting – just an *Oh yeah don't forget* type of footnote to everything else. All Possesseds were going to try to contain the demons coming through the gate at point of entry. Same idea as had been mumbled by the crazier Possesseds at the very discovery of the synagogue. If they could pull it off, there wouldn't be any need to chase them through the city. If they couldn't pull it off, they might cancel out the outward force that propelled the demons from the gate, leaving them all swimming around in one building.

Estimates suggested about 130 demons per gate opening. What happened when you let 130 demons loose in a space of 5,000 square feet?

"I think we both need something to eat before then," Harper said.

Bryan was pretty sure he hadn't eaten in twenty-four hours. "Gonna agree with you for once."

The elevator doors dinged and opened, and in the group that came out of it was Cam. He seemed absolutely astonished to see Bryan.

"Jesus," he said. "Am I glad to see you."

"What have you heard?" Bryan grumbled as the elevator left without him and Harper.

"That you turned up in the lobby raving and bleeding a river." He looked Bryan over. "You don't look hurt."

"It wasn't my blood."

"What?"

Bryan sighed. He wanted to give Cam the story, but he was tired of telling it and, if he was being honest with himself, he was having trouble keeping it straight at this point. "They're going to release a statement at the synagogue this evening, before the gate containment."

Cam's face fell, leaving him looking wounded. "I'm going to have to wait for an official statement?"

Bryan chewed his lip, noticing that two agents now waiting at the elevator were listening in. Not even bothering to be discreet. They were looking right at him. What version of the story could he even tell Cam?

Tell him everything, so he can blab to everyone what you did.

"Ivers? You okay?"

"I'm fine!" he snapped. He twisted around, heading for the stairwell, and after glancing at Cam, Harper followed. He didn't feel fine. He was thinking of the way raw muscle ground between his teeth. He felt like vomiting again.

He and Harper got there last, as late as Bryan could make it. He wanted to deal with as little social niceties as he could. Twenty-two Possesseds, including Hussein and Harper, gathered at the front of the synagogue, just waiting in the street. Everything within a mile's radius had been shut down and evaced. The media was having a field day. Bryan had driven through a sea of reporters and cameras that was breaking waves against the police patrol ringing the area. They knew now that there was a "gate" that the demons were coming through, but little more. That didn't stop them from tossing out theories, though. And of course the office was to blame for not finding it sooner, and for putting the people living in the neighborhood in danger.

Joining the group, Bryan saw all eyes turn to him. At least there were no Spotters, save for Harper. Just Possesseds here, in case everything went tits up and the demons ran around trying to feed. Still, Bryan withered under the scrutiny.

"So, what the fuck's going on?" Skinner asked him.

That made him smile.

Gennisson was even there, all wrapped up in bandages, bones still mending but with a smile on his face. He clapped Bryan on the back. "Greene and Kressin got in a fistfight over how many demons you fucked up."

"C'mon, guys," Bryan said weakly.

"Alright, everyone!" Hussein called, clapping his hands for attention. "We're all here. Let's gather around."

Bryan looked to the west. Houses and trees blocked the sunset, but he guessed there were forty-five minutes to go before dark. He realized he was dreading the sunset, as if something was waiting for the sun to vanish. Only the gate, he told himself.

They all circled around Hussein to hear the story, and Hussein laid it out for them. An Eternal had attacked Ivers. He had beaten it back with the help of his own demon – no mention of being overtaken. He had learned from the gamma during the fight that an Eternal cannot be destroyed – no mention of the conversation Bryan had had with it on Hussein's couch, though Hussein didn't know that part.

Connors had already been told most of the tale, being one of the three who had guarded the office lobby all day, and the only one of those three asked to stay awake to join this containment. Still, he looked like he might have a heart attack. Everyone else was silent and wide-eyed when Hussein finished. Word of the eternally Possesseds had gone around in gossip since Bryan's interrogation, but those things had been in some other world beyond the gate. Not this world, not this city.

"We don't know yet if other Eternals are in Chicago. Don't let your guard down at any time and travel with a partner whenever possible. We will find a way to defeat these things, given time, but meanwhile, do not engage this Eternal. Wound it if needed and run. I don't want any dead wannabe heroes."

Hussein stopped, took a breath, and seemed to debate whether or not to keep speaking. He looked around at all of the frightened expressions and continued. "The Eternals on the other side of the gate are strengthening the doorway. Eventually, at some point in the future, the doorway will be strong enough for them to all come through. We have to find a way to stop this or to destroy them."

Chatter broke out. Somebody shouted, "But you said they can't be killed!"

"Shut up!" Hussein ordered. "The last thing that would help right now is for all our Possesseds to panic. Yes, there are some mysteries, but we will find the answers to them. I'm telling you the situation because I know you wouldn't be here if you weren't strong and capable. I fear, in fact, that you are *too* strong and *too* capable, and will run at these mysteries and get yourselves killed. So, I repeat, do *not* engage this Eternal. Wound and run."

He looked around again as if asking for questions, but no one said anything. Bryan caught Cam's eye on the other side of the crowd, and they looked at each other with mutual determination and a little fear.

"Now, about tonight," Hussein continued.

It would run about the same as when they'd mass-contained the college building the night Bryan had caught the gamma. There would just be a hell of a lot more demons, and the Possesseds would be pushing against whatever force propelled them out over the city when the gate closed.

"What if a beta comes through the gate?" someone shouted.

"Or a gamma," someone else muttered. The chattering started up again.

"Then we're screwed," Hussein yelled. The chatter stopped. "You want to sit it out, then? On the slight chance something other than alphas show up?"

He looked around at them, locking eyes with a few – deliberately, Bryan knew. Hussein knew who would need that last stare-down.

No one objected any further.

"Okay, let's go in," Hussein said, waving them on. Then he motioned to Bryan and Harper as they started walking.

"I know," Bryan said to him. "I'm just here to watch." Honestly, after his most recent experience, he was relieved at the thought that he wouldn't be possessing.

"Right, no possessing. You neither, Kiyoko."

Harper's mouth dropped open. "But, sir—"

"Don't *'but sir'* me. You two are the eyes here. Be aware of how things are going and watch our surroundings."

"That's more of a job for Connors," Bryan said doubtfully.

"It's a job for a Spotter and that talkative gamma. Tell it to pull its weight."

Bryan's breath caught, but Hussein was already walking away towards the synagogue and didn't notice.

Harper let her own breath out in a huff. "Great, now I've been pulled down to your level. Sitting out work."

"Fuck off, Harper," Bryan growled. "I don't want this, either." The words weren't entirely truthful.

"No fighting," Connors ordered as he passed them, rounding up the tail end of the group.

Bryan and Harper grumbled insults under their breath, but set off up the stairs to the doors.

It was the same as the night they had all gathered to watch the gate open: three groups taking turns possessing, observing. Only, this time they were here to act. Once the gate opened, the group possessed at the time had maybe five seconds to begin containment and alert the others that it was time. The other two teams had only a couple of seconds to possess, get through the pain, and help with containment. It wasn't actually enough time, but it was the best plan they had. Everyone was on edge whether they were possessed or not. Only ten minutes in, someone panicked, thinking the gate had opened, and everyone possessed... only to discover that the glow of a mouse in a corner had set the agent off.

"Christ, people!" Connors exclaimed as they regathered themselves. "We're not looking for something so tiny as a mouse! You'll know the gate damned well when you see it! Stop getting worked up!"

This is where we are, Bryan thought. *Connors is telling people to not get worked up.* Indeed, Connors was wringing his hands so hard that he might work them off his wrists.

Hussein interrupted the ribbing of the faulted agent and got the room quieted down again. The only sound came to be paper rustling, mostly from Connors's book.

Again, Bryan got that feeling that something was waiting. Not for sunset – that had already happened – but for something else. For the gate? They were all waiting for the gate. He was just paranoid from the beta and gamma watching him.

But they weren't watching him. Their focus was elsewhere. The gate?

Voices snapped him out of his thoughts. The third team taking over. They possessed and cried out, and the second team put their demons away and gave sighs of relief. Slowly, silence settled in again.

Bryan was off to the side and behind the teams, closest to the entrance. Harper was positioned in the same way, but opposite him. He looked at her and, for some reason, practically willed her to look at him. But she didn't notice; her vision was firmly fixed on where the gate would appear.

Which is where you should be looking, he told himself. He looked forward and reached out to the beta and gamma again. They were watching the entrance.

He spun around, and Harper did look at him then, but he didn't notice. He was looking at the doors, propped open in case a rapid exit was required of anyone. He fully expected to see something or someone there, though he couldn't place why.

Nothing was there.

He gritted his teeth and thought fiercely at the two demons: *What are you looking for?*

They didn't answer right away, and he had the impression they were uncertain themselves.

Someone is out there, one of them said. Bryan was annoyed to find that he couldn't tell which one had spoken up.

Who? Bryan demanded. His thoughts were on the woman – the thing – in the rain.

Not her, the two demons said together.

That should have relaxed him, but it didn't. *Who, then?*

They're waiting.

"For fuck's sake," he snarled aloud. "Just tell me–"

"It's here!"

"Now!"

"Possess!"

Twenty people shouted twenty different things, and everyone – Bryan included – turned their attention to the gate, or in Bryan's case, where he assumed the gate was. He felt the wind blow out from it and smelled its emptiness, and saw everyone wave their arms around as if this were a concert, but he knew the demons were there in front of them, spilling out of the gate. Then the silent, invisible explosion of the gate's closing rocked them all.

As he was thrown off-balance by the blast – not by any force, but by an idea of the blast – he knew with absolute certainty that the thing that had been waiting was here, was behind him, and was leaping.

He spun and shielded himself with his arm. It bit down to the bone and tore the muscle away and

Bryan fell to the floor, a mess of pain and confusion. It went for his throat.

But then it stopped and reared up instead.

"Ivers! Get away!" Harper shouted.

Bryan looked her way and understood. She had possessed and was containing it – him. It was a man, its face smeared with Bryan's blood.

Bryan crawled out from under the thing, but already, it was looking to Harper. It would contain her, too. And Bryan knew she couldn't win that battle.

But then Skinner and Coates – *a rookie*, Bryan thought, *what is he doing?* – were there, having turned away from the synagogue demons to help Harper.

They'll die.

The others were still struggling with the demons, trying to capture them one by one. A few people were getting double- or triple-possessed and working through it. They couldn't help.

They'll all die.

No, Bryan thought. *They have it.*

The thing was indeed frozen in place, hunched over, trying to rise.

Wasn't it?

He couldn't tell anything about it. He couldn't see its power. Without a demon in him, thing and people together all just looked like normal people, no aeons and no containing fire.

You need me.

A memory of blood filling his mouth darted through his mind.

I can't possess. Not again.

They'll die.

Skinner and Coates vanished in a spray of blood as Bryan watched. They didn't even have time

Black Heart

to cry out. Harper did cry out, and was slashed in ten places, but she was further away and missed the brunt of whatever the thing had sent out. As it was, she was blown back against the far wall.

I can get rid of him.

It was winded, but gathering itself, rising from the floor.

I can't possess.
I can't possess.
I can't—
Everyone will die.

His arm didn't work. He pawed at his bag until it opened and the decks spilled out. He fell to his knees on the ground, and the thing was straightening in slow motion, but he was slower.

Here.

His hand fell on the deck and tossed the two cards from it and, for a split second, he didn't know which card it was.

He didn't want to know.

I can't...

HERE.

He snatched it up with his one good hand and put it between his teeth.

Oh god...

He ripped it open.

Steppen Sawicki

Chapter Six

The pain was incredible, but he didn't cry out. It fit him; it was supposed to be there in his heart and veins and every nerve. The thing in front of him leapt for him – he felt that more than saw it. He threw up a barrier and, though the thing broke through, it was bounced back. By then, Bryan had snapped the arm off of a pew. He swung it with all the force he could pull from himself and struck the thing in the head with a satisfying *crunk*.

It went down, skull cracked, skin torn from the scalp, but didn't stay down. It was only slightly fazed. Bryan tried to hit the thing again, but it both blasted him backwards and ran for him. The only thing that saved him was another barrier he put up to save his bones as he struck the wall, along with a temporary loss of coordination in his enemy due to the injury Bryan had inflicted on it. As it was, the windows above Bryan shook and shattered as the blast hit them, showering him with shards of glass that ground into his palm as he pushed himself back up.

He lamented giving up his knife after the first Eternal fight. If he had it now, he wouldn't be wasting all this time. As he rose to his feet, the thing closed the distance between them. The blood running from the wound on its head was rippling as it drained out.

Bryan knew it was because some of the blood was rushing back into the scalp, two currents running against each other.

He still held the chunk of wood. He swung it and only grazed the thing as it stepped back. Then it threw up containment around Bryan, and Bryan did the same back. Barely two feet from each other, they wrestled each other with their powers, leaning forward and projecting everything they had.

He didn't have time for this. If the Possesseds captured all of the demons, he wouldn't have anything to work with. And then this would all have been for nothing.

The crack of a gunshot filled the room and the thing fell, its containment dropping from Bryan so quickly that Bryan nearly fell on top of it. Harper ran over to stand over it and fired four more rounds point-blank into its skull.

Had she had that gun from the beginning, or had the office issued it to her after he had gone nuts? Why hadn't she told him?

There was no time to dwell on it. The marks from the chunk of wood were already stitched back together, and the bullet holes wouldn't be there for longer than a few seconds. Bryan grabbed the thing's foot and pulled it towards where the gate had opened, dragging it through the blood and gore that had once been Skinner and Coates, leaving a trail of red down the aisle. He noted the aeon glowing in that trail, and nearly stopped to marvel at it and at the aeon in Harper. Bryan had seen lifeforce before, but not like this, with such a hunger and need for it stirred in him.

"What are you doing?" Harper asked, following him.

"Getting rid of it." His voice was deep, rich, as if it were two voices speaking at once.

He shouted to the Possessed to get out of his way, and shoved them aside if they didn't listen. He saw their eyes dart to him and back to their task, and he saw wild fear and determination in them all. They were leaving this to him. Skinner and Coates had tried to help – *had* helped – but now they were dead. The rest couldn't do anything; they could only do what was in their job description. They were counting on him to figure out something for this other problem.

He couldn't fuck up this time.

The thing kicked, and Harper fired more rounds into it.

"That's all I have!" she shouted.

"That's good enough," Bryan said. "Barrier yourself and get to the platform."

Instead, she grabbed the thing's other foot and helped him drag it along. But she did think to barrier herself. By the time they got it onto the platform, it was twitching again.

Bryan looked around for something to strike it with, but Harper snatched up the podium with demonic and likely adrenaline-fueled strength and brought it down on the thing's skull, smashing it completely.

"Jesus," Cam said. He had jumped up there with them. So had Hussein. They both looked like hell. There were two demons currently housed in Hussein, but he was taking it. He had to – he couldn't put either of them away while keeping up such a strong barrier around himself.

Bryan didn't have a barrier. The demons didn't seem interested in him. He had known they wouldn't be.

But why?

He didn't have time to think about it.

"You'll have to throw him in," he shouted at the three around him. He didn't *have* to shout. Sure, there was chaos going on, but besides cries of pain, there was little to be said when capturing demons. But the energy in the room seemed to command shouting.

"Throw him where?" Hussein shouted back.

Bryan didn't answer. He knew now, the words the hooded figures in the dead place chanted. It was like he could finally think clearly – like he had never thought clearly in his life prior to this moment. Even as acid coursed through his veins and his muscles sang, his thoughts were clear.

Soft clicks came from the thing. Its skull was knitting back together, the brain seeping back in through the cracks.

"Jesus," Cam said again.

Bryan spoke. It wasn't English. It wasn't any language of this world. It was a language from worlds upon worlds away, not even of this universe. He stumbled the first couple of times, his mouth and throat unused to the sounds and getting the feel of them. Then he had it.

Every demon not yet captured flew to where the gate had opened, called there by his words. A new gate opened, formed of the demons. Because that's what the gates were – a funnel made of demons, linking one Earth to the next. How had he not known that?

Harper and Cam and Hussein lifted the body as Bryan went on repeating the words, willing the gate to stay open and the demons to swirl into nothingness. Because this gate didn't link to another Earth. One Possessed didn't have that kind of power. This gate went nowhere; it went only to the space between Earths, and that was good enough for this.

The thing was together now, its eyes focusing and its mind realizing what was happening.

As it was tossed through the gate, it grabbed Harper's wrist, and she went with it. Cam caught her, but fell in halfway himself before Hussein caught him by his other arm.

Bryan halted his speech for the briefest of moments, wanting to stop. Wanting the gate to close them off. Harper would be gone, and Cam might be pulled in as it collapsed. He would be rid of them.

Why would he want to be rid of them?

He had to fight against himself to keep speaking until Harper was pulled back out, blood flying from her arm where the thing had clawed at her. Finally, Bryan stopped and fell to his knees. Opening a gate wasn't meant to be a one-man job. He was spent from directing the demons.

The demons rushed out from the synagogue, the force of the gate closure blasting them out over the city. They hadn't gone through the gate – there had been nothing for them on the other side. The other Possesseds hadn't expected it and couldn't contain it. A few of them were knocked to the floor – not from a physical cause, but a mental one; it *felt* like a weight had been thrust against them.

Then it was silent in the synagogue. That horrid dead dust spun in the air, kicked up by all of the commotion. Agents put their demons away in their totems, taking breaths of relief at being alone in their own bodies again. Everyone stared at Bryan. He felt guilty of something he couldn't put a name to.

Hussein stood up from Harper's side, putting both of his possessing demons away. He spoke too loudly for the space, as if he had forgotten the madness was over. "Connors, get everyone outside and assess. Whoever can hunt tonight, give an assignment." His meaning was clear: anyone who was able to emotionally process what had just happened to Skinner and Coates needed to save whatever civilian lives they could tonight.

Connors had been staring not at Bryan, but at the trail of gore that spread down one aisle. He squeaked out an affirmative at Hussein's order, then came to himself and barked everyone out. And everyone stole last looks at Bryan as they filed down the aisle that didn't have human remains in it and out the doors. To avoid their gawking, Bryan looked to the three who had tossed the thing through the gate. Cam had a wide-eyed look of near panic, as if the crisis was still ongoing. Harper was a mess. Hussein was wrapping her tattered arm. She was covered in splashes of blood from head to toe – her own blood. One slash had struck her across the left cheek, leaving blood to drip from her chin.

The blood was alive. It pointed out that the woman was alive. That all three of them were rich with life. And he was still hungry. He was lightheaded and hungry from his own blood loss.

He stood and took a step towards them before realizing his intentions. He moaned and turned away, stepping down into the aisle.

Cam followed and gripped Bryan's arm as he tumbled against a pew. His touch was so warm, so close. It would be so easy.

"Don't touch me!" Bryan's voice was guttural. It rebounded off the walls and shook the place. He thrust Cam away so hard that the man flew back and struck the edge of the platform. He fell to the ground and coughed in the dust. Bryan looked back at him and saw that he shone with green light – enticing green light that meant life and sustenance – and he took a step back towards him.

"Put it away, Bryan."

Hussein was standing now, watching him. But keeping some distance between them. It wasn't the distance of a few feet anymore; it was the distance between worlds.

"Why?" Bryan asked. He felt a grin pull at his lips, baring teeth. Teeth that could rend meat.

Horror crossed Hussein's face, there and gone. Then he stood straight and stared him down. "Because you work under me and you'll follow my orders."

Bryan lost his grin. He tottered on his feet. That was true. But it also wasn't true. He didn't have to listen to Hussein. He suddenly hated Hussein for telling him what to do when it wasn't his place, not any longer. But the hate was love, and he loved Hussein already.

He turned away to look down the aisle to the entrance doors. He heard the faint barks of orders from Connors, far away, far away from him – the threat.

Could he put it away? What part of him was it housing in? What parts? Every part?

"Put it away," came Hussein's voice from behind him.

He didn't have to listen. Not anymore. Perhaps in another life, but not now.

He could devour them now.

He shook his head to clear the thought, but it didn't leave. He began taking steps down the aisle. His cards were ahead, to the left of the entrance. But he didn't know yet if he would go to them. He just walked to give himself time to decide. His thoughts were no longer clear. This wasn't a path to opening a gate, to getting rid of a threat. What he might do was a threat to himself, to his very identity, which he could no longer separate from the demon. The pain in his body seemed to respond to the turmoil in his head, and it tore at his inner flesh until he was struggling to take steps. But the pain was also pleasure, separate and the same. And he was angry at the demon for forcing him into this, but the anger was also peace, separate and the same. And he hated and loved what he had become. He understood all this and didn't want to leave it.

He knelt beside his cards, picking up the blank deck. Hussein and Harper had followed him, and Cam came following further behind. They watched and waited to see what he would do.

But when he pulled a card from the deck and willed the demon in, nothing happened. He paused and tried again.

He gasped for breath, and looked up at Hussein.

"It won't go," he said, both terrified and delighted.

Hussein glowed so brightly. He opened his mouth, closed it, opened it again. "It's just like first possession. You have to figure out how to thrust it out."

But what am I thrusting out? He looked down at the card again, and he wanted to know now. He wanted it out. This wasn't him.

But it is.

He gripped the card in both hands and willed it out. Even without knowing where it was in him, even as it ripped at his insides... even as it stripped him raw and tore so much of him as he crushed the card in his fist and wept and screamed.

As he fell, Harper ran to him, screaming herself. She caught him and shook him, but he was awake. He looked up at her and she gasped, her eyes filling with tears. He saw now that her glasses were gone, lost in the void with the Eternal.

"Ivers," she choked, "you..."

His own tears were already drying, his eyes blank. Everything was blank.

"It took me with it," he said, and there was nothing in his voice.

Hussein insisted he be given local anesthetic only, which probably seemed like a good idea, but Bryan was certain it wouldn't make a difference whether he was knocked out or not. And either way, he didn't care, even if the surgery on his arm did take several hours. He stared at the ceiling as the doctors worked at trying to save the severed nerves and torn muscle. Not bored. Not anything.

And then he was put back in a hospital room. Full circle. But the morning sunlight through the window was too bright, the walls shining. He screwed his eyes shut against it all until he heard the door open. It was Hussein.

"Close the blinds," Bryan said. They were his first words since he'd spoken to Harper in the synagogue, and Hussein was visibly relieved to hear them. The tension in his shoulders relaxed as he went to the window and drew the blinds closed. Even so, the room was still too bright.

"The doctor says it's looking great," Hussein said, pulling a chair alongside the bed.

"I already know you have a nasty habit of lying," Bryan said.

Hussein looked at the bandaged arm as if avoiding Bryan's eyes. "Well, of course, there's damage, but you should retain some mobility."

Bryan looked at the arm, too. It was still numb, as if not really there. But then, all of him felt that way. "How is Harper?"

"Some deep wounds, but nothing vital hit. Stitched up much quicker than you were. I set Connors over her to keep her down and resting, but she'll probably be storming in here any moment." He looked at Bryan's face, but Bryan's gaze was still fixed on his arm. "She says... that your aura is vastly diminished."

"Well, at least it's not gone entirely." Bryan said the words as if commenting on the weather.

"But it... took you."

"It overtook me, and then left with a portion of me, yes."

Black Heart

"But you're still here." Hussein's voice was desperate. He was probably in denial.

Bryan wasn't in denial. This was just how things were now.

"I'm not like, say, Gennick." Bryan looked back at Hussein. He was still radiant with life – dimmer than when Bryan had been possessed, but glowing. That hadn't left with the demon; rather, it was a part of the demon that had been left in Bryan. It hurt to look at that life. He was a starving man with a meal before him. "I can speak and I know what's going on around me. But I was overtaken just as Gennick was."

Hussein averted his eyes, and leaned back and covered his mouth with a hand. "I shouldn't have agreed to the containment."

"Don't blame yourself. None of us could have expected an ambush."

"We knew the Eternals were out there and that they're after the gamma. I should have anticipated this."

"Hussein."

He waited until Hussein looked back at him.

"I *chose* to do what I did. Everyone was busy capturing. Their backs were open, and that thing could have killed everyone there." He remembered the splotches of blood and guts that had been Skinner and Coates. "I only regret that I didn't possess sooner."

Hussein swallowed hard. "That gate we threw it into, that you opened. Was it to that other Earth?"

Bryan shook his head. "One Possessed can't open a gate between Earths. It takes many Possesseds to do that, and hundreds of free demons. That gate didn't go anywhere."

"How could it not go anywhere? It must have gone somewhere."

"Well then, it went to the space between Earths. Which is nowhere."

"But it's gone? It couldn't find its way back?"

"That would be impossible on its own. No, it's gone for good."

"So, we have a way to get rid of them." Hussein looked to the blinded windows. "If we had enough Possesseds and enough free demons, *could* we open a gate to the other Earth?"

"Yes... all that's needed is large enough numbers and the words I spoke. But what would be the point?"

Hussein's face fell. "There would be too many Eternals waiting on the other side."

"If we even made it through. As I said before, it's risky before the gate is stable. Few make it through. And what would we even do there?"

"I don't know. Drop a nuke or something."

Bryan tried a weak smile. At least he could still do that. "Now you're sounding like me."

"Just wishful thinking."

Hussein's phone rang and he jumped as if it had stung him. He answered it as he went out into the hall.

Bryan wondered if maybe Hussein had wanted a reason to leave the room. It had to be pretty disconcerting to be speaking to him right now. It felt disconcerting enough to *be* him.

There was a commotion outside the door, with Hussein shouting. Bryan thought he must be shouting at his phone until someone shouted back. Then the door opened and Harper was entering the room.

"I'm already in!" she yelled at Hussein. "You want to stop me?" She slammed the door and spun around. And then she saw Bryan, and stopped.

"You don't have to fight over me," he said.

Her cheeks flushed. Without her glasses, it was more obvious. "Sorry. I shouldn't have slammed the door."

"Already forgotten."

She stepped towards him slowly, as if approaching a spider or snake and unsure of whether it was venomous or not.

And she did radiate life at him.

He looked down at his arm again. "I would ask what I look like, but I think I already know."

She stopped a few feet from his bed. "There's still a portion of the demon in you, isn't there?"

"Yes, part of it stayed with me. Part of me went with it. Maybe that's why I'm not comatose." He looked up at her. Someone had clearly gone to her apartment and brought her a change of clothes – her clothes from the synagogue had been ripped to shreds and drenched in her blood – so it was hard to tell, but Bryan knew she was covered in bandages underneath. There was one on her left cheek, as well, over a gash so deep that it was sure to leave a scar. "Are you okay?" he asked her.

"Oh, who the fuck cares about me?" She came the rest of the way to the bed, rounding it to sit in the chair and grasp his good hand. "I thought you were gone back there. I was *positive*. Your aura was so weak. And then you looked at me and spoke. How are you here?"

"I'm not. Not really."

"I know. You are and you're not."

He smiled. That was it exactly.

Hussein burst back into the room, looking oddly triumphant. "Finally, some good goddamned news!" he announced. "D.C. and Vancouver have found their gates."

"What?" Harper gasped. "How?"

"We've been sending out samples of the dust from the synagogue. Our colleagues have been using it as a compass of sorts. Seems that alphas store memories, too – you just have to give them a strong enough stimulus to pull them up. Anyway, D.C. and Vancouver found their gates last night, and L.A. thinks they came close before the sun came up. They're going to try again tonight. The samples to Mexico City and Cordoba are still hustling through customs, but they should be receiving them tomorrow. The found gates have the same dust, which can be sent elsewhere. Exponentially, we should reach all cities within five days."

"That's great," Bryan said, "but how will they do anything about Somalia and Syria, or North Korea? You can't even enter those areas, let alone find a gate."

"We're already brainstorming that. If we get stable enough capturing directly at gates, we might can free up enough agents in the world to tackle the overrun places. This is just a first step."

"That's incredible," Harper said. "This could completely halt demon-caused deaths."

Hussein clapped Bryan on the shoulder – his bad shoulder, but it was still numbed up enough not to bother him. "It's all you, Bryan. You found the place."

Bryan was still wondering if all Hussein said was possible. He said nothing.

"Now," Hussein continued, "to break you two out of here. Since here Kiyoko is, walking around and arguing with me."

Harper went to her apartment upon release. Before leaving Bryan, she squeezed his good hand and gave him a smile that was probably meant to be reassuring, but instead was filled with sadness. Bryan barely noticed – he was staring at the life coursing through her hand grasping his. He turned quickly away from her, sick at the thoughts in his head. Only afterward did he realize that he had effectively brushed her off.

He didn't go to his apartment. There were still Eternals out there, after him. He was escorted to the office instead, where he fell asleep on Hussein's couch. He didn't dream, and woke even more tired than he had been when he'd laid down. The room was empty. The clock on the wall read 6:30, but he got up anyway to check through the blinds. The sun was setting, dusk heavy over the city. Most of them would be at the synagogue, except for whoever was guarding him downstairs. He wasn't sure where Hussein might be. But, clearly, Bryan himself wasn't invited to the containment. Good call.

Bryan looked over the room. His bag was resting against the couch, but his cards weren't in it. Hussein had taken them to quarantine. Bryan might have argued, had he not been so out of it. He was still out of it — 'out of it' might be his default mode now — but he wanted his cards back. He needed them. Or needed one of them.

He stood there at the window, staring at his bag for seventy minutes until Hussein walked in. He jumped when he saw Bryan, despite having left him in the room earlier.

"Did you sleep?" he asked.

"Yes," Bryan answered.

"Oh." He studied Bryan, the desk between them. "You don't look it."

"You're one to talk. You didn't sleep at all, did you?"

Hussein groaned and relaxed. The same as he had done earlier, the same as Harper had done earlier. Everyone was testing the waters any time they walked into a room containing Bryan. "When would I have done that? We're tracking packages of dust, coordinating new ways of containment, and then there's Lori and Tom," he said, referring to Skinner and Coates. He hung his head and walked the rest of the way to the desk, where he flung the folders in his arms down. "And all of this needs to be communicated to the public in the most positive light."

"You were double- if not triple-possessed last night," Bryan said. "I don't know how you're still standing."

"No rest for the wicked."

"Get some sleep right now."

Hussein sighed and rubbed at his eyes. "I'm waiting for word on the synagogue."

"I'm here. I'll get the word and wake you up." He thought about that, averting his eyes. "Unless you don't want to sleep with me around."

"Why would you say that?"

"I know what I look like. I know what Harper told you."

"And what do you say about it?"

Bryan looked at him again. Hussein shined green. "I look at people and I think how wonderful it would be to devour their life."

Hussein's eyes widened almost imperceptibly, but he kept his posture. "But that's not you. I know I can trust you."

Bryan rounded the desk, keeping his eyes on Hussein. "That's a lie. You don't trust me. I've been overtaken twice and I'm still standing. I make no sense. And it *is* me. It's part of me now."

Hussein didn't budge, but there was a flash of fear in his eyes. But, he was Possessed. And no Possessed trafficked much in fear of demons. At least not up to this point.

Bryan passed him by. "Lock the door," he said, "and get some sleep."

Outside Hussein's door, he didn't know what to do. If he didn't figure it out, though, he knew he would stand there all night staring at the wall, like he had stood at the window and stared at his bag for over an hour. He called Connors and told him to forward word on the synagogue containment to Bryan's phone. Connors's voice was tinny and strained at the concept of speaking with him, but Bryan hoped he had listened.

He went to quarantine, or at least to the floor where it was located. He stood in the hallway and tried to catch some glimpse of the gamma or – if he wasn't able to see the gamma – even the beta through the doors and walls. Tried to imagine a card lying on a table, to figure out if he was in there with it... the part of him that was missing and maybe now a part of the gamma, just as part of the gamma was now a part of him.

Then two agents exited the elevator, glowing beautifully, and he moved on in order to stay inconspicuous. He may have felt something as he'd reached out to where his cards might be, but it may also have just been him wanting so badly to feel something.

He wanted to go sit in on the classes, for the quiet droning that would provide, but he didn't want to run into Sonia. He also wanted to go to the lobby and find out who was on watch, who wasn't at the synagogue and was guarding him. But if the Eternal was scoping out the building, it was best to stay away from entrances and windows.

He wanted to go back to Hussein's office and curl back up on the couch.

He stopped in the hall, nowhere in particular. There was nowhere for him to go.

He didn't belong here anymore.

At 12:40, he got word that the synagogue had been contained. Hussein was rubbing sleep from his eyes when he answered Bryan's knocks. The emails waiting for him told them that D.C. had perfectly contained their own building – an empty church – at 10:30. L.A. was certain they had found their own gate

Black Heart

in a ruined Sikh temple and had Possesseds gathered and waiting for it to open.

"I'm not used to all this good news," Hussein said, shuffling the papers on his desk. "I'm waiting for notification of a meeting on how to manage all this good news."

"Can I have my demons back?" Bryan asked. He wasn't aware that the question seemed to come out of nowhere. It had been on his mind all night, and now was a strategically good time to ask — while Hussein was in a good mood.

"No," was all Hussein said, his demeanor changing entirely.

"Why? You're taking risks keeping them separate from me. They could escape the totems without—"

Hussein pointed to the door, not looking at him. "Not arguing this. Get out."

The old Bryan would have argued. This new Bryan got out, went to quarantine, and told the woman at the desk to release his demons. But what he had suspected was true: Hussein wasn't allowing them out or Bryan in. He felt stupid for even trying. But he'd had to try. He felt like he had to break in and forcibly take them, but he made himself turn around and walk away. He passed the elevator and went to the stairs. Inside the stairwell, he stopped and leaned back against the door, and he had another moment where he knew he should be doing something the normal Bryan would do... but he didn't.

He should have been crying.

He should have been angry that he wasn't crying.

He should have been punching the wall.

Instead, he stood in the stairwell, feeling only a vast loneliness with his missing half worlds away or maybe gone forever – and maybe holding that card wouldn't do a thing to help him.

And what if he went further, and tore the card?

He felt dizzy and sat on the floor. He realized he hadn't eaten in over twenty-four hours, not since he and Harper had grabbed some quick Chinese noodles, and he was hungry. But it wasn't that desire for life; it was just a pain in his stomach, and it felt good to feel anything at all that wasn't either a need to kill or that loneliness. So, he sat on the concrete and relished the hunger like it was the best feeling in the world, until three hours had passed and he knew he would finally have to eat something.

He went to the cafeteria and, although there were few people in there at 4 AM, they all turned to look at him and then turned back around to whisper. He went to the sandwiches and stared at them. They all looked unappetizing to him because they weren't what he really wanted. But if he stood there staring for too long, everyone would have more to whisper about. He grabbed a sandwich at random and turned.

Andrade was there, and she yelped and stepped back when he spun around even though she was already several feet away from him.

"Ivers," she rasped, her eyes like dinner plates. "I wasn't sure it was you."

"It is," he said, stepping towards her and meaning to pass by her. "What do you want?"

"I... nothing." She backed away again.

He stopped.

They watched each other.

"I'm sorry," she finally said. "I have to go." She spun around before he could respond and nearly ran from the room.

She had looked like she was about to cry.

Bryan paid for his sandwich, which he wanted even less now, and was heading for the door when Cam and two other Possesseds walked in laughing. Cam saw him right away and shouted his name, still half-laughing, and everyone in the room looked again.

Cam hugged Bryan, and though Bryan could barely stand the touch of another living being, he was able to tolerate it with minimal cringing. Maybe he would learn to deal with it.

"Nobody knew if you were okay," Cam said. "Where have you been?"

"Around the office," Bryan said, backing away to put some distance between them. "What are you doing here? Shouldn't you be out hunting?"

"Nothing to hunt! We closed out everything at the gate. Rest of the night has been clean-up of whatever was already out there. Calls have been few and far between. Half of us got sent home. But I wanted to see how you were, so I came back here."

"I'm fine." Bryan walked around him, heading for the door. "You should go home."

"Wait, Ivers." Cam grabbed his arm and he jerked away, not expecting the contact this time. "Hey," Cam said. "Sorry. Are you okay?"

"What do you want, Cam?" Bryan asked sharply.

"I just... wanted to talk to you." He looked wounded. "I know you know what's going on. I needed to talk about it."

"I can't do that right now." He turned to the door again.

"Please, Ivers."

Bryan stopped and looked back at him, seeing him as an aeon, but also as Cam. There was anxiety etched in his face. Bryan sighed. "I owe you, don't I?"

Cam smiled through the worry. "Yeah, you do."

They sat in the courtyard, though the wind was nigh freezing. Bryan sat with his back to Cam so he wouldn't have to look at him while he ate.

"Damn," Cam said. "It's getting cold."

"You brought me out here to talk about the weather?" Bryan took a bite of the sandwich. It tasted like nothing. He couldn't even tell what was in it.

"Sorry." But then Cam said nothing more for a full minute.

Bryan chewed and swallowed. "Christ, Cam. What is it?"

Again, he didn't speak right away. Then, finally: "Remember when you recruited me three years ago?"

"I didn't recruit you. I found you. You recruited yourself."

"Whichever. I joined, and then once I started capturing, I finally saw you again. And I told you I was scared. You thought I meant I was scared to be doing the job and you were really pissed off. And I had to convince you it wasn't that that I was afraid of."

"You were afraid of us never being able to capture all of the demons," Bryan interrupted him.

"And you told me that was impossible. That we were recruiting more Possesseds all the time. That we were capturing at a good clip. That the demons wouldn't overrun us."

"Well, we found the gates. Hell, you guys got off early tonight." But Bryan knew where the conversation was heading.

"Yeah, and D.C. and L.A. and Vancouver found their gates, and we're heading the demons off at the pass." He paused. "But I was there when you and the gamma were interrogated. And I was there when that Eternal attacked you. I know that both more demons and more Eternals are on their way."

"We still have time."

"We don't know that." Cam's voice was a thin veneer over panic. "We don't know when the gates will open for them all to come through."

"We're working on it."

"Are we?"

Bryan had quit bothering with his sandwich. It sat cold in his hands. He needed to reassure Cam somehow, but how? What *were* they doing? More of the same. Capturing. Just capturing and capturing and capturing. That wasn't going to stop the gates from opening.

"I'm scared again," Cam said. "I haven't been lately, but I am now."

Bryan turned to face him, and he made himself look past the glowing aeon again. Cam's eyes were wide, like he was fresh out of training again. "It's a process," Bryan told him. "We just found the gates. We're studying them. You've seen the tech guys with their set-up. We have to figure out what makes the gates tick and find a way to use that against them. To close them for good."

"You really think we'll do that? Figure that out?"

"We already know the gates themselves are made of demons. We work with the damned things every day. It's just a question of manipulation." The answer sounded good. He was practically convincing himself.

Cam smiled and looked at the ground. "Yeah. You're right. Just demons."

"Right."

Cam watched the ground for a minute as Bryan chewed on his sandwich some more.

"That was nuts," Cam said. "What you did. Maybe if you can make a gate, we can close them."

"Maybe. It's a start." Bryan didn't explain further — that it had been a gate of little use, to nowhere. He was there to keep Cam in the positive. But with the mention of that gate, he knew what was coming next.

"Are you okay?" Cam asked. "That was your third time with it. It didn't go easy, judging from what we saw."

Had Cam heard his words to Harper? Had anyone? Or had he spoken them quietly enough?

He pasted a smile on his face and lied. "I'm fine. Tell me about the containment tonight. I need some good news to tide me over today."

Cam told him while he finished his sandwich.

◆

At 5:30, he went back to Hussein's office. Harper was sitting outside, and she leapt up as Bryan approached.

"Don't tell me you were waiting for me," he said.

"I was," she admitted.

"For how long?"

"An hour. Maybe two."

"Just sitting here?"

"I assumed you wouldn't want to be searched out."

Well, she was right about that. "Are you checking on me under orders or for yourself?"

"Can it be both?"

He sighed. "I guess so. I hear containment went well without me around to attract any undesirables."

"It did. They were talking about having the students join us tomorrow."

He suddenly wanted to be there for that, but he wasn't sure why. He normally didn't bother with the students. Was it because of Sonia? Or just because he couldn't go? "Why did they send you out there tonight?" he asked. "You're injured, and shouldn't you be glued to me now?"

"They wanted someone familiar with what happened last night, in case another Eternal arrived. I think they thought I would know what to do."

Bryan thought of Skinner and Coates vanishing in a spray of blood. "Would you have?"

"We all know the words you spoke to open that gate." She averted her eyes and actually shivered, but kept talking to play it off. "So, anyone would do as well as me."

He studied her, but she didn't look back at him. "What did you see beyond the gate?"

He thought she might not answer, but she said, "Nothing. Absolutely nothing, stretching on for forever. A vast expanse of nothing. And that thing's trapped there for eternity."

"Do you feel sorry for him?"

"I don't know," she said quietly. "How could I not? You didn't see that place."

"He killed Skinner and Coates." He spoke with anger, as if Harper had taken a side against them.

"I know." She was looking down at the floor. "Forget it. It's Spotter stuff."

"Right, I know how Spotters are." He was thinking of Andrade running away from him in the cafeteria. Spotters, weak and malleable.

She finally looked at him. "Christ, Ivers. I didn't come here to fight with you."

"Then why did you come here?" Bryan snarled. "Come to stare at me? At the freak? See how he's doing today?"

He stepped towards her, wanting to snap her neck.

She could see it in him. She backed up, her eyes wide.

He stopped and hung his head, closing his eyes to avoid looking at her... both at her life and at the expression of fear and hurt on her face.

"I'm sorry," he said. "I... you should go home." He turned and opened Hussein's door before she could respond, and nearly ran into Hussein.

"Whoa!" Hussein exclaimed. "I thought I heard shouting."

"Sorry." Bryan noticed Hussein had his coat and briefcase in hand. "Where are you going?"

"Home," Hussein said. "Ruggeri tattled on me. Told everyone I look like hell." He turned to Harper. "Do I look like hell?"

"You do, sir," she said.

"You could fudge the truth a little bit, you know? Anyway, the demons in the city are actually in check. No emergencies. They're throwing me out for the day. Assignment: sleep." He clapped Bryan on the shoulder, haltingly. "I'm afraid you're still trapped in here, Bryan."

"It's fine." It wasn't really fine. Bryan wanted to go home, too. But he wasn't going to bother Hussein with that. "You're going to actually go to bed when you get home, right?"

"Yes, yes. Don't hound me. I'll see you two in the evening."

He left. Bryan tried to duck through the door after he did, but Harper stopped him from closing it.

"I'm sorry, Ivers," she said, "but I have to ask. Are you okay?"

He put on that weak, fake smile. "Yeah, I'm fine. Just tired."

She nodded. "Okay. Get some sleep."

"You too."

He closed the door. Had that been a lie? Hadn't he wanted to rip Hussein's arm off when he'd touched his shoulder? He had just hid it better than earlier.

He went to the couch and fell asleep with a blank mind, numb and raw.

He didn't dream.

He woke at two – still numb, but cold and deathly tired. But he couldn't fall back asleep. He lay there until he couldn't bear his blank mind anymore. It was like he was meditating, but without a sense of wholeness. Instead, he was in pieces.

He went to the cafeteria. It was some time after noon, so few people were there. Most people awake and working right now were on the lower floors and in the lobby, doing daywork or guarding him. Guarding him on the off chance that he might provide some new piece of information against the demons and the Eternals and the gates. He had no more information. He was emptied.

He turned on the TV and switched it to CNN to find out what the public knew about all this. Wolf Blitzer was reading information off. The gates were being found and contained at the source. But where did these gates bring these demons from, and how long was there to contain them? A woman came on for an interview and complained, asking, "Are we passing on this problem to our children? To our children's children? Are we going to just keep containing these gates every night? The office needs to step up their game...."

Your children and children's children won't be around to worry about the gates, Bryan thought.

No mention of the Eternals, either here or on the other side of the gates. Bryan's breath caught when word of a Possessed going crazy and attacking a woman came up, but it had happened in Hanoi. Nothing about him. No mention of impending doom. They all talked about the gates as an inconvenience, like it was the federal deficit they were discussing. The office was keeping a good wrap on things. He watched until he zoned out, staring at the TV like it was a wall. He came out of the state with a start, and found that three hours had passed.

"Good evening," Hussein said as he entered his office. He paused when he really saw Bryan. "You haven't just been sitting there all day, have you?"

"No," Bryan lied. Or half-lied. He *had* gone to the cafeteria. After which he had returned to Hussein's couch to zone out some more. "Did you sleep?"

"I did." Hussein was still looking at him. "Did you?"

Bryan had already decided to tell him if it came up. "I sleep, but I feel as if I haven't slept. I can't dream."

Hussein set his coat and briefcase down and went to him, sitting opposite him in a chair. Not beside him on the couch. "It did something to your subconscious. Took that, too."

"I won't get it back, will I? Even if I get my cards in my hands."

"Everything we've ever learned says no. The minds of the overtaken aren't stored in their totems. They're destroyed. Consumed."

"And I knew that. I was in denial. Even if I thought I wasn't." He looked at Hussein. "This is who I am now. Half a person."

"You've done so much, Bryan."

"I know. I worked longer than most. I just expected to be overtaken, not... split."

"Maybe you still have more to do."

Bryan managed an empty smile. "I never thought you one for fate."

"Not fate. Just possibility. You're the reason we're so close to solving this."

"*Are* we close to solving it?"

"Closer than we were. We're bringing in some experts tomorrow – professors and scientists. Going to see how these gates operate. Maybe physics can give us an answer."

"Weren't they still unsure whether the demons were energy or matter?"

"They're not unsure; they're debating." Hussein balled his hands into fists. "But we're figuring things out. We're *moving*. After all the years I've been doing this, we're finally out of the rut. We just need a little more time and we'll have all the pieces."

Bryan wanted to believe in his optimism, but the key word was *time*. They had no idea how much time they really had.

They both went to Conference Room B to watch the containment. Ruggeri was there, as well, and Bey, and Harper. They all studied Bryan – even Bey, though she had no Spotter sight.

"I see you got some rest, Hussein," Ruggeri said.

"I did, you snitch." Hussein grinned at her. "Now, leave me alone."

She smiled back. It was typical banter between them. Bryan wasn't sure how they tolerated each other.

The inside of the synagogue was livestreaming on Bey's laptop, the people breaking into three groups – preparing. A smaller group stood behind the rest: the students.

"Yesterday went awfully smoothly," Bey said, drumming her nails on the table. "We're not used to things running smoothly."

"Better get used to it," Hussein said.

"Don't jinx this. Believe me, I personally would much rather see things go smoothly."

"It would be a nice change from the chickens with their heads cut off approach," Ruggeri said.

Bryan paid no attention to their conversation. He watched the people moving in the synagogue. They all milled about, relaxed. No deaths expected tonight. There was something he didn't like about it.

Harper leaned over to him and whispered, "What's wrong?"

"I don't know," he whispered back. "Are the Spotters there tonight?"

"About a third of them."

"And all the Possesseds?"

"Except for the four guarding the office and a couple watching totems in quarantine. Why?"

"I don't know," he repeated. He watched the scene unfold with a numbed dread, helpless to affect anything happening on the screen. Sunset came and the first team possessed. Twenty minutes passed and the second team possessed. Someone entered the conference room and handed Bey a report, and Bey read out the news of the night. L.A., Mexico City, and Cordoba had found their gates. D.C. had already contained theirs for the night. On the laptop screen, the third team possessed. Bey and Hussein chatted about who was sending gate dust to where. Cantrell, Wallmann, and Utterklo arrived, and Cantrell made disparaging comments to Ruggeri. The first team possessed again.

And the entire time, Bryan was on edge.

It wasn't until the third team possessed a second time that the gate opened. Everyone in the conference room hushed and leaned forward as people on the laptop screen barked orders to possess. It was strange to see it this way, with nothing of note to actually view as everyone in the synagogue was rocked back by a force that was invisible, as they all stood and some waved their arms about at air. Some shouted "Over here" or "Help with these" as the students watched and whispered to each other. To anyone with lesser knowledge of the scene, it would have looked ridiculous.

But everyone was holding their ground. No one appeared to be in danger. So, why did Bryan still have that sick, nagging alarm?

"I have to say, Hussein," Cantrell said in that rasp of his, "your team is actually performing decently for once."

Hussein leaned back in his chair. "Why, Cantrell, that's actually civil of you *for once*."

"Don't get me wrong, Hussein. I don't want to see these nightly excursions busted apart by department infighting. Getting all of these Possesseds in that little space." He waved at the screen. "It's incredible they haven't killed each other."

"He has a point, Hussein," Ruggeri said.

Hussein watched the screen. "It's not them killing each other I'm worried about."

"We couldn't have predicted Skinner's and Coates's deaths," Bey offered.

"Couldn't we have?" Cantrell argued. "We knew those things were out there. *Are* out there."

Bryan was watching Hussein. He saw his eyes darken, and saw him getting ready to blow. But he didn't get the chance. Harper leapt to her feet, knocking her chair back. She cracked a walnut shell in her teeth and almost fell back down.

"In the hall," she said, quietly, though all eyes were on her, as if she'd shouted. "Sir, possess."

Hussein jumped up and brought out a match, snapping it.

The door crumpled into itself like a black hole had appeared inside it, splintering into a ball that was then blasted into the room. It was like a shrapnel bomb going off. Harper shielded herself, and Hussein shielded Bryan and Ruggeri, but the directors were pumped full of splinters of wood. And in the doorway stood the woman – the Eternal. Bryan could see a hint of her crimson aura. He would have seen it earlier, had he not been staring at the damned laptop.

It happened so fast, and Bryan saw little of what was actually happening. He wasn't possessed, couldn't see or detect the energy thrust against energy, and Hussein and Harper both jumped in front of him and blocked his view.

But Harper was tossed back into the wall, her already injured arm striking a stake of wood that stuck out. She howled and fell with the chunk through her forearm. And then Hussein was shielding the two of them.

Ruggeri fell in a spray of blood and hit the floor already dead. Bryan was spattered with blood, but it wasn't from Ruggeri.

Hussein fell in front of him, slashed in a dozen places, and as he fell, his demon leapt into

Bryan. And that was how Bryan knew Hussein was dead.

Bryan saw the Eternal now – hood thrown back from the force of the fight, hair long and red, eyes burning. Bryan felt an incredible rage pound through him, but inside the rage was calm. He bounded over the table towards the thing and it slashed ribbons of manifestations at him, but he bounced most of them away. The ones that did find him and cut him didn't bother him. He would see this thing destroyed again. Like in the rain in the street.

She tried to fight him off with tooth and nail, and he fought with the same. He tore her arm and she snapped at his neck and he clawed at her face and she bit his side.

She paused for the faintest moment, as Harper tried to contain her, but it was long enough for Bryan to get his teeth in her neck and tear it open. He ripped into the muscle and bone, but with a purpose to mangle. He didn't swallow the blood or flesh because he knew it would do him no good to ingest it. He was brutal, but his thoughts were clear. He knew what he was doing and why.

When he stopped and stood back, he took inventory of the room. Hussein was dead, but he'd known that already. Everyone was dead but Harper, in fact, who stared at him with her eyes wide. When his own eyes fell on her, she backed up hard against the wall.

"It's okay," Bryan said. "I'm still me. I just had to immobilize her." He looked down at the body. The bits and pieces and blood were already dripping and pooling back into the thing. "You'll have to keep chopping her up," he told Harper. "While I find out if anyone in the lobby is still alive."

"What are we going to do with it?" Harper's voice shook. It sounded odd coming from her.

"We're going to get some damned answers," he said.

Everyone in the lobby was fine. Nothing was amiss. They all balked at blood-soaked Bryan and two of them possessed, unsure of what to do as he approached.

Bryan wanted to scream at them, *You let her in!* But he recognized that he was soaked in blood with a demon in him and that that wouldn't be the best course of action.

"She got in," he said, struggling to keep his voice level. "She's upstairs, in pieces. What the hell were all of you doing?"

The guy who had jumped at the mouse the other night – Bryan's mind had lost his actual name completely, perhaps when the gamma had left him – spoke up. "We saw no one save agents enter and leave."

"Bullshit!" Bryan spat.

"It's true," Jones chimed in from beside the metal detector. "I saw only people I recognized tonight. Not even a member of the press came by."

"Whatever. All Possesseds get upstairs. *Now.*"

The three Possesseds looked terrified of him, and at this point, that suited him just fine. They followed him to where Harper was stabbing the body with forceful blows of energy Bryan couldn't see. Mouse actually cried out and ran to Hussein.

"Check all the bodies," Bryan ordered.

"Hussein's dead," whined Mouse.

"I know that. Check the rest."

"Cantrell's breathing," someone said.

"Of course, that bastard would survive." Bryan pointed at the one Possessed still standing at the door, as if he didn't want to come in. "You, call 911 and get the first person you come across in the hall to take over with Cantrell's health. Then join back with us. Everyone else, we're moving this Eternal elsewhere. Somewhere we can fit all the Possesseds."

"Where?" Harper gasped, out of breath.

There was only one room in which they could comfortably do what Bryan planned. "Cafeteria."

Chapter Seven

Mouse was hard at work in his turn to chop up the prone body of the Eternal when Connors walked into the cafeteria. The trail of blood that had been dragged through the halls into the room had already been sucked back into the thing.

"This is very unhygienic," Connors said, unperturbed, perhaps numbed by everything that had happened recently. "Where's Hussein?"

"Hussein's dead," Bryan told him.

Bryan had expected to be hit with the realization once he put the demon away. But the demon was away and, even unpossessed, Bryan was still empty about Hussein's death, as if it were someone he didn't know who had died. The bite wound in his left side hurt worse than the loss of Hussein. He didn't know whether this was just another thing in the long list of things wrong with him or if this could be some new stage of grief. More than anything, he was angry that he didn't feel anything.

Connors practically dropped his book. He, at least, could clearly be affected by the news. "Dead? How did this happen?"

"I'm not going to repeat it every time another Possessed enters the room. Let's wait until everyone's here."

Connors looked about to argue, but conceded. "They're all rushing over here. I suppose the urgent call was warranted."

"Did the containment work out?" Bryan asked, as if making polite conversation.

"It did, but who gives a shit?"

Bryan only nodded.

It didn't take even an hour for everyone to arrive. They had all taken the call to return to the office seriously, and they all took in the view of someone carving up a body in the center of the space in their own way, from displaying raised eyebrows of indifferent interest to open-mouthed shock. But only Connors had had the guts to say or ask anything. The rest uneasily watched the Eternal bleed, re-stitch, bleed again, and so on.

"Everyone's here," Harper said.

Bryan turned to her. She was calm and composed again, though the bandage on her arm was soaked through with blood. Bryan was likewise covered in both his and Hussein's blood. His own bandaged arm that had been stitched at the hospital was singing – he had attacked the Eternal with it without regard for its injury.

"Tell them what happened," he told her.

She shook her head. "They don't know me. They should hear this from you."

His heart skipped a beat. "I can't."

"It wouldn't be right for me to tell them."

She was right. He knew it. But he didn't want to do it.

She got a chair from where they had all been shoved against the walls and Bryan climbed onto it, nearly toppling it over as he did. Everyone in the room had turned to watch him before he had even cleared his throat. It was around sixty people, the majority of them Spotters that could read his aura. He broke out in a sweat.

He couldn't grieve Hussein, but he could get the shakes at the idea of speaking of his death before a crowd. It was ridiculous the parts of him that remained.

"Everyone, um..." He realized he didn't need to call for attention. All save Harper, who had taken over cutting up the Eternal again, were staring at him. He cleared his throat again and tried to start. "While containment was being done tonight, the Eternal on the floor there somehow snuck into the office and attacked several of us in a conference room. We, uh, captured it. But before we did, it harmed Cantrell, and it killed Bey, Wallmann, Utterklo, Ruggeri, and Hussein."

There were gasps and an eruption of voices, and Bryan had to hold his hands up for attention, though he almost fell off the chair again doing so. When the talk died down, he continued.

"All Possesseds are going to contain this Eternal while I put some questions to it. There are things we need to know to go forward, and we have a way now to find out those, uh... things." His voice dropped as he added, "Let's make sure they didn't die for nothing." He climbed down off the chair before anyone could ask him anything, and then dove through the people to Harper and the Eternal. The crowd parted for him like a Red Sea.

Connors clapped twice. "All right. Spotters get back. Possesseds possess and contain that body." He shuffled over to Bryan and appeared to almost grab at his arm before reconsidering. "Are you sure about this?" he whispered.

Bryan nodded. "If everyone here contains her at once, she won't be able to do a thing. Against two or three, she could have a chance. But not against a roomful of Possesseds all at once."

Connors wiped sweat from his forehead. "I hope you're right."

Harper stopped her slashing as everyone circled around and possessed. Once it was quiet again, Bryan turned to her. She looked ready to keel over. Manifesting energy was hard work – both mentally and physically – and she had also fought the Eternal while it had been on its feet.

"You should put yours away," Bryan said. "You must be exhausted."

"I'm fine," she gasped, her hands on her knees.

He stared her down for a few seconds, then waved at the chairs and tables against the wall. "You want me to get you a chair?" he snapped.

She glared at him as she tried to mask her gasps for breath. The bones and blood on the floor click-clacked and slupped and moved together.

"Fine," she spat, and put her demon away. Clearly, she was worn out, or she would have fought him.

He looked back at the body. He knew everyone was working on containing it – he could see it on their faces, frightened and determined and concentrating. And he could feel it. He wasn't possessed – and he didn't dare possess intentionally – and he shouldn't have been able to tell they were doing anything, but he felt the power of the containment before him. It made him nervous and itchy.

The room was silent as the body came back together, congealing into a semblance of a person, but a person broken and bloody. It jerked and twitched, and each time it did, people in the audience jumped, but it was only the muscles restructuring and the bones popping. Bryan could hear Harper's breaths beside him, and he couldn't tell if it was some sort of preternatural hearing due to what he had become, or if she was stressed enough to breathe that heavily.

The thing heaved as it sucked in an enormous gasping breath. A couple of Possesseds in the front row of the circle stepped back, and the containment wavered but held. The Eternal smacked its bloodied lips and its eyes blinked open. It continued to rasp breaths as its ribs knit back together, and it looked around as much as it could, frozen in containment as it was. Its eyes fell on Bryan last. Those eyes weren't hateful or spiteful; they only regarded him coolly. More coolly than the other two times they had looked at him.

"How did you get in here?" Bryan demanded.

She breathed in to speak, and coughed blood out. Then she tried again, and her voice was thick and deep with an accent no one in their world had ever heard. "I broke a window on the eighth floor. Made handholds up the side of the building."

Of course. He had been silly to blame the guys guarding the lobby. She could carve handholds out of concrete with manifested energy. Probably with pinpoint accuracy.

"How long have you been in this world?" Bryan asked.

"It has been the blink of an eye," she responded.

"That tells us nothing."

She grinned. The blood that had covered her face was gone now, making her look almost human. But her eyes were all wrong. "Because you know nothing. You do not know how it is to live through the eons."

"That's right. We know days and weeks and years. So, answer the question."

"A month, then."

"It was a huge risk, crossing over. The gate isn't stable yet. You could have waited."

"I couldn't. The hunger... there's nothing back there."

Bryan's voice deepened. "Because you ate it all. You've only yourselves to blame."

"Spare me your ethical concerns. You eat. So, too, do we. We eat and then we move on."

"You destroy and then you abandon."

"What does it matter? The worlds go on. More all the time. And we have to starve while the gates stabilize."

"How long does it take for the gates to stabilize?"

"Two thousand years."

"Two thousand? Why so exact all of a sudden? I thought a day was a week was a blink of an eye."

She gazed at the ceiling as if drugged, as if she didn't even feel the containment. "When it first began, all were thrust back in time, two thousand years and two thousand worlds back. The path has remained the same even if the vehicle changed."

"What the hell does that mean?"

"Nothing. Nothing to you." She turned her head slightly to look at the Possesseds around the circle.

"No!" he barked. "You look at me."

She did. Her eyes burned through him.

"How many others have come here so far?" he asked.

"Many. None. What does it matter?"

"It matters because we have to clean up you bastards."

She laughed a long, rumbling laugh. "You can't do anything to us. We are forever."

"We'll find a way."

"Oh, plenty have tried."

A shiver went through the circle around Bryan. It was true; what could they do? Perhaps others had done exactly what they were doing now; tried to get answers and gotten nowhere and died when the gates had opened.

Bryan stressed each word as he spoke. "How many Eternals are here?"

"Ah, you want the statistics." She bared her teeth at him in a grin.

"Yeah, give me a fucking statistic."

"Estimates are, fifteen cross before stabilization."

This time, Bryan shivered, as he envisioned Eternals sitting at computers, tallying up numbers. Did they do things other than eat? He hadn't considered it.

"Fifteen cross successfully?" he asked.

"Successfully, yes."

"How many aren't successful?"

"Oh, fifty or sixty or so." She looked up at the ceiling again.

"Fifty or sixty lost between worlds."

"It is nothing," she said bitterly. "We are too many as it stands."

"Clearly. You demolish a planet in not even two millennia."

"I say, we are too many."

Bryan could have asked how many. Probably *should* have asked how many. But he didn't want to know, and didn't want everyone in the room to know. There was something they *had* to know, however, regardless of who heard it.

He swallowed hard and asked, "When do the gates stabilize?"

"I don't have to tell you." She smiled at him almost sweetly, as if addressing a child who just didn't understand. But the eyes were still wrong. "But it doesn't matter. It won't be stopped. So many have tried."

"When?" He meant to demand this, but the word caught in his throat and he barely got it out.

"In this time zone, in this world, 8 AM, November twenty-first."

Bryan's head swam. That couldn't be right. "What year?" he pressed, trying to deny it.

"This year, you fool."

It was 4 AM on November thirteenth.

The room broke out in a commotion. Mouse shouted, "That's in eight days!" as if no one else had figured it out.

"You're lying," Bryan breathed out.

"It matters not whether you believe me, just as it matters not whether I tell you. It will happen all the same."

He had barely heard her. The room had exploded.

"*Shut up!*" he yelled. The Possesseds and Spotters all shut up and looked to him, for guidance or help or something he couldn't give. He had nothing to tell them.

Eight days.

He turned back to the Eternal. In the confusion, she had managed to roll onto her side, but that was all. Enough Possesseds had kept their wits to keep her down.

"How do we close the gates?" he asked.

"You don't."

"It's in your interest to tell us. If the gates are opened, this place is dust in two thousand years. If we close them, you eat forever."

"Forever? Nothing outside of us lasts forever. Everything falls to entropy."

"A lot longer, then."

"And then I would be hungry forever, without all of the others to stabilize the gates we would build here."

"But you could eat now."

"You do not yet grasp the concept of eternity. It is hard enough going hungry for centuries at a time. But for eternity? No one wishes for that."

"But you risk it, crossing before stabilization."

"Yes, because the hunger is so great. It is a paradox you wouldn't be able to work out as you are." Her eyes bore into his. "But it matters not. No one can close the gates. Not when they were begun, and not now."

"You just said you wouldn't tell me if there *was* a way. How can I trust you?"

"Trust me or not. It doesn't matter."

He would have put his hands to her neck and bashed her head against the floor, but the containment was between them, and though any normal person would have been able to pass it, he couldn't. A growl rose in his throat.

"The gamma," he said. "That's the key, isn't it? That's why you're trying to capture it."

"The gamma?" She looked at him quizzically.

"The youngest demon," Harper spoke up. Bryan jumped at her voice. He had forgotten the others were there.

"I know what you're calling a gamma, fool. You aren't the first to give them such names. I only don't see why I would want one."

"Why else would you come after me?" Bryan asked.

She looked at him in confusion for a moment, and then burst out laughing. It was sickening. It sounded like sobbing.

Bryan was taken aback, and said nothing as the sobbing laughs rolled around the room.

"Is that what it told you? That we were after it?" She chittered once more and quieted. "We have hundreds of 'gammas' in the past world. Many will pass through the gate in time. We have no shortage of them and care not where they are or what they do."

Bryan's mouth was dry. "Then why..."

"I said we are too many. Let us multiply and we will be many more, forever and ever. We are after you, to kill you, because you are becoming one of us."

Bryan reeled, and Harper caught his arm. He snatched it back from her and spun around. He couldn't look at the woman lying on the floor with her blazing eyes. He couldn't breathe. He had to get out of there. He didn't see the crowd he thrust aside and fell against and shoved out of his way; they were only faint glows and he wasn't hungry; he was only suffocating.

In the hall, he gasped for breath and fell against the wall. His vision was red and black and faint green. He thought he might vomit, but he didn't. Harper had followed him, but she had nothing to say.

He went up four floors, through the stairwell he had collapsed in yesterday, hungry and hopeless. Harper trailed him wordlessly. He was repeating a new mantra in his head: *It's not true, she's lying, it's not true....*

He burst into quarantine so that the woman at the desk jumped in her seat. When she looked at him, she leapt up and nearly fell backwards over her chair.

"Let me in," he said in a voice that wasn't quite his.

"Mr. Hussein said, um," she stuttered and gulped.

"Hussein is dead. Cantrell is in the hospital. All the other directors are dead." He stepped towards her as he spoke, and she backed against the wall. "I think procedure is out the window. Now, unlock the door."

"Then... maybe Ms. Ruggeri..."

"Is also dead," Harper broke in. "Please, open the door. It doesn't matter now."

The woman – Sekander, her name was Sekander, Bryan remembered now, detachedly – took in all this information and considered it, looked hard at Bryan, and then finally nodded.

Three Possesseds were watching the gamma. They jumped up when Bryan entered the room. Bryan didn't even notice. He shouted at them to leave. They might have argued, had Harper not taken them aside and spoken to them. Bryan didn't bother to listen to what she said or to notice when they left. He went straight to the table and snatched up the card.

You lied to me. The thought was fierce and burning.

The reply was cool. *Of course, I did.*

You planned this.

Yes.

Bryan had to fight an urge to tear up the card. That would have the opposite effect of what he would be going for. *You wanted this?* His accusation had been tossed out in anger – a wild anger he hadn't felt for days – but the response made no sense to him.

Certainly. Any demon would.

Bryan shook his head at the card. *No, demons seek to be free, to take over and feed.*

What is the ultimate freedom for a demon, the best way to feed? You've only seen failed attempts, your agents in the sanitariums. But done correctly, with a body and mind that can withstand the rigors of the process, a new consciousness arises, free and unrestrained. My initial capture was unexpected and unwanted, but a second possession of you made me realize I could achieve eternal possession.

Bryan forced himself to breathe. *So, it's true.*
You were trying to become Eternal.
Both of us. We will be Eternal as one.
Bullshit. I'm not who I was.
No, you've changed. And I've changed. We are becoming each other.
Stop talking like it's happening! I'd never agree to this!
We've already come close. To where hate is love and anger is peace. Where joy is pain and pain is comfort. The process just needs one more push, and we would be complete.
And why would I let you?
Because you hate me, and you love me, just as I hate and love you.

Bryan could swear he felt the thing inside the card grinning at him, from within the red hearts and the threes.

And because, it went on, *we can close the gates.*

Bryan dropped the card. It fluttered to the floor and landed face-down.

"Liar," he said aloud. "You're still lying."

There was no answer, but he didn't know anymore whether or not it was because he wasn't holding the card.

He turned to leave.

"What did it say?" Harper asked.

"It says it's none of your goddamned business," he snarled, pushing her out of the way.

By the time he got to Hussein's office, the anger had subsided and he was numb again. He shut the door and fell against it, sliding to the floor. He was exhausted, from all the exertion and death and lack of deep sleep, and the worst was yet to come.

Eight days to figure out how to close the gates. It was impossible. They needed more time.

Unless he believed the gamma. But he didn't.

He didn't.

The gamma.

He needed to do something with the gamma.

But what?

How?

He woke up still on the floor. Sunlight was leaking through the blinds. He had spaced out again, and he hadn't seen to the Eternal at all after the interrogation. He left the room cursing and saw Harper asleep at one of the desks right outside. She stirred when she heard him, but didn't wake up. He didn't want to wake her, and she might not even know what the situation with the Eternal was. She might have followed him and sat there the whole night and morning.

He had been an ass to her.

He left her alone and went to the cafeteria. The place was clean. The tables and chairs were back in their places. The lower floor agents were having lunch. It was disorienting.

"Like it never happened, eh?"

He turned around to see Connors. "Where is she?"

"We cut her up and put halves of her brain and heart in those air-tight, moisture-resistant containers we put old tokens in. Piled them and the rest of the body in quarantine."

Bryan breathed again. "I'm sorry. I should have been here to see to that."

"You had other things on your mind." He looked hard at Bryan, but Bryan didn't notice. He was

Black Heart

looking at the center of the room, where the Eternal had laid, imagining her being chopped into sections as half of the Possesseds and all of the Spotters got ill.

"It's true, isn't it?"

Bryan spun back to Connors. "What?"

"About you, that the gamma was trying to... make you into one of those?"

"The gamma confirmed it." Bryan stared blankly at the center of the room again. People were starting to notice him there and had begun whispering. He saw their aeons flicker as they concentrated on him, and he wheeled around and walked out to escape their gazes.

Connors followed him, clearing his throat. "I'm so sorry, Ivers. If we had only seen this coming..."

"We couldn't. All we've seen is agents turned to vegetables. Who could have guessed?" He lowered his voice, though no one was around to hear. "But I can't possess anymore. It was risky this time, to catch the Eternal, but that was an accident and I didn't mean for it to happen. But if the gamma's primed me to be some sort of vessel, it's possible any demon could knock me over the edge."

Connors opened his mouth to reply, but Bryan interrupted him before he could say anything.

"We still have the physicists visiting the gate tonight?" Bryan asked.

Connors started at the question. "Yes. Yes, of course."

"Maybe they'll have something to say."

"But... Ivers, don't you think other physicists on other worlds have already tried?"

"I opened a gate. There must be some way of closing a gate we just haven't encountered yet." He thought of what the gamma had said before he had tossed it away. Was it really possible, or had it just been leading him on? "We can open a gate tonight and dispose of the Eternal. I don't want it around, even if it is all chopped up."

Connors nodded in quick jerks. Probably, no one wanted it around.

Bryan looked back to the doors of the cafeteria. "They don't know yet."

Connors followed his gaze. "No, not yet. But the information will leak out. Too many of us were there to hear it."

"And the other gates. The people at those will need to know, too." Bryan took a deep breath and leaned against the wall. "How do we not start a panic?"

Connors thought about this. "No one outside an agency will care."

Bryan scoffed.

"It's true. The media never did believe any new development about the demons unless the death count was high enough. Now, there are monster Possesseds that will eat everyone when the gates let everything through? They'll think we're pressing for funding." He paused to run a hand over his bald head. "And if it does start a panic, what does it matter in the long run?"

They were silent for a moment. When Bryan spoke, his voice was quiet. "What can I even do? I can't possess."

"Hussein was supposed to be heading a conference call this evening with D.C., L.A., and Vancouver. I think you should be on that."

"What?" Bryan was actually shocked. "I can't do that."

"Bull. It's the sort of job you should have taken long ago."

"I meant, what can I do at the gate? Not sitting at some desk."

"What are you going to do at the gate? Watch? At a desk is where you can help us."

"What's a Possessed gonna do at a desk?"

"It's where Hussein was."

Bryan looked at him. Connors was a bundle of nervous energy, fidgeting with his hands, sweat standing out on his forehead. More nervous than usual. All of the agents were going to be more nervous than usual, Bryan realized, and more irritable, and more hopeless.

"Yeah, but..." Bryan paused. "How many people will be on the call?"

"Maybe five or ten in D.C., and another five in L.A. and Vancouver each. I don't know the specifics; it was Hussein's work. But they need to hear what's happening even if Hussein's gone."

Bryan paled at the number, but Connors misunderstood as he turned pale himself and rubbed his hands together. "You don't think they can do anything? I mean, I'm sure other Earths before ours tried all this same stuff, and no matter how many cities... I mean, if you think it'll cause only a panic, maybe we shouldn't..."

Bryan straightened. He was causing a panic all by himself. He couldn't break down now. "Don't blubber. I'll inform them and see if they have any initial ideas. They might think of something we haven't, or find something we haven't."

Connors nodded quickly, like a bird.

"But if I blow up at them, it's your fault."

"They'll probably blow up before you even start talking. A lot of people on the call will be Possesseds."

"Well, way to make the discussion impossible."

He was going through Hussein's emails when Harper walked in. He had kept the door open for whenever she finally woke up.

"You're a pretty sound sleeper," he said to her.

"You're not," she said, looking him over. "You haven't slept in days."

He leaned back in the chair and told her the matter of his sleep and lack of REM.

"I had assumed you were just avoiding sleep," she said.

"I have been chasing it with gusto; it's just always a mile ahead of me."

She nodded her head at the computer. "What are you doing?"

"Trying to make some sense of the five hundred different tasks Hussein was overseeing. The man should have had a secretary. *Two* secretaries."

"You shouldn't take them on if you're not able."

"You mean if I'm grieving him."

"Yes. Someone else could—"

"I'm not grieving him."

She blinked at him. "What?"

"I don't feel jack-shit about him. The man practically raised me and I don't care that he died right in front of my eyes. It's like he was a stranger, but I care more about strangers than I do about this. I care *more* about the fact that I don't care." He clicked open another email, but it was only about another new recruit. "That's how fucked up I am."

"That can be a normal part of the process."

"But I'm not normal. There is no normal part of my process." The next email was from Wei in media control on keeping the news stations away from the synagogue. Hussein had requested that their police liaison see if the cops were available, or otherwise, asked if Ruggeri could spare some Spotters to play the part in cordoning off the area. Bryan would have to respond to that one – they didn't need cameras around tonight, watching them open a gate to toss in some mystery tubes and boxes, and they didn't want anyone wondering what was in those tubes and boxes.

"What can I do?" Harper asked.

He looked up at her and seemed to see her for the first time since she'd walked in. He'd been able to change into spare clothes Hussein had brought him from his apartment back when the Eternal had been running rampant. Harper was still dressed in tatters. Her arm was haphazardly bandaged and large spots of blood bloomed on the gauze. Seeing that, Bryan felt that hunger again, worse than ever. He could *smell* the blood. He had to look away.

"Your arm," he said. "It's going to get infected."

"It doesn't matter." Was that hopelessness in her voice? Or just her usual poker-face?

But she was right. It didn't matter if her arm was falling off. It wouldn't matter in eight days.

"I can't look at it," he said. "It makes me.... Just get it fixed up."

From the corner of his eye, he saw her look at her arm and realize what he meant. "Ah," she gasped. "Of course. I should have... I'm sorry."

"It's not your fault." How could he expect her to think of his tainted reactions? "Just... could you be back at four?"

"Four? That should be doable. Why?"

"I, um... I have to be on a conference call."

"Am I needed for it?"

He fought an urge to shout at her and instead waved his hands as he said, "Look, just be here, okay?"

"Okay," she said, and without another question, she turned and walked out.

"Why weren't we notified?" Cowen demanded from D.C. He sat in the middle of a row of D.C. office reps, all of them glaring on sternly. They sat in a block on the monitor, right above the blocks of only slightly less people in L.A. and Vancouver.

There were only two people in the room with Bryan. Connors stood to the side, looking like Bryan felt. Harper sat beside Bryan, in a fresh change of clothes and with only a light scent of blood and flesh about her.

"There was no time," Bryan growled in reply. He had opened the call with Hussein's and the others' deaths, and gone on to say that the Eternal had been interrogated when Cowen had interrupted. "Which you'll understand if I continue."

"I think not," Cowen said. "We will—"

"We can't classify this information," Bryan spoke over him.

"Agent Ivers has the floor," someone said from Vancouver.

"Let him speak," said another from L.A.

Cowen was about to go on, but a woman behind him leaned over and whispered in his ear, at which point he grunted and quieted.

Bryan didn't speak right away. All the interruptions had reminded him of all of the people he was speaking to – not just the people on the monitors, but people off-screen, as well, who were watching from the sides like Connors was. Altogether, Bryan could count twenty-one people on the monitor, but he had managed to put them out of focus while he'd been talking, before he had been interrupted.

Harper kicked Bryan's leg under the table to bring him out of his stupor.

"Uh, yes," he spouted. "So, we questioned the Eternal, which was the same being that had... attacked me previously. We learned the following things from it."

He and Harper had made a list Bryan read from.

"One: These Eternals do indeed come through the gates from the previous world. According to this Eternal, up to fifteen may have already passed through and are on our Earth.

"Two: These Eternals cannot be killed. They cannot be destroyed in any way on any level. Like this Eternal, they will regenerate no matter what happens to them. There is no stopping them.

"Three: There are innumerable Eternals on the Earth lying beyond the gates. They have eaten and demolished everything on that Earth, and wish to pass through the gates in order to eat here on our own Earth.

"Four: These Eternals can all pass through the gates at once when the gates have fully stabilized.

"We have a date for when that will happen."

He took a deep breath and looked up at the faces on the screen.

"Coordinated Universal Time: 1 PM, November 21st."

There was silence.

"Um... that's all." He set his notes down flat on the table.

All of the people on the screen put their heads together and started murmuring so that Bryan couldn't hear. It made him as itchy as the containment in the cafeteria had.

"What reason," Cowen asked aloud, "did this Eternal have to tell the truth?"

"She... had no reason to lie," Bryan said weakly.

"That we know of. That she would allow herself to be captured eight days from the date of the gates... stabilizing... is odd."

"She didn't 'allow' anything. I had to—" Bryan cut himself off.

"You had to what?"

Harper spoke up. "Agent Ivers had great difficulty in capturing the Eternal. As has been stated, she killed several people before Ivers was able to apprehend her."

"Why did she attack the office in Chicago?" Cowen asked.

"We've gained a lot of information due to Agent Ivers," Harper went on. "The Eternals may see Chicago as a center of resistance."

Cowen raised his eyebrows. "Resistance is a strong word."

"This is a strong foe."

There was silence all around. Bryan gripped the edge of the table. Harper had covered for him. Center of resistance, indeed.

"You want everyone to know," Cowen said, "or you wouldn't have broadcast this in front of three different cities."

Bryan grinned. "I can't deny that. We need more minds trying to think up ways to solve this problem."

"If we announce this to all offices and the world, and a little over a week passes with nothing happening, we'll look like fools."

The grin slipped from Bryan's face. "I would welcome that outcome."

Not everyone returned to the synagogue that evening. Some of the missing had written their notice letters and handed them to Bryan or Connors – letters stating that they needed time with their families or time to themselves if they had no families. In his past life, Bryan would have raved at them for leaving just when the going got tough, but today he only nodded at each new letter, until he couldn't even muster up a *goodbye* or *good luck*. Eventually, he only took the notes without recognition, tossing them onto Hussein's desk and turning back to the computer, where there were more letters in the form of email.

But even more didn't even give notice. They simply didn't show up for containment, disappearing without a word.

Connors was livid, and he took it out on those who did show up. When Bryan told him to calm down, he shouted at Bryan that he shouldn't be there, either.

"I told you, you need to be in the office."

"How would that look with everyone else missing?" Bryan asked flatly, taking Connors aside. "If you want me to take charge, I need to be here to show I'm taking charge and still around."

"I know that!" Connors yelled, and took a deep breath. More quietly, he continued, "I know that, but damn it, our crew's been cut in half in one day."

"I don't like it, either, but that's no excuse to panic. We need to keep the others around."

Connors laughed in that loud, round way of his. "*You're* telling people not to panic?"

Bryan couldn't laugh with him. Because he *wished* he was panicking. He was someone else now. He looked at the agents mingling in the synagogue, among the pews and under the broken windows. Besides Connors's outburst, there were few fights, and little actual panic. But there was an electricity in the air – an undercurrent of hysteria beneath the tense surfaces of the people. All voices were low and choked and worried. Bryan saw Cam, who tried to catch his eye. But he avoided the man's gaze and looked past him to see the professors from the university, setting up their instruments to the side of the room. And past them, Mouse, which was surprising. Everyone might have to stop calling him by that name.

There were half the Possesseds left, and even fewer Spotters. Perhaps ten Spotters. Bryan had gotten their notices, too, for the lack of a Lead Spotter. Their reasons for leaving had been a little different. In large part, they felt they served no purpose, with the capturing happening at the synagogue instead of throughout the city. They no longer had to track, only observe, and they didn't want to spend their final days observing a doomed operation. They didn't state the matter in quite such words, but Bryan knew what they were thinking and why they left.

He looked over the Spotters. There was Hix, and Krotki, and... Andrade.

"Connors," he said. "Go give some pep talks, okay? Tell them what we're doing."

"Like business as usual, sure." He left Bryan with an expression like sour milk, but that was his usual expression, so it was hard to tell just how hopeless he really felt.

He hadn't left for good, at least.

Bryan went to Andrade, and she noticed him approaching almost immediately. Had probably been keeping an eye on him all along. But she didn't balk at his approach, even if the other two Spotters with her did.

"Can I talk to you?" Bryan asked. It wasn't a rhetorical question. She might very well say no, that she couldn't handle being in such close proximity to him.

But she said, "Sure," as if nothing was amiss, and stepped away from the others.

"I'm glad you're here," Bryan said feebly, grasping for something to say.

"I have to be here. If there might be any way I can help...." She bit her lip in that charming way of hers, but Bryan was dismayed to find it did nothing for him. "I'm sorry for how I treated you before, in the cafeteria."

"No, don't be. I'm—"

"Still the same person. I shouldn't have freaked out."

"But I'm not the same person. You can see that. It's understandable—"

"It was mean and I—"

"-that you would—"

They both stopped, and Andrade took a deep breath and looked at the ground.

"What's important is you're here," Bryan finished.

She gave a thin smile and nodded, looking up at him in a way that was half-coy, half-melancholy.

"I wanted to ask you," he went on, "since Renella is gone, if you might look after the Spotters. I don't think I can... handle both groups."

"I think it's really something that you're even handling the Possesseds," she said. "I know it's not what you ever wanted."

"Ain't that the truth? I'm still not sure I'm doing it."

"Of course, you are. Everyone knows it. That's why they all went to you to hand in their notice. And I know that wasn't easy, either."

"You don't think they left because of me, do you?"

He was looking away from her, at the Possesseds. Mouse was throwing a fit over a splinter he had gotten from a pew, kicking at the structure while the others tried to get it out of his palm.

Andrade didn't touch him, but instead ducked her head into his line of vision. "They left for their own reasons. Because they needed to see their parents or their children, or because they didn't sign on to prevent the end of the world. Nothing to do with you. But those who are here believe you can do something to change what's happening."

"That makes me feel worse. How would I do that?"

"We don't know yet. We're all here to figure it out. So, to answer your question: Yes, I'll look after the Spotters."

"Thank you." He put a smile on his face, but it felt fake. "Would you take over the Possesseds, too?"

"Hell, no!" She shook her head emphatically. "No one wants that job."

That should have been funny, but Bryan didn't laugh and the good-natured smile fell from Andrade's face. Suddenly, Bryan didn't know what to say or do to fix the awkwardness. Just in time, Harper appeared.

"They're about to bring the Eternal in," she said.

"Right. Ah, Andrade here has agreed to head the Spotters. In case you need anything."

"Well, I suppose they need somebody. But what is she going to be heading? The Spotters don't have much to do."

"Harper..." Bryan warned.

"No," Andrade said. "She's right. But we need to *find* something to do to help. That's why we're here. I'll help however I can."

"I apologize," Harper said, looking Andrade in the eyes. "I didn't mean to be rude."

Andrade shrugged, the smile back on her lips. "You're Possessed."

"A poor excuse. Please let me know if I can be of any help to you in a Spotter capacity."

Andrade blinked at her as if confused. "Thank you. I will."

Harper gave a little nod of her head – a semi-bow – and then she and Bryan left Andrade.

"Way to make my apologies look inadequate," Bryan said.

"I can't help it," Harper said. "I really do feel awful when I do things like that."

"And I don't?" He'd meant it as a joke, however poor, but she stopped abruptly.

"I didn't say you didn't," she said, her voice suddenly harsh.

"You're doing it again," Bryan said. "I'm afraid I'm no longer a good sparring partner."

"I'm not–" Anger flashed in her eyes, then subsided. "Right. I'm sorry. I'm tired. Not that that's any excuse, either."

"Forget it. I shouldn't have brought it up. Anyway, your reaction back there made me wonder – did you not work much with the Spotters in Tokyo?"

"I was officially part of the Possessed contingent. For all my overlap, the Spotters really didn't have much use for me."

"I find that hard to believe. I would have welcomed someone like you in Chicago."

"You say that, but...." she trailed off and started walking again, towards the entrance, where the containers of bits of Eternal were being wheeled in on a dolly.

Bryan stopped her. "But what?"

Harper turned her eyes away and shifted her shoulders. It was very un-Harper of her. "It's not something you can easily put into words. But... in our job, we're part of our respective groups. But I'm not part of either group. I'm part of one group and part of the other group. I'm not *really* a Possessed and I'm not *really* a Spotter. People want all or nothing, and I'm neither."

"I know what you mean," Bryan said.

She looked into his eyes, her own being expressionless and unreadable. But maybe not entirely. "I suppose you do."

"Ivers!"

Bryan turned with a groan. Connors was there, breathing heavily as if he had just run a marathon instead of a few feet across a synagogue.

"Connors," Bryan said, "I believe I said no panicking."

"Ivers!" Connors hissed, leaning in close to him. "There's nothing in those containers."

Bryan didn't react. He wasn't sure *how* to react. "That's impossible," he said, not actually sure whether it was impossible.

"We were unloading them," Connors went on, "and I noticed they were particularly light. So I unscrewed the lid off one and... no body parts. No blood. Completely clean."

"Are you sure those are the right containers?"

"I saw them packed myself, like I could forget. And we labeled them. They're the same ones."

"Was anyone watching them in quarantine?" Harper asked.

Bryan and Connors looked at her blankly.

"Well, we've been so busy..." Connors said.

"Half our crew quit..." Bryan said.

"They were sealed so tightly...." Connors moaned. "I'm sorry, Ivers. It should have been a priority."

"Well, who would have expected that thing to open the containers, or whatever it did? Never mind. What do we tell the others?"

"Are you implying we don't tell the others what happened?" Harper asked.

"Well, that's why we're whispering, isn't it?"

The three of them went silent. It *was* an option to just pretend the containers were full and chuck them through a gate as if nothing were amiss.

"Wait here," Bryan said, and he went back through the crowd of agents, back to Andrade. He took her arm and dragged her over without a word, only explaining the situation when they were back with Harper and Connors, where he realized he was still gripping her arm and nearly jumped back.

Andrade, however, hadn't even flinched the whole time.

"God," she said when he was finished.

"What's the atmosphere here?" Bryan asked her. "Are they good or is everyone about to break and run?"

She looked around them. Skinner's voice rose above the others, shouting at Greene, and one of the Spotters moved between them to break it up. Nerves? Or just typical Possessed behavior?

"They're worried," Andrade said, "and a little scared. But determined. They're here because they chose to be, and they want to help. I think you can tell them. I think you *should* tell them."

"We don't have enough people here to be positive we can contain the gate outflow as it is," Connors said. "I don't doubt Andrade's perceptions, but they *are* scared."

"I have to wonder if it would be better if they don't know," Harper put in. "There's enough for them to worry about."

"But it's your decision, Ivers," Andrade said.

He looked over the containers piled at the foot of the platform. Containers only the four of them knew were empty. "I can't play a charade. I have to tell them. If I didn't and one of them died because of that...." He couldn't finish. Because, in seven days, a death or two wouldn't matter. But he climbed onto the platform and called for attention, and everyone looked at him, including the batch of scientists.

"The Eternal escaped," he told them all. "These containers are empty. As before, um, stay on your guard. We don't know what its next move will be."

Murmurs filled the room. "Is it here?" Mouse asked. "At the synagogue?"

"Uh... we don't know. We don't know when it got out. But... don't think this changes anything. We've got momentum on solving the problem of the gates. We need to work together now. Tonight, with the trainees to help us, we may have enough Possesseds to contain the demons. But even if we can't, we can still run some experiments."

He jumped into the plan for the night before anyone could catch on to the fact that, behind his hopeful words, he was hopeless. Whether or not they were able to hold the outward blast that propelled the demons away, either way, they would use them in the few seconds they were present to make another gate – a gate to nowhere. This would allow their guests to take a few measurements and see how things worked. When that gate collapsed, everyone was to let the demons go out over the city.

He looked up at the end of his speech. All were silent and staring at him. They were wide-eyed. Worried. A little scared. Also determined.

Okay.

Connors separated the remaining twenty-one Possesseds into three groups as if they were operating as usual, but they were groups of about six each, and only that large because of the trainees mixed in. Andrade took a group of Spotters and told them to watch the front yard for anything that might be trying to ambush the place.

Then, with the sun going down and having nothing to do, Bryan joined the academicians. They had brought in more equipment, piling it in between the office's equipment. The floor was a mess of wires

Black Heart

running to humming generators. There were perhaps ten college students sitting at monitors, and four professors overseeing them.

One of the students leapt up from the crate he was sitting on when he saw Bryan coming. "Agent Ivers," he said, "I hear you're in charge in light of Hussein's absence." He stuck out his hand, grabbing for Bryan's own. Bryan jumped back and the kid was left grabbing air.

"Oh, I'm sorry." He snatched his hand back and gave a simpering, apologetic look. "I forget how touchy you Possessed guys are."

"That's not something you want to forget," Bryan said in a low voice.

"Ah... sorry," he said again. "It's just not every day us normal folks get a chance to talk with office agents, never mind view a gate opening and measure a group of demons. I'm specializing in demonic studies at the University of Chicago."

"That's a thing?"

"Unofficially, yes, if you make your own major. We're trying to make it an official field, though. Our club tracks–"

"*Club?*"

"Yes, the Demonic Studies Club. We track the occurrence and location of demon activity. We've tried to set up a joint venture with the office, like for what we're doing here, but unfortunately, it couldn't be arranged."

"You mean we shot you down."

"You could say that. So, I'm really excited to be here. Oh, geesh, I didn't introduce myself. I'm Dan. Dan Grant." He stuck out his hand again, but caught himself and retracted it with another apologetic smile.

A woman in a dark suit stepped up to the two of them. She had long blonde-turning-gray hair tied back in a ponytail and the discerning eyes of a teacher. "Dan, don't bother the agents. We're strapped for time."

"I'm not... um." He looked back to Bryan. "Maybe I could talk to you after the gate? I'm just dying to pick your brain."

What a choice of words, Bryan thought. "Maybe," he said aloud, and Dan grinned and returned to his monitor.

"Doctor Rollins, chemistry," the woman said, holding out her hand.

Bryan frowned at it. "You never realize how many people want to shake hands until you don't want to do it yourself."

She held up the hand. "Say no more."

"Fuck. I mean, sorry. That was rude."

"You're not the first Possessed I've held a conversation with." She crossed her arms. "Is Agent Hussein running late?"

"Hussein was killed last night by a type of Possessed that can travel through the gates with the demons."

Rollins's hand went to her throat. "God. I'm so sorry."

"The office directors were also killed. Which is why I'm afraid you'll have to deal with me. My name is Ivers."

"I had no idea. Then... we're not just here to study the gates, are we?"

"We need a way to close the gates before more of these Eternally Possesseds come through. We *are* on a time schedule."

Rollins's eyes were wide. "What sort of time schedule?"

"A tight one." Bryan changed the subject before she could inquire further. "What's your familiarity with what's going on here?"

"Well... Agent Hussein sent some of the dust found in this area to my department. It is as he said – dead. Trace amounts of bacteria and mites that can be found in far greater amounts in more lively samples taken from other spots in the building, so it may only have those from sitting here and interacting with the environment and wind. Typical components for dust anywhere in the world – silicon, oxygen, carbon, phosphorus, so on. But very finely powdered. We should have found skin cells, pollen hairs, textile fibers, but there were none of any of those. It's as if it was manufactured in a sterile lab. The same dust was found in various abandoned religious buildings in demonically active cities the world over, where the gates appear." She turned to look at the platform. "As for the gates, I'll have no clue until I observe one."

"They're made of demons, so they say." A young man stepped in beside them, whipping his glasses from his face. "Dr. Maclin, astrophysics." He stuck out his hand. He looked too young to be a doctor of anything.

"Agent Ivers is not fond of handshaking," Rollins explained. "Or so he so painstakingly explained to me."

"Well." Maclin withdrew his hand with a wrinkled nose. "Quite the welcome wagon here. First someone shouts at me for 'making a racket' setting up, and now–"

"Brad, drop it," Rollins warned him.

"I'm just saying, they invited us."

"I'm sorry," Bryan said meekly, not knowing what else to do. Rollins looked at him in surprise.

Maclin watched him as if waiting for him to say more, and when he didn't, Maclin cleared his throat and spoke as if no argument had happened. "Has the office gathered any data on the demons as they form the gate? If these gates are wormholes, as we've wondered if they might be, the demons could be able to create their own electromagnetic field. Or, possibly, we could gain some insight into the formation of wormholes themselves. Or this could be something else entirely."

"We haven't had time to study the gates," Bryan said, his voice weak, as if he were still apologizing. "We've just been trying to contain them."

"Hmm. That's very pertinacious of you."

"Honestly," Rollins broke in, "you're every bit as disagreeable as an office agent."

"Well, we've been asked to work with no background information."

"I know," Bryan said. "We don't have much information ourselves. We've just been moving day to day. Or night to night. We just need to find a way to close the gates, with your help."

"Assuming we have the technology for such an endeavor," Maclin said.

"We *have* to find a way."

"Something is going to happen," Rollins said, "isn't it?"

"Yes, and that's all I can say. Please do your best." Bryan left them before they could comment further. As he joined Harper at the back with the trainees, Ward was starting his talk with them.

"I'm sure you've all heard the news by now," he started. "And you know that many of our colleagues have already resigned. It's why you've been bumped up to containment duty."

There were eleven trainees left, and likely to be less tomorrow when word fully got around and the reality of it sank in. Bryan looked them over and did a double-take when he saw Sonia. He hadn't even thought of her, and thinking of her now, he wouldn't have expected her to be here. But she was right there, giving him a nervous smile; he shifted his gaze, hoping he hadn't stared.

Ward continued, "This is the real deal. If you have any doubts, if you want to go home instead and spend these days with your family, we can't hold you here."

They looked around at each other, as if daring any of their peers to leave. But despite the fear in their eyes, no one did.

Well, they might change their minds after tonight, thought Bryan.

Ward walked them through the containment, as he probably already had five times before. His words echoed in the space as the sun set and the first group possessed. Then, all was quiet as the Possessed focused on the gate platform and the Spotters focused on the road outside. Bryan watched the doors, searching for any sign of a crimson aeon beyond them.

Hours passed. Four hours, which was too long to be on constant alert. Bryan was becoming increasingly aware that he should be mingling, giving pep talks, keeping spirits up. That's what Hussein would have done. So, he tried, but his words came out forced and tinged with anger, as if everyone there had done something wrong. Andrade had to take over. He went to the side and moped, aware that he was moping and not knowing how to do anything else. And two more hours passed.

It was 1 AM when the gate opened, and Bryan didn't notice. He'd been staring blankly at the synagogue doors, staring past the doors with his mind empty. He didn't know how long he had been that way, or if he would have noticed any Eternal that wandered into his field of vision. By the time Harper elbowed him, the gate had closed. He looked to the platform to see that the demons had successfully been contained and Connors was speaking the words to open it back up to nowhere.

Bryan looked back around. No sign of an Eternal, and the Spotters were watching out for one. Still, Bryan looked again, hard, and searched out that inner voice or instinct which had told him before when Eternals had been around. It was silent.

He turned back. There was no gate. Connors was talking nervously with Ward.

Bryan went down the aisle to join them. As he approached, Connors shuffled to him.

"It's not working," he wheezed.

Bryan thought as he walked. Around him, the Possesseds were already flagging under the exertion of containing so many demons at once. A couple of them were on their knees.

"We need everyone to speak the words," Bryan said.

Connors nodded flittingly. "Yes, of course. I should have thought of that." He raced back to the front and raised his voice, telling the Possesseds to join him in speaking the words.

They did, though many of the voices were strained, and several of the trainees couldn't multi-task and had to concentrate on containment only. The words filled and reverberated in the space, heavy as if they carried volume, but also empty and chilling. Something was missing. As one minute passed, and then another, voice after voice went out like a candle.

The gate didn't open, and the containment was faltering. They had counted on a second gate's closure to disperse the demons over the city. Instead, they were going to fill the synagogue when the containment failed.

And they didn't have enough Possesseds to catch them all.

Bryan looked to the Spotters dutifully watching the doors, and to the bank of equipment and laptops with a dozen civilians behind it.

"They'll die," Harper said from beside him.

That was just fine with Bryan. It would even help him. It was the worst feeling he had had up to this point: not caring about fifty or so people all around him. Not caring about anyone at all. Total willingness to watch them die or be driven mad. It would all be the same in the end.

He screwed his eyes shut and cursed himself. A couple of Possesseds gave up and quit the containment, as if they might run, and with his eyes closed, Bryan could feel the containment flicker and falter. He opened his eyes and stepped forward to the edge of it and spoke the words, desperately hoping it wouldn't work.

The gate opened immediately.

The pull of it produced a wind that whistled through the broken windows of the synagogue, but other than that, there was dead silence until Connors shouted, "Back to the plan! Drop wide containment! Start capturing!"

Bryan hadn't expected it to take so much out of him. He could only hold it open for half a minute. When he let it go, he fell to the ground, blacking out for a second.

The demons did as they were supposed to, and shot out from the synagogue.

But no one breathed a sigh of relief. No one helped Bryan up. When he looked around, every Possessed was staring at him. Even Harper, whose usually so-blank expression held accusation.

"What?" Bryan snarled at her, at all of them.

"Are you okay?" she asked. Her voice was cold. It was not a question. It was a demand.

He would have snapped back at her, but he had noticed her aeon, and it looked more inviting than ever. If he had been on his feet, he would have stepped towards her, but he was sprawled on the floor and could only stare.

Then he blinked and realized that everyone was watching him, watching whatever his own aeon was doing. He saw Harper standing closer than the rest of them, determined and apparently ready to fight him. Her hand was inside her jacket.

He wanted to just put his head back down, to curl into a ball and ignore all of them.

"I'm okay," he said. He wanted to cry, but he couldn't. He couldn't stand, either. "Just give me a minute."

They were starting to murmur amongst themselves. He wanted to order Connors to drive them out, but he knew he didn't have the strength to shout, and even if he managed to get the Possesseds and Spotters to leave him alone, the civilians were still here taking measurements. It was Andrade who went to Connnors, and – though he argued at first – he called for the Possesseds' attention and started handing out assignments for the night.

Only then did Harper kneel beside him. "It's starting to fade," she said, "but you looked..."

"Like I'd kill someone?" he snapped. "I didn't do anything."

"But you looked dangerous."

"I didn't do anything." He'd meant to shout it, but his voice tore and rasped.

"We had to be sure. I'm sorry."

"Everyone's sorry," he whispered.

"Can you stand?" She reached out to take his arm and he slapped her away weakly.

"Leave me alone," he said.

She held the hand he had batted away as if he had actually slapped it hard, and seemed to think of something else to say. But she couldn't think of anything and got up. She stood like a statue, hands folded, until Andrade finished with the Spotters and came to Bryan. He made himself stand when he saw her coming, though it was difficult and he nearly fell over, having to grab the pew beside him for support.

"Connors and two other Possesseds are going to return to the office with you," Andrade explained. "Along with a Spotter. I'm going to stay here and see what they've gleaned off the readings."

"I don't need anyone at the office," Bryan argued.

"Of course, you do. The Eternal is loose again. It'll be after you."

"It doesn't matter. The Possesseds need to be out capturing."

Andrade came to him and clasped his hands. It was too much for him. He was so weak, and she was so full of life. So appetizing. He snarled at her and tried to push her away, but she held on. He could see the green light in her and feel the heat of her palms and fingers and hear the beat of her heart. But she held on until he stood still, breathing heavy.

"You're still in there," she said. "I can see the demon, but I can see you, too. And you're just as important and needed as anyone else."

He looked at her again, and he could see her again, as a person with concern on her face. But he could hear the beat of her heart and it was racing. She had been terrified to keep hold of his hands, but had kept hold of them regardless, to prove this to him.

He looked down at those hands, and she squeezed them gently, her pulse slowing.

"That was a stupid thing to do," he said.

She smiled. "Us Spotters have to be a little bit stupid. Now, head back to the office. Connors will drive you."

Harper sat beside him in the back of the car. They were halfway to the office when she finally spoke up, quietly, though Connors was on the phone and not listening.

"She was right."

"Who?" Bryan asked, shocked out of one of his staring spells. He had been watching the people on the sidewalk. God, he needed to eat something.

"Andrade. I shouldn't have acted that way."

"It doesn't matter. Everyone else did."

"That doesn't excuse it."

"I almost snapped at her when she took my hands. You were right to be wary. It *was* stupid what she did."

"It was right for her to do it. It was something only a Spotter could do."

He turned back to her. She was looking out the window now, watching the people on the sidewalk like he'd been doing. He wondered what she saw. "You're a Spotter, too."

"I'm not."

He thought back to her words earlier. Not really a Spotter. Not really a Possessed.

Like him. Not really human.

At the office, they set him up in an inner room – one with no windows. Bryan liked it; it was dark. It had only the desk, desk chair, and a couch. The people guarding him set up right outside the door. He collapsed into the chair and fell asleep, and only woke when Harper returned with a pizza. As expected, he hadn't dreamed, and he felt worse than before he had fallen asleep.

"Shit," he mumbled, swiping the screensaver off his – Hussein's – laptop and checking the time. "I can't believe I slept for... an hour?"

"You were exhausted," Harper said, setting down the pizza.

"It didn't help. And the group's capturing. I should be tracking them or something. I don't even know."

"Eat first."

He ate as he read emails. The media was having a field day with the news that the gates would funnel in extreme numbers of demons in a few days. Connors had been right – everyone thought it was a grant grab. And everyone else thought it was an exciting, end-of-the-world prank. The academics seemed to be arguing it, seriously, as a culmination of rising demon populations, but no one was listening to them.

He was getting notifications of who was capturing what where, but the call center seemed to take care of the bulk of things. Still, he had to coordinate clean-up. Harper helped, putting calls in to the clean-up crew, taking notes on how many were dead and any property that had been destroyed. Towards the end of the night, Wei came in to talk about media coverage. At 8 AM, Connors showed Doctors Rollins and Maclin into Bryan's cave-like office.

"What happened to you?" Maclin asked him. "You get hit by a bus?"

It wasn't far off from how he felt. He'd been run ragged that night with work he had no prior experience with, and still on no sleep. It also crossed his mind at that moment that he hadn't shaved in days.

"No time for pleasantries," he said. "Let's get down to business. We need solutions on how to close these gates."

"Easier said than done," Maclin said. "Readings of the gate generally confirm what I already suspected. There was a faint electromagnetic signature to the thing, radiation readings, bending of light..."

"Which means?" Bryan waved his hand impatiently.

"It means we're likely to be dealing with a wormhole. Something we've only recently begun to produce in a lab in infinitesimal size."

"Fine, it's a wormhole. How do we close off a wormhole?"

"This is humanity's first experience with these on such a grand scale. I mean, this is incredible. To be able to view such a thing at regular intervals in stable conditions? This isn't something you just 'close off.' We're talking about exotic matter, non-baryonic particles—"

"Basically," Rollins interrupted him, "items we can only theorize about. We need time to study the gates. This is only the beginning of the discovery process."

"We don't have time," Bryan said, stressing each word.

"Right," Rollins said. "The gates will... allow more demons through in a few days."

"Yeah," Bryan said. "Secret's out."

"People are saying it's enough demons to destroy society," Maclin said. "I don't see how that's possible."

"It's not just demons we've been battling," Bryan said gravely.

Rollins and Maclin watched him skeptically, waiting for him to give more information. He didn't.

"Say we theorize," he said. "How would one close a wormhole?"

"That's just it," Rollins said. "With our current knowledge, current technology, if you want it in a couple days' time, there's no way."

Bryan growled. "Will you stop saying no and—"

"Hold on," Rollins interrupted him. "Let's look at this another way. What do we know? That demons can cross over through the gate from one planet to another."

"From one Earth to another," Bryan said.

"Either way, can — *could* a human cross from here to there?"

"The gate isn't stable enough. They wouldn't make it."

"That gate," Maclin broke in, "is unstable in the direction of there to here. But that instability doesn't necessarily go both ways."

"How could it not?" Bryan asked.

"Who says it does?" Rollins asked.

"Well, obviously..." Bryan stuttered, "of course, it... it just would be!"

"You're supposing the gate looks like this." Maclin picked up a sheet of paper from Bryan's desk and curled it to make a tube. "Equal at both ends. Uniform throughout. But if it were like this..." He made one end larger and the other smaller, almost in a cone shape. "Say this smaller end is the other Earth. They go in there and come out from this other, larger end, and somewhere in this big space is our Earth, but they could end up anywhere in this end of the cone. But if *we* went in, and came out this smaller exit on the other Earth, there's only one spot – or, a far smaller amount of spots – where we could end up at." He let the paper unfurl and set it back on the desk. "This is, of course, purely guesswork. We have no way of knowing whether this gate is a tube or a cone or a cone on both ends."

The room fell into silence.

Bryan shot up out of his chair so that everyone jumped.

"There's a way," he said, and left the room.

There was no one watching his cards, no one watching the gamma, no one watching anyone's totems. They had twenty-one Possesseds left and they all needed to be out capturing during the night and recuperating during the day. Quarantine was simply a lower priority; considering the world was ending, it didn't matter if, by some small chance, a totem broke and a Possessed here or there went mad. There was a very small chance of that happening anyway.

Keep telling yourself that, Bryan thought as he passed by empty rooms, each with a pile of totems in them. Those belonging to Laity, still in the hospital, and Rudd, on psychiatric leave, and Demasi, who'd had a complete meltdown last month – all of their totems unguarded.

And his own cards. And *his card*.

He walked up to it and stared it down. The demon inside was watching him, looking him over calmly. Bryan felt a pull towards it, towards its warmth and vivacity... the things he no longer had. And it was pulled towards him.

We've already come close.

Bryan stood away from the card, and reached out his hand to rest two fingertips on it.

Does anything pass through the gates going from this Earth to the other one?

It didn't answer at first. It was considering the question, its implications, and how answering would benefit it.

Of course, it finally responded.

Like what? Or who?

Rats, mice, insects, homeless people. Now, the last causes an enormous uproar.

People go there?

The Eternals rip each other to bits to get at them.

How often does that happen? How likely is someone to get through if they enter the gate from this side?

You assumed the gate is unstable throughout.

But it's not, Bryan guessed. *It's stable if you enter it from here.*

Not entirely.

How stable then?

From there, one travels from a point to a vast array of destinations. From here, it's the other way around. But the traveler can still fall off the path.

So, it's risky, but possible. How possible?

How would I know? I've only gone one way.

Bryan was already starting to feel sick, sore, and he knew the demon was leeching into him even as he kept his distance. He could feel it roiling around in his head. His eyes hurt as everything took on a faintly green tinge.

Black Heart

You know all this, Bryan thought at the thing. *You claim to not know more? Bullshit.*

I have seen the construct of the passage as I came through it. It has a beauty and an ugliness in its mathematical asymmetry, a holdover from how it began.

And Bryan could see it, vaguely, in his mind. Like a half-remembered dream. It *was* beautiful, but also hideous, cold, mechanical, and lifeless.

How did it begin?

With a theory. With a machine. It flung the people who made it 2,000 years back and 2,000 worlds over. I have seen them. They are the oldest.

And Bryan could see them, too, tearing the other Eternals to ribbons to get at a pigeon, their eyes filled with hunger – *starvation* – and endless suffering.

But clearly, there are no machines now.

No, the machines have fallen away. They use the demons now.

Bryan was about to ask how it knew all that, but he already understood, that it was in the chants to build the gates, to gather the demons. It was a blueprint.

Why these places? These cities? Chicago, L.A., Berlin, Tokyo, all the others. Surely there weren't machines in every large city on Earth in the beginning. Wouldn't it have started with one machine, in one city?

You have your totems. They have theirs.

What totems? What are they?

Lodestones. Steel and screws and circuit boards they have kept together just as they have kept their bodies together.

What are *they?*

He was burning up, his head pounding and his muscles tense. He knew the gamma was stretching this out to be with him, *in* him. But damned if a part of him didn't want it in him. He wanted to tear the card and let it out, to let it enter him fully so that they would be complete.

Pieces of the first machine, from all those ages ago. Without them, would the gates function?

Surely, they need them. Or why would they have kept them all this time, while everything else turned to dust? These items have memories themselves, of the machine they once were. They direct us into the gate.

Then... we need only destroy those totems. Damn you for not saying so.

There is a much easier way to stop them.

Bryan knew what was coming, and should have let go of the card, but he didn't want to leave, though it hurt every part of him to stay. *How?*

Let me in. It would take one word to close the gates.

Liar. How could one word stop them? Thousands of them have been working for thousands of years to structure all those gates.

And still their stability hangs on a thread. One command will force the program closed, will sever that thread.

It made so much sense, what it said. Bryan couldn't really tell anyway through the pounding in his head and heart.

But it did make sense. And it would be so much easier.

He was pushed back, losing contact with the card and the demon. He cried out as he fell to the floor, unable to find his balance. When he looked up, he saw a brilliant green figure. But he couldn't devour it, not as he was.

"Why did you..." he snarled.

"It was consuming you," Harper said. "It might have escaped the card."

Oh, why couldn't it have? Why had she had to snap that connection? He was empty again, nothing again. He wouldn't have needed to care anymore, about this planet or these people. He could have just been one.

He was in so much pain that he couldn't stand. He hung his head, and saw that the glow of a billion dust mites traversing the carpet was fading. He did care. He had to care. He wasn't Eternal; he was human.

"You're right," he said, only partly to Harper.

His cell rang, causing Harper to jump, but Bryan only noticed it on the third ring. He picked it up with a weak "Ivers."

"Sir," came a voice he didn't recognize, "this is Darzi down at the hospital. Mr. Cantrell is requesting you—"

"Requesting nothing," interrupted a voice in the background. "Give me that." There was some shuffling, and then Cantrell's raspy voice was clear, or as clear as it could get. "I'm *telling* you to get over here. I want some explanations for what the hell you think you're doing, Ivers."

Steppen Sawicki

Chapter Eight

Cantrell was berating a nurse when Bryan entered his room. The agent who'd placed the call to Bryan was standing by the window, clearly exasperated, but he breathed a sigh of relief at the sight of Bryan.

"Ivers," Cantrell exclaimed. The old man looked even older than ever before, and Bryan wouldn't have thought that possible. But with him lying in a hospital bed with a white sheet over his battered body and fluid lines running to his veins, he looked like he belonged there: old and wrinkled in a hospital bed. But he wasn't acting like he belonged there. "Tell this med school dropout I don't need any fluids. I should be back at the office, not tied to some bed."

"You're not tied to anything," Bryan said. "But you sure as hell aren't going anywhere."

The nurse went to Bryan and spoke to him as if he were Cantrell's friend or family. "Try to convince him. He keeps pulling his lines out." Then she left, and the agent by the window saw his chance to escape and scurried out after her, leaving Bryan alone with Cantrell.

"I'm not deaf!" Cantrell shouted after the nurse. "I don't need any of this sorry excuse for treatment! I need to take care of your mess, Ivers."

"You have a fractured hip, old man," Bryan said. "You better take anything they give you."

"Don't 'old man' me. This is all your doing."

"I didn't fracture your hip."

"That thing that did was after you." Cantrell pointed a bony finger at Bryan. "And you stood by as it killed all the rest of us."

Despite himself, or despite the lack of himself, that got Bryan's hackles up. "I had no demons to fight with. I could only attack it after Hussein's demon possessed me."

"Yes, and then you tore into it with your fangs like a damned animal."

"But I captured it. And we—"

"Got some vague information out of it and let it *escape*."

Bryan swallowed his rage. "It wasn't vague. We have a date for when the Eternals will pass through the gate."

"And what are we going to do about that?"

Bryan went to the bedside and stood next to Cantrell, telling him what he had learned. Cantrell's fiery eyes seemed to inspect him as he went over it all.

"And you got this from your better half?" Cantrell asked when he was done.

"From the gamma," Bryan argued.

"And you think it would tell you the truth? Just give away this weakness of theirs?"

"It's not one of them, it's—" Bryan cut himself off and lowered his eyes, unable to look at Cantrell.

"It's what?" Cantrell prodded him.

"Never mind."

"*It's what?*" he demanded.

Bryan didn't want to say it, but he knew Cantrell wouldn't let it go. "It's... not part of them. It's part of me."

"So, it's going to be nice and sweet to you? Tell you everything you need to know?"

"I could... experience what it told me. Like memories."

"You trust it?"

"In a way, I can."

"Then you're even more of an idiot than I thought, Ivers. It's a *demon*. It will tell you anything to get what it wants. And do you know what it wants?"

"Me," Bryan said weakly. He suddenly wanted to sit down, but he knew Cantrell would see that action as another sign of weakness – one sign among many.

"And it sounds like it's getting you, as sure as cats fight dogs. What else did it tell you?"

Bryan looked back up at Cantrell, but couldn't quite meet his gaze. "That I could close the gates with a single command... if I let it in again."

"And you believe that?"

"I don't know." Bryan felt like he had been defeated at something.

"So, what are you going to do about these lodestones?"

Bryan blinked at the change in discourse. "Sir? I thought you were saying the gamma lied."

"I said no such thing." Cantrell laid his head back on his pillow as if the conversation had exhausted him, but his words were still as biting as ever. "I was just pointing out your shocking lack of logic. Say there are lodestones at the point of each gate on the other Earth. What do we do about it?"

"Well, we need to destroy them." Bryan thought of Hussein's words: *drop a nuke or something*. "We may just need to send explosives through the gates."

"Oh, just explosives. How easy."

Cantrell said nothing further, just boring into Bryan with those piercing eyes until Bryan finally said, "Um... what?"

"You're going to send a bomb through?"

"Well... it's an idea."

"And you'll hope you're lucky enough for it to go off at just the right point in space and time? For it to actually make the journey?"

"We could, um... send several."

"How much time does it take to travel from here to there through the gate?"

"We don't know."

"How will you program these bombs, then?"

Bryan felt this was going nowhere. He stood straighter and nearly shouted, "What's your idea, then? That's better than mine?"

"Answer my question."

"What? Programming? Time? I don't know! I don't know how we'll do it!"

"That's because you're young and naive and think everyone's going to be saved in the end." Cantrell pointed a shaky finger at Bryan. "I'll tell you how you're going to do it. You're going to send agents to carry and set off those bombs."

Bryan felt the blood drain from his face. He would have finally fallen into a chair had he had one, but instead he had to wobble uncertainly on his feet. "I... but they'll die. We can't do that."

"I never heard those words from Hussein!" Cantrell spat. "Hussein knew what was at stake. He knew what was required. He sent men to what may or may not have been their destruction every night."

"I'm not Hussein! I'm not even... I didn't ask for any of this!"

"No one does." Cantrell suddenly turned his head to look at the window, the light from which was starting to give Bryan a headache. His voice grew softer – or as soft as his could get – and no longer accusing. "Do you know what I did before the offices came about?"

Bryan was again stunned by the change in topic. "Yeah. You were the chief of police in Detroit."

"And Hussein tapped me to head this sorry agency. You had maybe forty demons in your cards and barely spoke a word a day. Do you know what Hussein told me?"

Bryan shook his head.

"He said, 'Cantrell, you and I are going to hate each other, are going to want to punch each other's lights out. I'm going to think you're a rotten S.O.B. But I need you to tell me the hard stuff, because people are dying, and I'm going to have to send people off to die. But you'll tell me when I need to be told.'"

He turned back to Bryan. "So, *you* tell *me*. Is there any other plan?"

Bryan shook his head.

"Stop bobbling your head and speak."

"No," Bryan got out. "This is our only chance."

"Then do it."

"I'll do it. I'll go through and–"

"You don't get to volunteer. The agents going there will need to be possessed."

"But I'm—"

"Unreliable. Whether you possess here or there or on the way, we don't know what you'll become or what you'll do."

Bryan hung his head, ashamed. Cantrell was right. He was unreliable. He might well arrive on that other Earth possessed and decide to join the other side. That was what the gamma was after, anyway.

"How many are you thinking?" Cantrell asked.

Bryan thought, and hated himself for the answer. "Three. One might fall off the path on the way, and a second might be struck by the strangeness of it all and not detonate in time. With three, we can be pretty certain one of them will make it there and detonate."

Cantrell nodded. "Then send four."

He announced it in a shaking voice in the classroom, two hours before sunset: They needed four volunteers to ferry explosives across the gate to the other Earth. They would not be returning, but they would likely save humanity. The other gate cities were being advised to do the same.

Four people per gate.

Thirty-six gates in the world.

One hundred forty-four people.

That was less than the number which would die tonight in Chicago alone from demons, but it still hurt. He said so to Harper when they both were back in his tiny office.

"People are more likely to sympathize with other people of similar social standing," she said.

Bryan glared at her.

"I just mean it's normal to feel that way," she said, looking abashed.

There was no containment to watch that night. They didn't have enough agents to contain at the gate. They were falling back on old tactics – chasing down the demons as calls came in. Wei relayed that the public was demanding to know why the gate wasn't being contained and civilians were dying again. The same old regular problems. It was like they were regressing, except that they had a plan. A hideous plan.

Andrade came in halfway through the night, while Bryan was on email trying to work out the logistics of getting enough explosives to produce a crater in Chicago. She knocked softly on the open door to announce herself, and Bryan looked up to see her aeon burning bright and tantalizingly.

"Checking in with Possessed Central," she said.

"The report is we're screwed," Bryan growled.

"What a coincidence. I have the same to report from my department." She smiled weakly at him, but he couldn't smile back.

"We just don't have the numbers," he said. "We've now got nineteen agents including trainees, stretched over the whole city." He nearly winced at the number. Nineteen agents, and he was expecting at least four of them to volunteer for suicide.

She practically read his mind. "Would it help to have some Spotters on the gate mission? I know you left them out of the announcement for a reason, but a few of them could be willing to help."

"That's not feasible. Whoever goes through the gate could be possessed on arrival or even on the way through." He shrugged. "It's why I'm not a candidate."

"That's the only reason you're not sending yourself, isn't it?"

He deflected his eyes to the laptop in order to avoid looking at her. "I'm not good for anything but pushing paper these days."

She sat on the desk, leaning over to put her hand on his. "I know this has been hard on you."

He risked a glance at her, and this time saw *her* beyond the aeon. She was bedraggled, her hair in a tangled bun and circles under her eyes.

"It's been hard on all of us," he said.

She gazed into his eyes; her own were deeply sad and tired, but still glowing with that life and sympathy. "We've all aged a decade or two in the past few days, haven't we?"

"You wear it better than me, though." He realized what he had just said and felt his cheeks grow hot. He remembered that Harper was sitting on the couch – not looking at them, but listening.

Surprisingly enough, Andrade's face flushed, too. She took her hand back, and instead of prodding him, she changed the subject. "Do you think the mission will really work?"

He wondered, and said, "I don't know. I don't even know if we'll get enough volunteers."

"I wouldn't worry about that," she said. "These are Possesseds, after all."

Black Heart

◆

First, Anna Molotch came in at 7 AM, and then Missy Moreno at 7:20. Bryan was surprised when Mouse — *Robbie*, Bryan told himself, *his name is Robbie* — showed up at 8:30 to say he would be the third. Bryan thanked each of them and shook their hands awkwardly as he told them to take the next night off. They all said they would think about that. Each volunteer coming forth took a bit more out of him, as if they were demons scooping out a hollow in him bit by bit.

Right before 11, he was in the halls and heading to a meeting dealing with the procurement of the explosives. He didn't have to be in on it, but sleep would do him no favors and he needed a distraction. He just hoped he wouldn't be asked anything. His guards were napping, all of them assuming the Eternal was enough like a demon to not fully operate in the daylight.

Which had caused him to wonder: What would happen in the daylight at 8 AM on the chosen day when the Eternals all came through, should that happen? On the other side of the planet, they would have darkness to march in, but here in the U.S., would they collapse in the street before the synagogue doors and pile up? Or were they all wrong, and the Eternal could pounce on Bryan in full daylight?

He had decided it didn't matter, and people other than him needed to sleep. He'd taken his chances and ordered naps for everyone.

So, he jumped when he heard his name shouted, and spun with adrenaline pumping. But it was only Cam catching up to him.

"Christ," Bryan told him, "I thought you were the Eternal."

"What, calling your name before attacking?" Cam asked. "That only happens in the movies, man."

"Well... right."

"Have you been this jumpy all night?"

"No, I've generally been too tired to be jumpy. I was just... thinking of things. Speaking of which, shouldn't you be in bed?"

Cam shifted from one foot to the other. He didn't answer right away. "Well, see, I've been thinking, too. Thinking really hard. About how things have just been totally hopeless lately, and then you hatched this plan, and it seems like it might work, you know...."

Bryan knew what was coming, and wanted to say something to stop it, but he didn't know what. So, he only watched Cam and waited.

"And I think," Cam went on, "I think I want to volunteer."

"No," Bryan said.

Cam gave a nervous smile. "What?"

"No."

"Did you already get four volunteers?"

"No."

"Then... is the project scrapped?"

"No."

"Well then, say something other than *no!*"

"I'm not sending you."

Cam smiled again, but this time in irritation. "So, you're saying I'm not qualified. That it?"

"You're qualified." Bryan was aware that he had let this conversation go off the rails. He didn't want to fight with Cam yet again. Not over this.

"You think I'm gonna chicken out?"

Bryan shook his head. "I'd never think that."

"Then why?" Cam was shouting now. "Why not me?"

Bryan's voice was barely above a whisper. "I don't want you to go."

"That's it? Man, I don't *want* to go. I don't want *anybody* to go. But you can't tell me I can't."

"Cam, you won't be coming back if you do this."

"I *know* that." He threw his hands up and sighed heavily. "Don't think I haven't thought about that. But my family's here. My mom and my sis, they're both just an hour outside of city limits. And we've got five nights. I gotta do something."

"You can do something else."

"Like what? Capturing demons like everything's normal? Quitting the office and passing the days getting drunk off my ass? You don't even have the four yet. Who'll do it if I won't?"

I will. Me. It should be me. Bryan turned away from Cam as if he would leave. But he just stood there.

"I'm going, Bryan," Cam's voice came to him, and when Bryan didn't answer, he walked away.

When they asked Bryan in the meeting whether he had four volunteers, he said yes.

The plan had been put into rapid effect the world over: Every city with a gate had at least four chosen volunteers as well as the necessary explosives. They would all enter on the evening of the seventeenth. All on the same night, so it would be a surprise attack. The times the gates opened would be staggered, as always. The hope was that the Eternals would have no lines of communication with each other, and no way of knowing what was happening across the countries. But whether the Eternals had a way of communicating with each other or not, the agents' only way to go over was based on time zones and whenever the gates opened.

Get in, get over, detonate.

There were cities that they wouldn't be able to get to, in Somalia, Nigeria, Columbia. The demon populations there were just too dense, and the places would have to be invaded by large numbers of Possesseds that those cities just didn't have at the moment. That was to be taken care of the next night. Agents had already found the gate locations, flying over the areas in daylight while the demons were sluggish or hiding from the sun. Far more agents from the surrounding gate cities were needed for this plan after the other, more accessible gates were taken care of; a mass of agents would have to protect the group as a whole from waves of demons once the sun went down, at least until the gate opened and hopefully until the sun rose again. But nobody had much hope for the latter to work out.

Had it been about to happen in Chicago, they'd all have been screwed. There were ten Possesseds left, or would be after tomorrow night. But agents in other cities hadn't seen and heard the Eternal spelling out their doom. Those agents had hope, and perhaps a few agents around the world were even blissfully skeptical this whole situation was even happening, that the world was ending.

Black Heart

Anna was the only volunteer who decided to work the night before the plan. Bryan tried to talk her out of it, but she insisted.

"It's why I'm going through that gate anyway," she said.

Missy, Robbie, and Cam were nowhere to be found that night, which was more like what Bryan had expected. He both assumed and hoped they were getting drunk off their asses in one last big blowout.

In the meantime, the city was dying. There weren't enough Possesseds and there were too many demons left over from the previous nights, and more to come tonight. Bryan cursed the difficulty and red tape involved in getting enough explosives to flatten several city blocks four times over. It could have all been done tonight, otherwise.

But it gave Cam and the others one more day.

To what? Change their minds?

He shook his head to drive the thought away, and Harper glanced up at him from her laptop. She looked like she would have said something, but Bryan's cell rang right at that moment, and for once, he was glad of it.

It was Wei, wanting to run him through the announcement pegged for the next morning and see if he wanted to add anything. He didn't envy Wei's job, even beyond the obvious "sit in front of a camera" part. The public was getting furious at what they saw as a lack of action on the part of the office, especially with knowing where the gate was and how to contain it. But they couldn't just say they couldn't control the demons at the gate due to a shortage of agents, so they were trying to steer all conversations towards how more demons were passing through as the gates headed towards stabilization.

That was another problem. The public had caught wind of the plan. That had been expected, what with having a plan spread over major cities all over the planet, but opinion was divided over whether the volunteers were heroes to be cheered on or sacrificial lambs to be saved from slaughter. Without a doubt, police would be needed on site tomorrow.

The night passed in a blur of disasters – apartment buildings and housing developments and stores turned to graveyards and nobody to take care of them. Bryan wanted to be out in the thick of it, capturing, but that was impossible now.

Or was it?

It was only a guess that possessing with any demon would allow it to take him over. After all, he had been possessed by Hussein's demon when he'd died and nothing had happened. Suppose he could work as normal, could be saving lives, but was holed up in the office due to a feeling?

But the Eternal was out there, too. If only he hadn't let it escape.

Sometime after the sun rose – though Bryan couldn't tell in his windowless room – a commotion sounded in the hall, of several people shouting. Harper and Bryan both leapt up and Harper took out a walnut shell, running to the door just as it burst open. She nearly possessed before she realized it was just Missy, Robbie, and a couple of other Possesseds.

"Ivers!" Robbie shouted. He was plastered. "You're not getting out of this party!"

Bryan wanted to protest – this was hardly the place for a drunken party – but couldn't, not to

Robbie. Robbie, who had been so nervous about volunteering for the mission and had told Bryan he wasn't sure if he would be wanted for it.

So, Bryan tried to ignore the growing crowd and work, but the more people who showed up, the more beers were shoved in his face, until even Harper told him he should take a break. He relented and went to find Cam. Instead, he found Missy, Anna, and again Robbie, and shook all their hands and thanked them. They were drunk and likely wouldn't remember him thanking them, but he did it anyway. No one knew where Cam was.

He stood against the wall and drank his beer, though it tasted like nothing. He wondered whether he was still able to be drunk, or at least to feel drunk, all the while staring at the aeons of the bodies before him and thinking of how much better than beer they would taste. And then Andrade joined him.

"Hey," she said, leaning against the wall with him.

"Sorry if they interrupted your work," he said.

She shook her head, sending her brown curls bouncing over her shoulders. "They need this. You may have noticed there's more than a few Spotters here, too."

"Yeah." Had he noticed? Noticed individuals? They all looked like life luminescence to him.

He could feel her studying him. She finally put a hand on his shoulder. He tried not to jerk away, but the warmth and weight of it was like a firebrand.

"Are you holding up okay?" she asked.

It was a variation on *Are you okay?*, but that wasn't what bothered him. He knew he could grab that warm hand on his arm. He could pull it, and bring her arm to his mouth. He could bite it, and tear it, and fill his mouth with blood and his muscles with life and finally taste something.

He did jerk away then, and left her without a word. He had to leave the crowd. It was all greens and pulses, stronger than ever. Too many of them all together in a mass.

He went to the roof, thinking he needed fresh air. But when he opened the door and the sunlight fell on him, he felt like his eyes and his skin would catch fire. He slammed the door shut and held down a scream. *Whatever.* It was cool and dark in the stairwell. It was becoming his hideout.

Were the others looking for him? They'd said he wasn't getting out of the party, but he had. He'd had to. They were still pretending he wasn't all that different. But he was. A slight touch on his shoulder had made him want to rip apart a crowd.

What had happened to him blanking out for hours? He would have welcomed that right now. But his thoughts had been a jumble since...

Since he last talked to the gamma.

Could it still affect him even if he didn't possess with it?

Two hours later, he returned to his office. Three Possesseds were hanging around, but they were all asleep.

Harper was awake, though, typing away. She didn't look up as he entered, but spoke. "The explosives are procured and prepared."

"Mm," he let out as he went to the desk.

"You should rest," Harper said.

"I just sat in a stairwell for two hours."

"To get away from a party, which was a source of anxiety. That's not restful."

"What? I should sleep?"

She looked up at him. "You should take a break."

He *was* tired. He wanted to fall asleep, even if it would do no good. He wanted to be ignorant of tonight's plans, just for an hour or two. He went to the couch and fell into it, though he didn't lay down. He and Harper sat in silence for a full minute, and when Bryan spoke, his voice seemed to boom in the silence.

"We're really doing this. Sending people to their deaths."

After a pause, Harper stood and approached him, and she sat down next to him. "They're giving their lives to save so many more."

"You shouldn't get so close to me," Bryan murmured.

"I think you need some proximity to a person."

He chanced a look at her. Her aeon was enticing, but he didn't need it. Maybe because there was just her and not a roomful of aeons. Maybe because he was just too tired. "Is that how you're reading me?"

"You're tired, and you're sad. You know one of those people more than the others, don't you?"

He stared down at his hands, realizing for the first time that they had a faint red glow about them; not just green but reddish-green. "Cam's my best friend. Hell, I *found* the guy. He followed me into this mess. I should have known he would.... I mean, he practically jumped at the prospect of being a

Possessed. No doubts. Just wanted to help." He looked again at Harper. "Did you see him today? At this silly party?"

She shook her head.

"Maybe he changed his mind," Bryan went on.

"I doubt that."

"Yeah." He looked at his hands again. It was an ugly color, that rusted green. Like corroded metal. He wondered whether he was ugly in Harper's sight. He thought of how ugly it was that he was using this kamikaze plan. He wondered whether Hussein would have agreed to it, would have strapped bombs to human beings and sent them to a dead world to die among a billion demons.

He didn't know. He didn't know if Hussein would have done it.

"Ivers."

He jerked out of his thoughts, looking at her. As he did, tears fell from his eyes. He sniffed and wiped at them almost frantically, but Harper took his hands.

"It's okay," she said.

"No, you don't understand." His voice broke as he blinked tears away. "It's because I spoke to the gamma again. I can think and feel a little bit more again, but it's not really me."

"You can't know that. These emotions could be you slowly returning."

He shook his head. "You really don't understand. I'm sad, but that's not why I'm crying. I'm not crying just because I'm sad about Hussein's death and this plan. I'm also crying because I'm overjoyed. I'm sending people to die and I'm so happy about it.

It's giving me this thrill, like I'm on a rollercoaster that's cresting a hill, and it's gonna happen. They're going to die and it's because of me. I'm gonna do it."

Harper had dropped his hands. Had shrunk away from him ever so slightly.

And he was smiling.

He realized it and forced the expression from his face as he looked at Harper, both of them stunned.

"I'm sorry," he said. "You shouldn't have known any of that. It wasn't fair."

She thought about this, then said, "No. I'm glad you told me."

"Why?"

She looked around the room, seemingly for something to rest her eyes on, but there was only a desk with a pile of papers and blank windowless walls. "Remember what you told me? That we're all the same? We're all just looking for that break. Fighting a hopeless fight so we can find that break."

Had he said that? That felt like another Bryan, an age ago.

She slid close to him, though he nearly jumped away as she took one of his hands in both of hers.

"I don't care," she said, "about how you feel about sending those people through that gate. Maybe you have some fucked-up feelings about the result of it. But I know your *reason* for sending them, and it's not so you can get some sick pleasure out of it. It's because this is our break, humanity's break, and you're making the hard choices and doing what needs to be done. Just like Hussein would have."

Her words were so harsh, so like her, but she was also so right. Like she knew him. Like she had known him for years instead of weeks. Her hands were gripping his tightly, so tight that it almost hurt and so warm they almost burned. Her face was so close he could read every inch of it, and her eyes so cold but so deep and fathomless. He needed her. He leaned towards her, intending to kiss her.

She drew back, taking her hands with her. "What are you..."

"I'm..." he stammered.

"Ivers..."

"...kissing..."

"I'm gay."

"...you." He stared at her in shock for a split second, and then buried his face in his hands. "Fuck. I'm sorry."

"And even if I wasn't..." she went on.

"I know."

"...we're both Possesseds."

"I know. I'm sorry."

"I mean, what was even your intention?"

"I know. I don't know. I'm sorry." He flopped down on the couch, bringing his legs up behind Harper so that she had to duck and slide away to make space for him. "You're right. I should sleep," he said before he realized she hadn't said he should sleep. He dug his face into the back of the couch and screwed his eyes shut as if the sun were in them.

Stupid. Stupid. Stupid.

He felt Harper rise from the couch, and for a moment, she stood there as if looking him over. Reading him.

Stupid.

Then she sat on the couch again. No, not sitting. She laid down behind him and put her arm over his waist.

His eyes flew open, but he couldn't move to face her. "What are you doing?" he exclaimed.

"I'm going to sleep. Be quiet."

He wanted to leap up from the couch; she was too warm, too present. But he wasn't looking at her, couldn't see her the way he was pinned, except for her hand on his stomach. And it did look tempting, but he wanted something else more than food: contact with a human being, someone who knew him and didn't care that, deep down, he was a monster. Someone who would hold him regardless, because they knew what he needed.

He closed his eyes, and he slept.

And he dreamed.

That evening at the synagogue, Anna, Missy, Robbie, and Cam were being prepped for their actions like they were going to act in a play. The bomb squad had cordoned off a truck in the street that contained four vests composed of seventy pounds of TNT each. Close to sunset, they would be brought in and strapped to the agents, and then everyone would wait for the gate to open.

No one in their time zone had been sent through yet – the operation was starting in Brasilia Standard Time, with Brasilia and Cordoba. From there, it would spin around the world, agents marching over as the gates opened in their respective cities, whenever each gate happened to open.

When Bryan entered the building, leaving behind the flashing cop lights holding back reporters and protesters, the bomb squad was showing the four how to detonate the explosives with the flip of a switch. They were all so calm and attentive, and on seeing them, Bryan shivered as the autumn wind blew through the broken windows and stirred the leaves on the floor.

Before they were loaded up, the four were left to roam for a bit, to say goodbye and shake hands and hug. It was the only reason Bryan had showed up. It took a while for Cam to notice him, but when he did, he hurried over.

"I didn't think you would be here," he said.

"I didn't get to see you yesterday," Bryan said. "They all threw this horrible drunken party outside my office, but you weren't there."

"Yeah. I was with my mom."

"Oh. That makes sense. Does... does she know?"

"I didn't tell her, but..." Cam looked down at his feet. "I think she knew something was up. Me just showing up to spend all day and night with her, and with this operation plastered all over the news. But we didn't talk about it."

Bryan looked to the doors of the place, where any minute the bomb squad would be filing in with their bombs. "I can't believe you're doing this. I mean, not in like, 'that guy - who would have thought it,' but in like... you're actually doing this. You know."

Cam smiled at him. "Yeah. I know. But somebody has to do it."

"But I don't like that it's you." *And I don't like that I like it happening.*

"Man, I don't like it either." Cam laughed, a touch bitterly.

The doors slammed open. There they were, bringing it all in. Everyone turned to watch.

"You should go get ready," Bryan said, not looking at Cam. Not able to.

"Yeah." Cam stood beside him for a moment, as if waiting for him to say more. Then he left.

Bryan saw the other three standing in the midst of a congratulatory sea of Possesseds – *Good luck with that job we couldn't bear to shoulder*. He didn't approach them. He didn't know what to say. He saw Andrade, but she was busy with the Spotters. He wouldn't have known what to say to her, either.

The place grew quiet as the bombs were strapped on, as if, at the sight of them, everyone had finally realized what was about to happen. When they were all suited up, they climbed onto the platform and stood, and everyone remained silent as if a religious rite was about to be performed. For the next five hours, the only sounds were Connors telling teams to switch off and the resulting cries of pain and discomfort.

At twenty minutes to midnight, the four entered the gate. In Bryan's vision, they simply took a step forward and vanished, swallowed up by nothing – what Bryan in his half-demon state could only perceive as a vague shimmering of the air. One second Cam was there, the next he was gone. Bryan couldn't even see his face.

The four agents gone, the gate closed with the shimmer dissipating. The remaining Possesseds weren't containing the demons – Bryan didn't want to jeopardize the mission by messing with the gates –

and the demons swept out from the synagogue, as if from a bomb blast that no one felt. In the ensuing silence, agents looked anywhere but at each other, as if not able to face anyone.

It was a good thing that no one looked at Bryan; if anyone had, they would have seen the smirk stretched across his face.

Chapter Nine

Morning came and no anomalies were reported. The plan had gone off around the world without a hitch. The rest of the plans – involving drop-zoning into the overrun cities – would take place that evening. Bryan felt both sick and ecstatic; he had done this – he had found the first gate and sent groups of suicide agents over. It was all his fault and achievement.

It was late afternoon and everyone else was asleep when a knock sounded at his open door. He looked up to see Sonia standing in the doorway. Her aeon was dim, exhausted.

"Am I interrupting anything?" she asked, weariness even in her voice.

"No," Bryan said. "Door's usually open."

"I know you're busy." She fell onto the couch. "I'll take a break. You were capturing tonight."

"Yeah."

"Are you doing okay?"

"Yeah."

"You don't look it."

She cast her eyes down to look at her lap. "I'm tired, but I feel I should be doing something."

"You're new at this. Extremely new. You should stop if you're worn out. There will be far fewer demons to roam tonight, so they can do without you. It's just clean-up now."

"Actually, that's why I'm here. Well, that and feeling I should do something. I checked in with the lab after work tonight—"

"The lab?"

"Sorry, I mean the analysts, the guys who are looking over the data we've been gathering at the gates. I've been hanging around there a bit during the day."

Bryan nodded. Doctors Rollins and Maclin had been hanging out there a lot, too, comparing measurements. Bryan had seen them there and they had seemed almost melancholy, investigating a branch of science that was nearly done with.

"There's all the usual readings," Sonia went on. "Radiation, heat, wind speed..."

"I can guess that you know more about it than I do."

"Basically, all the usual stuff. But last night something out of the usual range was recorded. A lot of guys in the lab think it was caused by people entering the gate, that the two are connected. And it's so slight that it couldn't have interfered with the explosives equipment, but..."

Bryan held up a hand. "Back up. What was recorded?"

She took a breath, as if this was of great import. "There was a short burst of electromagnetic energy that was slightly stronger than usual."

"But you said it wasn't strong enough to interfere with the explosives."

"Not as we read it. It's so very slight, just out of the expected range."

Black Heart

"But it worries you enough to tell me. If it were more out of range, would it affect the explosives?"

"If it were a larger pulse, it could render the electronics on the bombs useless, keeping them from detonating. But it's not that severe."

Bryan was chewing on his pen. It was a new habit of his, done hard enough to leave marks. "Do we get the full range of readings on what happens in the gates?"

Sonia swallowed, fear finally exposing itself on her face. "If we read something that happened on the other side of the gate, how could we get a complete reading from here?"

Bryan knew what she meant – he had wondered it himself. Were their readings exact? He trusted the equipment, but he didn't trust the gates. If an electromagnetic pulse was generated on the other side of Chicago's gate – on that other Earth – would the full force find its way through the gate to here?

Or would some of it get lost on the way?

The agents roamed the city that night, capturing leftovers – demons that had escaped them previously. Everyone took to it energetically; there was an end in sight, and nothing hopeless about the struggle this time. Even Connors was less fidgety. Bryan didn't pass on Sonia's misgivings to anyone but Harper; it could very well mean nothing, that spike of energy. But his and Harper's eyes were glued to a monitor displaying a live feed from the synagogue. Only the "lab" guys were there, along with one

Possessed and one Spotter, just to keep them safe from any demon that might wander back in. They milled about the screen, gesturing and laughing.

It wasn't that they'd all expected the plan last night to be foolproof. All four volunteers could possibly have veered off-course and not made it to the other side. If only one had made it, their equipment could have malfunctioned. More explosives were already prepared for use the next night if needed. But without enough agents to contain at the gate, it was pointless to gather everyone there on the off chance that it opened. They were of better use capturing.

"Hold on," came Connors's voice from the hall, and then in the room, "hold on. Ivers, are you even watching your mail?"

Bryan jumped at his name as if guilty of something. "What? Why?"

"You'd know if you were watching it. Potts got a bit overexcited and collapsed. Thankfully, he was putting his possessor away when he did. But Logan Square is now open."

"Oh. Um...." Bryan turned to his laptop. "Um, who's in Humboldt? Can we–"

"They're busy. Which you would know if you were paying attention." Connors waved his hand at the feed on Harper's laptop. "Why are you wasting your time with that? If the gate opens, it opens. You aren't going to change that by staring at that screen."

"I know, but..." Bryan shook his head and dropped the subject. He didn't want to worry Connors, and besides that, the man was right. Nothing would change, whether he watched the synagogue or not. Still, he only managed ten minutes of actual work before he was staring at the feed again.

"You're too stressed," Harper commented, reaching for the laptop. "Maybe we should turn this off."

"No." Bryan went to pull it out of her reach, but stopped himself. Harper raised her eyebrows at him and he sat back. "You're right," he went on. "But still..."

"The pulse was likely just an anomaly in the regular construct of the thing. The readings bounce up and down whenever it's open."

"But this was right when they went through."

"A coincidence."

He peered at her skeptically. "You really believe that, or are you just trying to destress me?"

She looked back at the screen. "I don't know. But I—"

She cut off, her mouth opening in shock and her eyes on the feed. Bryan looked to it to see wind tearing though the synagogue, sending papers and peoples' hair flying. Bryan couldn't see it, but he knew the gate had opened. And someone was on the platform, lying there as if they had fainted. The camera's view was too wide, and Bryan couldn't tell who it was or discern its aeon.

"He came through the gate," Harper said weakly.

Bryan snatched up his cell, hands shaking as he pulled up Reddy's number. It only rang once before it was picked up.

"Reddy here!" the Possessed in the synagogue shouted. The wind was starting to die down on the screen, but the agents had gone to the platform and were kneeling next to the figure who had come through.

"Get away from it!" Bryan shrieked into the phone. "It's an Eternal!"

"It's not," Reddy said calmly. "It's Cameron Knowles."

Bryan insisted on going to the hospital. He said it was necessary to get all of the information quickly, but surely everyone saw the real reason – he had to see Cam for himself. The ride there and the walk through the hospital doors into the stuffy, heated air of the lobby was surreal, as if it had just hit him that what had happened – everything that had ever happened – was out of the realm of possibility. Approaching the agents in the hallway put a defense up in his head: He would speak to them and they would tell him they'd been mistaken, that this was somebody else they had found or that they hadn't really found anybody. Maybe he would wake up and it would be one of his rare dreams.

But when he got to them, Reddy said, "He's woken up now. He's very calm. We heard you were on your way and decided it would be best to wait for you."

"Did he make it over?" Bryan asked.

Reddy nodded, fear in his eyes.

Bryan went into the room, Harper on his heels. It was Cam lying in a bed, hooked up to an IV and quietly speaking with a doctor. He saw Bryan, but didn't smile or give any other indication of emotion. His aeon was bright, as if nothing was wrong.

The doctor stood as Bryan introduced himself and asked how Cam was. "Dehydrated," the doctor said. "But other than that, physically healthy. I suggest psychological counseling, though. He appears to be in some shock. I know you want to interview him, but I'm not sure that's the best idea right now. Give him time."

"No," Cam said, "there isn't any time."

"He's right," Bryan said, and went to the bedside. Connors and a couple of others filed into the room after him and began setting up a camera. Bryan glanced at it.

"Are you okay with recording this?" he asked Cam.

"It doesn't matter," Cam said, his voice flat and dead. His face was the same – cold and emotionless. Bryan couldn't tell if the camera really bothered him or not.

"I'm so sorry, Cam," he said.

But you're not, he told himself, and nearly cringed at the truth in the thought.

"None of this is your fault," Cam said, as if to preface what would follow.

He said nothing more until someone behind the camera announced, "Recording now."

"All four of us made it. It was instant; we took a step and we were there, like crossing a threshold in a doorway. It was pitch-black, and the air was so thin it hurt to breathe, but we knew we were there because we could see their aeons stretching on for miles, though we couldn't see anything else. And we could hear them chanting. I flipped the switch on my pack. It was crazy, expecting to die and going on ahead with it. But nothing happened. I flicked it again and nothing happened. We all started yelling at each other to set the bombs off, but none of them were working.

"I thought they were going to kill us right then and there, in the dark, before we could even catch a glimpse of anything. But when they came to us as the gate closed, they stripped the bomb jackets from us and threw them away into the crowd. We couldn't see the jackets themselves, but the crowd swarmed around where they landed, and they scuffled over them – aeon on aeon, reds in the black, and I didn't yet understand why they were fighting. They were all shouting and murmuring in some sick, guttural language I'd never heard.

"I was waiting for my eyes to adjust, but they couldn't. It was too dark. I could only see the aeons, pale red and weak. I looked up and behind me, and could see no moon, no stars. We were in a covered area, possibly a building, but I couldn't see enough of anything to tell.

"More Eternals started to press forward, and the ones before us who'd had taken our jackets turned and snarled at them. Some fought, gnashing and screaming like feral animals, but none were allowed to get to us.

"It was still so hard to breathe, but I *could* breathe. I don't know how, but maybe they had some way of making oxygen in the building. I thought I could hear some machine humming distantly after things quieted down. They wouldn't tell me anything about that. But I'm getting ahead of myself.

"Once they were all spent fighting over us, one spoke to us in English, as if it was just making conversation. 'You can put your demons away,' it said. 'We are shielding you.'

"We didn't, at first. I think we all thought it was a trick. But a trick to what end? Surely, they were just going to eat us anyway. So, one by one, we took out our spare totems – who would have thought we would use them? – and put our demons away.

"That's when it hit me, what kind of position we were in. With the demon in me, I'd felt like I had actions I could take; I was indignant, I was confident, and I was in a place I had once considered home. I put it away and the freezing cold of the night enveloped me and set my teeth chattering. And the darkness around us was silent; the Eternals barely spoke to each other, just shuffling around. And any moment, they could strike out of the dark and kill us. I couldn't see them anymore, couldn't see their aeons... it was just blackness all around. It was like being in a dark house at night, worried that something might be lurking behind you, but I *knew* there were things lurking there, right in front of me and right behind me. I fell to the ground and felt behind me for the others, and found someone's – I don't know whose – hand, and we held on to each other.

"That voice came again from the dark. 'I will take your totems.'

"'You knew we were coming,' I heard Anna say.

"'It was always a possibility,' the voice said with no jest, no satisfaction. He was just stating facts. 'It has happened before, and it will happen again. The demons give off an electric and magnetic current. Creating an EMP with them is simple.'

"'Everything we could do,' Anna went on, 'you've seen it.'

"'Yes.'

"A wild series of explosions sounded, rocking the ground and sending dust down on our heads from above. I thought I could see the light from them, but it was hard to tell. It's hard to tell anything when it's that dark.

"'They're feeding off the energy from the bombs,' the voice explained. 'The ones that didn't get blown up, anyway. Not as filling as life energy, but we take what we can get.'

"*And you're going to feed off of us*, I thought, but I couldn't bear to say it. None of us could.

"One more explosion went off, this one even closer, and we gagged on the dust that showered down on us.

"'Kill us already!' Anna shouted at the voice in the darkness.

"It didn't answer. It said no more. The voice's owner might have already left. We demanded some answers from the others around us, but none would speak to us.

"'What can we do?' Robbie whispered between us, his voice shaking. 'Where's the lodestone?'

"'We can't do anything,' Anna said. 'We don't know where the lodestone is kept outside of gate time, or even what it looks like or what it is.'

"We fell silent. We had no weapons, and even if we'd had our demons, the four of us together could hardly have taken down one Eternal. There were a

Black Heart

hundred Eternals around us, thousands perhaps – it was impossible to know, they were so quiet in the darkness – looking us over, trying to work out how to get at us. Others surrounded us, guarding us and occasionally speaking to each other in that awful language, but they wouldn't respond to our own questions. I reached out at one point and my fingers brushed against the fabric of clothing, but the thing clothed in it jumped and hissed at me, and I didn't bother to reach out again. We were trapped in our little circle, in a dark space that felt both tiny and infinite at the same time.

Some outside our circle of guards did try to get at us; they snuck up like cats stalking birds. Sometimes we could hear them, their breaths chuffing as if smelling our scent. But sometimes we didn't hear them at all; sometimes we only heard an Eternal from the group close around us leaping on them to fight, both of them screeching and howling. As daylight came and sunlight filtered in around us so dimly we still had to strain to see, we could view them.

They were hideous. Gaunt and shriveled, the bones of their cheeks jutting out against the skin and their eyes wide and red. Mad eyes. Hungry eyes. And then we could see the fighting, the skin and blood flying until the stalker ran away – or was dragged away. Then the Eternal guard that had fought them off would turn back to us, us clinging to each other in our fear and helplessness, and it would bare its teeth at us – filthy, blood-stained teeth. And we knew they were enjoying this... our reactions, our fear, our helplessness. It was a moment of excitement in their long years of nothing.

"The crowds thinned out as the day wore on, hot and stifling in the enclosed space. And we could see that now, too, in the dim light – a huge space like a warehouse of a factory. But it looked about to fall apart, practically just rubble and strips of metal piled over our heads with pillars of stones stacked to the ceiling. It's a wonder it didn't fall when the bombs went off. That horrible dust drifted in the air constantly, making it even harder to breathe. Our 'guards' fell asleep in a pile around us. No concern at all about what we could do; they just laid down and went to sleep right next to us. Though there were less Eternals in the place than had been there to open the gate, they still crept closer to us, studying the sleeping guards to make their move, but if they came too close, the guards would wake up and chase them away. Except when they didn't. One snuck in very quietly, and would have grabbed Robbie, but Missy jumped between them and was dragged off. She punched and kicked at it, but it was like it didn't feel any of it.

"It couldn't drain her – couldn't take the life energy from a Possessed. But it could rip her leg and stomach open. Her screaming woke the others and they tore at the attacker, chasing it off.

"God. Missy. She lay there on the baking floor, her insides spilling out, her blood seeping into the dust and gravel. She spit up blood and looked right at me and... her eyes. I've seen people die. I've seen *so many* people die. But this... she died for nothing. No point to it. We had gone on a suicide mission and failed, and she was gonna die anyway, having done nothing. I saw it in her eyes. The woken Eternals fell on her and she screamed again. They left nothing. They even broke her bones open to get at the marrow. They sat around us, cracking them and sucking them dry.

"That was it for us. Any thought that we could do something to affect some change was gone. Robbie broke down and cried, but me and Anna... I think we were just numb. Anna told Robbie to shut up, and then we all sat there, drenched with sweat and struggling to breathe and waiting for whatever to happen.

"Eventually, the crowds began to thicken again as the sunlight faded, and there was even more fighting as they tried to get at us. But our guards were awake and tore them all apart until the darkness descended again.

"Bit by bit, they all started speaking. Chanting to open the gate. Thousands of them, until they were all in unison. All dusty, throaty voices. It was just another sickening thing in a line of sickening events. I finally threw up.

Our guards put up shielding to keep the gathering demons from us; that was the only reason we didn't get possessed. Not that it would have helped us any if we had.

"Anna was shivering, but I knew it wasn't from the cold. At some point, she could take no more. She stood up and shouted, 'If you're going to eat us, eat us!'

"'No,' came the first voice that had spoken to us. 'We're sending you back.'

"Anna sputtered, trying to ask why, but the Eternal cut her off, apparently already knowing what she would say. 'We get bored. Tell them we're still coming. Find something new to do. Give us a challenge.'

"'We won't make it back,' Robbie argued, his voice shaking again.

"'We only need one of you on this world to make it over to get the message across.'

"Anna fell back down and didn't speak again.

"They went on for hours, and the demons gathered and blew around and coalesced in the space before us and pressed against the shielding that was holding them away from us, until we really were nearly suffocating. Until we couldn't take anymore. Then the gate burst open.

"They broke our totems and tossed us in.

"I was in there for months or years or a lifetime. I don't know. I didn't get hungry, though I was thirsty from nothing to drink in that dusty other world. I never slept, though I was entirely spent. There was no time there. There was no color or temperature. There was nothing. I had only my demon, and being an alpha, it wasn't interested in language, though we grew to know each other. But it couldn't overtake me, maybe because there really was no passage of time for it to work in. I didn't know until I came to this side that only seconds had passed. In the gate, I thought I must have been lost in the void, and that years had passed and Earth was already demolished. An age in seconds. And they must still be there, Anna and Robbie, there in the nothing."

In the hall, Bryan stopped and looked down the corridor. It was silent, only a nurse and the agents to be seen. Victims of demonic attack didn't get a second chance. They didn't get put on oxygen and ferried to the hospital to fight for their lives. They were sucked dry as bones, there one second and gone the next. The silence of the hallway pressed that into Bryan's mind.

"It's over," he said to Harper. "We have two nights. We don't have anything new to do."

"We'll send out this video," she said. "Someone might have an idea."

"Do you really think so, or are you just saying that?"

She didn't answer, as if she wasn't sure herself.

He thought about the silence in the corridor, about Cam being surrounded by Eternals and the darkness and the nothing. "I have to talk to it again."

"You can't!" There was a note of panic in her voice. "It's changing you every time you do. Even you know it."

"I do know it. But I have some things to say."

"Like what? That it lied again? What purpose will telling it that serve? It wants you to go back to it, no matter what your accusations are."

"Maybe I can still get something out of it."

"It'll get something out of *you*."

Bryan turned on her. "You know nothing about it. You haven't had to live with it. You haven't had it in your head. So, don't tell me what not to do."

She grabbed him by the collar and slammed him against the wall. The agents at Cam's door gave them glances and sighed at the Possesseds' behavior, but Harper spoke low instead of shouting. "I've heard my father's voice every day I've been partnered with you, telling me I'm not doing enough. Telling me I need to let him in so I can do more, so I won't disappoint him. I hear him in my dreams. Sometimes

I'm not even sure if I'm remembering my father as he really was or if it's the demon. Every day I've been here, I've lived with it. And you know why it does it? Why it tricks me and leads me on? Because it wants me. Not to help me, not to help any of us. To help itself."

She let him go and he slumped against the wall. "It has no answers," she said.

"I know," he admitted.

The sun was rising as they left the hospital, and when it hit him, Bryan shouted and covered his eyes as he threw his coat over his head. Harper had to lead him blindly to the car. It felt as if the sun was emphasizing Harper's point. The demon was already such a part of him; what would more talking with it do? But when he fell into the car and Harper sat beside him, she had the grace not to say 'I told you so.'

They dived into a rush to stop the second round of bombings. Bryan had to speak with Cowen in D.C. and relay Cam's story, and then there came a flurry of additional phone calls. Agents were being choppered into Nigeria and Somalia, and they had to be informed to pick everyone up and get back out of the zone. It took most of the day, and even with all the fresh demons roaming Chicago, it seemed the most important task – to make sure no more agents went through the gates.

The volunteers in Bogota had already gone through. The remaining agents who'd been there to support them throughout the night had been overpowered at some point, leaving them all overtaken or comatose by the time morning broke. That had been expected, and they had all known the risks going in, but they hadn't expected that it would all be for nothing.

In the afternoon on the nineteenth, Bryan lost Harper and went to his gamma. But he didn't go close to it. He just stood watching it as if it might bounce off the table.

There is a much easier way.

If it was so easy, why hadn't it been done before?

Simple, he thought to himself. *Because you'd become Eternal, and you wouldn't want to close the gates. You wouldn't damn yourself to eternal starvation just to save some lesser humans.*

He could sense a protest tickling the back of his brain. The gamma, feet away, trying to argue. But he was right and he knew it. How many of those Eternals beyond the gate had been in this situation, had grabbed hold of their demons and become one of the mass?

You're different.

Had he thought that? Or had that been the gamma speaking? He turned to leave and nearly ran into Harper.

"I knew you'd be here," she said.

"You're right," he said. He was thinking of her words – *Sometimes I'm not even sure if I'm remembering my father as he really was or if it's the demon.* "It has no answers. Just the usual bullshit."

But he wasn't sure if he was right.

Back at his office, Sonia was waiting. Her eyes were red and puffy. She'd been crying.

"Any news from the lab?" he asked her, nonchalant. He wasn't hopeful for a positive answer.

She shook her head. "The readings haven't deviated other than to signal the EMP when Knowles went through two nights ago."

Knowles. Not Knowles *and* the others who'd been lost forever.

"Then why are you here?" He hadn't meant to demand it, but the question had come out that way.

She stood to face him directly, but she was far too tiny. Even standing straight like this, she had to look up at him. "I wanted to let you know that if there's any way I can help—"

"You want to volunteer," Bryan finished.

"Yes."

"For what?"

"For... any ideas you might have."

"There are none."

Her eyes widened. She lost her straight back. "But there must be something..."

"There's nothing."

"But somebody..."

"There's nobody with any idea. Go home and see to your grandmother." He passed by her and sat at his desk, flicking the screensaver off of his laptop.

Sonia stood in the center of the room for a full minute, until she found she had nothing more to say, and then she turned and left.

He jerked awake to a hand on his back. He twisted around ready to jump on whatever was there, adrenaline pumping as if he had been woken in a jungle rather than an office building. Andrade leapt back, startled by his reaction.

"I thought you were asleep," she said, grasping the hand that had touched him as if he had bitten it.

"I was," he said, his heartrate starting to slow down.

"Oh. Well. I didn't mean to frighten you."

"You didn't. I was just..." *...about to attack you...* "I've just been jumpy."

"Oh." She studied him, and he realized his lie had been pointless. She knew what was on his mind.

He turned away from her. "Okay, that was a lie. I was about to pounce on you."

"I know. That's... sort of why I'm here."

"Huh?" He looked back at her, but she turned away to sit on the edge of the desk. It was so unfair that she could read him so well and he could only read that she was alive.

"What are we going to do now?" she asked. "The office, I mean. Humanity."

"If you're asking what our plans are, we have none."

She twisted around to face him. "None?"

"None."

"But we had a back-up plan, surely."

"There was never a back-up plan. This was our one shot."

"But Knowles was *there*. He saw them. He was among them. We know more now."

"We know they are too many who are too prepared. We know we have no chance against them."

331

She laughed, running her hand through her hair as she did. "You're just being Bryan. I'm sure there's something we've been cooking up."

"Bowers wants to send tanks over."

"But the EMPs...."

"I don't think he knows how tanks operate."

They watched each other for a moment, until all trace of the laugh left Andrade's face.

"Is there really nothing?" she asked. She sounded so weak and hopeless.

"I'd lie to you if I could."

Her eyes went down to the desk and her finger traced a line in the woodgrain. "But that's what I like about you. Everything's real and out in the open."

God, she was killing him. What was up with her? "That's certainly not how you are," he spat, suddenly angry.

"I know," she said, unbothered by his accusation. "I know that I–" She stopped and bit her lip, looking up at the ceiling.

Bryan had to turn his chair to look the other way. It wasn't right for her to do this now, to tease him like this. "You shouldn't be working," he said. "You should be with your family."

"They're all in California," came her voice from behind him. It sounded far away, dreamy. She was thinking of something else. Was she looking at the ceiling still, or at him?

He glanced at his monitor. It was 5 PM. "You have tonight and tomorrow. Hop a plane."

"I don't want to."

He stood and turned to face her. "Then what do you want?" he shouted.

She took several deep breaths, watching him watching her. Then she said, "Kiss me."

He wasn't sure he had heard her right. "You joking again?"

She shook her head. "No jokes. Not now. Not tonight. I want you to fuck me."

"I'm not... me," he argued, dumbfounded by her wording.

"I know what and who you are. I can see it. I want it." She stood and took a step towards him, close enough that he could smell her in hints of sweat and sex. "Kiss me."

He grabbed her so roughly that she cried out, but he covered her mouth with his and the cry turned to a moan. He lifted her and set her back on the desk, and as she struggled to loosen his tie, he felt her all over, rougher and rougher, but she moaned again and breathed harder. He could feel her aeon light and airy around her, but he couldn't touch it. It was too wispy, like spiderweb. If he touched his fingers to it, it melted away between them. He tried to catch it and failed and growled. He grabbed her shirt instead, tearing it open, and she practically screamed. He chewed at her neck and felt her pulse under his lips, and then he had to move back to her mouth, though he bit that instead and blood hit his tongue.

"Yes!" she cried. "Like that!"

He didn't hear her. He was tasting the blood. He was trying to grasp her energy. His hand ran over her neck and his fingers felt her pulse. He twisted her hair in his other hand and yanked her head back, and put his teeth to her neck. But he didn't know what he was doing; he missed the vein entirely, so that some blood came but not enough. He needed more. He lowered his head again.

She was screaming. She was screaming and pulling at his hair, trying to push him away. He stumbled back and fell to the floor. He looked up at her, but he could only see her aeon.

And her blood, flowing between the fingers she held to her neck.

And her eyes, wide and horrified, staring at him.

She climbed backwards over the desk, her eyes on him. Then she backed towards the door, bringing her breathing back under control.

"I'm sorry," she said when she reached the door. Her voice was incredibly steady. "I shouldn't have pressed you."

It's not your fault, Bryan wanted to say. But he couldn't speak. His mouth was filled with blood.

She opened the door and left.

By the time Harper arrived for the night, Bryan had cleaned himself up along with the blood on the desk.

"Andrade says we have two Spotters tonight," she said. "How many Possesseds do we have?"

"Four," he said. "Not that it matters."

"Andrade is hurt. What happened?"

"I attacked her."

Harper didn't speak at first, and Bryan didn't look at her.

"So, that's why she wouldn't tell me," she said. "She said it wasn't important."

"Isn't it, though?"

"Is it? Is anything?"

He passed a hand over his face. "Is it even worth hunting tonight?"

"I don't know."

He looked at her then. She was slumped over slightly, and though he had expected her to be watching him, she was watching the floor instead.

"You don't have to be here tonight," he told her.

"Neither do those four Possesseds and two Spotters and Andrade. But what else would we do?"

So, they worked until the Possesseds were too exhausted and the Spotters had ordered them home. The gate opened and closed, and measurements were taken that didn't deviate from the normal. No one was placed on watch over Bryan. They didn't have enough people. Even the non-Possessed and non-Spotter agents were fleeing the office like rats from a sinking ship. Everyone was giving up. There were no more plans.

Still, Bryan knew there was another way. Another damned way.

I told you not to listen to it, came Hussein's voice.

I know, Bryan thought at the memory. *Fuck, I know.*

It lies.

I know.

But you don't really know. What are you really thinking of doing?

Bryan jumped, so that Harper looked at him. This wasn't memory. Hussein was actually speaking to him.

"Stay here," he told Harper, heading to the door.

"I'm going to need a reason," she said.

"I can tell you I'm not going to see the gamma."

He went to quarantine. He passed by his deck of alphas, passed by his gamma, and went into the room with his beta. It was set now, and wouldn't be able to break out unless the card was torn by hand. He couldn't speak with the gamma, not without risk. But the beta was just a beta. He had seen better tricks than what it had to offer. But still, he didn't touch it; he only stood before it.

It only wants you, Hussein — the beta — told him. Just like Harper's beta spoke to her in her father's voice, Bryan's beta was using Hussein's voice.

"Would it work?" Bryan asked aloud. "Would I be able to close the gates?"

You wouldn't want to. You wouldn't care.

"So, it's not possible."

Not with a gamma. It's too aware.

Bryan gritted his teeth. "And you're not?"

Gammas still have this idea that black and white are separate. Immature. It thinks there is only one way to go about this.

"What's the other way, then?"

You wasted too much time with that gamma. All is lost now.

He knew it was intentionally teasing him, so he led it on. "There must be something. Tell me."

I would have to search in you several times. Several nights. How could it be done now?

"But if we did that? What then?"

I have seen other worlds. It has not.

"Answer the question."

I am answering it. You must know their construct, not only of this gate but of the other, older gates. When we would understand each other, then we would know how to close them all.

"Other gates? What could they do with—" Bryan cut himself off. There was only one reason that the older gates would matter. "You're saying they could go back. The other gates are still open."

They're still there. Not open, but they can be opened as easily as opening a door.

"Then what would happen?"

They could travel back to their first world. Start over.

"What would that mean?"

Who knows?

"You sound awfully cognizant to accuse the gamma of being too aware."

The gamma needs you. I need you, but I also do not need you, as they are the same thing.

Bryan understood that. It sounded so right. He wanted and needed the beta as much as he hated and reviled it.

Maybe, if we started now. Maybe it's still possible.

The card was in his hands. Bryan screamed, dropping it. He had no idea when he had picked it up.

Maybe there's still time, it echoed in his mind.

He left the room, slamming the door behind him. He shouldn't have gone to it. He should have ignored it, as Hussein had told him.

Still, Hussein's voice lingered and bounced around in his brain. *You're wasting time. You're wasting time.*

◆

Harper was speaking quietly to someone when Bryan got back to his office. He looked in to see her and Cam on the couch, his hands in hers. She was telling him something Bryan couldn't hear. She saw him at the door and said to Cam, "Okay?"

He gave a thin, empty smile and nodded.

They were talking about you.

Was that Hussein's voice, or the beta's, or the gamma's? Or just his own? Did he have his own voice anymore?

Harper stood and left the room, and in passing by Bryan, she stopped for a moment but seemed unsure of what to say, and so she walked on out.

"Shouldn't you be in the hospital?" Bryan asked Cam as if in accusation.

"I'm perfectly healthy," Cam said. "Physically."

"Did you think of anything that could help us?"

Cam looked down at his hands. "No."

"Dammit, Cam, then go be with your family, not here. We don't have any ideas, either."

"I can't...."

"There's nothing for you here." Bryan stormed to his desk as if that was the end of it.

"My sister keeps a gun in her house," Cam blurted out.

Bryan stopped so quickly that he rocked on his feet, as if the words had struck him. He looked at Cam again, who kept his head down, slumped over. Bryan suddenly felt sick for suspecting him of... something. He didn't even know what he had been suspecting. He had just been automatically suspicious of his being here. He went over to Cam and sat beside him.

"It's really hopeless," Cam said. "Isn't it?"

It's not.

"I don't know," Bryan said out loud.

You do.

"But you just said the office has no ideas."

But you do.

"I'm thinking still. Just thinking. Okay?" Bryan swallowed. Cam looked so lifeless, despite his aeon. Hopeless. This wasn't the Cam he had sent marching through a gate.

"I can't see all those things again," Cam said. "And what they do. How they eat. I won't."

"You won't have to," Bryan argued. "Give me time."

Cam looked at him, his eyes empty and sad at the same time. "You will think of something, won't you?"

You know what to do.

"Yeah." Bryan nodded. "Yeah, I–"

"Just don't become one of them."

Bryan's breath caught. "What?"

"They've been telling you to. But that's not the way."

Bryan's eyes narrowed. "Is that what Harper told you?"

"She didn't have to. I was there when we interrogated that Eternal in the cafeteria. I know you think you can use that. But I've seen them, so many of them, and they were just outside one city. How many of them thought they were going to help their planets?"

Bryan stood. "You don't know anything about what I think."

Cam peered up at him. "Am I wrong, then?"

Yes, you're wrong. We can end it.

"Bryan!" Cam stood suddenly and caught Bryan as he nearly fell over, dizzy.

"I don't know what to do," Bryan said, gripping Cam's arm.

"Then let it be," Cam told him. "Maybe no one can do anything. It's not all on you."

It is. It is.

"Just give me time," Bryan said.

Chapter Ten

Wei came to Bryan's office before Harper returned. There were riots and looting in eighteen different countries, Wei told him, and minor riots and looting in areas of Chicago. People were gathering outside the offices, though the crowds had been disturbed in Moscow and Jakarta when flocks of demons had happened by.

"What can we say other than 'Don't panic?'" Wei asked him. But Bryan got the feeling the question was rhetorical. Wei took out a pack of cigarettes and a lighter. "You mind?"

"Not anymore," Bryan said.

"Good answer." Wei put a cigarette to his lips and lit it. "You want one?"

"I don't think I'd really enjoy it." Bryan leaned back in his chair. He had sat in it for so long these days that it was killing his back. "Main thing is making sure our agents don't get harassed by anyone in our crowd outside. We still need to work."

"What for?"

"What are you still working for?"

Wei blew out a puff of smoke. "My sanity. It helps, pretending I'm working with business as usual."

"Well, there you go."

Harper walked in then and stopped when she saw Wei. "Can I have one of those?" she asked him.

Wei gave her one and lit it, and then left to do his work.

"I didn't know you smoked," Bryan said.

"Not in four years," she said, letting out the smoke with a sigh.

"I have to ask you something," he said.

She raised her eyebrows. "Okay."

"Can I have your gun?"

Her frown deepened. "Can I ask you why you want my fucking gun?"

"When all those demons come through the gate, whichever one gets to me first is going to turn me Eternal. I have to prevent that."

She thought about that, looking at him so intently that he wanted to squirm.

"Have you ever fired a gun before?" She looked around for somewhere to flick her cigarette ash and found nothing, and so she flicked it onto the carpet.

"No," he admitted.

"Then you'd probably miss."

"So? So I should take pills or something?"

"I'll do it. We'll go together."

He stared at her in shock.

She took a particularly long drag and let it linger. "I'm not risking turning into one of those fucking things, either."

He hung his head. "I'm sorry. I never did find any way to stop this."

"It wasn't all on you."

"I had the gamma. I didn't ask it the right questions."

"It wasn't all on the gamma, either. It only crossed a gate once."

Black Heart

The beta didn't.

"You look awful." Harper stamped out the cigarette on the desktop. "Get some sleep."

"It's twenty-four hours until the gates open. How can I–"

"So, you'll sit there all day sulking and blaming yourself, and fall asleep on your keyboard? At least use the couch."

He couldn't argue with that. There was nothing for him to do if he tried to stay awake. He stood, unsteadily, and started to the couch. Halfway there, he stopped and couldn't face Harper as he asked. "Would you stay?"

"Only if you promise not to tear my neck open."

He flinched at that, and she noticed. "Sorry," she said.

"No, you're right."

She sat on the far end of the couch and pulled a knee to her chin. "I'll sit over here."

He nodded, lay with his head to the other side of the couch, and fell asleep almost immediately.

He dreamed of the endless waste. On the crest of a hill, he could see below him the figures traversing the dust, the full moon swallowed in their black robes. Above him, the stars were innumerable, so deep and so bright in the clear stillness. There was no oxygen, and so he gasped for breaths he didn't need – dream breaths.

His demon was beside him. It was a woman here, with long black hair and an angular face and freckles that would have looked more at home under red hair.

He was angry at her. Furious. But so furious he couldn't put it into words or even screams. He was frozen with rage and could only watch the figures go back and forth below him.

"Don't be angry," the demon said. "I told you the easy way. You chose the harder route."

He said nothing, his vision red.

"Of course, there was a chance it could fail," it went on. "I had never seen it attempted."

"Have you seen an Eternal's birth attempted?" he asked venomously.

"No," it admitted. "But it's simple enough."

"Not if I want to keep myself."

"It won't be yourself and myself. It will be a new being, complete. You have never understood that." It looked at him with such sorrow in its eyes that his anger was eased ever so slightly. He was furious and hated it, but he loved it so much more.

"Don't think I don't want to be with you," he said, as if it was the one who needed placating, rather than him. "I do, so badly. I have to fight against it every day. But I don't know what we'll become, what the end result of all this would be."

It did look petulant then. "Your talk with the beta."

"I already knew beforehand. If someone had wanted to close the gates by becoming Eternal, the gates would be closed already."

"You're different," it said. "Can't you see that? I can."

He was becoming angry again. "You do nothing but lie. You don't care what I become."

"I only want to be with you."

"You want to eat," he spat at it. "You want the gates open so you can eat forever. And you hate me as much as you love me."

He stood and descended the hill, eyes down to the dust. He was unsure of which side he was going down, down to the Eternals or to the unknown plain behind him that held darkness and oblivion. The demon called after him as if it couldn't follow.

Harper had slid off the couch and was now curled up on the floor. Bryan checked the time: 11 PM. Nine more hours, and no one had woken him. Perhaps no one was out hunting tonight. Perhaps even Connors had thrown in the towel, though he had told Bryan previously that he'd be at the synagogue at 8, waiting for the armies to march through.

Bryan had asked him why. He hadn't had an answer.

Just had to see it for himself, probably.

Bryan slipped silently from the couch and out the door. Harper didn't stir.

He went to the lobby and was shocked to see security running a full shift as usual.

"What are you guys still doing here?" he asked Jones.

Jones shrugged. "Our jobs."

"But..."

"Yeah, we know. But someone's got to be here to keep the crazies out." He stuck a thumb at the doors, where two cops were standing around outside chatting. "Protesters finally went home for bed at 10."

"Good. I was worried I'd have to fight my way out."

"Why would you want to?" Jones asked incredulously. "Whole city's gone nuts."

"I should see it." Bryan clapped him on the back. "Thanks, Jones. For everything."

"Just doing my job."

"We all were." Bryan exited the doors, unclipping and pocketing his badge as he went. The air outside was stale and held a hint of far-off smoke. The sky was hazy and glowing with the reflections of ground light, almost like it was daytime and the dimness was only due to clouds. The cops eyed him as if they wanted to ask him a few things, and doubtless they did want to. But he didn't look at them.

The further he got from the office and the pair of cops, the more damage he saw – smashed windows, wrecked signs, pummeled vehicles. But whoever had done it all had moved on to another area. He only saw a few scattered suspicious types, with scarves over mouths or blunt objects in hand, and they didn't acknowledge him.

He meant to walk aimlessly, but regardless of that plan, he ended up at a bar he'd once had to clean up, years ago. He remembered it because a woman had attempted to stab him while he'd been working. She hadn't been possessed, just mentally ill and drunk. The bar's owners had refurbished the place quickly, and a week later, it had been as if nothing had happened there.

Tonight, the windows and door were smashed and kicked in, but the lights were on inside. Not hoping for much, he went in. There wasn't much alcohol behind the bar, much of it having been scattered over the floor. A man stood among the remains, opening a bottle of vodka and pouring a great amount into a mug. He was a large man with large arms that could snap a neck, and hard lines on his face placed there by plenty of scowling.

"Got some of that for me?" Bryan asked, straddling the one upright stool at the bar.

"This one's all for you," the barman said, and slid the full mug over to Bryan. He got another glass from under the bar and upturned the rest of the contents of the bottle into it.

Bryan held up the mug. "To you, for staying open through all this." He took a gulp and coughed. It had been a long time since he'd had anything besides cheap beer.

"Ain't my bar." The man drank from his own glass. "I just wanted a drink. But the bastards chased the owner off, smashed half the bottles, and stole the TV."

"I don't want to watch TV anyway," Bryan admitted.

"Damned right. I can see what's happening with my own damned eyes."

"You believe any of this?" Bryan asked, at ease with this tough, cursing man. "About tonight being the end of the world?"

The man's hard eyes turned to hurt. "I don't care anymore. Demons took my wife two years ago and my daughter last week. The world's already over for me."

Bryan looked down into his glass. "I'm sorry." He wasn't sure how much he was apologizing for.

"What can you do?" His voice lost its edge as he spoke. "If it were a human being that had killed them, I could scream at them and punch them. Ask them why. But what do you do to a demon?" He shook his head. "Nothing. Can't do nothing to a demon."

Bryan couldn't say anything.

An ancient man with grizzled gray hair stumbled in and blinked at the barman in surprise. "You're not Arnold," he accused.

"No, I'm not," the barman said. "Want a drink?"

"Of course, I do," the old man replied, as if he'd been insulted. Bryan stood up another stool for him and the guy eased onto it painfully. "Look at this place. Look what they've done." He waved his hands at the mess in the bar with emotion.

"It's a damned shame," the new barman said. Bryan still wasn't sure whether the man had had any part in the destruction.

"Don't think I haven't seen this coming," the old man lectured them. "People go a little bit crazier every year. Every year, the demons get a little bit worse. And when the news got hold of the things being real, it was just like tonight! People lost their minds!"

"You think it's true, then?" Bryan asked him, once again wanting to test the waters.

"What? The gates? Of course, it is. You can't see all I've seen and not see where it's been heading."

"I'm sure you've seen a good lot," said the barman, who was certainly old enough to have been around for the beginning of the demons. Bryan assumed he must be humoring the old man.

"I remember when the things were running around with no control at all. Nobody was catching them. They just went and ate and then went on to the next victim, and all the cops and doctors just couldn't figure out why all these dead people simply collapsed into dried-up husks."

They *had* been capturing back then, Bryan recalled. But he said nothing.

"They thought it was some *disease*," the old man went on. "Like a virus could do that. You've seen them. Well, on TV at least."

Bryan noticed how the man had caught his words there, but didn't point it out.

"A lot of good it does us, knowing what it really is," said the barman. "A lot of good the offices did."

The old man waved a hand dismissively. "They did what they could." It wasn't the response Bryan would have expected from an old guy.

"Bullshit." The barman banged a fist onto the bartop and displayed a baseball bat he lifted from behind the counter. "If any of them were to show their faces right now, I'd let them know how well they did."

"Do you know someone in the office?" Bryan asked the old man.

"Place tried to recruit me!" he exclaimed. "After my brother died. They couldn't kill me. The demons, I mean."

"But you turned them down?"

"I was already seventy-eight years old. Nearly had a heart attack from the excitement. What was I going to do, chase demons with an ambulance following me around, should I finally keel over? No, once was enough."

They fell into silence at that, sipping their drinks. The barman broke the silence by asking the old man what he'd used to do in his younger days.

They passed hours in idle chatter about days past. It was as if they had established a rule without speaking of it: no demon talk. Bryan told them he pushed paper at an insurance company and had women trouble, and that his father had just passed away from cancer and a car accident had sliced his arm open, and the two men nodded at the normal problems he wove. When the old man – Bryan never did learn their names – said he had better go home, the barman stretched and said he had better be off, too, though he didn't say where to. Out in the 4 AM breeze, Bryan breathed deep, as if the air were fresh, though it was just as smokey as earlier. The old man was already hobbling down the street, eager for bed.

"I'm sure you've got work to get to in the morning, eh?" The barman winked at Bryan as he tapped the end of his bat down on the sidewalk – *tonk, tonk, tonk.* "Lots of insurance forms gonna be heading your way."

"That's for sure." Bryan winked back at him. "I'd best go to bed, too."

They both looked up at the hazy, glowing sky. God, it was good to pretend to be normal, to just be a regular person on a regular night in a regular world. To be just like this guy beside him – an electrician who drank too much and was quitting smoking and whose asshole boss had taken pity on him because his family... had been killed by demons.

The fantasy ended there, didn't it?

"It's a hell of a thing," the man said.

"Yeah," Bryan agreed, assuming he was finally talking about the demons and the gates again. "It was good to talk, though."

The man looked at him. "Naw, I mean – *Look out!*"

The man shoved him out of the way, and a crimson blur sailed past Bryan inches in front of his face. It knocked the man down, snarled, and tore his flesh open in a spray of blood. As he sputtered and coughed red, it turned to Bryan. But Bryan already had the baseball bat in his hand. He only had one arm to use, but as he was now, it didn't matter. He swung it at the Eternal and it connected with a *crunch* that Bryan found wholly satisfying. Bits of skull and brain were sent flying into the street and the thing collapsed as Bryan fell to the side of the man.

He was still struggling for breath, bubbling through the blood in his mouth and throat. Bryan pressed his hands to the gaping wound and blood welled up between his fingers. He had the suddenly fierce desire to lap it up, and he had to shut his eyes, though the image of the green lifeforce remained, burnt onto his retinas.

"I'm sorry," he said, his voice breaking. "I'm sorry. I'm sorry."

It was all he could say as the man died on the sidewalk.

When he rose, the Eternal was chittering and squelching together, trying to take shuddering breaths. Bryan picked up the bloodied bat in a bloodied hand and brought it down on the thing again, over and over, until his muscles refused to go any further. The bat tumbled to the ground – *tonk, tonk.*

The thing was a grinded mess. He didn't have much time.

"Not gonna be like you," he said to it. He started running.

Chapter Eleven

The way to the office wasn't clear. One demon drifted down the street as if going for a leisurely stroll, but Bryan could see three more in the buildings beside it. He had to double back and take the next street over, and two miles later, the same thing happened. This time, five demons were clustered in the road and sidewalk, chasing the stray car that happened by. Bryan saw them far off enough that they posed little threat to him, but it wasted his time by redirecting his route. He could have just taken one of them and allowed them in. It would have saved time. But he had already chosen.

The cops at the office doors stopped him until he pulled his badge back out. He wanted to shove them out of the way and shout at them: *You just saw me, you imbeciles.* Instead, he told them they should come inside; the streets were unsafe. As he darted in the door, they gave him fearful looks, as if to say, *Even the office guy is panicking.*

Not panicking. Just in a hurry. He had three hours until it would be gate time, but the real problem was the Eternal. Maybe he should have pulled its heart out and stuck it in his pocket, but perhaps that would only have drawn it to him. He could have tossed it away somewhere. Whatever. He hadn't been thinking clearly.

Was he thinking clearly now? He was certainly drunk, or at least had had enough vodka for a normal person to be drunk, but he wasn't a normal person. He was thirsty as hell, though, and as he reached quarantine, he realized he had a burning cramp in his side that he hadn't noticed previously. Everything had been about getting here, all his attention focused on getting here and on getting to his demon.

He snatched up the gamma. It was overjoyed, it was horrified, it was thrilled, and it was terrified. Bryan understood.

One word, right? he asked. *One word to close the gates.*

Yes, now, it begged him.

No, not yet, he told it, shoving it into his jacket.

Why?

He had no answer to that. Perhaps it was only habit. It was a very common mistake in his profession – to wait.

As he turned to leave, the beta screamed desperately in his mind in the voice of his sister.

I lied! I only need to enter you once! I lied!

Bryan ignored it. He had already chosen, had chosen long ago.

When the elevator doors opened on the lobby, they opened on Andrade. She was gasping for breath, having run down the staircase to catch him. He started at the sight of her and backed into the elevator guiltily. She could see what he was like now, how close to the demon, and more so, it was possible she could see the demon itself burning a hole in his pocket.

"Where are you going?" she asked, though she knew. Her eyes were already filling with tears. Her neck was bandaged.

Without a word, Bryan shoved past her into the lobby.

She followed him as he made his way to the front desk. No one was there. "You can't. You can't do this."

He went behind the desk into the back room, which had been left unlocked, and grabbed a set of car keys. When he turned back, she was blocking the door, tears falling freely now. He went to shove her out of the way again and she thrust her hand into his jacket.

He broke her arm. He didn't mean to; he just turned on her as if this tiny woman really had the means to take a card from him by force. He snatched her arm, and a *crack* sounded as she screamed and let the card flutter to the floor. All of security ran over, but they were unsure of what to do. Bryan stood at the desk with a ring of people watching him with accusing eyes and Andrade crumpled before him, her forearm at an angle. Still, she reached for the card, and again, in a panic, he snatched it from her reach, and then he fell before her and grasped her in his arms, failing to baby her broken arm because she cried out again. But he had to hold her one more time... he had to tell her he was sorry, because he never would again.

He couldn't tell her he was sorry. His voice was caught in his throat.

"Bryan," she sobbed, grasping him with her good hand, "don't do it."

He stood and ran to the garage, where he found the car matching his keys. His hands were shaking so much that he dropped the keys twice, once on the pavement and once on the floor of the car. On the road, he realized just how drunk he was, and that combined with his rushing made it so that he swerved in and out of traffic and miraculously avoided a hundred accidents, even if he did clip the sides of two cars, breaking their side mirrors and his own so that he had none. He jumped at the sight of demons everywhere, though half of them were just his imagination egged on by the gamma, which was convinced that some other demon would get to Bryan before they could make it to the synagogue.

"You're not helping!" Bryan shouted at it as he dodged another car. Its horn blared at him as he careened around it.

You left the Eternal. It will be there. It will be waiting. Just let me in now.

"Quit nagging me!" But he knew it was right. He knew because *it knew* it was right. He should take it now. That would be the sensible thing to do. But he was frightened.

Someone was in the street in front of him. He turned the wheel to go around them, but–

It's her!

the figure was crimson. An intense wave of force came out from it and Bryan's car flipped end over front. Bryan tumbled and glass showered in a flurry around him. The car landed on its top and spun, finally coming to a stop after what felt like minutes but had only been seconds.

Bryan was amazed to find that he had remembered to buckle his seatbelt. Still, he had smacked his skull into the ceiling hard enough that he was dizzy, and coupled with the effects of the vodka, he was nearly senseless. Someone was shouting at him, but he couldn't tell who or what they said – it was all a fuzz in his brain.

He unstrapped himself and rolled onto his stomach, coughing at the dust from the airbag. He crawled out the window, glass digging into his palms and leaving streaks of blood on the concrete.

...here! She's here!

Bryan figured out the voice in his head too late. Nails dug into his shoulder and flipped him over. A hand squeezed his throat as red hair fell over his face. He fumbled into his jacket pocket, his intention transparent to the Eternal.

She plucked the card from his fingers and flicked it to the side.

It landed just out of his reach.

So, it was over.

"What took you so long?" Bryan grinned up at the Eternal. He wanted to laugh. It was over. He wouldn't have to decide after all.

She actually grinned back down at him. "Had to disperse on an atomic level to escape the canisters. Easy enough to do, but the reconstruction takes days."

"Oh," Bryan said, and then he did laugh.

She laughed along with him. "You gave a good chase. I enjoyed it."

She thrust her nails into his stomach then, bursting through the skin and muscle with preternatural strength, and ripped out his intestine. She brought it to her lips, tearing into it with strangely human teeth.

Bryan coughed and gagged and grasped the air fruitlessly with his hands. A scream slashed through his head – the gamma. He saw and felt his torn-open insides but it was like something happening far off, not to him even though it was to him.

The Eternal's head jerked up, and then her whole body sprang up and away from him. Somewhere, a gun sounded out muffled shots. There were muffled screams. And a muffled voice.

I'm here.

Bryan turned his head to the side, aware of a searing pain in his torso. He saw his card through blurred vision, resting in a pool of blood and glass.

I'm here. It's okay.

Bryan opened his mouth to speak, but it hurt too much. *It's over*, he thought at it.

It's not.

I'm dying.

Let me in.

He threw his hand out to it. It lay inches from his fingertips. He would have laughed again, but he only spat blood.

You're too far.

That doesn't matter.

"Ivers!" A handed rested on his cheek gently. He looked up and could just discern Harper's face. It was spattered with blood. "Ivers. You bastard. You didn't come back and I knew."

He turned back to the demon, but Harper grasped his head in both hands and turned it back to her.

"No," she said. "I won't let you." She reached behind her for something on the ground.

Let me in.

You're too far. Bryan's head fell back to the side, not through effort but because that's where it fell. All of his strength was gone. The muffled clicks of Harper reloading reached his ears.

No, I'm with you. You need only let me in.

No. Horror gripped him, turning his heart. He wasn't supposed to have to decide. Not anymore. He was dying. He was supposed to be free. It wasn't supposed to be his choice. He shouldn't have to choose.

Let me in.

His tears fell as Harper put the gun to his temple.

The card burst like a firework, but it made no sound. The sound was that of Harper's screaming.

The pain was incredible, as if the searing in his torso had spread to all the rest of him – every limb and digit and even his head. He was momentarily gripped by panic and fear and the inability to function, but then he passed through that and the pain was a part of him. It belonged, and he was whole. He was himself, more himself than he had ever been. He could see now that he had been only a part of a being previously; that accounted for the loneliness he had felt, the desire to be close to other partial beings, and the fear felt in dark rooms at night that something was out there which could overtake him. There was no Bryan and no gamma now. He was simply he. He could remember being a child at the cabin on the lake, with his mother and father, and he could remember being born of the waste, of the absence of life in the dust and mud, and both memories were him.

He was putting his body back together – soaking in the blood and raveling his insides back in, even pulling the bits of intestine out from the stomach to throat to mouth of the other Eternal, who was a mess herself but was also knitting back together. A human aeon was there, had moved away from him and cowered on the ground as he rose with blood still flowing like rivers through cracks in the pavement, running up his legs and into his stomach. The aeon screamed again and crawled backwards away from him.

He stepped towards it. It was a stunning green thing, so close to aeons that he had glimpsed before but also nowhere near them at all. It danced and shook before him, nervous. It would be his first meal as...

It was Harper. The image seemed to focus and click into place: suddenly Harper, pointing the gun at him. Her hands were shaking so badly that she would surely miss if she did fire. There was more emotion on her face – shock, horror, sadness – than he had ever seen.

He could still eat her. It wouldn't matter. He could eat what he wanted of these incomplete beings and join the others and move on to the next world and eat more.

It was the logical choice.

But he knew Harper. Harper had listened to him in his self-doubt as he'd told her his failings. But those weren't failings, he recalled; they were only part of becoming Eternal. Harper had held him as he'd slept. But he didn't need anyone to hold him now; he was one. Harper had been about to kill him to prevent him from becoming whole... would have sent him into the nothingness of death. So, why shouldn't he kill her? Why shouldn't he kill everyone?

She thought she had been saving him.

She was going to shoot him, and then herself.

It was why he had done this, taken all of himself. To save them. The humans.

But that was irrelevant now.

Wasn't it?

If he saved them, how would he eat? What would he do once the planet died and the sun died, as well, and the universe expanded to its full?

He looked up at the sky, the damned sun lighting up the heavens in the east. He gritted his teeth so hard that they cracked, and then they went about repairing themselves.

It was madness, what he was considering. It was wrong. It would damn him forever.

Why did he choose this?

Why had he chosen this?

Harper had shifted the gun in her hands. She closed her eyes and put the point of it under her chin.

"Don't do that," Bryan said. His voice was deep crystal, new and faultless, and yet there was something off in it.

Her eyes flew open. They stared at him, bloodshot.

"You have to watch this one." He gestured to the other Eternal, who was about to sit up at any moment.

"What?" Harper gasped. "What are you... what are you going to do?"

"I'm going to close the gates."

Again, he took off running, leaving her without even waiting to see whether she had comprehended or not. He knew what to do to close the gates; he had known all along. He hadn't lied to himself on that, except for one thing: It would take three words to close the gates, not one. For all the worlds his fellow Eternals had crossed, the gates were fragile, wisps of energy linked to crumbling bits of machinery that themselves were held together by the forces of the demons. And the fools had never bothered to unlink each city's gate from the others. It would be like tapping a domino and watching all the others fall with it. Effortless.

One command will force the program closed. His own words to himself, as he had faced himself in quarantine what felt like ages ago or the blink of an eye. His words to himself as he had ached to be complete and as he had been terrified of the prospect. But he had known, even then, that it was certain to come to pass. He had always known.

He ran quickly, rejoicing in the speed he was capable of and how the lactic acid ran in his muscles. He looked about him at the vibrant green life-energy and the occasional red of a stray demon and had to tell himself *Later.* Later he would have time to feed.

But not on everything.

Epilogue

It was midnight on Monday, September 1st, and Kiyoko was leaving the office for the night. Andrade had relieved her of duty, and though she had been livid at the dismissal, a part of her was nevertheless glad for the break. They could afford to take breaks now; the demons were more or less cleaned up, only the stragglers needing to be captured. The rest had wandered outside the city, where the county and forestry branches would have to track them down. The gates no longer functioned – they were closed forever.

She climbed the metal staircase to the Elevated platform, thinking again of the reports. She hadn't been able to be there, of course. She had been tasked with keeping an Eternal down until 8 AM had come and gone, wondering the entire time whether or not he would truly do as he'd said he would. She had wanted to believe him, but at the same time, she hadn't believed it possible for him to subvert what would, at that time, have been his nature. Plagued by doubt, she had stood over the Eternal, cutting into it over and over again.

The others had had to tell her what had happened at the synagogue. Connors had been there, along with Sonia Reeves and two other Possesseds, and two Spotters. Forty minutes to gate time, Ivers had walked in, sending the two Spotters present into a panic. But he hadn't attacked; hadn't even looked at any of them. Reeves had actually described him as looking dejected. He'd gone to the front of the place, stood next to where the gate would be, and stared at the floor. Connors had tried to speak to him, but he hadn't responded, and the Spotters had pulled Connors away and explained what Ivers now was.

They didn't know what he was going to do. He might very well have been there to welcome the others like him, or start fighting with them because, just maybe, Eternals liked to do stuff like that. The sun was starting to light up the inside of the building, pouring in through the broken windows, and Ivers had to kneel in that awful dust and cover himself with his coat. When eight o'clock rolled around, everyone decided it was best to act as if he wasn't there and prepare to possess, wait for the gate to open, and go down fighting, much as it hurt to be Possessed in the daytime. But as soon as the gate opened, it closed. Reeves was closest to Ivers, and had heard him speak what she thought might have been three words, though it was hard to tell.

Then Ivers stood, with extreme difficulty, and dragged himself to the back rooms of the synagogue. His coat fell from his head as he rose and everyone there could see the deep burns etching into his flesh.

Reeves followed him into the dark, silent rooms, and saw him hide in the darkest one, but he only told her not to come near to him. She knew he had caused the gates to close, though no one else did and she had to tell them what she suspected, until Kiyoko arrived and confirmed it.

Black Heart

When Kiyoko had gone to look for Ivers where Reeves had left him, he'd been gone.

The train was slowing towards her stop. She leapt up to stop her thoughts and nearly toppled over as it braked. There was no use thinking about it all now. Ivers had made his choice and it was done.

So, why did her heart ache?

Walking to her apartment, she forced her thoughts onto other things – the agents shipping down to Columbia to clean up the overrun area, the capturing she had done tonight, the fight she and Connors had had over the last doughnut in the cafeteria. She didn't even like doughnuts. She breathed in the early morning air, which was finally smelling more like brackish city air rather than smoke and burning fuel. The police force had been just as busy if not busier than the office, getting people convinced that the gates had in fact *not* opened, that the demons about were just remains and not Eternals. Because the general public still had little to no idea of what the Eternals really were.

She brought her eyes down from the sky and saw someone up ahead. They looked wrong – no color or shape, with only a clear, crystalline structure about them. Her heart leapt. But it was too far away to really tell. As she approached, the aura would surely fill in. It was just the city smog playing tricks with her eyes.

It couldn't possibly be an Eternal.

She reached into her bag, grasping a walnut shell between her fingers. Not her beta; that beta was back at the office in quarantine, and to hell with the damned thing. These were just alphas in her bag, blissfully silent. The person or thing ahead of her hadn't noticed her, and seemed to be distracted. But as she came closer to it, nothing about it changed. It remained vague and featureless. An Eternal. She took out her shell and held it close to her teeth.

"Who's there?" she shouted, her voice enormous in the stillness.

It moved quickly, as if surprised, diving between the buildings.

She pulled out her revolver, as well, and with it and a demon prepared, she inched forward.

"Show yourself!" she said.

It came around the corner of the building, peeking out at her. "Harper?" came his voice.

She could have fainted. She could have cried. But she stepped forward and called, "Ivers?"

"Yes." He stayed close to the alley, out of the glare of the streetlights. She had to come to him, and could only see him due to his aura.

"What are you doing here?" she asked.

"Waiting for you." His voice was slightly off. Deeper and eerie. Missing something.

"Then maybe you should have been watching for me. What were you even doing?"

Though he was in the darkness, she could see him shrink a bit. Embarrassed. "I was... watching the leaves. I'm still overwhelmed by so much aeon all the time."

"Because you were in the waste." It was a statement to test him.

"Yes. Because I was in the waste. But also... my human self never got to see the full picture. Everything's so... beautiful."

"And appetizing."

He didn't answer right away. "Yes, but I wasn't going to say so. I don't expect you to understand."
"You really are different from them."
"I'm not really."
"You are. None of them did what you've done."

He went silent for a long time. She watched him, trying to find something in that empty aura, and it did seem to fluctuate so slightly and quickly that she had no hope of knowing whether it was something she was truly seeing or just something she was hoping to see.

"My human half," he finally said, "took precedence. That shouldn't have happened. I think I still can't see things as they really are."

"As they really are?"

"As the same. All one and the same. Perhaps I never will. Perhaps I made the wrong choice."

"But you saved us all. Us and countless worlds."

"Not that choice. I mean the gamma or.... Never mind. Is the office holding up?"

He was changing the subject, but she let him. She had pestered him enough to have built up an idea of him. "Connors is about to have a meltdown, but we've almost caught everything anyway."

"I've seen you guys capturing. I'd say you have two more nights of real footwork."

"You've been watching us?"

"I haven't seen Cam, though." There was a flash of something in his aura, quick but definite.

"He's been in touch, but recuperating. He thinks he's not up to capturing at the moment."

"I want to see him, but... I don't think he'd want to see me as I am now."

"He will, after some time." She wasn't sure whether that was true, and hadn't discussed Ivers with Knowles at all.

"And... Andrade? How is she?" Another flash – an idea of temperature more than anything else. A chill. He was thinking of what he had done.

"Her neck got infected, but she's on treatment for it now."

"And her arm?" He even sounded pained; she didn't need to see a sign of it in his aura to know it.

"Healing. She'll be fine."

"Tell her I'm sorry. Please. I never did tell her."

"She doesn't blame you for any of it."

"Maybe she should."

Kiyoko stepped towards him with her hand out, but he shrunk back.

"Don't," he said.

She stepped back, all the way to the gutter. "Then come out here. Don't be so secretive."

He came out onto the sidewalk – eyes down, hunched over. The streetlights barely got to his face. But he looked so like Ivers. He was even wearing a tie, like he was about to head in to work. But his eyes held something bestial and vicious underneath.

"And you?" he asked. "Are you going back to Tokyo?"

"I don't know. Everything's up in the air right now."

He seemed disappointed by the answer. She could see that now that she could see him in the light.

"Will you come to see me again?" she asked him.

He looked up at her, his strange eyes wide, shocked. "Why?" He said it like he suspected an ulterior motive.

"Do you have a reason not to?"

"No, but... I don't know why you would want to see me."

"Give me your hand."

He laughed, baring teeth. "No."

She held out her own, motioning with it. "Come on."

He straightened and tried to stare her down, but she motioned again, until he sighed and took his hand out of his pocket. He looked away as she took it. It was scorching hot, so hot it felt it might burn her if she held it too long, but she knew that was only illusion. She interlaced her fingers with his and held them both before his face, so that he looked at them and at her, animal hunger in his eyes... but also pain, sadness, loneliness.

"Okay?" she asked.

He nodded.

"You'll come see me?"

Again, he nodded.

"Good." She let go of him.

He turned away and slowly walked away from her, down the sidewalk, the light of the lamps pouring over him.

"Ivers!" she called.

He looked back.

"Are *you* okay?"

He seemed to think about it before answering. "Someone once told me, not too long ago, that a person could get used to a lot of pain." He looked up to the trees – the leaves he had been studying before Kiyoko interrupted him. "I am okay and I'm not. But that's what life is."

He turned away, and he left.

THE END

Black Heart

Steppen Sawicki

Author's Note

Thank you so much for reading! I hope you enjoyed this novel, and that you'll check out my other works at www.SteppenSawicki.com. A prequel to *Black Heart*, titled *Black Flame*, is available, along with my first book-slash-series *The Fallowing*.

Thanks to my editor Jennifer Collins. I don't know what I would do without her. Thanks to my cover artist Fay Lane for the awesome cover. Thanks to my friends: Jenny, for reading and telling me it gave her nightmares; Danny, for coming along on writing excursions and complaining about being at Starbucks; and Emily, for helping me with formatting, which I just could not work out.

Lastly, thanks to my mother for the horror genes and the love.

Made in the USA
Monee, IL
10 January 2022